K.L. REICH

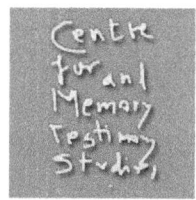

Memory and Testimony Studies Series

As a catalyst for interdisciplinary research and a space of confluence for scholars, artists, and community agencies working in the field of memory representation, this series undertakes comparative explorations in the often contested interpretations of remembering and forgetting in relation to traumatic history.

Series editors:
Marta Marín-Dòmine, Director, Centre for Memory and Testimony Studies, Wilfrid Laurier University

Colman Hogan, Co-Director, Centre for Memory and Testimony Studies, Ryerson University

Send proposals to:
Lisa Quinn, Acquisitions Editor
Wilfrid Laurier University Press
75 University Avenue West
Waterloo, ON N2L 3C5
Canada
Phone: 519-884-0710, ext. 2843
Fax: 519-725-1399
Email: quinn@press.wlu.ca

K.L. REICH

JOAQUIM AMAT-PINIELLA

Translated by
Robert Finley and Marta Marín-Dòmine
with an introduction by
Marta Marín-Dòmine

 WILFRID LAURIER
UNIVERSITY PRESS

Wilfrid Laurier acknowledges the financial support of the Government of Canada through the Canada Book Fund for our publishing activities.

The translation of this work was supported by a grant from the Institut Ramon Llull. Translated from Catalan by Robert Finley and Marta Marín-Dòmine.

LAURIER
Inspiring Lives.

LLLL institut ramon llull
Catalan Language and Culture

Library and Archives Canada Cataloguing in Publication

Amat-Piniella, J. (Joaquim), 1913–1974
[K. L. Reich. English]
    K.L. Reich / Joaquim Amat-Piniella ; translated by Robert Finley and Marta Marín-Dòmine ; with an introduction by Marta Marín-Dòmine.

(Memory and testimony studies series)
Translation of: K.L. Reich.
Includes bibliographical references.
Issued in print and electronic formats.
ISBN 978-1-77112-017-3 (pbk.).—ISBN 978-1-77112-019-7 (epub).—
ISBN 978-1-77112-018-0 (pdf)

    1. World War, 1939–1945—Prisoners and prisons, German—Fiction. 2. World War, 1939–1945—Concentration camps—Austria--Mauthausen—Fiction. 3. Prisoners of war—Spain—Fiction. 4. Prisoners of war—Germany—Fiction. I. Finley, Robert, 1957–, translator II. Marín-Dòmine, Marta, [date], translator III. Title. IV. Title: K. L. Reich. English

PC3941.A716K3 2014   849'.9354   C2014-900211-4

Cover design by Daiva Villa, Chris Rowat Design. Front-cover image by Richard Corkrey Photography, www.rfcphotography.co.uk. Text design by Carol Magee.

© 2014 Wilfrid Laurier University Press
Waterloo, Ontario, Canada
www.wlupress.wlu.ca

CONTENTS

INTRODUCTION

Joaquim Amat-Piniella was born in 1913 in Manresa, a city near Barcelona, the capital of Catalonia, today an Autonomous Community within the Spanish State.

In his youth, Amat-Piniella was part of the lively political climate that followed the proclamation of the Second Spanish Republic in 1931. During this period, he was engaged in cultural and political activities geared towards the national reconstruction and cultural renovation of Catalan society. A jazz enthusiast, he co-founded Manresa's *Hot Club,* and he was key in the creation of the avant-garde review *Ara.* His political journalism and art reviews appeared in the daily newspaper *El Dia,* which became, in 1931, the mouthpiece of the *Esquerra Republicana de Catalunya* (ECR), a party of the moderate left still active today and at that time the largest party in the Catalan Parliament. The ECR was and still is profoundly anti-monarchist and forms part of the broad coalition of parties seeking independence for Catalonia.

During the uprising of 6 October 1934, led by Catalan President Lluís Companys against the most conservative parties in the Spanish Republican government, Amat-Piniella was arrested and held at the Model prison in Barcelona, along with many others, for almost three months.

In 1936, with the outbreak of the Civil War—the moment when the principles of the Popular Front were put into practice in those areas actively resisting fascism—Amat-Piniella interrupted his law studies in Barcelona and enrolled as a volunteer in the Republican Army.

The fall of Barcelona to Francoist troops in January 1939 signalled the final phase of the war, which ended in April of that year. The victory of the Fascists under the self-proclaimed "Generalísimo" Franco (his title a grandiose gesture intended to emulate the status of his allies, *Der Führer,* Adolf Hitler, and *Il Duce,* Benito Mussolini) resulted in the flight to France of huge numbers of Republicans, who feared being executed or incarcerated by the new regime, which intended to persecute those who had participated directly or indirectly in the fight against fascism.

The first massive entry of exiles into French territory took place between 8 and 9 February 1939, when the French government opened its border with Catalonia. While the actual numbers remain uncertain, historians estimate that almost half a million men, women, and children crossed into France, where they found themselves placed in makeshift internment camps on the beaches of the southern littoral or, in the case of most women and children, transferred to "refugee" centres elsewhere.[1]

Amat-Piniella crossed the border later, on 14 July 1939. After being sent to various camps, he was placed in the 109th Company of Foreign Workers (*CTE, Compagnie de Travailleurs Étrangers*), destined for work near the Maginot Line.

In June 1940, many from these companies found themselves detained by the occupying Germans and sent, along with captured French soldiers, to various prisoner-of-war camps.[2] From there, most of the Spaniards, Amat-Piniella among them, were sent to Mauthausen. Spanish contingents were sent to Mauthausen during 1940 and 1941. Another wave of Spaniards came later, accompanied by French Resistance fighters captured in 1943. Of the roughly seven thousand Spaniards sent to Mauthausen and its satellite camps, only two thousand survived. Of the approximately ten thousand Spanish men, women, and children sent to Nazi camps other than Mauthausen, almost half died.[3]

Amat-Piniella entered the main camp of Mauthausen (Austria) on 27 January 1941, arriving from *Stalag* XI-B in Fallingbostel, between Hamburg and Hanover. The Spaniards had been separated from the French soldiers detained with them in prisoner-of-war camps.

Once in Mauthausen, Amat-Piniella was assigned, through the mediation of his friend Josep Arnal (José Cabrero Arnal), to work at the *Effektenkammer* or camp warehouse.[4] Arnal, a draughtsman on whom Amat-Piniella would partly base the character of Emili in *K.L. Reich*, had been requisitioned to draw pornography for some German officers; when he vacated his position in the *Effectenkammer*, he arranged for it to be filled by Amat-Piniella.[5] However, in the fall of the same year Amat-Piniella was transferred to the quarry. After three months of harsh conditions, he was again transferred thanks to the intervention of some of his contacts, this time to Barracks 11 under Cesar Orquín Serra, who would become a source for the character of August in *K.L. Reich*. Orquín, a Valencian anarchist who knew German and who showed great initiative and courage, convinced the SS that for the Spaniards to become more productive they would have to be better treated. Having convinced the SS, Orquín was able to organize external *Kommandos* to work for Austrian industries. Amat-Piniella worked in two of these *Kommandos* set up by Orquín, and although the conditions were harsh, the deportees in them had more generous rations and greater chances of survival, a circumstance that Amat-Piniella describes in *K.L. Reich*.

Before Mauthausen was liberated by American troops, the *Kommandos* were transferred to Ebensee, where Amat-Piniella was liberated on 6 May 1945, one day after the liberation of Mauthausen's main camp.

Like most Spanish survivors of Mauthausen and its satellite camps, Amat-Piniella was rehabilitated through Paris. In 1946, after wandering through France, faced with an uncertain future, for returning to Spain was very risky for those who had fought for the Republica, he established a temporary exile in Andorra. There, while recovering from the physical and emotional distress common to all survivors of the Nazi camps, he completed *Llunyanies* (Distances), a collection of poems he had begun while in the camp, as well as the first draft of *K.L. Reich*. In 1948, he decided to end his exile and rejoin his wife Maria Llaveries in Barcelona, despite the harsh political climate, which would persist until 1975. Maria Llaveries died three years later, leaving behind their three-year-old son. Amat-Piniella never recovered from her loss.

Amat-Piniella maintained close relations with Mauthausen survivors living in France, mostly through the *Amicale de Mauthausen* in Paris and the *Federación Española de Deportados e Internados Políticos* (FEDIP, Spanish Federation of Deportees and Political Internees), founded in Toulouse, France, in 1947. He also played a role in the founding of the *Amical de Mauthausen y otros campos* (Amical of Mauthausen and Other Camps), headquartered in Barcelona. The *Amical* in Barcelona remained underground from its founding in 1962 until it was legalized in 1978 with the end of Franco's dictatorship.

Amat-Piniella's first book was *Ombres al Calidoscopi* (1933). After the war he published *El Casino dels Senyors* (1956), *Roda de Solitaris* (1957), *La pau a casa* (1959), and *La Ribera Deserta* (1966). A posthumous edition of *Les Llunyanies (Poemes d'exili)* was published in 1999.

K.L. Reich was first published in 1963. In 1965 it received the Fastenrath Prize for the best Catalan book; the award was celebrated in Paris at a ceremony that Amat-Piniella was unable to attend.

Joaquim Amat-Piniella died on 3 August 1974 in Barcelona.

Mauthausen, a town in Upper Austria on a bend of the Danube, is famous for its surroundings and often praised by commentators for its beauty—a rhetorical stance that contrasts starkly to the horrors associated with the Nazi concentration camp of the same name.

The history of the main camp at Mauthausen begins with the *Anschluss*, the Third Reich's annexation of Austria in 1938. The camp was to be built near the Wiener Graben stone quarry, three miles from the town of Mauthausen. At the end of April 1938, the SS founded the company

Deutsche Erd und Steinwerke (German Earth and Stone Works) to quarry granite using prisoner labour. In August 1938, the *Inspektion der Konzentrationslager* (Inspectorate of Concentration Camps), the SS body in charge of the camps, transferred roughly three hundred prisoners from Dachau, mostly Austrians, to begin constructing the new camp. By the end of 1938, Mauthausen held nearly one thousand prisoners. One year later, the number had increased to more than 2,600 and now included political opponents of the regime.

The number of inmates held in Mauthausen and its satellites steadily increased in the years that followed. Then, beginning in the second half of 1944, thousands of prisoners were transferred there from camps farther to the east. In the spring of 1945, as the eastern camps closed down, their inmates were transferred to the main camp at Mauthausen in what were known as "death marches." The result was overcrowding in Mauthausen, Gusen, Ebensee, and the other still active camps. The mortality rate rose steeply as a result of starvation and sickness.

Although the exact figures remain uncertain, it is estimated that 200,000 prisoners passed through the Mauthausen complex (the main camp and its satellites) between August 1938 and May 1945. At least 95,000 died there, of whom more than 14,000 were Jewish.

Hartheim Castle was also part of the Mauthausen complex. Located twenty-five miles from the main camp, it had previously served as an asylum for the mentally ill. In 1938 the castle was taken over by the SS and reconstructed to accommodate a crematorium and gas chamber; it was then put to use as part of the Reich's euthanasia program as well as for medical experiments. (The SS dismantled the gas chamber at Hartheim on 12 December 1944 in order to eliminate evidence.) Prisoners were also gassed in the "ghost trucks" that transported them from Mauthausen to Gusen. Also, approximately 10,200 prisoners were murdered in the gas chamber at the main camp, constructed in 1940. Mauthausen was one of the only western camps to have a gas chamber.[6]

The Mauthausen quarry became infamous for the 186 steps the prisoners were forced to climb and descend carrying heavy stones, which at times were close to the weight of their emaciated bodies. The quarry was also the scene of collective tortures and murders, above all against the Jews, who were systematically sent to work and die there. One section of the quarry received the name of "the parachutist's wall" for the prisoners, mostly Jews, were forced to jump off its ledge to their deaths below.

Mauthausen had been constructed primarily to incarcerate criminals and other "elements" the Third Reich considered "unredeemable." These included Soviet prisoners of war and Spanish deportees as well as Polish, French, Dutch, and Italian prisoners. It was not designed to be an extermination camp, meaning that it was not conceived for the systematic annihilation of Jews, although they were subjected, as in the whole Nazi concentration camp system, to the most brutal ill-treatment.

On 19 August 1941, Reinhard Heydrich published an edict that divided Nazi concentration camps into categories. Only Mauthausen and Gusen were designated as *Stuffe III*, or "work to death" camps, the harshest classification. Deportees to Mauthausen also died from torture, execution, starvation, and medical experiments.[7]

In 1940, the Nazis began to open satellite camps close to Mauthausen, subordinated to the main camp and located in the vicinity of various factories. Prisoners from the main camp were transferred to these satellite camps to work. By 1945, Mauthausen had fifty satellite camps; among the most notorious were Gusen, Ebensee, Redl-Zipf, Ternberg, and Vöcklabruck.

It has been said time and again that Spaniards entered Mauthausen as "stateless" prisoners, and that designation is current to this day in the memorial discourse about the Spaniards in Nazi camps.[8] According to historian David Pike, the German government refused to concede Spaniards the status of prisoners of war because Germany was not at war with Spain.[9] Because of this, Spaniards were given the blue triangle, which, within the concentration camp system, designated them as "emigrants."[10] Interestingly enough, for Spaniards an "S" was superimposed on the blue triangle indicating their origin, a detail that in principle contradicts the designation of "stateless."

Historians and survivors have come to acknowledge the importance of the Spanish contingent, because they were part of the first *Kommandos* sent to build the main camp, but above all for the role they played in organizing Mauthausen's underground political network, which was led mostly by the Communists—a fact well illustrated in *K.L. Reich*.[11] From its beginnings, the aim of this network—and probably the only one practicable—was to provide support and promote solidarity among the Spanish deportees and to find ways to place them in less onerous tasks. However, over time the organization was able to perform some heroic acts, such as smuggling out photographs that later served as evidence at the Nuremberg trials.[12] It also managed to safeguard the camp's archival materials by copying the original registration cards and hiding those copies away.[13] These two actions would be key in reconstructing the history of Mauthausen and the list of its victims.

The visual record of Mauthausen has three parts. The first consists of photographs taken by the SS, including the identity photographs taken of the prisoners on their entrance into the camp, and shows the daily routines of life in the camp. These images, which suggest a clean and orderly camp complex, mainly show inmates going about their work. Although they are undeniably a record of a "penal colony," nothing in them speaks of the brutality of the Nazi system. The SS were meticulous in organizing the *mise en scène* of their records, and the main objective of these photographs was to keep Berlin informed of the progress in camp construction. Other SS images provide a record of inmates supposedly killed while trying to escape. In most cases, however, those photographed had been executed by various means—by being thrown against the electric fence, machine-gunned by guards, or thrown from a height in the quarry. These pictures were intended to form part of the official response to any inquiries into prisoners' deaths. Most are inscribed "Attempted Escape" on the verso.

A second set of images is comprised of photographs and newsreels taken in the days following the liberation, mostly by American troops. These images, some of them quite well known, etch themselves in the viewer's mind for the pathos of their subjects: emaciated bodies, people in despair, some trying to eat, others on the verge of death. Very often these images are interpreted incorrectly as part of the record of life and death in the Nazi camps.[14] As is true with all of the camps, there are no existing images that depict the real, day-to-day existence under that regime.

A third set of images are those that Francesc Boix took with his Leica in the days following the liberation. These are the most personal of all; they seem to have been taken not simply to show the horror but also, and above all, to show the joy of liberation and the restored dignity of the survivors.[15]

That Joaquim Amat-Piniella is not widely known in North America is hardly surprising, for his most important novel, *K.L. Reich*, a fictionalized account of his experience in Mauthausen written in Catalan, has until now never been translated into English or any language except Spanish.[16]

The lack of translations notwithstanding, it is striking that *K.L. Reich* has not had the reception it deserves in either Catalan or Spanish culture. The so-called memory boom that mushroomed in Europe in the 1990s, and that in Spain—and for that matter, in Catalonia—seems to have reached its peak at the turn of the century, did not redress this situation.

The protracted fascist dictatorship that Spain endured from 1939 to 1975 furnishes one explanation for the book's low profile. During this period, all written materials, both literary and non-literary, had to pass state censorship. The censors took into account both morals—the contents had to align with the fundamentalist Catholicism imposed by the state—and ideology. Works could not contain any hint of opposition to the Francoist regime. Those that were authorized for publication often suffered the elimination or modification of characters, paragraphs, and chapters.

Considering the convoluted laws of the publishing market—laws that were geared towards sales rather than literary merit—and the roadblocks that were and still are raised in Catalonia and Spain against the memory of those Spaniards who were sent to Nazi camps, the history of the publication of *K.L. Reich* deserves a brief discussion.

K.L. Reich was published in 1963 by the publishing house Club Editor, first in its Spanish translation and some months later in the original Catalan. Carlos Barral in Barcelona, a highly influential editor of books in Spanish and a friend of Amat-Piniella, was responsible for this first Spanish edition. Interestingly enough, Barral also committed that year to publish *Le grand voyage,* by Spanish writer Jorge Semprún, a memoir about the transport that sent him to Buchenwald. Semprún, who lived most of his life in France and wrote most of his works in French, had been caught by the Gestapo while working with the French Resistance and was subsequently deported as a political prisoner. As Semprún wrote later in one of his best-known testimonial works, *L'écriture ou la vie,* Barral had tried to have *Le grand voyage* published in Spanish translation in 1963; however, the censor would not allow it. In response, during the public presentation of the Prix Formentor in Salzburg, on 1 May 1964, Barral presented a copy of the book made up of blank pages to Semprún.[17] In the case of *K.L. Reich,* Barral did get approval to publish, in 1961.

The manuscript of *K.L. Reich* published in 1963 was the culmination of multiple drafts that Amat-Piniella had been working on since 1946. This rewriting mostly involved polishing the style and eliminating or compressing paragraphs. A letter that Amat-Piniella wrote to his friend, the poet Agustí Bartra, exiled in Mexico, indicates that by 1948 he had completed a final draft.[18] Later, in June 1953, Bartra, who had read only a fragment of the novel, which had been published as a short story, offered Amat-Piniella the possibility of publishing *K.L. Reich* with a new publishing house he hoped to establish in Mexico to promote Catalan works that either had been rejected by the Spanish censors or, because of their subject matter, had not found a publisher.[19] In the end, this project did not succeed; however, it is clear that in July of that year an enthusiastic Amat-Piniella responded to Bartra's offer and sent him a copy of the novel, inviting him to make whatever changes he deemed necessary, with the proviso that he wished to further revise the text.[20] It is also clear that Amat-Piniella's friend and editor, Albertí, had sent the text to the Spanish censors at least once, in 1955. Interestingly, a report in the *Archivo General de la Administración de Alcalá de Henares* in Madrid authorizes publication of the manuscript that year; this authorization, though, would later be "suspended," according to the censors' records.

If we consider the final manuscript to be the one submitted to the censor in 1955, it took eight years for the book to be published. A hint of the obstacles, beyond those raised by the censors, can be found in yet another letter to Bartra, dated May 1958, in which Amat-Piniella states that he now thinks the novel will find a publisher, not only because the censors will allow it but also because a new generation is showing interest in reading Catalan books and in writing in Catalan.[21]

We should also consider the complex political situation of the times as it related to the publication, in Europe, of the memoirs of concentration camp survivors. After the war and well into the 1960s, the public tended to view the camp survivors as political heroes resisting Nazism. In camps like Mauthausen and Buchenwald, the percentage of political prisoners was high, most clandestine organizations were communist-led, and most accounts were both homages to solidarity and proofs that these prisoners remained politically active even while interned.[22] The complex bonds between memory, the history of the camps, and political beliefs are awaiting broader analysis; let it suffice here to say that, as Régine Waintrater has pointed out, the first published testimonial works focused on the political resistance in the camps rather than the specific experiences of the Jews.[23]

In *K.L. Reich,* the Spaniards at Mauthausen are shown to be politically active but divided by ideology. Specifically, the narrative sets out a conflict between anarchists and communists, an extension of conflicts that began even before the Spanish Civil War and that persisted throughout its course.

Amat-Piniella was undoubtedly aware of the difficulties of depicting this conflict and of the reactions the novel was likely to receive from survivors, many of whom were highly engaged politically. For this reason, it would perhaps be misleading to describe the version published in 1963 as a maimed product of censorship. For one thing, we know that Amat-Piniella kept a file of paragraphs excised from earlier drafts, paragraphs that, for reasons unknown to us, he did not want to publish. There is no evidence at the *Archivo General de la Administración* that the censor had marked these paragraphs as requiring redaction. But it is also true that some of these fragments depict the political leaders in the camp.

It must be pointed out that the *Amical* in Barcelona had, among its members, a number of influential former militants and Communist Party sympathizers. There is evidence that the *Amical* showed interest in *K.L. Reich*,[24] and one cannot help but think that some of its members would have read many of its scenes with discomfort or dismay.[25]

In 2001, thirty-eight years after the first publication, the Catalan publishing house Edicions 62 published the 1946 typed-manuscript version of the novel, and decided to reinsert four of the fragments that Amat-Piniella had deleted from his first published version. This decision served as the publishing house's justification for marketing its edition as "uncensored." This edition, produced by David Serrano, who had previously defended a dissertation on *K.L. Reich*, appeared at a time of growing public interest in recuperating the past as it related to the Spanish Civil War and its immediate consequences. The back-cover blurb seemed to perfectly suit the new mood of openness to memorial accounts: "David Serrano presents us with the whole and original text, written in Sant Julià de Lòria between 1945 and 1946, containing all the fragments and variations that were not included in the version that saw the light in 1963."[26]

This marketing strategy had an immediate impact: in very short order, Serrano's edition came to be considered the "real" one, and surpassed the 1963 edition in terms of sales and public reception.

While the notion of recuperating a manuscript lost to censorship might appeal to potential readers—an appeal of which marketing agents are fully aware—we believe that further analysis is required if we are to understand all of the elements and circumstances that made the publication of *K.L. Reich* and its further circulation difficult. We are faced with the rather bizarre circumstance of two editions competing for legitimacy.

For our translation we have decided to work with the 1963 edition, for Amat-Piniella considered it the definitive one. That edition also offers the most polished use of Catalan, as it was very likely reworked with the guidance of the Catalan editor Joan Sales.

K.L. Reich is a fictionalized re-creation of the experience of a Nazi concentration camp, with the focus on a group of Spanish prisoners. Although the camp's name is never mentioned, Mauthausen can easily be identified from the narrative's topographical and physical descriptions, as well as from various scenes that re-create well-known historical events. In the text, the letters "K.L. Reich" are stamped on all of the objects belonging to the concentration camp system. This mark is deeply etched into Emili's eyes as he works in the *Effektenkammer*, the Civilian Clothing Warehouse to which he has been assigned. In borrowing this stamp, the novel effects a transposition between objects and narration.

As Amat-Piniella states in the preface, his intention was to give a general account of the experiences of Spaniards in Nazi camps, using the tools of fiction. His characters cover a wide spectrum of experience and behaviour, from executioners to victims. It must be pointed out that many of the book's characters are based on real individuals. This level of referentiality, set against the background of a fictionalized memory, serves perhaps as compensation for the absence of the first person narrative voice that has come to be expected in testimonial accounts.

The use of the extradiegetic narrator identified with the main character, Emili, provides the narration with ample scope for depicting the full spectrum of the behaviour and the moral and political choices made by the various characters. Emili judges and condones, pays homage and shows pity. It is not inconsequential that Emili's name echoes that of Rousseau's Émile, hinting at the moral need for a "social contract" in order to avoid the corruption and abasement of power. All the more important within the concentrationary system in which the "spirit of the camp," as defined in the novel, compels each individual to confront the moral choices entailed in the daily struggle for survival: what Primo Levi conceptualized as the "grey zone."

From a canonical standpoint, testimonial literature requires that the "I" of the author meet the "I" of the narrative voice, following the well-quoted definition established by R. Dulong: the voice of the text should testify for the "I was there" of the author.[27] However debatable this statement may be, it is true that fiction necessarily disappoints this expectation with its requirement that a testimonial account provide an apparently unmediated relation between experience and writing.

Reflections on the relations between truth, testimony, and text, and analyses of the conditions that make possible the transmission of experience, are part of an ongoing debate that began with the accounts of the soldier-survivors of the First World War, followed later by the first works of testimonial literature about the Nazi camps, and soon after that by the literature of the survivors of the Gulag.[28]

Although the scope of this debate exceeds the aims of this introduction, it is worth mentioning the position of French writer Jean Cayrol, himself a survivor of Mauthausen, with whom Amat-Piniella might be said to have shared certain experiences.[29]

In an article published in *Esprit* in 1953 titled "Témoignage et littérature," Cayrol lays the groundwork for an argument that opposes truth to fiction in writing about the camps. Cayrol refers to the experience of life in the camps as the "monster impossible to describe"[30] and says it defies every attempt to shape it into a fictionalized form:

> Nous songeâmes en 1943, alors que nous étions enfermés, à décrire dans une fiction ce que nous supportions, et nous comprîmes rapidement le ridicule de ce projet. Nous n´étions pas des héros de roman dociles mais ingrats.[31]

Cayrol's categorical invective against fiction—specifically, those works that attempt to sate the reader's curiosity—expresses the conviction that the experience of the camps is intrinsically intransmissible, ill-suited for the stability that fiction presupposes and produces. And Cayrol goes even further, interpreting the social demand for fiction as a defence against the uncanny effects that might result from reading about the true dimensions of camp experience.

Conversely, Amat-Piniella has faith in fiction to convey some of the truth of the experience:

> We have chosen the form of the novel because it seems to us the most faithful to the inner truth of those of us who lived through those circumstances. After all that has been said about the camps with the cold eloquence of numbers and all the stories that have appeared in the press, we believe that through the lives of some few characters, real or not, we have been able to give a truer and more vital impression than if we had limited ourselves to an objective exposition.[32]

Amat-Piniella wrote those lines in the isolation of his exile in Andorra at a time when very few accounts of the camps had been published.[33] Most of the first testimonies to appear were being written at that same moment, addressing a need to narrate the experience that Robert Antelme described as an "*hémorragie d'expression.*"[34] A number of important works would come out of this first surge. In France alone, Annette Wieviorka has recorded 104 testimonial works published between 1945 and 1948 written by deportees to the Nazi camps.[35] In Italy, Giuseppe Mayda records 27 works published between 1945 and 1947 dealing with various aspects of the deportation, with special emphasis on *Si fa presto a dire fame,* which had been written secretly in Mauthausen by Piero Caleffi.[36] Since these works had not yet been published, Amat-Piniella could not have read them when he was writing his own. However, he aligns with writers of early testimonies such as David Rousset in granting fiction the capacity to convey truth. As Rousset stated in the preface to *Les jours de notre mort* (1947):

> Ce livre est construit avec la technique du roman, par méfiance des mots ... Toute fois la fabulation n'a pas de part à ce travail. Les faits, les événements, les personnnages sont tout authentiques.[37]

Indeed, most of these written accounts, whether fiction or direct testimonial, rely on the first person singular.

This flood of testimonies soon produced enough texts to make a commentator in *Les Temps Modernes* exclaim:

> Encore un livre sur les camps de concentration! Après ceux de Rousset, de Kogon, et de tant d'autres on croyait que tout avait été dit. Même s'il reste encore quelque chose à dire, nous aimerions qu'on se taise. La guerre est finie. Nous avons le droit de goûter la paix sans qu'on vienne nous la gâter.[38]

Writing fiction—or better, fictionalizing a real experience—seems to have been a way for Amat-Piniella to combat the resistance to knowing about the camps and to better portray the states of mind through which the survivors had passed. It seems that fiction depends on the author's acknowledgment of the entirety of the camp experience: since the whole is impossible to transmit, one must surrender to its fragments. One might say that the often remarked "unspeakable" nature of the experience of the camps is in fact one of the ways to come to terms with what Lacanian psychoanalysis has described as the Real, understanding by that term the dimension of subjective experience absented from language and hence structurally outside discursive representation. The subject loses his/her place as an "I" to become part of the magmatic and undifferentiated Real, structurally *indicible.*

One might argue, paradoxically, that in acknowledging the impossibility of relating the experience as a whole, one opens the path to the very condition of its transmissibility. Through writing, the subject becomes the "I" subtracted from the Real. In other words, the gap between language and the "essence of the experience" is the necessary condition for the narration to exist. Fictionalization of lived experience is indeed one possibility—and perhaps a necessary one—of the transformation of this essence into language made memory. The main purpose for writing *K.L. Reich,* we are told, was to narrate the "intimate truth" of the experience of the camps, a truth that for Amat-Piniella could be transmitted only by means of the organized structure of a novel.

It bears noting that the partly omniscient narrator is, after all, a limited witness of the camp, and that while characters and situations are often exquisitely detailed, the narrative's reach is circumscribed within a very specific microcosm. The lens through which we view the camp is focused by a desire to provide meaning for the excess of suffering and death. As Primo Levi and Germaine Tillion have pointed out, such a will to meaning was, given their ideological bases and discourses, the privilege of the political deportees, since the Jews were confronted by an ontological "why?" without any possible response.

The need to extract some meaning from the experience—a need that often takes on a theological dimension in *K.L. Reich*—can be perceived both as a strength and, paradoxically, as a weakness. If this is so, it is perhaps because the contemporary reader, confronted with a multitude of testimonies, has come to find this search for meaning fruitless. Needless to say, one has to contextualize this need, and in the case of *K.L. Reich* it is important to keep in mind not only the vicarious immediacy of the writing and the narrated experience but also the seeming permanence and moral exigency at that time of a political idealism that nowadays and among younger generations seems distant and diluted.

As part of the corpus of the literature of deportation—that is, the literature of political prisoners as opposed to the literature of genocide written by Jews—*K.L. Reich* offers unique insights into the "psychology of the political deportee." The experience of the Spanish prisoners in the camp followed on their political defeat in the Spanish Civil War. It is not surprising, therefore, to encounter in the work instances of irony often verging on cynicism. At the same time, the use of irony allows for a detachment of both the narrative voice and the main character, and this serves to place everyone—principal narrator, secondary narrator, and reader—both inside and outside the camp. This narrative device allows the reader to accept certain incongruities—such as the numerous scenes in which Emili reflects on his inner state of mind—that can be grasped only if the text is understood as an *après-coup,* idealized reconstruction of the experience.

It is precisely this distance, textually constructed through Emili's physical and mental wanderings, that enables Amat-Piniella to depict the camp through a series of metonymically linked tableaux, some of these depicted simultaneously from different angles as if through the lens of a camera.

But there is more to it than that, for if an element has to be underlined in *K.L. Reich,* it is the role of the gaze, with regard not only to its place in the narration but also to its epistemological relevance. One need not stress that the concentrationary system was designed to deprive the subject of his/her symbolic and imaginary attachments, to render the subject an object submitted to the *jouissance* of the Other/other. However—and this is a troubling aspect introduced by Amat-Piniella—where language failed, the gaze remained active. And it is precisely through the gaze that the reader is brought into the bowels of the camp.

In *K.L. Reich* the gaze exists on at least four dimensions. First there is the gaze that observes the torture inflicted on others. This gaze generates a tension between identification with the gaze of the torturer and that with the gaze of the deportee, who has been spared the torture and who observes the changes in his reactions as he gains experience in the camp. This evolution, or rather involution, is exemplified by the growing coldness of the inmates as they are forced to witness executions and tortures. This detachment from the suffering of the other can be perceived not only as part of the psychic strategy for survival, but also as a consequence of the concentrationary system, which sets the individual in a sort of "concentrationary hypnosis,"[39] thus numbing the senses and alienating viewer from meaning.

Second, and contrary to this "benumbed" gaze, there is the active gaze placed at the service of the act of witnessing. Emili makes the decision to look in order to remember after his friend Francesc pleads with him on his deathbed: "Remember … remember all of this … when the war is over. Remember me!" From this moment on, looking becomes the equivalent of filming, and remembering becomes an act of resistance, of extracting and detailing the horror from what is otherwise perceived as part of the normal daily routine of the camp. Looking, thus, means exerting one's capacity to bring oneself "into focus" in order to differentiate the magmatic horror of the inside from the possibility of giving it meaning and judgment through the language of the outside. Looking therefore prefigures writing, pointing at the passage that goes from witnessing to narrating.

There is yet a third role of the gaze: to document through extradiegetic narration. Here we find a fictionalized documentary gaze that, through the eyes of the omniscient narrator, penetrates a zone to which only the victim and the perpetrator have access: the gas chamber, the crematorium, and the infirmary where Francesc is murdered by an injection of benzene. The importance of these fictional scenes documenting real facts must be stressed, especially when we consider that even in the 1960s the existence of a gas chamber in Mauthausen was still being denied.[40]

Fourth, and probably most relevant, *K.L. Reich* succeeds in presenting one of the most troubling aspects of the camp: the attraction that horror and the suffering of others can arouse in the viewer—in other words, the camp as the site of *jouissance*.[41]

It is probably in fiction's dual capacity to elicit curiosity while potentially downplaying moral empathy and ethical reflection that the novel's detractors find their footing. However, Amat-Piniella seems to have had the courage to put his finger on one of the most lacerating aspects of life and survival in the camps: the inability to avert one's gaze from the suffering of others—from the "orgy of blood," as it is so often referred to in *K.L. Reich*.

It is through the narrative development of one of the novel's most moving and disturbing scenes that this scopic drive is implicitly problematized and ethically resolved.

The death of Francesc is preceded by a scene in which he is brutally beaten by an SS officer. Francesc will never recover from his injuries, so he is declared "incurable" and sent to be killed. The moral and ethical dimensions of his death catalyze Emili's will to testimony. Francesc's punishment at the hands of the SS throws into relief a sequence of causes and effects.

Earlier, Francesc had been transferred to a better position in the camp, a circumstance about which he feels some guilt. The day his beating takes place, he sets out on the simple task of collecting some water in a bucket. On the way, he feels his senses awakened by the wind. It is at this precise moment of distraction and excitement that he witnesses the scene that is going to seduce his gaze: an SS officer tormenting a Jew. Here, in a very subtle narrative play of psychologies, the SS officer discovers Francesc's gaze and commands him to take his turn as torturer. When Francesc refuses to follow this command, he himself becomes the new object of torture, and this will lead to his death.

The scene's complexity can be synthesized along a number of axes: first, it textualizes, as stated earlier, the potential seduction of certain scenarios set up by the torturers; second, it implicitly imparts the moral need to analyze this seduction and to neutralize it with an ethical perspective; and third, it depicts the Jew as the paradigmatic object-victim of the concentrationary structure.

Thus, rather than deploying narrative techniques that parallel those deployed by cinematography, *K.L. Reich* forces the reader to look at the excess—the *surplus de jouissance,* to put it in Lacanian terms—that the camp offers to the eyes. It is, needless to say, a negative offering, a looking into what should be forbidden. Here Cayrol's insight is most pertinent: "le regard d'un deporté, souvenez-vous-en, était bien celui d'un homme qui a trop aperçu; un regard qui saute les obstacles, qui contemple ce qui l'aveugle" (17).[42]

"You get calluses on the eyes," one of Emili's companions in the quarry says to him. "It's the eyes that do the real work." As readers, we too are forced to look, forced to reassess our role in regarding the suffering of others. This is probably one of the most disquieting lessons of *K.L. Reich* and where its ethical value is to be found.

—*Marta Marín-Dòmine, Toronto, March 2013*

A NOTE ON THE TRANSLATION

Translation, like its etymological sibling metaphor, denotes the carrying across from one place to another: a text richly displaced that hearkens to its origins and at the same time leans into new meaning in a new context. In our translation of Joaquim Amat-Piniella's *K.L. Reich*, we have tried to respect and to trace this distance the text has travelled in order to conserve rather than erase the sense, for an English-speaking reader today, of a somewhat foreign sensibility at work in this Catalan testimonial novel drafted in 1946. Catalan is an old and tremendously resilient language. It lies at the juncture of Spanish, French, and Latin, though it leans a little closer to the Gallo-Romance line that includes French and Italian than to the Iberian-Romance heritage of the Castillian Spanish that surrounds it geographically and has for long stretches of time suppressed it politically. And so it is at the centre of the constellation of Romance languages that inform one half of English's double lexicon. The English of our translation tends toward this shared Latin lineage as a way of underlining the presence of the Catalan text behind the one you have in your hands. The sustained effect of this on a contemporary reader is of a certain formality and reserve: it can produce a sense of detachment not only as regards the narrative voice in relation to what it narrates but also for the reader in relation to what is being narrated.

This orientation of the target language, we feel, has served the translation well in a number of ways. For one thing, it brings the feeling of the English text closer to that of the literary register used in *K.L. Reich* in its language of origin. It also more easily accommodates important idiosyncrasies in Amat-Piniella's own style that tend to exaggerate the inherent formality of mid-century literary Catalan. A writer passionately interested in science, Amat-Piniella strove for a kind of objective clinical precision in his descriptions, especially those concerning the body. For example, we first meet August, one of the book's central characters, sitting on a table in the barracks in which he, as an interpreter, holds a position of privilege, and wondering how that privilege might be put to use. He is described thus:

While thinking about this, August's almond eyes shine and his legs swing restlessly back and forth. His strong neck sinks between his shoulders, his arms propped against the table, and the position makes more obvious the creases of the occipital zone at the base of the skull. Through his skin, which is very dark, one can see the contraction of the muscles in the hollow cheeks, and the lips, vaguely Semitic, tighten to widen the slash of the mouth.

Or later in the book, the thoughts of one of the main characters who is laid out under an operating room light and reflector in the infirmary are set down in this way:

> The only real thing was the concave gaze that was absorbing him, and annihilating him, that erased from his mind all trace of time and the dimensions of space. Death was a mirror! Cold, shiny, virtual, an illusory image, the inverted reflection of an absurd world, of men working with jerky movements around a table where another man was lying down.

If the use of "occipital zone" and "virtual" (in its precise optics application) seem somewhat arcane in a contemporary idiom for fiction in English, it is important to realize that they would have similarly seemed so in Amat-Piniella's Catalonia. The precision and the emotional coolness of the terms are characteristic of the book and, we feel, of the author's struggle to maintain a disciplined gaze from the moment that he chooses to take up the burden of bearing witness to the events around him at Mauthausen and its satellite camps.

A reader may also be struck by some distancing elements that occur in the text as it balances on the border between narrative fiction and testimony. Drafted in the year immediately following Amat-Piniella's liberation from the camps, the novel was revised over a long period of time and, notwithstanding the visceral immediacy of its action and Amat-Piniella's intensely visual imagination, there is often a kind of slippage detectable between the incarnate fictional world of the novel and the testimonial reflection or commentary of the narrator: things are often set off at a little distance. For instance, the surprising appearance of the adjective *aquell*, as in *aquella multitud*, "that multitude," to refer to a group of prisoners of which the author is in fact a part and in which the narrative voice is otherwise embedded, can jolt the reader out of the immediate action of the novel to a vantage at a remove from recalled events. Similarly, more self-conscious shifts in voice, sometimes even to direct address to the reader on the part of the narrator, and shifts in tense such as are found especially in the closing pages, tend to underscore the book's double nature as a testimonial novel. The same might be said of the book's highly anecdotal structure, which moves the reader around the camp in a way not governed primarily by plot but perhaps by a desire to give as complete a picture as possible, to provide as much evidence as possible, of camp life.

It is our feeling that all of these qualities and their slightly awkward presence in the novel underline important characteristics of Amat-Piniella's mode of approach to his subject. They are important to the book both as part of its meaning and as part of the remarkable complex of abilities that allowed Amat-Piniella—surely exhausted in mind and body and spirit after four years of civil war, a year in French work camps, four years in the German concentration camp system, and with the prospect of permanent exile from his homeland before him—to sit down in 1946 and bear witness in such considered detail to the extraordinary expression of human evil and resilience that the camp life in Mauthausen was, to sit down and relive those years and their horrors.

After the book's eventual publication in Spanish and in Catalan, Amat-Piniella said of the protracted process of writing it: "It is a very long and bitter experience, trying to explain, to give testimony to what was the life and the death of the thousands of Spaniards that went through the Nazi camps."[1] The writing of *K.L. Reich* was by no measure, one imagines, a cathartic exercise. It is, rather, a supremely disciplined engagement with the human capacity for evil, not only in the writing, which bears witness, but in the witnessing itself. In the inverted morality of the camps, where the whole force of camp life was designed to nullify the very humanity of its victims under the dreadful rubric of a life of pain, hunger, exhaustion, and sudden, arbitrary, and brutal death, in a world made to deafen the prisoners to their fellows and their own selves, our author somehow retains the ability to observe and to remember and to parse nuanced feelings and responses to the full range of human experience and to stay keyed to the complex political and ideological ambitions of those around him and of the age. This is an incredible achievement. Part of the discipline necessary to that work, we feel, is registered in these particular qualities of Amat-Piniella's writing we have tried to preserve in the translated text. That is to say that these characteristics of his voice are not just ways of speaking about things, but ways of thinking about them, of apprehending them. It may be that they were also, at the time, aspects of a sustaining discipline discovered in the call to bear witness, a way of holding on through the long years of his incarceration. But this is not a book about surviving, it is a book about a triumph, *"el triomf real de l'Home,"* the triumph of "the Man," as Amat-Piniella calls him in the closing pages of the book, and also of the witness who, in spite of the oppressive and poisonous atmosphere of "the spirit of the national-socialist camp," sees, remembers, and records.

"My book does not seek to deepen wounds or differences, but to unite people before cruelty,"[2] says Amat-Piniella. The book's invitation, like the voices of the camp itself, should properly be represented in a Babel of languages. Its story belongs not to a people but to a time that is our shared inheritance seventy-five years later. We are very grateful to have been given the opportunity to set it down in English. Our thanks to the Amat-Piniella family; to Maria Bohigas i Sales, managing editor of Club Editor, the publisher of the 1963 version of *K.L. Reich*; to the Institut Ramon Llull; to Lluis Llobet and Cesca Gelabert, directors of the Centre d'Art i Natura, Pallars Sobirà, Catalonia, for getting us to Andorra; to our respective universities, the Memorial University of Newfoundland and Wilfrid Laurier University; and to everyone at Wilfrid Laurier University Press for their careful, close, and thoughtful work. And our thanks, always, to our families, where their stories touch this story.

— *Robert Finley*

K.L. REICH

Wehe dem mürder!

Goethe

To Pere Vives i Clavé, murdered by the Nazis on the 31 October 1941, for brotherly love.

To General Omar N. Bradley, head of the American forces that liberated me on 5 May 1945, as testimony of my gratitude and admiration.

AUTHOR'S NOTE

It was not until the fall of the German Third Reich that the magnitude of atrocities committed by Nazism since its rise to power thirteen years before finally came to light. It was then that the stories, uncovered documents, statistics, photographs and films, the proceedings at Belsen, Dachau, and Nuremberg, and the testimony of those who had lived through and been rescued from them, became irrefutable proofs of those monstrous acts. And today, when only fanatical racists can still doubt the reality of these events, we see how time and new international problems have pushed them to the back of the drawers of History.

It is not our fault that this book is being published only now.* If, today, we bring it before the public despite the waning urgency of its subject matter, it is because we believe that before something can be forgotten, it must first be known. And what almost nobody knows of these events is that, among the millions of people from all nationalities who met their deaths in Hitler's camps, there were hundreds, perhaps thousands who were Catalan. Without counting camps other than the ones we know first-hand, in Mauthausen and its satellites on the Danube 70 percent of the 7,500 Catalan and Spanish exiles who were interned died from starvation, overwork, and abuse. Detained by the Germans during the fall of France in 1940 as military workers on the French fortifications, the Spaniards were sent to prisoner-of-war camps along with the French soldiers, from there to be sent on to the SS extermination camps as stateless undesirables.

The astronomical figures for the Jews, Gypsies, Russians, Poles, the French, Czechs, etc., who died in Nazi camps do not diminish the importance of the Catalan and Spanish portion of that overwhelming carnage. Our 5,500 dead at Mauthausen, along with the thousands of others who may have fallen in other camps, ought to be taken into account in the measure of the Peninsular effort in the cause of liberating Europe.

---

*Furthermore, the original Catalan version of the text has come out some months after a translation of it. There is no need to say that our wish was that these would appear in their normal succession: the original first, the translations to follow. However, while the authors and editors propose, it is others who dispose.

Our objective with this book has been to give an idea of the life and death of these citizens of the world who created, in the face of National Socialism, the International of pain. We have not tried to construct the history of any specific camp, but rather a set of scenes, situations, and characters we met with in the four camps we passed through during four and a half years, taking the camp at Mauthausen as our chief model. Four camps, out of the countless ones that existed throughout Germany, especially interesting to readers in Catalan countries because of the particular stamp that the presence of our citizens made upon them. These are stories of suffering, of terror, of death, but also of hope. The miserable and yet epic life of a multitude of men who, in the most weakened and powerless state, found the resources to oppose the enemy's intention to annihilate them. It is a mixture of picturesque and dramatic elements that shows the confluence of races, nationalities, and individuals forced to live together in the most straitened circumstances. The shifting fortunes of a fierce contest that lasted more than four years between the destructive forces of the camp and the ordinary men who began by resisting them, managed to neutralize them, and ended by vanquishing them.

We have chosen the form of the novel because it seems to us the most faithful to the inner truth of those of us who lived through those circumstances. After all that has been said about the camps with the cold eloquence of numbers and all the stories that have appeared in the press, we believe that through the lives of some few characters, real or not, we have been able to give a truer and more vital impression than if we had limited ourselves to an objective exposition.

To succeed in this task will have the double value of adding our own voice to the judgment that the whole world has passed on Nazism, and to address the most fervent homage and the most heartfelt memorial to lost companions. Millions were murdered because they loved freedom: all of them contributed with their deaths to the final victory.

—Amat-Piniella, Barcelona, October 1963

CHAPTER I

It was a biting cold. No need to pinch oneself awake. Toes jammed for three days in damp boots and dirty socks surrendered without resistance to the frozen ground. Without its honed edge, the dawn might have seemed unreal to those hundreds of men, shaken from their sleep. Through fog that thickened as the day dawned, nothing but the loom of the surrounding landscape could be made out. Diffused light from the snow seeped into the early morning. A thick pillow, smooth and undulating, covered the steep roof of the station. The railcars, immobile on their invisible tracks, looked like rows of gigantic corpses abandoned under the drifts. On the other side of the road, on which the new arrivals were struggling into a ragged line, rose the sheer cut of the scarred hillside.[1]

They wore the motley "uniforms" of the French Army: some sky-blue (from the First World War), others dark-blue, still others khaki, with belled coats, and on their heads they wore berets, two-pointed caps, balaclavas, and even the red caps of the Senegalese.[2] They milled about, anxious and confused, in a vortex of panic, each trying to find a place, among the suitcases, bags and bundles, in the wavering line. The snow churned under their hobnailed boots, its pure white ground into the muddy road, while only the clink-clink of their army dishes, their tin cups and water bottles tied to packs and suitcases, broke the dawn silence. In contrast to that same silence came the guttural and terrifying commands of soldiers in the green uniform of the German Army, who, with their rifles at the ready, their fingers on the triggers, cordoned off that mass of prisoners. New voices, foreign, full of hidden menace to men who did not know the language.

    —And the overnight case? —one of the prisoners asked his companion.
    —Didn't you bring it?

Emili rolled his eyes and, under his balaclava, smiled fatalistically.

    —Then you might as well give up on having anything to wash your face with, —he said, hefting his heavy knapsack from the ground.
    —They'll have soap. Don't worry about it.

—What worries me, Cisco,[3] is we won't be needing it. I don't like the look of this.

—Like it or not, we'll have to lump it. We'll soon see what's up.

Francesc looked at his friend's red nose, which stood out even in the thin light, and tried to catch his eye. He smiled. He knew Emili's tendency to see the dark side of things. True, the treatment when they got down off the train had been rough, surprisingly rough, but he didn't want to jump to conclusions. He preferred to think that the guards had only been annoyed at having to get up so early, or at the cold, or at the foul temper of the officer in charge.

—Germans aren't barbarians, —a lieutenant had said to him when he took him prisoner—. We've got a great sense of comradeship. You'll see.

And it was true, in the prisoner-of-war camp from which they'd come the Spaniards had been well treated, even with a kind of deference. The fact of their having fought in a war, their industriousness, the quaintness of their habits in German eyes, these were all probably reasons. But why then, as they got down from the train after a three days' journey, had this new type of German appeared, so different from the one they'd come to know? Why the blows from rifle butts, why the kicks and the beatings, the shouting, the threats? Everyone would have got off the train just the same, without the big rush, and the line could have been formed more easily, maybe, and with less confusion and fear.

—They must be getting trashed up at the front —someone suggested.

Emili piled up his luggage and prepared to wait patiently until the recount was finished. He had never trusted the Nazis, despite the sheep's clothing they put on in the occupied countries. It always smelled like a ruse. The brutality here confirmed it. "Why didn't I get away when I could?" he asked himself bitterly. It was clear now how stupid he'd been to ignore a fellow prisoner's advice when he'd suggested they escape together. He shrugged his shoulders in resignation but couldn't shake off a depressing sense of foreboding. There behind the fog a terrible secret lay waiting.

The forming up was taking forever. Etched against the thickening fog, the dense black line of prisoners could be made out, marked at exact intervals by green-grey smudges, the carefully placed sentries, their rifles cocked.

—*Atención !* —somebody yelled,— *Atención!*[4]

The silence deepened. An interpreter was speaking, the one who'd already taken charge at the prisoner-of-war camp.

—The commander of the unit responsible for our custody wants us to form up well and quickly. The slower we go, the colder we get. Follow the orders; you can see this is no joke.

At the prisoner-of-war camp the roll call had never added up. One escapee more or less never seemed to matter very much. The officer would sign off on the report from the prisoner in charge without any fuss. Here things had changed and nobody knew why. One after the other the officers, junior officers, sergeants and even common soldiers made their separate counts. When they arrived at the end of the column they would compare results and, not having reached an agreement as to the exact figure, would immediately start the count all over again.

Even more astonishing than this grotesque operation was the "language" the guards used with those who, out of line or distracted, obstructed their task. When they met with an interruption such as this, they would repeat out loud the number they had reached, so as to remember it, and then strike out randomly with their fists to right and left.

Once the counting was finally done, the column had a hard time to get moving. They'd spent three days without sleep, without hot food, and the cold climbed up their legs and closed like a vice. Some were jumping up and down or stamping their feet. Others blew into their hands to warm them, or swung their arms, slapping themselves vigorously on the back. A boy close to the two friends in line dared to light up a cigarette. A guard started yelling at him from his surveillance post:

—Put it out —said Emili— He's talking to you, you idiot.

But one of the sergeants was on top of him before the boy even had a chance to pretend ignorance, and with a punch to the face he made blood spout from his nose. Emili caught a glimpse of the officer's collar.

—Did you see —he asked when the sergeant had gone— We're in the hands of the SS.
—You're joking!

The camp too was sunk in that morning's fog, a fog that ate away at the faint green of the Blocks. A single storey built of wood, long and narrow, and ranged in rows on terraces cut into the hillside, the Blocks hovered like a shadow at this hour of the morning. Their chimneys, two to a Block, spewed the thick black smoke of coal just lit, and it dispersed little by little into the heavy fog.

In the dining room[5] of Block 13, August, the Spanish interpreter, was helping with the cleaning duties that had been assigned to a group of boys: cleaning the windows, dusting the cupboards and the tables, sweeping up, making the metal buckets shine ...

—It's Spaniards coming in today, —said August—. Fifteen hundred of them.

The *Stubendienste*[6] stopped for a moment. That they were Spanish was no surprise, but the number seemed extraordinary.

—Fifteen hundred! —said the boy holding the broom—. A good batch for baking in the crematorium!
—Shut up! Maybe you've got a brother with them —said the one cleaning the windows.
—What do you want me to do, cry about it? Every day they come, and they all walk the same road. Besides, I don't have any brothers.
—Then stop mouthing off.

August let them argue. He abandoned the closet he'd been cleaning, even though it wasn't his job, and sat down on the edge of a nearby table, his legs dangling. His eyes didn't have the resigned, empty look that marked the gaze of most of the prisoners. He was the interpreter of Block 13,[7] and if the small measure of security this position afforded him was not enough, he was also a man who knew how to go at things with the spirit of an adventurer. An adventurer who had always had luck on his side. Of a very Mediterranean temperament, a rebel by nature, free of the prejudices of his well-to-do family, he'd lived a life of complete independence from a young age: his father's money was there waiting for him while he spent his time doing as he pleased. And what good times they'd been! Calling himself an anarchist, sporting a beard and sandals, sometimes a vegetarian, all just for effect; running away from home to be a pianist in a cabaret for a lark; entering the trenches in the very first days of the Civil War and distinguishing himself in one of the International Brigades[8] by voicing such extreme opposition to the communists that he got himself condemned to death, now that was really something. For this latest performance, he was now going to spend some time in a Nazi extermination camp. If he'd always managed to get out of trouble before, why not now? Used to taking everything that came his way as an opportunity to shine, social, political, and violent upheavals constituted a perfect setting for him. What was important was having something to observe.

Sitting on the table, August kept turning over in his mind what would happen in the camp if the influx of Spaniards continued at this rate. Men like him, more or less fluent in German, would be in ever greater demand, and to be an interpreter meant to have influence. The Germans, that is, the SS who ruled on one side of the barbed wire and the German prisoners who ruled on the other, often preferred letting their interpreters run things for them rather than the constant bother of having them translate everything. It was just a question of getting in little by little, of gaining their confidence, behaving intelligently, making oneself indispensable, and so using one's role as an intermediary to gain direct and executive control. A risky enterprise, August knew this well enough: any fall from grace would lead straight to the worst of deaths. But for him the risk itself was the biggest attraction. To gain power in a Nazi camp and transform the most inhuman penitentiary system in the world into a regime where it was possible to save the lives of at least some of his unfortunate compatriots, this would be an entirely unique experiment in the history of Nazi barbarism, an achievement worthy of the greatest of statesmen.

While thinking about this, August's almond eyes shine and his legs swing restlessly back and forth. His strong neck sinks between his shoulders, his arms propped against the table, and the position makes more obvious the creases of the occipital zone at the base of the skull. Through his skin, which is very dark, one can see the contraction of the muscles in the hollow cheeks, and the lips, vaguely Semitic, tighten to widen the slash of the mouth. Such an experiment is just the kind of thing to stir up a man like him. After finishing their cleaning the boys warm their hands at the stove. The *Blockälteste* (the German prisoner in charge of the Block) snores heavily, curled up on the table, his head cradled on his arm.

This dining room only seems hospitable by contrast to the snow and the fog outside. From the bleak and draughty dormitory, a current of cold air flows in, and along with it the smell of fermenting straw. Through the door, which someone has left open, one can see a huge scaffold of straw pallets, constructed with great care and hung with blankets in the guise of curtains. Empty since the previous day, the Block awaits the new tenants that August has just announced.

—Shut the door, Miquel —he yells.

This morning the boys have managed to do two complete cleanings of the Block. Everything has to be polished, shining, neat: everything that the prisoners never touch, every table at which they are never permitted to eat, every stool on which they never sit, the floor on which they never walk, the cupboards that contain nothing, the stove exclusively for the comfort of the *Blockälteste* and his deputies. A Block is not meant for living, only to be nice and clean when there are visitors needing to be convinced of the model installation of a Nazi camp.

To be able to accommodate today's arrivals in even minimal living conditions, this Block and a few more besides would be necessary. There isn't enough room for so many, but the established order will not be jeopardized by this little detail. The dining room will remain as it is now, neat, empty, and shaken by the snoring of the *Blockälteste*. The prisoners will cross it to get to the dormitory, where they will be crammed in like cattle, and again to get out to the street, where they will spend the greater part of each day. They will always cross it in Indian file, over a carpet of empty sacks, with their boots in their hands, their heads uncovered, and in silence. The filth is horrendous; the camp's apparent cleanliness and order, a cruel refinement.

All of a sudden the silence, so profound that you might think the camp entirely deserted during these work-hours, is broken by an unusual cacophony: whistles, bells, shouts, doors slamming, feet running in the lanes. *Blockälteste* 13 jumps up from his table as if propelled by a spring, puts on his cap, crosses the dining area in a breath, and, still half asleep, runs out onto the street.

—They must have arrived —August says to nobody in particular—. I'm heading over.

He doesn't want to get caught up in the rush. He leaves the barracks without hurrying, and he tries to follow the paths that others have left in the snow that whitens the streets, immaculate in patches, elsewhere marred by all the coming and going. The smoke of the crematorium drifts down over the camp and mixes with the fog. The cold is so intense it forms crystals in the air, a cold that dispels the torpor of the stove. Fifteen hundred victims more, fifteen hundred men right now absorbing the same impressions that he had the day he arrived here. Impressions that, by different routes, all lead to the same end: a mix of fear, perverse curiosity, and bewilderment.

The camp was situated on top of the highest hill in the region. The surrounding terrain gave the impression of a rough sea suddenly solidified: not mountains but waves more or less pronounced, clothed here and there with swathes of forest that stood out at this season against the white snow of the open stretches. After four or five months of winter, the green grass of the great rich pasturlands would emerge, along with the houses, scattered but numerous, with their red terracotta roofs.

But the fog that day erased the contours of everything in the background, and it was impossible to tell where the earth left off and the sky began, all of it the same colour of lead, the colour of cold.

The journey had been long and exhausting, and the endless procession of the fifteen hundred men was now finally coming up to the barbed wire of the external precinct. The climb up the steep and icy road had been hard, laden as they were with their belongings and with the heavy burden of their fear. The guards had never stopped screaming at them and whipping them the whole way up, the pace had been too fast, and some had taken a lot of punishment. It should be no surprise, then, that at the entrance to the camp, fatigue and anxiety could be read in their faces, in their heavy gait, and in their silence.

—Home at last! —said Francesc with irony.

The permanent enclosure of the interior precinct was still under construction. The huge sections of cut stone wall weighed on the spirits of the new guests; the morning took on a bluish tinge. Breaking the monotony of the walls, half-built towers rose up at regular intervals. From these the sentries would one day be able to survey the scene in more comfort than they could now from their rickety wooden watchtowers. On the other side of the walls the snow-covered rooflines of some large barracks complexes emerged.

From the external barbed wire, one could see through the entrance and pick out the little black silhouettes of workers at the base of the wall, prisoners whose task was to make their own prison stronger.

The control bar lifted to clear the way before them. The new arrivals hadn't eyes enough to take in everything around them. For them, neither cold, fatigue, nor pain from the rain of blows existed anymore, only that avid curiosity that overwhelmed all other feelings. Their senses were lit up, their attention perfect: the secret was opening before their eyes. A concentration camp—nobody doubted anymore that this was where they were—was welcoming them, decked out in the best attire of its terrible regime. The antifascist pamphlets had talked a lot about the

German concentration camps, but no one had imagined anything like this, a huge fortress, stone.

The road climbed another hundred metres, skirting the new construction to end up at what was strictly speaking the main entrance of the camp. The prisoners, still in formation, advanced like a black snake along the snowy path. The stench of burnt leather caught in their throats. Emili and Francesc had not spoken for some time. Their heads were bowed under the weight they carried on their backs, but from time to time they would look up to observe the sights which that unique landscape offered them. Emili was the first to notice a small group of three or four men—he had to make a conscious effort to call them "men"—who, having come up along a secondary road, were waiting to cross over once the column of new prisoners had passed.

—"Look!" —he whispered.

They were dressed in blue-striped rags, with striped caps pulled down to their ears, their faces burnt by the icy wind, their lips and the tips of their noses purple with cold, shivering through their entire hunched bodies, but what was most remarkable was their cadaverous thinness. Their bones stuck out, not only from their skin, but out of the rags that covered them. From out of their too-short trousers stuck ankles grotesquely swollen, and the wooden clogs that crippled them; clumps of ice crusted on the soles made their balance uncertain, those human carcasses.

Francesc swore under his breath.

Then one of the living skeletons opened its mouth:

—*Sois españoles?* —it asked with an Andalusian accent.

The voice came out of his mouth as though delayed, and there was no correspondence between its power and the scarecrow that was making use of it. Nobody had the courage to answer him. The man repeated his question until he got tired. His voice and body together, presiding over the passing column, offered the newcomers a summary image of an existence to which fifteen hundred more men had been condemned.

—Did you get a good look? —asked Emili finally.
—What faces! —exclaimed Francesc, thinking he was seeing things—.
And he spoke Castillian ...
—We'll end up like them.

—Maybe they're just the sick ones …
—A great consolation …

The group's observations broke loose bit by bit in a crescendo of voices as they gradually overcame their astonishment. Tight voices, as though escaping constricted throats, the voices of children who are afraid of the dark and of being alone. Words without meaning, but on which everything depended for both speaker and listener: that they were still alive, that they were not wearing the striped pyjamas, that they did not have those spectral faces.

—This is a slaughterhouse!
—Bastards!
—They should finish us right now!
—Murderers!
—Not even a rat would survive this!

More groups of prisoners cut from the same cloth began to appear along the roadway. All of them worked with the same slowness, the same heavy rhythm of forced labourers: a passive rebellion, the only kind of rebellion possible against work from which one could expect no benefit but only a progressively ruinous exhaustion. Some of them cleared away snow with shovels and brooms, others were carrying construction materials on stretchers between them, and still others hefted impossibly large stones in their arms and shuffled in and out of the construction site at the base of the wall. They dragged their feet, their bodies curled in on themselves against the cold, their faces wracked by days, weeks, months of pain. All of them watched the column as it passed by, taking advantage of this moment to rest. In their deadened gaze one could sense an extra-human expression between pity and a strange happiness: "Now it's your turn" —they seemed to be thinking— "Too bad for you! You'll soon know the lot that's fallen to you."

In each work group one individual stood out for having no tools in hand. Like the others, he wore a striped uniform, but a new one, and he wore a blue or black peaked cap in the German style, and he often carried a club or a rubber tube in his hands. These individuals were clearly another category of prisoner since, to all appearances, they gave the orders. Their guttural shouts, which none of the newcomers understood, could only be meant to keep the work moving. "They're probably *cabos de vara*"[9] Emili thought. He'd only ever seen them before in movies.

—They always have the same dog-face —he said out loud.

The road climbed more steeply now, and to each side, there were barracks surrounded by ant-like activity. The green of the SS uniforms was the dominant colour here; probably these were the outbuildings, housing and kitchens for the troops. At the crest of the hill was the wall they had seen from afar. Two great towers with windows, their roofs vaguely Chinese in appearance, framed the great doors of the main entrance. To the left, the wall suddenly ended and was replaced by electrified barbed wire, a fact made clear by the porcelain insulators. Once the entrance was crossed, the new arrivals found themselves in a huge courtyard or, better, in the middle of a broad road complete with sidewalks, that ran between low, uniform barracks on one side, and large buildings with chimneys on the other. It must be from one of these chimneys that the acrid smoke with its stench of burnt leather was coming. A bizarre cacophony of bells, whistles, and shouts startled the new arrivals. From all directions, more people like the *cabos de vara* they'd already seen came running. When they arrived in front of the SS officers or sergeants who were organizing the manoeuvre, they squared up and took off their caps, showing their shaved heads to be as squared as their shoulders at attention. They received their orders with mechanical gestures, exaggerated as if making a parody of it, and with a click of their heels, they would invariably utter a word of two syllables. Then they would turn and run frantically up and down, emitting hoarse little shouts that sounded like the crackle of gunfire, only to reappear in front of the officers and start their puppet show all over again.

—Perhaps we're in an insane asylum? —asked Francesc.
—They're right to keep it fenced.

Then came the recount, repeated fifty times, and the arbitrary interrogations that nobody could answer because nobody knew the language and that therefore usually ended in beatings. The herding dogs ran back and forth, barking more loudly whenever they were approached by the uniformed men giving them commands. At one point the voice of a soloist rose above the madness, a German prisoner who spoke an effeminate Castilian. He was the official interpreter of the camp.

—You have just arrived in a German concentration camp, —he said calmly—. You are here to work and to obey, and obviously there is no point in complaining about it, as you seem so fond of doing. There's no need for you to ask questions; everything is prohibited and the punishment for those who want to be clever is very severe. Remember that the slightest mistake is often paid for with your life. Here you are going to be under the most rigid discipline it is possible to imagine; you are never going to laugh again …

—Faggot! —said Emili.

CHAPTER II

"Block 12," announced the lettering over the door. The newcomers were entering in small groups to go through the formalities of their arrival. Emili and Francesc had been waiting their turn for a good while. Lined up in the snow, after so much, their mouths pasty and their lips dry for the lack of a proper hot meal, they were starting to feel the overwhelming weight of their fatigue. It was bitterly cold, a fine snow coming down with increasing intensity, and their feet, after having warmed up a little in the run from the station, were again beginning to feel icy pins and needles piercing the skin. The two friends noticed that most often when prisoners from the camp approached them, if they were the well dressed ones, nothing happened, but if they weren't, they were violently beaten away. They were surprised that some of those who did manage to get close to them were Spanish; they would ask after such and such a person, or about the people from a certain village, and answered the questions posed to them in turn with the superior air of those in full command of the uses and customs of the house. Each explained things in his own way, but all of them recounted the most unthinkable horrors with complete equanimity. The newcomers felt as if they had fallen into a deep well.

—And you say they're going to take all our things?
—You'll be stripped of everything. Here everything is forbidden.
—Just what that faggot told us.
—But pretend that it's not the case. Just try not to get caught …
—Keep your eyes open.
—Photographs?
—None.
—Why don't you hide them for me?
—Don't mess with me. I'm not an idiot.
—And tobacco?
—For now you'll be able to keep it, but the *Blockälteste* is going to take it as soon as you get to the barracks. Don't even think about holding on to anything.
—Why no photographs?
—Ask Hitler.

—And money? —asked someone who had made a good deal of it in the prisoner-of-war camp.
—What would you do with it?
—Buy things from the canteen.
—They've only got tins of shoe polish and combs.
—Combs? But everybody's bald!

Without asking a single question, the two friends had learned the first law of the camp: they would have to give up everything they had.

—We're going to die from the cold in those pyjamas they're giving out —said Emili.

Their luggage wasn't worth much: old uniforms of coarse material, and dirty, some books they'd picked up in the French barracks that had served as their prisoner-of-war camp, cooking implements, worn out shoes ... Nothing and everything. Everything they had.

—My drawing materials —Emili lamented.
—Ask to have them put aside. You never know ...

A German prisoner divided the men into two rows; now it was time for the two friends to go in. They proceeded into the dormitory of one wing of the Block. A dormitory in name only, it had no furniture, only a great mound of clothing, knapsacks, parcels, suitcases, plates, and canteens that a few prisoners were separating lazily into piles. A nauseating stench of sweat hung in the air, inadequate as the windows were, even wide open, to ventilate the room. The German prisoners, with their shaved heads, never stopped screaming at them to hurry up, meting out kicks and blows all the while.

Emili and Francesc sought out a corner where they could get undressed in peace. They gathered what they could in their arms and, completely naked, with goose bumps and chattering teeth, went through to the dining room next door. Here, the tables had been set up for paperwork; some seated prisoner-clerks were taking down their affiliations. Another prisoner held open a big paper sack into which yet another haphazardly stuffed the treasure from each piece of luggage. An SS supervising the operation looked over anything of value and, if he liked it, put it in his pocket. Emili showed him his drawing instruments and the folder with some of his drawings in it. He tried, by miming, to make the officer understand that he would like to keep them. The SS had a look at the drawings.

—Gut, prima! —he allowed, thinking it was praise that Emili sought from him.

And he looked with a hint of admiration at this man who in spite of belonging to an "inferior race" had hands that could produce "something like that." But pencils, paper, and folder all ended up in the paper bag in any case.

Still naked, with their belts hanging around their necks and the little tobacco they still had clutched in their hands, they crossed over to the other wing of the Block. Here the dining room looked like a barbershop in a nudist camp. An SS lounged in an easy chair pretending to carry out a medical check, and with a single glance, declared all of them as fit. These unwilling Adamites then had to line up and submit to the hands of the various barbers charged with shaving them. When it was their turn, they would sit on a stool until their heads had been shorn; after that, they stood up and offered their armpits, then their chests to the clippers; and finally they had to climb onto the stool to have their pubic hair shorn off. The windows were locked shut because the doctor was afraid of catching a cold, and the stench from all the bodies was making them dizzy.

Emili fell to a Spanish barber endowed with the characteristic loquacity of the guild. The man never took a breath.

—Today you're a big group that's come in —he said while running the clippers over Emili's head—. Soon everyone in this camp will be Spanish. Where are you from? Catalan, right? It's not so good here, especially in winter. Very cold. Myself, I can't complain: doing what I do I am spared work in the quarry. You're not a barber are you? No? Too bad. At least for now, barbers are making it.

The way his clippers kept nipping the skin was nearly unbearable. Emili winced and tears welled up in his eyes.

—Stand up —commanded the barber after finishing the first stage of his torture.

The draughtsman ran his hand across his head and scratched it. He noticed that some hairs remained longer than others.

—The equipment, you know —the barber apologized—. It doesn't matter; here there's no call for vanity.

Emili climbed onto the stool and spread his legs.

—Higher —ordered the barber— That's it ... People here starve. Many die. The Spaniards, when they are just about finished, are taken off to another camp. Now to the right ... Good, good. They say it's a rest camp! Just to make fun of us. They're all killed. Nearly done here. At the beginning it's very hard, but you get used to it. Or you die. It's all a question of luck and of being able to keep the spirits up. It's five months now I've pulled myself through. There, finished. Now get lost.

Emili got down from the stool and rubbed the martyred zone.

—Ah! —exclaimed the barber—. You've got a moustache. Prohibited!

The draughtsman couldn't repress a grimace of repugnance. The clippers had gone into every nook and cranny of his body and of hundreds of other bodies and now passed inexorably across his mouth.

—Don't make such a face —counselled the barber, smiling—. Revulsion is a luxury here.

Once dressed in his striped uniform, Francesc, like the others, had to jump through a window that gave onto the laneway of the next Block, Block 13, to which he was assigned, and like most of those who had preceded him, he was betrayed by his wooden-soled shoes: stepping on the hard-packed snow, he fell flat on his back. The others had been waiting for this, and their laughter made him realize that, at last having found a bit of calm, he could take a deep breath and loosen his grip on himself a little. The groups that filled the laneway were recounting the morning's events with as much good humour as possible. A strained exchange that didn't auger well, but was the best that they could manage.

Francesc heard Emili's voice calling out to him. He had to study the faces in the crowd before he recognized him, and when he did, with some difficulty, he couldn't keep from laughing like the others. They had run out of winter uniforms, no warmer than the summer ones but a darker colour and so giving the illusion that they might be. In their place, they handed out a sort of striped pyjamas, patched and mended all over, too tight or too loose, too short or too long, that made an extravagant contrast with the snow now falling more and more heavily.

—What a look! —cried Emili.

—Yours and everybody else's. Zebras in the Arctic. A terrific disguise.

And, posing like a model, Francesc spun on his heel. The group laughed aloud. The draughtsman took him by the arm to make him turn. His jacket had a large stain in the middle of the back.

—It looks like an old bloodstain.
—More than likely —offered one of the group—. Chances are it's not tomato sauce.

The two friends walked away from the group and went on a little ways in silence.

—This is a mass gallows —said Emili.
—I'm not so surprised; we heard all about it, after all.
—But who could have believed it.

They'd gone up some stairs and found themselves on another terrace. Access to the streets across from them was blocked by barbed wire. On the other side there appeared some skeletal, half-naked prisoners. They looked Slavic. Everybody stared, but nobody said a word to them. By contrast, a bit farther on, in the last street, there was a big press of newcomers at the thorny barrier making a huge ruckus.

—That must be the barracks for Spaniards —said Emili—. They've had Spaniards here six months now, and a third of them have died. They take them to another camp, a satellite camp, and exterminate them en masse.
—Just what I've heard too. It must be true, but I don't want to think about it. Be ready for what comes, you know what I mean. There's always a hole to hide in and wait for a lucky break.

Emili smiled skeptically.

—The war isn't going to last long —insisted Francesc—. Remember what we read in the newspaper about Graziani on the Allied superiority.[10]

He paused and then, smiling, added:

—Cheer up, Emili. Count on it: by August, we'll be in Sant Feliu for the village festival.

—You're out of your mind.

They got to the end of the street where the crowd was larger, and the spectacle before them was astonishing. None of those unfortunates was older than fifty (the maximum age for entrance into the French work companies from which nearly all of them had come). In their present condition, all of them looked like ancients at death's door ... stiff, mummified. They danced around constantly from the cold, they flailed their arms to keep warm and talked relentlessly to the newcomers. Whether about their home regions or about the horrors of the camp, they spoke with the easy manner of those who have grown used to things, almost with a kind of pleasure at feeling important. Most of them, instead of asking for food, begged cigarette butts.[11]

—Let's get out of here! —implored Emili—. Please, let's go!

From time to time a flurry of snow drifted down. The low clouds made a compact ceiling.

—This damned smoke! —he exclaimed after some moments, fixing his gaze on the crematorium chimney—. If I have to breathe it much longer, I'll go nuts.

The new tenants of Block 13 were allowed into the dormitory a little while before lunch. The *Blockälteste*, nicknamed "Popeye," spoke to them through August, the interpreter, and told them that he would let them in on the condition that they were quiet; otherwise, they would be out on the street and stay there for the rest of the day.

In an endless string, the newcomers walked across the empty sacks that served as mats, their shoes in hand, bareheaded and silent, toward the empty, freezing dormitory. Here, the straw pallets and blankets that had been laid out made a kind of platform in the centre.

Because the room was far too small for so many people, the fug of human cattle steamed up the windows and the men soon started to warm up. Their initial silence was now broken by scattered exchanges in low voices. The situation, not much better than desperate, had triggered a sort of false levity in them, perhaps from a need to feel alive despite everything; a kind of contagious hysteria began to take over, and their voices grew louder and louder. After a while, it was like a shouting match in the room. One person even dared to light a cigarette. The *Blockälteste* opened the door:

—I said SILENCE! —he exploded.

And made his entrance, hands behind his back, torso inclined forward, taking long, slow strides. In a rush his gallows face brought back all the fear that the men had been trying to dispel with their joking and chatter. He was a simian type, prognathic, a product of the back streets of some port city. A longshoreman or a tavern bully. His German was rough and full of jargon. Spit sprayed from his mouth when he talked. At that moment, nothing could be heard over the clatter of their wooden shoes as they scrambled to their feet.

Behind Popeye's back, August gestured, making it clear that he had warned them this would happen. The German passed in front of the men in silence, as if he were a cattle dealer sorting out the best specimens at the market. He didn't stop until he came to the range of bunks. There, his eyes lit up with joy.

—Interpreter! Interpreter! —he shouted like a madman—. Who's done this?

He pointed with the index finger of his right hand at a blanket with its corner torn off.

—Who did it? Eh? Who? Don't you realize this is sabotage?

The word was all the rage in Germany. A broken dish, a slammed door, a hat misplaced, anything and everything was sabotage.

August translated Popeye's questions, but nobody answered.

—This blanket has just been torn, —insisted the *Blockälteste* in a fury—. Whoever did it must come forward. If not …
—Probably none of them did it. —August said in German—. They're scared to death. Nobody would have dared …

Popeye, as if he'd been waiting for just such a comment, launched into a storm of shouts, threats, and insults. He opened a path through the crowd and took great strides back and forth, adopted theatrical poses, and vomited insults at them. The men watched this performance with curiosity.

—We'll find out soon enough. No one leaves.

The *Blockälteste*'s acolytes (one from each wing of the Block) stepped up to organize the frisking of those hundreds of men.

—It's a pretext to pillage anything you've got left —explained August—. It happens every time a new group arrives.

Each and every remaining bit of "treasure" the men had been able to smuggle in with them, tobacco, lighters, penknives, fountain pens, photos, pieces of soap, were now being piled up in the middle of the room. The piece of blanket did not appear. August had passed the word that in the event there was an actual culprit, they must be sure he was not discovered, as he would most certainly be killed.

—Out on the street! —shouted Popeye— In formation! You'll stay out there in the cold until whoever's responsible for this sabotage owns up to it.

August didn't have time to translate the order. The three Germans had already started to lash out, punching and kicking to left and right. The doorway, terribly narrow for the two hundred men rushing to get through it, began to creak as if it would split apart. Many of them jumped out the windows in a panic. Some fell and were trampled by the others.

Once they were alone again, the Germans gathered up their booty and took it into the dining room to sort through it. Outside, it was snowing heavily now; nobody got anything to eat until late in the afternoon.

To simply stretch one's legs! To stretch them right out, to the point of disjointing them. Two hundred men who couldn't stretch their legs. Constantly in one another's way, they cursed, they hated.

The rules of the camp said that at this hour they must go to sleep, and the bell had already tolled silence some minutes before. Popeye had turned off the lights with no concern for those who had not yet found their places. The arguments, the protests, the insults between those who were struggling to find somewhere to settle and those who refused to give up any of the little space they had won with such effort, all of these were suppressed by fear of the punishment Popeye meted out for any transgression of the rules. Recent as their experience had been of an afternoon spent outside in formation, those hours standing immobile in the snow, any voice mounting in complaint was quickly silenced by a "shhh!" from the more prudent.

Now, with the stragglers finally settled, a relative calm descended. Some of the men breathed deeply or snored, others coughed, but these were just rustlings that gave form to the silence, the same way that the fug, dust, and sweat gave density to the bottomless night.

On the straw mattresses spread out on the floor, the principle of the body's impenetrability was put to the test. The blankets scattered over that floor paved with men lying side by side and head to toe made a uniform pattern and gave the appearance of a huge carpet decorated with two hundred decapitations.

Nevertheless, this was the time for dreams, a moment of escape to better worlds where concentration camps were unknown; it was short-lived, but the only thing like it, for those lucky enough to drop off to sleep.[12]

Despite his exhaustion, Emili couldn't close his eyes. The faint light that filtered in through the windows, the clouds of fug that whitened when they slid out through the open transom vents, the rhythmic breathing of his neighbours, the snoring on all sides, the shuffling of those going out to urinate, everything was keeping him awake despite his best efforts. Perhaps because of this, his forcing it, sleep slipped tauntingly away. His thoughts were all in turmoil, and the mental balance he needed and that he could have maintained if he'd been calmer in his spirit, dissolved into a gratuitous and incessant play of images, one on top of the other, constantly turning and starting over, all jumbled together in a kind of obsessive arabesque.

Francesc was breathing heavily next to him. Sleep was the reward for his courage. Francesc believed in happy endings: the lightning advance of the British Army and the national uprisings of the oppressed. He was sure he could see signs of how things were coming apart for the Germans. This said it all. Emili smiled when he thought of his friend's naïveté. The reality of the camp weighed down his dreams. The cold, the hunger, the exhaustion, the disintegration of the body, they were all there and stalked them all. A slow and agonizing death, no doubt, but shorter, much shorter than the war.

Those old men he'd seen dancing on the ice begging cigarettes from behind the barbed wire of the special camp, they crowded in like phantoms now across the carpet of sleepers right towards Emili where he was sweating and shivering all at once in his corner. He shut his eyes tighter, to keep the vision at bay, and the clear, perceptible silence of the two hundred men around him gave him an intimation of immensity. He too flickered in that closed space where just to breathe took real effort.

He had the ethereal sensation of his own absence. He'd abandoned his body where it lay among the other men, but his sensation, of being a guest of the universe, was undiminished. He grew and grew in the vacuum between the stars, and the starlight gathered in a vast aureole around his loved ones. Matilde, his wife, was laughing and seemed to be getting ready to dance alone, as he had once seen her do, and from the Earth, already so far beneath his feet, came a low and solemn rhythm, like that of the drums of mourning. From a pile of sponges in a fishing net the liquid colours of the rainbow poured out, and a man with the bearing of a gorilla, like Popeye, was beating them with a stick and opened a toothless mouth as if to sing. But now the body abandoned among the sleeping men began to stir, and Emili again felt imprisoned, as though within some elastic medium. Impossible to stretch his legs among so many corpses! Impossible to move, to stand up, to run, even while those ravening old men were getting closer and closer, begging their cigarette butts. They were just on the point of stepping on him; they paid no heed to where they put their feet, their eyes fixed on that white fog that poured through the vents. Emili distinctly felt the weight of one of them come down on him … He wanted to scream, and he did, loudly, very loudly.

He woke up soaked in sweat. His nose was stuffed up and he had to open his mouth and gasp for air in his panic. He thrashed his head back and forth on the pillow he'd made from his clothing. His whole body was in pain and his head felt like it was going to explode. It was then that he noticed the itching in his crotch and armpits. He scratched himself and thought, "the shearing." Then something stuck between his fingertip and nail, big as a grain of rice, soft and alive. "Lice," he realized with disgust:

Francesc woke up:

—What's the matter?
—You haven't found any lice?
—Go to sleep and leave them alone.

And their two hands found each other across the legs of the one sleeping head to toe between them, and across the stinking blankets.

CHAPTER III

August didn't know much German, but he did know how to handle people. He'd been trying for some time to convince Popeye to let the men come back inside, their having spent the last two hours out on the street taking the fresh air.

> —Real men, your Spaniards! —laughed the *Blockälteste*—. Five minutes in the open air and they're dying of cold.
> —Five minutes? —replied the smiling interpreter—. Your watch must have stopped! But I'll get my revenge when you come to Spain. You'll spend this five minutes of yours out in the sun. Enough to peel the skin right off your back!
> —Don't boast so much about your famous sun! —intervened the secretary—. I spent two years in the Sahara with no damage to my hide.
> —Because yours is too thick.

The secretary was a German prisoner detained as an "asocial." He'd spent some time in the French Foreign Legion, and all he knew about Spain was the existence of a boxer named Uzcudun.[13] August had got on his good side by telling him, in exacting detail, about an imaginary tour of duty he had made in the Tercio,[14] of which he claimed to have been an officer. The secretary was very fond of Africa as a theme, and the fact that August listened to him with the air of a connoisseur made him gentle as a lamb. August took advantage of this friendship to move the weaker men into the easiest positions, for the secretary was, in fact, the arbiter of the prisoners' lives, responsible as he was for organizing the *Kommandos* (work parties).

> —They need to get used to the cold —Popeye assured him—. It's not healthy to spend all day in the barracks. When the time comes for them to go out to work they'll be ready for it.
> —Yes —the secretary chimed in facetiously—. Let them go outside and play; there's fewer headaches then.

August told a dirty joke, and the Germans laughed over it for a good while. Then Popeye gave his permission.

—Tell them if there's any noise, half a dozen are dead on the spot—.

The men filed through the dining room according to the regulations. It had only been three days that those unfortunates had been in the camp, and they hadn't yet gone out to work. But hunger and cold were already starting to leave their mark on the less resistant organisms. Some of their faces showed livid welts left by the truncheons, the older ones trembled like leaves, and all of them, without exception, looked greedily at the stove, glowing with heat, planted right in the middle of the dining room for the exclusive use of the Germans in the Block. Some even dared stop for just a second, just long enough to pause in front of it and extend their frozen hands. This act alone now constituted a crime.

—Don't stop in front of the stove —August kept repeating like a chant.

Emili came in from the street primed for a fight. It wasn't the SS who were responsible for most of the tortures they were subjected to, but the German prisoners, capricious and demented as they were. In other barracks, the prisoners enjoyed relatively more humane treatment, and they spent their time indoors when they weren't working or forming up for roll call. A man got into line in front of him. He was over forty. Emili knew him from the prisoner-of-war camp and felt a strong kinship with him. Exhausted by what he had had to endure, half sick, this man was worn out from the cold. He rubbed his hands convulsively together, and his nose streamed. The poor wretch hadn't noticed Popeye glowering from his position next to the stove, guarding his treasure.

—Don't stop —August called out.

Either he didn't hear him or he didn't understand. Hardly had he paused when the German laid him out with a punch.

Emili didn't think twice. He threw himself at the aggressor and sent him reeling with a blow from his wooden shoe. The secretary raised his eyes from his papers and settled in to watch what promised to be a most entertaining diversion.

At last he'd found among the Spaniards a successor to the great Uzcudun. August was dumfounded: "What's he doing, the idiot?"

Popeye had collected himself and was staring at his opponent with a mixture of surprise, admiration, and rage. All at once, he charged at the draughtsman. Defence with the shoe got him nowhere; the German was twisting his arm, his face red with anger and his teeth clenched in rage. The shoe fell heavily to the floor.

Emili was not a weak man. He was tall, and his leanness didn't denote any lack of strength. His fine musculature gave him a slippery agility that allowed him to dodge the heavier Popeye's blows. But then he got caught full in the face. He tumbled to the floor amid a clatter of stools and tables. Half unconscious, he felt a piercing pain in his left side that left him momentarily breathless. Kicking him again and again, Popeye savoured his revenge.

The secretary, having got up and joined the crowd of spectators, many of whom had taken advantage of the situation to get nearer the stove, watched the scene unfold with the avid attention of an enthusiast. He liked the Spaniard's gesture. That somebody had dared, against the terrible Popeye, gave him a malicious satisfaction.

—Enough is enough —he said to the victor— Let him go, all right? The boy is very brave.

But Popeye didn't listen. His rosary of insults and abuse begun, it was not so easy to stop.

—What's he think, the filthy dog? —he shouted— Who makes the law here? It's going to cost you, this little joke! I'll crush you, you hear me, I'll crush you!

Even though the secretary repeated his call for clemency, the *Blockälteste* didn't stop pounding away at that inert body until his own exhaustion slowed him down. And after all, Emili, now immobile, had ceased to be so exciting.

—Out of here! —he shouted all of a sudden, when he noticed that the dining room was full— Out, you pigs! Get out, I said!

And then he picked up an iron poker from the stove. Everybody scrambled. Still shouting, Popeye stopped to look at his reflection in the mirror. There was a lump rising in the middle of his forehead and his face was covered in scratches.

—With his fingernails, like a woman! I'll finish you another day, you stupid dog! Filthy gipsy! You don't screw with me!

The secretary had gone back to his table and was smiling wryly. August was helping Emili into the dormitory.

—Where's my vaseline? —shouted Popeye, searching the cupboard.

It had been a long time since Vicent had come to the camp. Destiny had mocked him, making the day of his arrival coincide with the anniversary of his birth thirty-two years before. As if this was a sign, he didn't have the same good fortune as some of his companions—the lucky few—but instead met with difficulties as did the great majority. Accustomed, his whole life, to luxurious homemade paellas, to the rich fruits of l'Horta,[15] to good fish and nicely seasoned meat, he'd had to begin by substituting quantity for quality when he arrived in the French refugee camps. It had been just the same later on, during the months in the Workers Company. And here the Germans had captured him when they erupted across the Maginot line. Now, Vicent, or "València" as everybody called him, didn't even have the quantity. After three months on the concentration camp diet, one might say that he had consumed the last of his strength, having already lost all of his flesh. His blackened skin, darkened partly from the snow and sun, and partly from his indifference to washing, appeared flaccid and wrinkled in the places where the bones didn't shine through. He'd lost his good humour too, his farmer's loud, farting, laughing, back-slapping animal vitality. The blue shadows around his eyes extended little by little across his whole face, and his only expression was a covetous gaze at the morsels of bread that his comrades in ill-fortune were still chewing when he, a bit of a glutton and very hungry, had already swallowed his whole day's ration in two mouthfuls. Today he envies his companions who are lucky enough to be last at the soup pot and thus receive a thicker ration. Vicent would spend hours and hours talking with his wagon mates in the quarry about imaginary banquets, or hold forth with surprising passion on the poor qualities of the midday ration. He rushed in with a little wooden stick he always carried, to scrape the insides of the thermos flask, braving the whips of the German prisoners in charge of getting the soup pots back to the kitchen. At night, he would dream the details of an imaginary homecoming when his wife, Eugènia, would prepare a repast for him worthy of a Pantagruel, a Pantagruel from València.

Vicent was hungry, very hungry. When he finished the meagre litre of watery soup at midday, or that morsel of black bread that constituted his only supper, he was hungrier than before he began. He couldn't quiet the complaints of his stomach, which constantly twisted and gnawed on itself during the periods of digestive inactivity afforded it so generously. He suffered constantly, this same slow, silent torture without respite, and his body used itself up, growing thinner every day; his arms bent when he had to push the wagons, his knees refused to hold him up, and his eyes couldn't tolerate the light on sunny days. Vicent was one of the condemned, and he knew it. But facing death, he fought for his life like a cat turned on its back. Contemptible acts, hatred, meanness, selfishness without limit: thanks to the inversion of values only possible in a camp of slow death, these were the means by which he made his heroic protest against an unjust destiny, in short, against the cruelty of men. The vileness of his existence didn't bother Vicent at all: it bounced like a ball off his hardened will to survive.

That morning had been hard. He'd got up more tired out than ever and had had to make a huge effort to get himself to the door of Block 2 (the barracks for the privileged prisoners, the cooks, the warehouse workers, the clerks, in sum, for those who were not starving), where maybe somebody would take pity on him and give him the leftovers from the soup ration, the bone broth they were given some days for breakfast. But that day, nothing, and on returning to Block 13, he discovered that the companion to whom he had entrusted the collection of his own regular ration had slipped on the icy steps and spilled the contents of both of the bowls he was carrying.

To cry out, to moan about it, to object would serve no purpose. The resulting confrontation wouldn't return one drop of the wasted broth and was only going to make his obsessive hunger all the more acute and painful.

The work had been harder than ever as well. It seemed as if the quarry had come alive with activity, even if it was just a way to fight back against the cold, that cold that reached through the hardened layer of snow to the heart of the stone itself. Because of the cold, the jackhammers weren't working, but there was enough loose stone that the big diesels never stopped coming and going to the cut where Vicent was one of the loaders. Ten wagons each train, a hundred stones each wagon, and, on top of them, the *kapos* with their constant shrieking, brandishing their rubber truncheons, never letting up on those under their authority.

"València" could do no more. The cold had got into his bones and, with frozen hands, he loaded the wagons like an automaton. He longed only for that midday that never seemed to come. And still another train, and another one, and … Each time the ridiculous whistling of the engine, coming closer with its merciless clickety-clak. It had been ages now since somebody had told him it was eleven o'clock. Inside the wooden clogs, his feet were like a bridge for the cold climbing up his legs. The contractions of his stomach echoed within his own being the hollowness of death. Midday! Vicent imagined the rosy colour of the boiled turnips that would constitute his little ration in an hour's time, the regular shape of the machine-cut pieces, and he savoured, as though in a dream, the particles of potato, smoothed round by boiling, more floury than the turnips. It was almost as though he already had the aluminium bowl in his hands, filled to the brim with more than a litre because, finally, he'd had the good fortune to be the last one at the thermos and the prisoner in charge of serving the soup had given him two generous ladles-full. Solid food, without broth … His hands were slowly warming up, and his body was coming sweetly back to life.

—Get to work! Didn't you hear me? —shouted the *kapo* in German—. Faster, faster! At lunch hour you'll move quick enough! Move, slacker! Work, if you don't want me to beat the shit out of you.

"València" looked at him stupidly. The slave-driver's voice was completely puzzling to him just then. The truncheon no longer frightened him. The capacity for suffering has a limit, and Vicent had reached it. The *kapo* came up to him.

—Didn't you understand me, you idiot?

He whipped his ribs with the rubber truncheon.

When the quarry siren started whistling, Vicent was just finishing the loading of the last hundred stones of the morning. It was true that after one short hour he would have to start all over again, but this was too bleak a realization to think about now, at the best moment of the day, when he was going to get his food. Having forgotten about the cold, his fatigue seemed to fade away, and even his knees seemed to behave themselves better. Snow clumped to the soles of his shoes, he staggered as if he were drunk.

The sky was a dirty grey and the snow itself was dull; you could say the quarry was pillowed with it. The voices of the *kapos* chanted out the pace:

—*Links, zwei, drei, vier … Links, zwei, drei, vier …*

The column was moving much too fast for Vicent to keep up. It was so far from the quarry to the roll call square! But there awaited the thermoses, all in a row, ready for the distribution of their precious contents. In spite of the pain he felt in his legs, as if they would snap from the strain, Vicent felt untouchable. What did it matter if he fell out of step just now, or if the Pole behind him was making a scene to alert the *kapos* to this grave transgression?[16] Vicent gasped for breath, and the breath that came laboriously from his dry, open mouth, crystallized in tiny particles of ice on the turned up collar of his jacket. None of this was of any importance to him, because he was thinking of the smoky soup with its thousand good flavours.

The next day, Emili woke to the sound of the bell feeling like he couldn't move. He had trouble breathing because of the blood clots in his nose, he could tell that his right eye had swollen up, all his bones ached, and from time to time, a sharp pain pierced the side of his body where he had been kicked repeatedly. "I'm probably black and blue all over," he thought. And he got himself up with great difficulty.

Once the formation for the work *Kommandos* was finished, August took him to the infirmary, where a sympathetic doctor made sure that Emili didn't have any serious wounds. Back at the Block, the draughtsman asked for advice.

—Popeye is rabid —said August— Try to avoid him. He may try to trip you up. Luckily the secretary likes you, and if I ask him he will transfer you to another Block.
—Yesterday afternoon's reprisals are causing me a lot more pain than this, let me tell you.

There had been two long hours of rolling around in the snow, of leap-frog, of running up and down the length of the camp, of doing "*Mützen ab.*" To cheer himself up, Popeye had armed himself with a broomstick and was meting out blows all around, especially during the last of these exercises. This one required the four hundred men (two hundred from each wing of the Block), to put on and pull off their hats, all together, with Prussian exactitude. They had to do this hundreds and hundreds of times while standing at attention, and the slap of the hat against the thigh had to sound unified and energetic. Pity the one who lost the rhythm!

—*Mützen ab, Mützen auf, Mützen ab, Mützen auf ...*

When bedtime arrived, the enraged *Blockälteste* put a bucket of cold water at the barracks' entrance and announced there would now be a "foot inspection." Four hundred men had to wash their feet with the same water, without soap or towels. After the first hundred, the bucket was four fingers deep with thick mud. People scrubbed their feet with saliva or urine. According to what August had told them, even a little smudge, or a callous slightly darker than the surrounding skin, was sufficient cause for a beating.

Emili took all the precautions the situation required, and Popeye didn't want to earn a name for being unjust.

The third act came at midnight. Under the pretext that those who were getting up to use the toilet were making too much noise, Popeye decided to wake everybody up and, with blows from his stick, forced them outside and into formation. In the rush and under the rain of blows, nobody had had the presence of mind to remember it was freezing outside. Some half naked, most without their shoes, they stood at attention on the snow for a long half hour.

When he considered the consequences of his act, Emili recognized his mistake. August laid out his own personal approach for him.

—Blow for blow, they'll always win. They're stronger than us. It's only by using our heads that we can keep them in check, and who knows, someday maybe we'll gain the upper hand.

The draughtsman didn't grasp what August was insinuating. He only replied:

—I don't think they understand that, the language of intelligence.

Having let August go on his way and unable to go into the barracks, he walked back along the street in search of Francesc. The sun was showing its face through the fog rising up from the Danube, and even if a little faint-hearted, it shone down kind and sweet. Some, stripped naked, were catching the lice they found in the seams of their shirts. Others smoked their last reserves of tobacco. None of them spoke; none had anything to say. None of them knew anything of the outside world, and of the world inside, they knew everything. Their hunger, now starting to get painful, was the one topic that had a dependable audience.

He found Francesc leaning against the side of a barracks where the sun was strongest. His face was turned upward and he looked like he was sleeping, having given himself over completely to the voluptuousness of that heat. It was one of those faces that inspired trust. Perhaps because of the deep-set eyes, perhaps the long, square chin ...

—Sleeping or thinking?

Francesc turned towards him.

—You're back?
—It seems so.
—Your eye is getting blacker all the time —he said, smiling. And he asked— What did they say to you down there?
—That it's nothing.
—Nothing? Does it seem like nothing, carrying around such a piece of ID?

Emili, smiling as well, told him what he had seen at the infirmary and waited a long time for his companion to say something. But Francesc had closed his eyes again and didn't seem to have anything to tell him.

—You haven't heard anything? —asked the draughtsman.
—About what?
—About the stupid thing I did yesterday.

Francesc let some seconds pass.

—You protected a poor defenceless man. What do you expect people to say?
—I behaved like an idiot. The excesses of that scoundrel ...
—Don't dwell on it. Concentrate on taking care of yourself.

A fellow prisoner came up to them and said to Emili:

—Aren't you 4386?

The draughtsman had to think hard to remember the number that was stitched to the left breast of his jacket below the triangle of blue cloth.

—Yes —he answered—. Why?
—They've been calling you for an hour now at the barracks. My number's after yours.

The two friends headed towards the Block. Emili went into the dining room and Francesc, from outside, saw him talking to the secretary and a prisoner he didn't know, probably a German. Popeye was nowhere to be seen.

When Emili came out he was with the stranger and Francesc went over to him:

—Where are you going? Where are they taking you?
—I don't know. I couldn't understand them. It sounds like I'm going to the office.
—What for?
—How should I know! Maybe they want to ask me how I like the food.

He regretted speaking harshly. Francesc seemed worried.

—But just in case they let me go free, goodbye —he joked.
—Eh, you! —said the German.

He asked something that Emili didn't understand, but from his gesture he thought he was asking how he got his black eye.

—Yesterday —answered Emili, using one of the few German words he knew.

And he made a gesture with his closed fist.

—Are you a boxer?

And the German laughed with his whole round doughy face.
Francesc was left alone. He thought: "Popeye has found a way to make peace."

CHAPTER IV

Hans Gupper, "El Negre," had just arrived at his office. At around nine o'clock every day he left his house, a villa he had had the prisoners build a couple of kilometres from the camp, and made the trip on his motorcycle in just few minutes. He was the camp commandant and the most feared of all the SS there. A militant founder of the party[17] in Austrian territory, he had taken part in all the struggles of those times, most importantly in the *putsch* against Dollfuss, after which he'd had to seek refuge in Germany. He had returned to his own country during the *Anschluss,*[18] arriving in Vienna with a chest full of stars, stripes, and medals. Each rank and every decoration would have meant hundreds of lives sacrificed on the altar of "Greater Germany."[19] This flamboyant *Obersturmführer* of the SS had acquired his hero's laurels through the murder of Jews and communists.

Now, some years having passed since these heroic deeds, nothing in his demeanour suggested the least sign of satisfaction, but on the contrary a fundamental disillusionment and bitterness that he disguised as severity. He must have missed his good old days as a shoemaker, when he spent his time putting on half-soles and rubber heels, cursing Christian populism or social democracy with his friends, his clients, and his neighbours.

He cut a striking figure. With his officer's hat, the long fur coat that reached down to his ankles, the impeccable boots, the jingling spurs (for riding his motorcycle), and those enormous dogs that wove arabesques around him while he walked through the camp, and, above all, with the terror that radiated from his mere presence, nobody could deny that he was cut out for the job.

—Hans Gupper has entered the camp.

Word flew from barracks to barracks. *Blockälteste, Stubenälteste,* and secretaries all rushed to take their various precautions. They put in order what was already ordered, cleaned what was already clean, and hid what was already hidden. This last was the most important, because Hans Gupper was a clever old cat and knew every trick that the prisoners with "administrative responsibilities" used to move food, clothing, and all manner of things through their black market. When Hans Gupper uncovered an "organizer" (as they were called in the Germans' slang), the consequences were very severe. Hans Gupper had an iron fist! Once in the camp, he was heartless: he obeyed orders and he gave them.

Entering the dispatch office that day, he didn't take off his coat or hat. Only his gloves, and these because his fingers were stiff with cold from riding the motorcycle. He drank a cup of coffee from the thermos that the office boy had ready for him, lit a cigarette, and warmed his hands at the stove. In a corner of the office there was a scale model of the camp. When he had first come, there were only the prisoners' barracks, a barbed wire perimeter surrounding them, and a few barracks annexes on the outside. The walls, the great doors at the entrance, the gardens, the stairs, the garage, the blocks for the troops, and many other installations had been built under his orders. And that was only the beginning. He would build a model camp, a proto-camp. And there would be no shortage of lives to sacrifice to it, especially now that the Germans were advancing, adding victory onto victory.

Hans Gupper looked once more at the model, which represented both the work done and his program for its completion. At a glance, he calculated the time left, and the muscles in his face contracted into a grimace that might have been the beginning of a smile:

—Two years —he hissed—. I'll finish it in two years.

It was a question of accumulating the materials. With the first good weather, a big push. Stone, above all, more stone. The Reich couldn't provide much in the way of concrete or iron, but Hans Gupper had stone, good stone, and lots of it, and he had the men to quarry it, carry it, and build with it. He'd already shown that he knew how to organize a camp, and now he would build one in which the enemies of National Socialism would die better than in any other.

Not a man for dreaming, he soon turned his back on the model and went out. At that moment some prisoners were scratching away at the ice around the camp entrance, and when they saw him coming they picked up the pace. It was a beautiful day, but the officer was more interested in the progress of his work than in the sun that sweetened the morning. He caught sight of the workers and considered their extreme thinness. "If they ate more, they'd work better," he thought. He walked into the camp administration office:

—*Achtung!* —a voice shouted, and they all stood up.

Hans Gupper took in the ambience of the room at a glance, and he understood instantly that, only a few seconds before, nobody had been working, that somebody had been cooking food on the stove, that somebody else had rushed to put out a cigarette, and that it was the paunchy *Lagerälteste* (the prisoner in charge of the camp) who had been presiding over this little get-together. The "privileged" of that office, German prisoners who were there for common offences, were perfect bureaucrats.

—Carry on with your work —Hans Gupper said evenly.

They were more useful to him as executioners than as clerks; the SS felt the one task well done was really enough to expect of them.

He went over to the desk of the prisoner who was general secretary for the camp, and slowly, with that air of someone who gives an order only once, said:

—As of tomorrow, increase the stone-carrying teams to five hundred men. I want strong ones.
—*Jawohl!* —answered the secretary, and then went on to discuss a number of other matters pending.
—Come with me, Hermann. We'll go visit the works.

The *Lagerälteste* too said *Jawohl*. He was a giant of a fellow, obese, like a good son of Munich, and with a small, pointed head. The Spaniards called him "King Kong," and despite being a loudmouth, he didn't treat them as badly as some of the other prisoners in positions of responsibility did. He limited himself to applying pressure to his immediate subordinates, and so avoided getting either his hands or his reputation sullied.

—There is a lot of theft going on in the camp —Hans Gupper said to him after they had walked on a little way—. The prisoners should be fatter.

And looking at him out of the corner of his eye, he added:

On the other hand, there are some that are too fat.

King Kong preferred not to take up the innuendo.

—As far as I am aware, there's no stealing. The ration is sufficient. The prisoners are working hard.

—I know there's theft; I know the camp better than you do.

—It's difficult to stop it completely, *Obersturmführer*.

—Just make sure I don't have to intervene.

—I'll step up security and bring an end to any abuses —promised King-Kong.

The prisoners they met on their way took off their caps and glued their arms to their sides with Prussian rigidity. When they arrived at the construction zone, the chief *kapo* responsible for the camp works presented himself to give an update.

—Come, come along —said Hans Gupper—. I have something to say to you as well.

The *kapo* sighed with relief; to all appearances, the Commandant was in a good mood.

—Take me along to the new *Kommandantur*. I want to see how it's coming.

—You will see some changes, *Obersturmführer* —the *kapo* simpered.

—All the better.

Hans Gupper wasn't listening to the details the *kapo* laid out for him.

—Tell me —he interrupted—, to finish the south wall and lay the foundation for the big hospital during the three summer months, how many men would you need?

The *kapo* didn't answer right away.

—It's difficult to say, like this, off the top of my head.

—Approximately.

—I'd say with forty masons and five hundred labourers I could do it.

—Then get ready to work and to make them work.

They came to a half-built edifice, a construction of cut stone buzzing like a beehive inside. Hans Gupper had no illusions but that all this activity was due entirely to his own presence. "At this pace, it wouldn't take two years," he thought.

The masons placed stone on stone, and the labourers carried in the materials individually—or in pairs, on stretchers. Someone was set to tending the braziers full-time to keep the cement from freezing. Farther on, one could see a huge trough where a number of prisoners were mixing mortar with shovels and rakes. Dominating that hive of activity were the shouts of the *kapos* and the sub-*kapos*, and the presence of some SS acting as inspectors.

Hans Gupper compared the state of the work with what he remembered from his last visit and was satisfied.

—The work is good, and the wall is going up fast —the *kapo* offered.
—And these masons, where are they from?
—A bit from everywhere: some are Polish, but for the most part, Spanish.
—And the best?

The *kapo* struggled for a moment; he didn't know if his opinion would be well received.

—If I had to choose, I'd take the Spaniards, but I …
—Good, good …

The officer took a few more turns among the scaffolds, the braziers, the piles of stone and sacks of cement; satisfied with his visit, he dismissed the *kapo* and, accompanied by King Kong, went on to another worksite.

—Hermann —he said—, put together a census of all the Spanish masons in the camp. I'll need it tomorrow.

When August got back to the Block, Francesc literally jumped him:

—Do you know where he's been taken?
—Who?
—Emili.
—Who is Emili?

Francesc explained all that he knew.

—I'm afraid something's happened to him.
—I'll find out.

Francesc didn't have long to wait; August came right back with news.

—The German who took him works in the civilian clothing warehouse.
—Now I'm even more confused.
—Some administrative mix-up maybe —said August—. Did he have anything of value?
—Nothing at all.
—Clothes?
—Old, like everybody else's.
—Then I don't understand it. But don't worry; I don't think it's anything serious.

When he was alone again, Francesc smiled; it was clear that Popeye had had nothing to do with it. He took advantage of the sun having dried the stone steps of the barracks and sat for a bit. He felt exhausted, and he yawned from hunger. He reminded himself that he'd been through this before. But hunger in a way wasn't the issue. What he didn't understand was that cold cruelty, so admirably well organized. The Nazi mentality was beyond him: everything in his Mediterranean temperament rebelled against that inhuman machine.

A Nazi camp offered the internee one chance in a thousand of surviving. The men incarcerated there sought that one chance desperately. It was diabolical, the psychological incisiveness of whoever had devised that penal system. When men died there, they died clinging to the most miserable of existences, still waiting, even while their fingers curled and their skin stuck to their bones, for their luck to suddenly turn. It wasn't possible to laugh in the face of such a vision. To fight? A crazy idea, and a ridiculous pretence. To fight ... how? With what? Beginning where? He'd wait for luck as well, just like the others. A good *Kommando*, lighter work, more nourishment ... The secret of his future tightened around his heart.

He didn't notice Emili looking at him.

—Someone gave me a job! —he exulted—. In a warehouse of ... I don't know what!

And seated on the step beside Francesc, he went on to explain the great event. Somebody had discovered his drawings while going through the clothes. The SS in charge of that annex had seen them and had the artist sought out.

—He asked me if I could draw for him. Pornography of course! And all the time, I thought they were going to kill me ...

Francesc smiled:

—If you can save your skin with that ...

And, after a pause, he added:

—To denounce pornography! Tell me that wouldn't be stupid.

The colours of the camp had suddenly shifted. The two friends were happy. The hero's role is not always to one's taste.

The three big complexes that lined the right side of the avenue that also served as the roll call square contained, respectively, the wash house and disinfection unit, the kitchen, and the crematorium cells. The kitchen, in the middle, was well placed if one took into consideration that it was the axis around which the whole camp turned. A model installation: completely enamelled, nickel-plated, clean, polished, like an operating room. When the lids were lifted from the big pots, you would have thought you were facing a parade troop of a new species of oyster with a Prussian education. Out of that perfect kitchen came perfectly disgusting food: turnips fit only for animals and potatoes in their skins boiled all together in salted water until they formed a homogenous paste. The regulation margarine would disappear before it reached the pot; it was the gold standard of the underground trade.

The cooks were privileged prisoners. The Germans who had entered the camp first fought tooth and nail to keep this privilege. A cook was a master with servants, he wore a good uniform, smoked cigarettes that the civilian German population couldn't get hold of, got drunk when he felt like it (on the sly, of course), and could take care of his friends and his "little friends." There were cooks who had debtors and proteges even among the lower ranks of the SS.

In the cellar of the kitchen, however, not only Germans reigned. Many Poles worked there, and Spaniards too were starting to find their way in. The work consisted of peeling the turnips and potatoes. The light was feeble, and it was very damp. Water spilled out of the big sinks and soaked the floor, climbed up the walls, up the legs of the benches, into the prisoners' shoes, invading everything. It was a dungeon cell of huge proportions. One had to spend twelve or fourteen hours there at a time, working without cease at one thing or another, and in total silence. Nonetheless, the prisoners who worked there were considered worthy of envy.

Ernest had been studying for his high school matriculation when the Spanish Civil War broke out. One of the first Spaniards to enter the camp, he'd been picked by a Block secretary and asked to chose five men "for the potatoes." Ernest was a gentle boy, delicate, good looking, friendly. The *kapo* in charge of the potatoes quickly made him his personal servant: to polish his shoes, wash his clothes, make his bed, and cook his special meals. In exchange, Ernest was well dressed, smoked good cigarettes, and stuffed himself with food. He was very young and couldn't see farther than the end of his nose. He soon forgot his own companions and became oblivious to the conditions out of which he had been lifted. He came to think of his position of privilege as a kind of titled nobility:

—What do you think of these shoes? —he would ask one of the unfortunates who followed him around in case he let fall a crumb for them—. They cost me three loaves of bread. You think that was too much?
—Here, have a smoke —he would say the next day to someone else, handing him the butt of his cigarette—. For a carton of a hundred, they were asking a kilo of margarine. Expensive, but what can you do?

The day after that he would buy a shirt, or have a new cap made with a visor, in order to look like a *kapo*, or purchase massage oils, or have the legs of his pants let out by one of the SS tailors. He kept his kindnesses for the *kapo* who was protecting him. And this one was a real gentleman: strong and carefully groomed, perfumed, he had his head shaved twice a week, waved his hands dismissively, and had his clothes made to measure. Ernest laughed aloud every time his honourable friend raised his stick and flushed out the poor devils going through the garbage for potato peelings, which they would devour raw. Ernest was the chosen one of the god of that cellar, and nobody dared say a thing. Thanks to this position of "royal privilege," he found himself respected, flattered, and feared by men twice his age.

That morning, the *kapo* and Ernest had locked themselves inside the *kapo's* little room. A stove for cooking, a table, a closet, two stools, and a bed. The wooden walls that separated the room from the rest of the cellar were too thin to muffle the din of shouting and scrambling that accompanied the games within. Those peeling the potatoes nearby looked at one another and smiled maliciously.

The door opened suddenly and Ernest came out like a shot, flushed and shaking with nervous laughter. The *kapo*, chasing him, tripped over a bucket of potatoes and spilled the water. The prisoners working at that end of the bench had to raise their feet to avoid a soaking. The *kapo* took advantage of Ernest's hesitation at the men's complaints, picked him up by his collar, and, dangling him like a puppet, returned him to the office. Once the door closed, the laughter within recommenced.

One of the Spaniards peeling turnips commented to his neighbour: *"Estos juegos acaban en el catre."*[20]

Ernest was very young, yes, but old enough to know that this was true.

CHAPTER V

There were barracks with real beds and barracks without; in the first of these lived the privileged prisoners. A bed was not only a piece of furniture on which to rest at night, but also a sign of social standing. Even so, a bed brought with it considerable headaches, for the rules of the camp had turned "the making of beds" into a demanding art. One had to be able to convert a mattress stuffed with straw into a perfect parallelepiped. Blankets, checkered sheets, and pillowcases had to be made up in a special order, following the bias of the fabric, with corners squared and all carefully smoothed flat. The *Blockälteste* would then inspect the finished product, and the most minuscule wrinkle or fold out of place was enough for him to take hold of a corner of the sheet and, in the blink of an eye, destroy the patient labour of a full half hour with a single pull. If the prisoner was of a high rank, nothing more would happen; however, if he was only a "privileged" of the second order, the rebuke would be accompanied by a beating or, often, by a punishment that consisted in spending all Sunday afternoon making and unmaking beds. It should be said that the supreme aristocracy of the camp had servants to do their bed making for them.

Since he'd begun working in the warehouse, Emili's days had taken on a certain uniformity thanks to the bed he'd been given. To him, more than being just a place to sleep or a symbol of his rank, the bed signified a kind of synthesis. He was adept, and with his second try the *Blockälteste* had given his "okay," the equivalent of a certificate of aptitude. Once every day, the making of the bed. The count seemed easy and clear, but one morning, after several weeks had passed, Emili calculated that he had made his bed fifty-two times, and he couldn't help but be surprised. It was the same stencil laid out and printed fifty-two times, and the images, perfectly aligned and superimposed one on top of the other, gave no sense of the extent of their repetition.

But the landscape had certainly changed, and even though winter had been long and the snow slow to melt, after a merciless February a benign March of clear skies arrived. The little bit of the world that could be spied through the still unfinished wall was beginning to put on those fresh and brilliant greens that, while they were the colours of life returning, for

Emili were nothing more than a taunt at his own impotence. Looking at this landscape brought him a more exact impression of the inexorable passage of time, and his surprise from earlier that morning was turned upside down: two whole months had elapsed, and two months was a considerable amount of time lost. The images derived from nature as it changed could not be superimposed on one another like those of the bed. To finish the wall would be to facilitate the prisoners' slide into resignation; it would allow them to continue, uninterrupted, the dreams of their night vigil, it would isolate them completely from an outside world in which they could find only the pain of an insurmountable contrast. As long as the wall remained unfinished, the solution was to neutralize time's passage and take refuge between the four boards of the bed where the nap of the blanket always made the same pattern, where the colour of the furniture and the walls was immutable, where time moved discreetly, as though on tiptoe.

To get used to a concentration camp was the greatest of privileges, and there was no set way of doing it. Men who could find no protection, who were starving, who were going to die bit by little bit didn't suffer as much as others whose most urgent needs were taken care of: for them, it was the imagination that created the irresolvable problems and, worse still, left them without hope. For the unlucky there always existed the possibility of a change for the better. For the comfortably well off, the threat of a fall from grace took the joy out of their good fortune, and if they were perceptive, the sight of the irremediable suffering of others was already torture enough. In addition, hunger is a physical agony that is both absorbing and exclusive. Starving men think of nothing else, and if they do manage to fill their stomachs on a given day, they experience a temporary state of euphoria that the others can never reach because their yearning cannot possibly be satisfied within the camp.

To get used to a concentration camp meant being able to anaesthetize one's feelings with a drug distilled from the limitations of the place itself. One had to restrict the range of the senses to the world as it then was; one had to forget the exterior world one had lost, to let go of any interest in family, friends, belongings, the war, political ideals. It meant being able to fill life's every dimension with a purely vegetative existence. Once one had renounced everything, complete isolation held the only consolation possible. Confinement in the camp was a polar night of unknown duration; to adapt to it one had to ignore the very existence of light. There was a complete degradation of the individual: for the hungry, the obsessive mania to get food; for the privileged, submersion in a sewer of selfishness, greed, brutality, and vice.

The draughtsman liked to pass along a terrace that looked over the courtyard and, partly, over the external wall, for from there he could look out on the immense valley of the Danube as it cut its way through the foothills of the Alps nearly to the horizon. In spite of the risk of being there as a prisoner, to pass along that balcony constituted, for Emili, a brief escape to a world he could never resign himself to having lost. The privilege of getting used to the camp had no appeal for him if the price to be paid was the denial of the human condition. It was better to construct a discrete world, for himself alone if necessary, an inner world in which, with the help of the imagination, he could still have at hand those big green and blue spaces and the white of the faraway peaks.

And on that day of the coming spring, two months after his arrival in the camp, the draughtsman set out to actively resist the spirit of the camp. Nazism was trying to annihilate its enemies physically, but, just in case it didn't manage the job completely, it had prepared surroundings for them that would annihilate them morally once and for all. Emili would try to overcome both tests.

When he was going to bed that night, he pulled back the blankets without regret; the fact that tomorrow he would have to make it up once again had lost, in his view, all the importance that it had had over the previous days. He felt above material annoyances, and the bed had ceased to be the clock against which to measure his tedium. It had now become an ally. From that moment on, he would find within himself the necessary solitude for his own private escape. That evening he lay down sure of the strength that was gathering within him.

Emili often witnessed scenes of violence. As a worker in the Civilian Clothing Warehouse *Kommando*, he had to be present for the arrival of all newcomers to the camp, and it was the exception when beatings were not meted out during the change from civilian to camp clothing, as though this were part of some sort of rite.

The measures taken that day had been extraordinary. While the seven new arrivals were getting undressed, all the officers and sergeants of the *Kommandantur* had come and gone through the door of the warehouse. Very few of them left without having tested the strength of their fists.

Even before they got on the shirts of their uniforms, the faces and bodies of those seven poor men were already completely smeared with blood. Emili didn't know German well enough to figure out the reasons for such a rough "interrogation." "They must be big shots," he thought. When curiosity got the better of caution, he took a parcel of clothes and went over to one of the newcomers, who was standing a bit apart from the others:

—German? —he asked quietly.
—No, Hungarian … Jewish. And you?
—Spanish.
—Spanish? —repeated the other, surprised. And, in very good Castilian, he added— And why are you here?
—For being stateless.[21]

An SS approached them with a whip in his hand. Emili pretended to be looking for a piece of clothing.

—What's your profession? —asked the soldier.

The draughtsman raised his head to make sure that the question wasn't directed at him.

—Doctor —answered the Jew.
—A doctor, eh …? —the SS said sarcastically—. You're going to fit right in. We need doctors, lots of doctors … to carry stones. *Ha, ha …*

With a single punch full in the face, he threw the Jew up against a stack of boxes four paces away.

—There, now you've got a practice. You can start by fixing your nose, *ha …*

The victim got up unsteadily. The SS's eyes were shining:

—Go on, go on, hurry up —he yelled like a madman—. Get dressed. You're going to work. Faster, Faster! No more playing lazybones!

The Jew obeyed, but, his nerves unstrung, he couldn't get his legs into his trousers.

—You want us to dress you too, you dog?

And he made him fall like a sack of potatoes with a kick to the groin.

—Oh, you're a comedian, are you? —the German was shouting—. Stand up! Do you hear me?

And he began thrashing him with the rawhide without watching where he struck. The Hungarian stood up, his eyes wide with terror. He was covering his head with his arms. The lash had cut a red furrow across the skin of his face, and the blood that gushed from his nose ran all down his half naked body. Immobile, he took the torture in silence. When the SS got tired of shouting, he went off in search of another victim.

Emili held the parcel of clothing between his legs, paralyzed with horror. It took some effort for him to say:

—Courage!

He didn't need it.

—Some day they'll pay for that, the lot of them —swore the Jew.

Once dressed, the seven unfortunate men were put up against the camp wall next to the guardhouse. When any of the SS entered the precinct they didn't think twice about using these "punching bags" to do a little training. The *Führer*, always fatherly, was seeing to the entertainment of his favoured sons.

By the following morning, after an evening and night in a Calvary of suffering, two of the Jews had died. The five survivors were made to join the disciplinary company carrying stones. Emili saw them passing by the door of the warehouse and would not have recognized the Hungarian doctor, he was so disfigured, had he not made a friendly sign to him.

In the evening, after supper, Emili took a turn through the roll call square with Francesc. He learned then about the tragedy's finale:

—I saw how it ended for three of them —explained Francesc— It must have been after their second trip with the stones. About fifty metres above where I was working there's a little sentry post. The three unfortunates went past it. They were holding hands and walked slowly with their heads held high. All of them singing hymns in full voice, crossing the barbed wire. The sentry shot them with his machine gun.
—And the doctor, how did he die?
—I don't know which one he was.

—He was the tallest.

Francesc explained that two men had loaded him up with a stone that must have weighed at least seventy kilos.

—He couldn't hold himself up —he explained—. When, after a terrible beating, he managed to struggle to his feet, his legs bent as though he were a rag doll. I saw the SS give him a piece of barbed wire and point him to the stonecutters' barracks. Somebody who was there said that he'd been given ten minutes. He said that when they took him down, the barbed wire was buried deep in under the skin of his neck.

Emili felt a chill. That stench of burnt wool seemed more grating than ever.

With the coming of the good weather, the food lost a good deal more of its already meagre consistency.

—The spring thaw has inundated the kitchen —joked one among the starving.

And Vicent, who had already broken a record for resistance, saw his suffering increase still further. In fact, the hunger was the same as always, but every time he held out his bowl and watched as a serving of turbid water with traces of turnip and potato was emptied into it, it reached directly into his mind by way of his eyes. It was obvious that no one could survive on murky water, and even while Vicent's intelligence was rudimentary, he was smart enough to grasp the immediate significance of his observations.

—Don't think about food —counselled those who weren't as hungry —. You'll suffer less.

How could he not think about his hunger when his legs were getting weaker by the day, when his head was always spinning, when his empty insides sucked him in like a whirlpool? He couldn't keep his eyes from following anything related to food; the clatter of plates and spoons was as musical to him as had been, years before, the sound of his village band. Was it a crime if he was the first to hear the whistle that announced it was time for the thermoses to be picked up at the kitchen? What could

K.L. REICH

he do about it if he was the best informed about the next day's "menu" or about the variable proportions of the soup's contents? Or if he knew precisely the number of ladles-full each thermos could hold? Or if, after watching them line up every day, he knew by heart the names of the lucky ones who were granted an extra portion from time to time for extra services rendered?

Vicent had improvised a set of scales with some bits of lath and string in order to make a more equitable distribution of the bread that was given out, one loaf for every group of three, after the final roll call of the day. And, if the division was off despite the scales, he would raffle off the pieces in front of witnesses, asking, "This one, it goes to whom?" with an almost liturgical intonation. Later, he would eat the piece that had fallen to him, always remembering to spread out on his lap a napkin torn from a paper sack, which allowed him to catch even the tiniest crumbs. The bread seemed like it had been made of sawdust and crumbled all in pieces.

The strategy of stopping at the wealthy Blocks to wait for leftovers brought him good results when the food was at its worst, and he didn't think anything of spending hours and hours there on days, like Sundays, when they ate their lunch in the camp. He seemed immune to pain when the *Blockälteste* came out with a broom handle and lashed out right and left, and he usually got the worst of it because of his weak legs.

Vicent would sniff the garbage cans from the garrison's exterior precinct, searching like a dog amidst the lice, straw, sawdust, and ashes for a little handful of potato skins or a crust of mouldy bread.

If his thoughts had had leisure to turn to matters other than hunger, and he had tried to compare the "València" of these days with the Vicent from before, it would have been difficult for him to do so. Was the papery skin he had now the same skin, taut and glowing, as before? Had his back always been so bent, as if the torso was folded over the empty stomach? And the black mood that had come over him and made him more irritable in his dealings with his companions every day? Vicent hadn't noticed these changes because nothing existed for him but hunger. When he fought with someone over some trifle, his anger, the torrent of insults that came out of his mouth, the holy rage that shook his thin body and drew its strength from who knows where, had, in fact, the most valid of justifications. If to be alive was his natural right, even his duty, then his irritability was nothing more than a defence against a society that plotted to kill him by starvation. Locked in and maltreated by those beyond the barbed wire, despised and ridiculed by his companions in misfortune, anyone at all was, by definition, the enemy. The privations of all kinds, the weeks on weeks of physical pain, these had distilled a hatred in his heart, a deep hatred that crested like a wave before his instinct for survival. Like a caged animal, he bared his long yellow teeth when necessary.

Vicent had been living in this state for a long time. His resistance was exceptional, when thousands of similar cases didn't last more than three months. Destiny was toying with his poor body. His suffering had gone past the point where the senses are numbed. Because of this, he had no notion that his was an extraordinary and inexplicable case of survival, as if the inactivity of his digestive system had paralyzed his conscious mind as well. Vicent knew nothing, understood nothing, remembered nothing. All he had was hunger.

August, also a Valencian, helped him out from time to time, but there were so many cases like his in the camp!

—Stop eating garbage, my countryman —he'd say. It's not helping your hunger, and worse, it's giving you diarrhoea.

That evening it was only with great effort that Vicent managed to climb the hundred and forty steps[22] that made the track from the quarry to the barracks. Two companions, as badly off as he, had had to just about carry him: a double sacrifice since Vicent had not stopped complaining the whole way up. The formation for roll call had been long, longer than ever, doubtless because the counts hadn't matched up. And once they'd broken ranks, Vicent had argued interminably at the entrance to the Block with those who, just like him, crowded around the door to be first in line for bread. At times like this, València became feverish; only a few minutes and he'd be in possession of his third of a loaf of bread and the nearly transparent slice of tripe sausage that went with it, and he could already feel the dry texture of the coarse flour against his tongue and taste the faint bitterness of the mixture. He was salivating heavily and felt the consequent slight tinge of pain under his ears. As Vicent took his place in the line and moved ahead little by little, he kept his eyes fixed on the table where the loaves of bread were lined up. He counted those in front of him and then looked to see which loaf, following the order of their distribution, would be his. A crappy one! Small, squashed, it would fall to pieces as soon as they tried to divide it. He cursed his usual bad luck under his breath and decided to elude it by any means possible. He needed to get out of line, and the pretext of going out to urinate would do the trick. Moving farther back, he'd try his luck again.

—Hey, hey! —protested those behind him who suspected his strategy—. Each to his place, we know your tricks.

València didn't move, and a few seconds later, his obsession dissipated. The *Blockälteste*, the brutal Popeye, was just shutting the door of his little private cupboard at the end of the dining room, behind the table where he usually ate with the secretary. From where he stood, Vicent caught a glimpse of two full loaves of bread, one on top of the other on the top shelf. No, he wasn't hallucinating. The cupboard was closed again, but the image of those two loaves of bread didn't fade from his retina. He took the ration he was given without paying much attention to its defects, as if supper had ceased to be important; then he gave his registration number, waited until the two behind him, with whom he had to share the bread, had given theirs, and went immediately to the dormitory. Vicent didn't argue about the division of the ration as on other days; he accepted the shares suggested by his two associates without a word.

Now, it has been some time since the lights were turned off, but Vicent, in spite of his immense fatigue, is not asleep. With his eyes open, he dreams. He dreams that he has managed to get into the camp's food warehouse, as had happened on another memorable occasion, on account of his having to take some boxes there. His sense of smell picks out, with great precision, the unmistakable odour of the canteen mixed with the smell of soft bread, and he perceives, as distinct as a little stream, the sticky sweetness that flows from the big five-kilo jars of marmalade. With a little imaginative effort, everything there can be his at bedtime. He'll begin with the long sausages wrapped in waxed paper, after this, slices of bread smeared with thick margarine and powdered with icing sugar, and he'll finish with marmalade by the spoonful. A dream, only a dream. And to think there are those who really do have access to all these objects of his desire. Not him, certainly! He doesn't work in the kitchen, nor in the warehouse, nor is he in charge of the Block. Why does Popeye have two full loaves of bread in his cupboard, two loaves that have been stolen from the prisoners by those who rule over them, and he, on the contrary, gets none of it, not a crust, not even a crumb? Every three days he eats a loaf of bread, and with the hunger he has, he could eat two loaves at once, one after the other, and still be hungry. His suffering is without remedy.

On getting up tomorrow, he will drink the watery soup or the "coffee" and hold out until midday when he will receive a meagre litre of murky water. Bread, the only even slightly solid food, he will not see again for twenty-four hours. Vicent wants bread, he needs more bread, he has a right to the bread that the one in charge of the Block, already stuffed with better food, keeps for his business dealings.

And Vicent gets up from his sack and walks among the bodies of his sleeping companions. Barefoot and wearing only his underwear, as if going to the toilet, he goes out of the dormitory and into the dining room. The silence and darkness are not complete; in the camp, they never can be. In the dining room are the bunks for the German supervisors, the interpreter, and the servant boys. He hears their measured breathing and someone coughing here and there. Light from the floodlights along the wall and above the roll call square angles in through the shutterless windows. The floorboards creak under Vicent's light step and an uncontrollable terror takes hold of him. He freezes there for several seconds, trembling like a leaf, listening intently. Nobody stirs around him. From the urinals, there is nothing but the sound of the drains. In the room everybody is asleep. Vicent shakes off the paralysis of his fear, and, with all of his senses put to sleep, walks towards the cupboard …

He will not be so stupid as to wait to soften the bread in his soup the next day; Popeye will have noticed the deficit and be carrying out his investigations. "València" will at last go to work with a feeling of plenitude in his tortured stomach; in the course of that difficult digestion, he will find in his discomfort a deep well of pleasure.

CHAPTER VI

Hans Gupper had good reason to be happy. The war was going well for the Germans, military preparations suggested that a massive new campaign would soon be launched, the construction of the camp was moving along at a good pace, and setting up the hospital was going to give him an excellent opportunity for new commissions. And last but not least, he'd just been informed by telephone of the arrival of a large shipment of prisoners that was going to furnish him with manpower that had started to run short. Everything was going well; even the weather was good. With these excellent prospects before him, the officer pushed open the door of the barbershop.

This annex, exclusively for the use of the SS, had been situated in a section of the complex next to his office. The modest parterres that surrounded each of its barracks were lush with grass and punctuated by yellow flowers.

When an officer entered a room, everybody stood to attention until a little sign of the hand gave them permission to return to work. Hans Gupper made this sign as soon as he crossed the threshold. The chair reserved for him had been made ready with the softest of cushions, and the *kapo* of the *Kommando*, a big-bellied Viennese barber who had grown vain from his privileges, prepared, as usual, not only to shave the officer, but also to deliver, non-stop, all the camp gossip. Hans Gupper listened only from time to time, and as he was in a good mood, he smiled.

Facial massages and creams were a mania for the Germans. Among the *parvenus* of Nazism, material excesses were common: the immoderate use of luxury goods of a distinction and refinement that in earlier times would have been the sole preserve of the rich and powerful. There were SS officers who ate with their gloves on, their opulent brass rings on the outside, the better to show them off. Because the military uniform didn't allow much scope for personal decoration, the desire for ostentation often found its expression in the creams and pomades of the barbershop. These concoctions were of poor, wartime quality, but this was no deterrent for the flamboyant aristocrat. The important thing was to be well perfumed and have the skin well oiled. Hans Gupper was the Commandant of the camp, and, as was appropriate to his social standing, he was settling in for a massage with a French-made cream he had found at a good price during the invasion of France, fresh jars of which he supplied to his barber as it was used up. For the Viennese, that cream was a real treasure. A prisoner in the kitchen or in the warehouse would have given anything to get a jar of it. The Commandant's face cream! There wasn't enough bread or margarine in the whole camp to pay for it!

The *kapo* had been thinking for some time about setting a jar aside, as an investment, and as he saw that Hans Gupper was in a good mood, he thought now might be the moment to try his luck:

—*Obersturmführer* —he began—, I'd like you try out a new massage cream I've got hold of. I'd even say that it's better than the French one. A base of natural herbs ...
—I don't want to try anything out.
—It's ... it's that the other one ... it's all gone.
—But I gave you a jar last week.
—I don't know what to say, *Obersturmfürher*. I'm very upset ... but the jar was broken.
—You're lying to me.

The *kapo*'s smile took on an ugly servility:

—I wouldn't dare. Lie to you ... I'm not that crazy.
—Fine then, come by my office later on.

The *kapo* thought he was in the clear and returned to his work. However, Hans Gupper had stopped smiling, and when he got up from the chair, he started walking around the room drying his face with a towel. His affected indifference was making the *kapo* nervous.

—How are your supplies?
—Good, very good.

The officer had opened one cupboard and looked through it with great care. He opened the other cupboard and ran his hand along between the packets of towels and gowns. He poked around in there for a good while. The *kapo*'s face had turned pale.

—Next time, you should do a better job of hiding what you steal —Hans Gupper said with a terrible smile.

A white jar was placed on the glass table top. The officer's expression turned hard:

—What did you want with it?

The *kapo* put on a dramatic face:

—It must have been these Spaniards. They told me they had broken it and I believed them. This always happens to me, because I am too …
—Shut up! Being a thief is one thing, that's why you're here. But lying is something else again. I won't have it … —and then, in a curious combination of Spanish and German, he shouted:— "*Espanyòler!*"

He pointed at one of them, the nearest one:

—You, you.

A man of about thirty-five turned to face him.

—Did you know that this was here?
—I don't understand —replied the Spaniard in awkward German.

This was the best way to get out of a difficult situation. Hans Gupper smiled almost imperceptibly and again addressed the *kapo*:

—Tomorrow, the disciplinary company. And from now on —he added, looking at the Spaniard—, you will be my barber.

The Spaniard put on a stupid face and the officer tried to explain himself by gestures. Soon he realized that the situation was absurd: the prisoner had understood everything perfectly from the start. He finished by asking him his name:

—Rubio —answered the Spaniard.
—Barcelona? Madrid?
—Madrid.

Hans Gupper took his hat and got ready to step out into the street.

—Good workers, these Spaniards —he said to nobody in particular.

Everybody stood to attention for the regulation shout of *Achtung!* Outside, the sun was spreading its warmth. Hans Gupper went to collect his motorcycle; he was having lunch that day with his family.

Since Emili had gone to live in the "privileged" Block, Francesc often met up with August, especially after supper, the time of day when the few social gatherings that were allowed in a concentration camp took place.

The interpreter had been good to Francesc. Through his relationship with the German *kapos*, he'd managed to get him a relatively quiet work assignment, with food privileges and everything. It wasn't so strange, feeling as good as he did, that Francesc wanted to chat a little, even if it was with August, a man geared more to speeches than discussions.

That evening, sitting on the interpreter's bed in that corner of the dining room where all the Block administrators slept, they had begun by talking about cooking, about vegetarianism, and about the war.[23] Emili arrived when August was talking with uncharacteristic passion about "British deviousness."

From his table nearby, Popeye, who had just finished supper, raised his head and smiled in greeting. Nothing but this subservient smile remained of the threats from some months before when Emili had left his mark on Popeye's head with a wooden shoe. Werner, a German working in the civilian clothing warehouse, and who spoke French, had explained it exactly:

> —You Latins cannot understand us. Resentment is a feeling that belongs solely to individualistic peoples. Offence, dignity, and honour are concepts that make no sense to most Germans. Your Calderón makes us laugh.[24] We are too used to being obedient and accepting our place in the hierarchy. For us, the only limit on the powerful is the authority of those that are even more powerful. The weak endure the abuses of the strong, and, as if the whole country were a huge barracks, each makes sure that whatever power he has is felt by those beneath him in revenge for what is, in turn, imposed on him by those above.

What might be more surprising to you is that a weak German, when raised to a higher rank, would not think twice about making peace with those who had previously tormented him. Resentment is an extra-military emotion, and we don't have any capacity for it. The one promoted will make use of his authority with rigidity and objectivity, and the one left behind will endure his situation as impassively as he did before, when he was the one in charge. And between two people of the same rank, relationships always depend on the fear they have of each other or on the favours they can do for each other.

Popeye certainly had an important position, but Emili was now working in the *Effektenkammer,* and it was rumoured that he enjoyed the direct protection of a certain SS officer. There was, therefore, a levelling out of hierarchies. Popeye was a prudent man (ältester), and when the draughtsman passed by, he smiled.

—Be careful! The bed's going to collapse! —cried August when Emili sat down.
—Good news —said the draughtsman—. The English have started a new offensive in Africa.
—Just like I said —August jumped in—. The English are making a game of this war. Forward today, backwards tomorrow ... biding their time and hoping it will spread, that the United States, Russia, Japan ...

The discussion soon had them all wound up. Emili was interrupting August to defend England, and Francesc was attacking the USSR for having caused the war in the first place with the German–Soviet Pact.[25]

—Russia can't stay out of it with the German expansion into south-eastern Europe. It will have to intervene, for certain.

Francesc assured them that all communists, including those in the camp, were convinced that sooner or later they would have a decisive part to play in ending the war.

—Those in the camp? —asked Emili, surprised.
—You didn't know they're organized?
—The Spaniards?
—Who else? Certainly not these German reprobates or the Polish Catholics!
—Always the same obsession —scoffed August— They organize themselves all over the place. Don't take it too seriously!

Francesc explained that the communists were moving to coordinate aid among themselves, to do away with "privileged" positions in the internal administration of the camp, to save their own people, to strengthen their ranks, to organize, to seek contacts on the outside. He concluded:

—They believe that the prisoners in the concentration camps will have a big role in a final revolt of the fifth column.[26]

—Pie in the sky —August jeered—. The only thing they'll have a big role in will be bringing on an SS intervention.

Emili thought it would be better to get all the Spaniards together regardless of party differences.

—You'd give the game over to the communists and compromise the lot of us —said August—. Nonsense like that is only going to get in the way.

—And if each separate group did as the communists are doing? —suggested Francesc.

—And continue the civil war right here? What we should do is gain the trust of those in charge in the camp and, with their complicity, begin to change their thinking. It will take skill and patience ...

—A lot of patience! —Francesc interrupted—, by the time that's done, we're not going to be around to see it.

—When the camp has no one in it but Spaniards, which I've been told is a real possibility, the SS will have no option but to rely on our cooperation. That will be the moment to show our skill.

—And if what you've heard isn't true, and we stay in the minority?

—My solution could actually work; separating into small groups across political divides would be collective suicide.

It was getting darker. The *Blockälteste* shouted at the servant boys to start clearing up for the evening. The three men had to move out of their corner to let them sweep.

—Come on out for a cigarette —said Emili.

On the street, night was falling peacefully over the camp. The stars were coming out one by one, disinterested in the human affairs below. The three friends smoked in silence. Probably, if they had spoken their thoughts aloud they would have agreed that their worries of a moment before were insignificant within the universal order that was mirrored in the calm of the night. Thousands of men were dying, devastation and misery were reigning over all of Europe, and, in spite of everything, sunset had come once again, night was falling as always, and as always the sun would rise tomorrow. Hope was born from the certainty that emanates from all perennial things. Time slips slowly by, but out of the serene succession of the days and nights would come the solution to the problems of the present moment. Months would pass, and years, and centuries, and when the world had long forgotten that war, still the sun would set each evening and rise each morning.

One had to keep one's feet on the ground. When, after a few words more, the three friends went their separate ways to sleep, August continued to turn over in his mind plans for winning influence in the management of the camp, Francesc promised himself to talk to his comrades from the anarchist unions, and Emili still held to his idea of a unified Spanish front.

The *kapo* from the crematorium woke on the verge of throwing up. Blood hammered in his temples, and soon he was shivering all over from cold. Something indefinable was preventing him from waking up completely. He made an effort and shook his head despite the shooting pain that every movement produced. "I slept on the floor," he said to himself, surprised. Another effort and he managed to sit up. His mouth felt pasty, and it reminded him of times when he had woken up hung-over. He tried to remember: "I wasn't drinking ... It's been years since I've had a drink." He checked his pocket watch. One o'clock; he still had a few minutes left. He leaned over the table and looked at the cups of "coffee" that, as on every other night, he had shared with the *kapo,* Seppl, and Peter from the Sanitation *Kommando.* All at once, he understood: of the three, he had been the only one to empty his cup. In a flash, forgetting his pain and with the uncertain steps of a drunk, he crossed the room and went down the metal stairs. He wasn't mistaken: the grating to the underground heating gallery was wide open. In a corner on the floor, he saw a pile of striped clothes. He didn't want to know anything more, and, like a madman, he flew out into the street.

The bell clanged loudly and the searchlights along the top of the wall lashed the night. The windows of the Blocks came alive with light and silhouettes. The SS on guard duty were running in and out of the camp, back and forth from the crematorium to the Blocks, and from the Blocks to the administration office. The voice and the great bulk of King Kong dominated that strange chaos. Between whistle blows, he was shouting like a raving lunatic:

—Meeting of the *Blockälteste!* Meeting of the *Blockälteste!*

A little later, the *Blockälteste* returned to their respective Blocks and ordered everybody to form up. The men, asleep only moments before, started coming out of the barracks, so many of them that it seemed impossible that they had all been lodged there. The Germans in charge never let up rushing them along, landing blows left and right. The crowd, half asleep, was like a swarm of numb flies.

—Roll call on the square! —were the orders.

And the human contents of each of the Blocks flowed through the streets that led onto the square, in columns of ten and to the sing-song rhythm of *Links, zwei, drei, vier ...* The operation took a long time, but when everybody found his place in the formation, all that broke the silence were the commands of the *Blockälteste* trying to tighten up the lines. Dry, grating, staccato voices, they rose above the square like the barking of dogs or like the shouts of a savage tribe excited before battle.

Once the count was done, everyone would learn why they'd been turned out. The raw light of the searchlights threw them in relief and etched the impeccable lines of the formation. Thousands upon thousands of men, bareheaded, immobile, in line, their eyes still sticky with sleep, grumpily awaited the outcome of this operation by the SS, who never ceased their running back and forth.

A motorcycle arrived with a roar. When the engine stopped, they could hear the click of heels and the "news" being shouted out. Hans Gupper had arrived. The SS demonstrated their zeal by intensifying their pointless scurrying here and there. Orders and counter-orders came one after another and echoed through the square like cracks of a whip.

August was listening to Popeye's explanations:

—What are they saying? —Francesc asked, forming up next to him.
—We're all set —exclaimed August without answering.
—Why?
—Two men have escaped. We won't be allowed to break ranks until they find them. It's the rule.
—And if they aren't found?
—So far, they've always been found.

And after a moment of silence, he added:

—Once, before the rest of you were here, three men escaped and we stood for eleven hours in the snow.
—Such luck!
—Silence! —yelled Popeye.

Hans Gupper went past them headed for the crematorium. Slow long strides, as if he were walking on springs. His two dogs gambolled along beside him, and several SS followed along behind, visibly animated by an event that broke the monotony of their life as zealots. At the head of each section, the *Blockälteste* saluted with a smart click of the heels.

—Seppl? —exclaimed the secretary—. It's his *Kommando* that did the tunnel work, isn't it?
—And so he knew the way.

After a minute, Popeye added:

—It seems the crematorium *kapo* was involved.
—But he didn't escape.
—He was drugged. He's a coward, you know that.
—He's going to sing, and he's going to say what he knows and what he doesn't know too.

Francesc had the conversation explained to him, but since he didn't know any of the people involved, the story left him more or less indifferent. His only thought was that it was going to be very difficult to find the fugitives at night. If they had to wait until dawn, and even then only if the search party was successful, the situation was going to be hard to bear. His lower back and his legs were already hurting. "And I'm strong," he thought. For the poor wretches that could barely stand up straight in ordinary circumstances, the coming torture was going to be too much.

Hans Gupper returned from the crematorium. The abandoned accomplice now formed part of his entourage. The interrogation was about to start. Minutes later, several orderlies went by bearing an instrument adequate to the task: a trestle, or "horse," similar to those used to hold saddles.

—It's the chair of the twenty-five —August said.

Francesc had only heard about it. It was the most common form of torture in the concentration camp. Any mistake, any small lapse in discipline, forgetting to remove one's cap in front of an SS, "requisitioning" some potatoes, breaking a tool by accident, any little thing was enough to put a man over the trestle and apply twenty-five lashes to his buttocks with an ox-hide whip. Among the most vigorous of the SS there was a kind of sportsmanlike rivalry when it came to playing the torturer. The victims were forced to count the whip strokes out loud, and if they lost their heads and made a mistake, they had to start all over again from the beginning. Once the last stroke had fallen, the supplicant had to square up before his tormentor.

All through the square, the cracks of the whip rang out clear and sharp with the heavy rhythm of hammer strokes on an anvil; it was as if someone were beating a leather cushion. Suddenly, a terrible cry tore through the silence of the multitude, a cry that dragged on for several seconds, a howl. The crematorium *kapo* was getting a triple series. Every three lashes of the whip there was a number for him to pronounce, and his words were spilling out deformed by the pain, guttural and unintelligible; however, not one of the men rooted to the square failed to keep the exact count. For most of them, the *kapo* was just one more German miscreant, a prisoner who had become the tormentor of other prisoners. But, for that moment in time, the whole camp bore a sense of solidarity with him. When the torturers interrupted their work to ask him if he was ready to confess, everybody agreed that the count stood at seventy-five lashes. This kind of moral support would continue as long as the man remained silent. When he was no longer able to resist, even to save his life, they'd despise him.

The *kapo* was holding up longer than his reputation as a coward would have led one to expect. The whip could no longer be heard, though his plaints had become even more dreadful. Now they were the prolonged moans of a wounded animal, sometimes shrill and piercing, sometimes stifled, as though just echoes of the screams that had come before. August conjectured:

—He'll have been hung up by the wrists. Tied behind his back. They pull down on the feet until the shoulders come out of joint.

Some time later, the moans were drowned out by the barking and yelping of the dogs. A shudder ran through the assembly like an electric current. The dawn looked like an etching by Goya: everything on a ground of raw light, and all thought numbed by the insidious hammering of terror.

They'd been standing at attention now for some three hours, and to the east it seemed the first light of dawn was showing itself. The prolonged immobility and the night's chill were becoming very hard for the weakest among them. And the hours for rest were slipping inexorably away, reveille approaching and with it the order to go out to work without having slept at all. Francesc thought about the hard day to come. He thought about the men that would fall for the last time. He wanted to set things in a context, to find explanations: that was how he distracted himself, how he got through these tests. The trap that the Nazis set with these collective punishments was obvious: the more unjust they were, the more dense with terror, the more spectacular the *mise en scène*, the more efficient they ended up being. To annihilate body and soul together. Francesc marvelled at how the Nazis seemed to know exactly how to organize the extermination of their enemies. To bear up under the exhaustion was, for the time being, the best opposition to the exterminators' designs.

There was a swell of voices and movement in the last rows of Francesc's group. Popeye headed over, furious:

—Silence! —he ordered— What's going on here?

A man had fainted and two of his companions were struggling to hold him up. Popeye gave orders, August translated, and the sick man was removed from the formation and left stretched out as he was on the damp earth.

—He'll recover —the German grumbled.

Others were fainting here and there throughout the formation, and when the new day shone its indifferent light on the vast assembly, the open corridors between the groups were filled with unconscious men.

Meanwhile, the *kapo* of the crematorium had come staggering out of the office, barely able to hold himself upright, his arms dangling, his head sunk between his shoulders, and his legs rigid so that his clothes, blood-stained and in rags, would not rub against the raw flesh of his buttocks. He was put with his face to the wall. Once the search was finished, he would go to the *Arrest*, to the punishment cells, a prison within the prison from which very few came out alive.

And with a simple blow of a whistle, the formation by Blocks shifted to the formation by work parties, and the prisoners had to go out to work without their statutory quarter litre of "coffee."

CHAPTER VII

The hundreds of Dutch Jews who had just arrived inaugurated the season of the great slaughters. Hans Gupper's camp, constructed after the annexation of Austria into the Greater German Reich, overlooking the waters of "the beautiful Blue Danube," had begun to welcome the Gestapo's favourite victims.

When the Germans invaded Holland, they sent out a call to Zionist youth offering them freedom in exchange for work and collaboration. The invaders had put on sheep's clothing, in a massive propaganda campaign, they announced the creation of a "Camp for Voluntary Workers," where Jews could quickly redeem themselves. The incautious who fell into the trap were rounded up, their affiliations, addresses, and references recorded. They were treated well enough. But given no work. Soon they saw their parents, friends, and acquaintances arriving to keep them company. The Germans knew how to make good use of the information they obtained. This is how it happened that, when the time came to "go out to work," whole families went to their deaths.

Three hundred Dutch Jews, some of them boys of fourteen and fifteen, had entered the extermination camp weighed down with luggage, food, money, and jewellery.

—Keep your eyes peeled —Werner said, smirking at Emili for whom all of this was completely new—. Keep your eyes peeled my friend, because today's performance is going to be beyond compare.

The Jews had to strip after having first emptied their pockets, opened their suitcases, and untied their parcels. The SS, who had turned up in numbers, hesitated for a few seconds, staggered by the horn of plenty that had been poured out before them. Suits, dresses, lingerie (made of silk!), deluxe cigarettes, boxes of vitamin candies, chocolate bars, candied fruit, watches, rings, tie pins, wallets full of florins, and ... gold coins!

Without any respect for the usual hierarchies, the free-for-all began. A simple *Rotenführer* (an ordinary soldier, first class) would fight over a watch with the highest *Obersturmführer* present. SS and German prisoners competed on an equal basis when it came to spiriting away a fountain pen or a dazzling solitaire.

—What did I tell you? —shouted Werner, sarcastically—. Jewish gold! What a lie! If gold has a race, it's Aryan, the purest of all! —And he burst out laughing until his little eyes were just pinholes—. Racism is an inspired doctrine.

It wasn't that the SS were much concerned about keeping up appearances; however, to be sure that no one could say they were taking things for free, they made an effort to demonstrate their anti-Semitic fervour as they came and went from the melee. So they would punch and kick the first Jew they happened to meet, but without dallying over it; then they would move on quickly to sorting through the treasure horde for loot, and take their leave at last with another little demonstration of sacred fury, but only a little one, in order to avoid any sudden movements that might empty their pockets. After a little while, they'd be back. Chocolate, above all, obsessed them.

—Look after my chocolate, *espanyòler* —one of them yelled at Emili, who was filling the paper sacks. Some were devouring it right there, by the mouthful.

Once the rush was over and they'd returned to the warehouse, the draughtsman sat down on a pile of paper sacks and lit a cigarette. Werner came over to him:

—What did you think of that?

The rest of the prisoners of the *Kommando* were busy with the remnants of the festivities.

—I never would have believed it.
—You have not yet lived long enough among Germans.
—Even the hungriest of the prisoners would've been more restrained.

Werner sat down.

—Do not be surprised —Werner said in his halting French.—
Germany is a nation as primitive as the Congo or the remote Pacific Islands. Our civilization is purely materialistic. That is to say, non-exis-

tent. The regime has murdered our spirit, and nothing is left us but scientific progress, industrialization, survival of the fittest, idolatry of the State, and an oligarchy that is ambitious but wholly without talent. And there you have it: all of this leads to an urgent need for chocolate!

And he added, after a little pause:

—If Hitler had said that London was a big chocolate store, and not the capital of England as is claimed by the Jews and those who are unpatriotic, today we would be the rulers of the British Empire.

Emili smiled. Werner was German, from Saxony, a former watch manufacturer who had made long sojourns in France and Switzerland. When it came to criticizing his compatriots, he was not only witty but eloquent. He missed the good life and the freedom of spirit that he'd found in the West. Accused of smuggling Swiss watch parts, he'd been sentenced to three years in prison as a "bandit." When released, he was immediately interned in the camp, the green triangle of the common criminal blazoned on his chest. He'd been a prisoner now for five years, the arbitrariness of which he attributed to disagreements with his family. He insinuated, without giving details, that his wife had accused him of being anti-Hitler so that she could have the business to herself.

Emili agreed that German nationalism was based on misery, the point of departure for all movements focused on territorial expansion.

—The great advantage of the German people over more Western nations —said Werner— lies precisely in this lack of everything. A soldier who is hungry, and the longer the better, gives much more of himself than a soldier who is full.

He paused to light a cigarette.

—To some extent —he added in an apologetic tone—, Spanish soldiers are courageous for a similar reason. But I don't want to make odious comparisons.

Emili felt compelled to disagree:

—For our part, no one would declare war to take away what belongs to others.

—Not now, because with this intervention of the masses in political leadership only nations that are collectively covetous are capable of aggression, and you Spaniards, you are not greedy. It is the same in Italy. In spite of il Duce, the Italians keep running away from the English. By contrast, we Germans are the first among covetous peoples to have set out on the road to the Orient; the Japanese bring up the rear. We are, as we have always been, the invaders of Rome. It's obvious: we disguise our appetites with pompous ideals, imitating the development of the old Western states when they first began their own wars of aggression, but the truth is that none of the great pronouncements of our politicians holds the least importance for us; here nobody believes them, neither those who govern, nor those who are governed. Führer, ministers, generals, soldiers, and even the village women, all of them are fighting this war in order to pillage rich neighbours, exactly as our ancestors did before us.

—You're not very indulgent of your compatriots.

—I have stopped being German; I renounce the glory —Werner replied, with irony—. I don't like chocolate, to be precise. But I do like French wines, and yours too; your spicy Mediterranean food, and your spirit, even spicier. Doubtless it's because I'm still German, and therefore lacking in every good thing, that I seek out the riches of my neighbours. But my weapons are different. Nothing is really conquered with tanks and with planes. I prefer to insinuate myself peacefully.

Werner smiled and his eyes seemed even smaller:

—The Germans can only improve their situation —he concluded— the day they abandon the military advantage of their own misery, the day they stop being German and renounce, as I have done, their country. Then they will follow my program and ...

—Before that they might need to lose a few more wars.

—They will lose them, they will lose them —Werner affirmed with conviction.

All day long this mountain rain that enriches the valleys and saddens the heart has been falling. It's a light, steady rain, silent, cold, and penetrating ... The flowers themselves, the grass, the fruit trees, all seem to complain of the sadness that surrounds them. From the window where Emili has set up his drawing table, he's been able to observe, for hours, the lawns and flowerbeds arranged in the space between the barracks, and he's been watching the sudden quick movements of the flower stems, made, to all appearances, without external cause. A community of feeling has coalesced between him and the plants; he too protests against the sadness of the day.

Today is the anniversary of his marriage to Matilde. A June day, Barcelona spread out beneath a brilliant sky and emotions overflowing. Melancholy makes his discontent even more intense. The privileged situation he enjoys, while so many others are dying every day without remedy or consolation, has weighed him down for a long time now with a vague feeling of indignity. What are his special merits that he's spared the fate of the others? Because he draws. More precisely, because he draws in a despicable genre, because an SS scoundrel protects him, he lives, and lives well in comparison to his comrades. He recalls the arguments that once served as his excuse for accepting the job, and, discouraged, realizes that in avoiding the collective destiny by accepting a shameful task he has placed a burden on his conscience that grows heavier each day. Vain scruples, some would say, and perhaps they'd be right. His own personal sacrifice wouldn't fix a thing. But he feels sullied. And can't see his way clear. To set things right with a grand gesture? He'd only let himself begin it if he had the will to carry it through to the end. The same force of will that should have prevented him from accepting the job in the first place. To step back now, to rethink it, would be ridiculous.

He's come into the Block without any desire for supper or for his evening stroll. He's lain down on his bed, a refugee from bitter hours of contemplation, and he wants to read. Impossible to concentrate. His mind carries him to far-off lands, across countless farmers' fields, meadows, rivers, and mountain ranges. He's being suffocated by the hollow, corrosive grey of the present, and even more so today, his memories stirred up by these hallucinatory colours. His longing takes on an unprecedented violence; never before has he felt so lost, so orphaned, so alone.

Matilde, too, would have been pensive all day, and maybe, who knows, even less hopeful. What explanation could she have for the lack of news? For ten months now Emili has not been able to send a single word. All the detainees in Germany are allowed to write home except the Spaniards, doubtless because of the nature of their abduction and to conceal the arbitrary exercise of authority that led to it.[27] Their families will wait in vain in many cases since those absent will remain so forever. Maybe this is what Matilde thinks about Emili; maybe she has spent the day crying in her sewing corner … "To go on living would at least spare her this uncertainty," thinks Emili. The evocation of Matilde is so painful that the man clenches his fists and pounds the straw mattress. He is alone in his own despair, and he wants to be even more alone. The murmuring of his companions in the Block, the conversations of those eating their supper at the tables behind the row of cupboards, the footsteps and slamming doors of those coming in and going out, all of these are a desecration of the peace in which he wants to dissolve his soul, of his reaching for an absolute that would explain everything, of his search for a vital meaning that as yet eludes him. "If I could hate," he thinks. Not a cerebral hatred, not an imposition of the will, not for the sake of appearances, but a real feeling, hot, from the gut. It's the epoch of hatred. "I'm out of step" —he says to himself—. "The strong these days are the ones who know how to hate. Can I only love? Not that either. The one is tied to the other. Love is in the past as well. I love the memory of love. My God, how did my soul become so parched?"

Francesc's voice cuts in like a knife:

—Asleep at this hour? Wake up, lazybones.

Francesc grabs his feet to yank him out of bed.

—Leave me alone, don't bug me.
—What's that?
—Leave me alone, I said!
—Are you sick?
—No.
—If you're not sick, then out of bed! It is not eight yet.

And he gives his feet another tug.

—I want to lie down. Leave me be.

Emili's voice is plaintive. Francesc gives him a mocking smile:

—Well, well, you *are* sad today ...

Emili gives up on his dreams. He gathers himself together.

—I've been lost in thought.
—The rain.
—Are you going to tell me why you're here?

—You're not glad to see me?
—You seem in a good mood.
—I've just met a real character.
—A Polish prince?
—No, brother, no. The brains behind the communists.

Emili remains indifferent to this pronouncement.

—And who is he? —he asks condescendingly.
—Rubio, the barber for the SS.
—I don't know him.
—He's no ordinary guy. He's sharp, very sharp.

Rubio's communism was a curious expression of his mercantile character. A barber by profession, when he was still very young he'd left his scissors behind in order to dedicate himself to perfumes. At the beginning, just a homemade eau de cologne; later on, a vast and growing industry. He devoted his spare time successively to bulls, to soccer, and to politics. Marked with vaguely humanitarian sentiments from the time of the Republic, above all a man of action, he avoided the moderation of the socialist intellectuals and aligned himself with the then nascent communism. Methodical, tenacious, inflexible, his temperament was well adapted to the bureaucratic style of the Party, and he learned how to combine two apparently contradictory sets of objectives. He attracted people to the Party in the same way he attracted customers, and vice versa. Austere as he was, not in the least vain, for him politics was a job that called for sacrifice and dogged labour. Now in the camp, Rubio did just as he had done in Madrid: he sought out new customers and did his best to keep them.

One evening after supper, he showed up at the door to the kitchen. It was the time of day when the "Potato *Kommando*" was finishing work. When Ernest came out, Rubio got started:

—I've been told you're now the *Kommando* interpreter.
Congratulations. You'll be in a position to do a lot of good for your comrades.

Ernest took out a packet of cigarettes.

—You know I don't smoke —said the barber, but then thought better of it—. Here, I'll take one.

During the Civil War he'd known one of Ernest's elder brothers, later killed, and he had promised to watch out for the boy. They'd come into the camp together.

Ernest knew that Rubio hadn't stopped just to congratulate him. He was too used to being lectured by his "guardian." The barber started by praising his protege's abilities in his German studies, applauded his efforts, and ended by talking about the need to work, each from his own vantage, to take care of the others. His words were smooth and practised, and he used them to wrap his listener round as though with a dancer's veil.

> —It's vital —he finished.
> —Yes, I know —mumbled Ernest—, but I don't own the kitchen …
> —Good, very good … now first find out what resources we can count on. And then we'll take the time to talk about it all. The important thing is that you're ready to help me. I'm a good judge of character, and I've known from the outset that I could count on you. I don't pay much heed to malicious talk, you know …
> —What do you mean?
> —Nothing at all, don't panic. I don't make judgments so lightly. They can say what they like, I think you've done very well to cultivate the *kapo's* friendship.

Rubio continued this little discourse, speaking with his distinctive mellifluousness. The young communist has to be active, steadfast, and self-sacrificing —he was saying— and certainly "diplomacy" was called for when it came to reaching certain goals, but once these had been attained, one should go back to a strict moral discipline.

> —You have to be an example —he added— I'm sure you know what I mean. You've got the position you have because the *kapo* trusts you. Now, little by little, you have to distance yourself from him. We don't want people talking.
> —The *kapo* is a good friend, and I'm not going to distance myself for no reason.
> —His friendship is not doing you any good … or us either.
> —It's just gossip …

Rubio's voice turned hard, although he kept the amiable grin fixed on his face.

—I know well enough what is and what isn't gossip. The *kapo* is a prison rat and knows exactly what he wants from you.

—I won't let you talk about him this way.

—I made a promise to your dead brother —said Rubio sweetly—, and it would be unfair not to tell you about it. You're a communist …

—I'm a prisoner like everyone else.

—And also a communist, and it is through me that the Party is talking to you …

—To hell with the Party!

—We can't tolerate your embarrassing us. You know full well that such frivolousness can't be forgiven.

—I have no reason to change.

Rubio was quiet for a moment.

—Very well. Is this all you have to say?

Ernest didn't answer. He gave his cigarette, which had gone out, a studied look, and threw it on the ground.

—We'll talk —said the barber, taking his leave—. I hope you'll think it over and change your mind. If you want to count on us …

—I know what I need to do.

Rubio let it go for now, but with a view to renewing his efforts another day. The interpreter's position in the Potato *Kommando* had a decisive and strategic importance in his plans. When, some minutes later, he passed by the door of the "privileged" Block, he saw a comrade with his metal bowl under his arm.

—Are you waiting for somebody? —he asked him.

—Sometimes they give away leftovers from the soup.

—You come here every day?

—Yes.

—How many times have you been lucky?

—Once, three or four days ago.

—You'd do better to get some sleep.

Rubio turned to go, but then reconsidered.

—Smoke?

The other nodded.

—Here, a cigarette.

And he gave him the cigarette that he'd slipped into his pocket earlier.

CHAPTER VIII

The Austrian daybreak is always cool, even in June, and even more so if one has to be out in the street, stripped naked, at six in the morning. To the Nazis, this was a minor detail. The order had been given: "Next Sunday, at six in the morning, everyone is to be ready for a general disinfection of the camp. Prisoners will leave all personal belongings behind in the Blocks, without exception, and gather in the garage courtyard until the operation is completed. The doors, windows, and vents of the Blocks will be sealed with tape supplied by the camp office. The *Blockälteste* will be responsible for the discipline of their personnel and for ensuring that the present order is carried out."[28]

If the garage courtyard had something of the penitentiary about it, it was in the high walls that surrounded it on all four sides and in the stone stairway that linked it to the main entrance. That morning the sentries at each corner of the gallery that capped the walls had criss-crossed the lines of fire from their machine guns. There shouldn't have been much room to spare with so many people concentrated there, but at this early hour one could have squeezed in twice as many. It was no ordinary performance. The multitude huddled together against the walls, and each sought in that massing of bodies the warmth that the early morning denied them. Their skin tightened with goose bumps, and the few words that anyone dared utter were stuttered through chattering teeth.

—Still no sign of the sun? … —this was the one question, and it was posed only by the most talkative.

Thousands of naked bodies! Even without energy to analyze the situation, Emili realized that his disgust, his revulsion before this spectacle of which he formed a part, wasn't only because of the pervasive prospect of a completely naked and more or less skeletal multitude, nor because of the stench from the lack of basic hygiene, nor because of the inevitable contact of their bodies with one another, but rather because of something more intimate and personal. It was the feeling of being stripped, the humiliation of being deprived of even the slightest protective covering, the repellent touch of one's own skin when rubbing it to sooth the cramps and shivering.

—Look who's coming down now —said Francesc.

One might have said that the martyrs of a Roman circus were descending into torment. Emili couldn't help smiling, despite himself. Wrapped in white sheets, like cartoon ghosts, the sick from the infirmary were coming down the stairs. Their progress was slow on account of their infirmities, and it lent them something of an air of solemn majesty. The stronger ones carried stretchers bearing those who couldn't walk. Some leaned on others; more than a few fell and rolled down the stairs.

—They've been dressed in their shrouds ahead of time —observed Francesc.
—The SS know what they're doing; the cold will save them the trouble of finishing them off.
—They're parasites. Today's cleansing is going to be thorough.

The sun was gaining height now and gilded the western half of the square. Soon the torture from the cold would be over and torture from heat would begin. The clusters of men were breaking up, their gestures loosened, and the square gradually filled. Conversations sprang up, and lips regained the confidence of their movements. Some couldn't resist the temptation and, hands no longer stiff with cold, they filled their mouths with the piece of bread and margarine that would be their only food for the day.

The two friends decided to take a turn about and stretch their legs.

—Wasn't it you who, just the other day, presented us with a defence of nudism? —Emili mocked.

Francesc laughed.

—This isn't nudism —he objected—; this is a fairground for infirmities.

In the shadiest corner of the square, near the empty oil drums and a truck up on wooden blocks for repairs, gathered the newly arrived Dutch Jews. At least those who were still alive. They were not at all thin, but they had already lost their natural colour. Bruises, scabs, open wounds, and dirt darkened their skin and accentuated their racial characteristics. Despite the chill and dampness of the ground, very few of them were standing up.

Emili gave them a quick glance and shook his head:

—I can't understand why they go on living. What possibilities are left for them?

—The same as for the rest us.

—Their death is certain, more so than ours. At least, more immediate.

—Maybe, but for them as for us, time could be on their side. A sudden end to the war …

The two friends were slowly getting used to the fine gravel under their bare feet. Emili broke the silence.

—We're all afraid of death! Too afraid. Our indifference is cowardice. They kill our friends, our parents; we know that sooner or later we'll share the same fate, yet we're incapable of making a single noble human gesture.

—Ours is a pragmatic time.

—I'm talking about a gesture informed by individual valour.

—The romanticism of another age.

—It's sickening. If we survive, we'll be thought of as martyrs, heroes. We've just been careful, that's all.

—Suicide is no solution. We have to reserve the power that each one of us represents for a more propitious moment.

—But to hold ourselves in check this way, the weight of it will have us down on all fours.

—That will depend on the effort we make to stay on our feet.

—I'm the first to recognize my own impotence, but if I survive this, I'm always going to be haunted by not having been brave enough.

The sun was bearing down with all its strength as if it wanted to compensate all at once for the earlier chill of the morning. Muscles slackened, and a painful fatigue took hold of that lifeless multitude. The ground had dried up, and dust glued itself to their sweaty skin. Leaning over the railing that topped the walls, some SS were taking pictures. They would be able to show them off when they needed to sing the praises of National Socialism. Some girls in the Party uniform were with them.

A black point stood out amidst the dust-coloured multitude. A negro from Barcelona, born in Spanish Africa.[29] The officer who had spotted him from the balcony ordered that he be brought up to him. His robust and muscular body (the fact of his being the only negro in the camp had earned him a spot in a good *Kommando*) surprised the Germans. According to their racism, he should be thin-limbed, pot-bellied, and have a cannibalistic expression, and this boy was not only handsome but also cultivated. He spoke a number of languages and could get by in German. Once up top, he had to stand at attention for a long time while the group of SS, growing ever larger, satisfied their curiosity. Their prejudices were being shaken. One of the soldiers, young, lymphatic, with an unfortunate face, couldn't keep himself from testing to be sure his eyes hadn't deceived him; he moistened the index finger of his right hand with saliva and rubbed it hard on the man's skin. His face betrayed a mixture of disillusionment and admiration: the paint didn't come off.

Another attraction were tattoos. One could find "illustrated" characters everywhere among the German prisoners, most of whom were from rough backgrounds, and even more so among the Slavs, for whom tattoos seemed to be an obsession. Snakes, lions, palm trees, women, anagrams, torches, and symbols of all kinds were favourite themes for anyone wanting to enhance their nudity with a tattoo. On that day all the living pictures "of the house" were on display. Nobody was surprised to see a "connoisseur" delicately lift up the arm of a tattooed man to trace the finishing touches of a design into his armpit. Fortunately for the exhibitors, the Commandant's wife was not a collector of cigarette cases, purses, or screens made from the tattooed skins of executed prisoners, as was the case at Buchenwald.[30]

The hours passed slowly, each more heavily than the last. Now the sun burned their naked bodies without mercy. Dust rose through the human anthill and stuck to their bare skin. Thirst was rampant, and the only faucet in the square (the taps for the garage were inside) couldn't cope with the interminable parched line of men. For the hungry who had already finished their ration of bread and margarine, the thirst was really desperate.

Emili couldn't eat. The monstrosity of that heap of human flesh, the sight of those sitting on the ground tearing into their bread, their hands filthy with sweat and dust; the sight of his own naked body; the thoughtlessness of those who crossed through the groups of men sitting down to eat and let their naked bodies rub against their heads; the purulent wounds; the stench coming from the open trap of the sewer where everybody had to relieve themselves; the heat, the dust, the thirst, and the revolt against such brutal treatment that smouldered within him, these were more than enough cause to lose one's appetite. Francesc, on the other hand, calmer, maybe tougher, was taking things more in stride and doing honour to his frugal meal.

When, mid-afternoon, Emili came back from his trip to the latrine, Francesc could see that his friend couldn't take it anymore. A grimace of disgust constricted his features.

—What's the matter with you? —he asked.
—Shit! —the draughtsman exclaimed, his voice tight—. I am drowning in shit!

He was looking at his feet, completely black from the overflow of the sewer on top of which he had had to stoop.

At that moment, a German prisoner wearing clothes, part of the group carrying out the disinfection, came rushing down the stairs. When he arrived at the bottom, those who knew him gathered around and pressed him with questions, most likely about when their torture might end. The prisoner answered them with a brief word, but then went on to talk about something else that caused discrete manifestations of joy among them. He wasn't taking much time with his listeners; he'd finish talking to one group and then go quickly on to the next. It was clear he was enjoying his sudden importance. His words flowed among the groups of Adamites like water along cracks in the pavement. Animated discussion gradually flooded that strange assembly. Emili recognized the phenomenon, that whirlwind that caught them up and made them forget about the heat, the thirst, and the loathing.

—Something's going on —he said.

The German came over right next to him.

—What is it, Rudy? —another German asked him.

What Rudy answered, excitedly, made Emili happy too, just like the others, but Francesc was still in the dark.

—So, what did he say?

Emili took hold of his arms tightly.

—Now it's really coming!   he said   The whole catastrophe! This is the decisive moment …
—Say it!

Emili laughed, and his eyes shone with the great courage that comes out of hope.

—Germany has attacked the Soviet Union. This very day.

CHAPTER IX

When the *Kommandos* returned from work a little before evening roll call, the prisoners were surprised to find a scaffold set up right in the middle of the square; two big trestles supported a crossbeam with three pulleys, from which dangled three nooses.

—This evening, "the theatre" —the veterans were saying—. They're going to hang the crematorium fugitives.
—In front of everyone?
—It looks like it.[31]

After roll call, with the prisoners still held at attention, there was a big influx of SS eager for some real entertainment. Hans Gupper presided over the performance with his dogs, while King Kong, along with the most diligent of the *Blockälteste*, took care of last-minute details, running here and there yelling constantly to show his zeal. The compact blocks of the formation filled the heavy evening air with emotion, an emotion that was silent, and a silence that was hungry, tired, and full of hatred.

The sound of a lively march started up behind the door at the entrance. The prisoners fond of playing music in their spare time had been gathered together and obliged to lend their talents to the festivities. The door was flung wide, and the soldiers who had gathered on the balconies of the Chinese towers burst into laughter. An open wagon, pulled by two prisoners and decorated with banners and coloured paper, was making its entrance into the camp. The two fugitives and their abandoned accomplice rode on it. The orchestra in front, and King Kong in front of that, baton in hand, marking the beat of the march. The wagon had placards hung from its railings: "We came back because it's better here," "We'll never escape again." The procession took a couple of turns along the avenues between the blocks of men in formation. The orchestra kept repeating its lively tune, and King Kong, flushed from the effort, conducted with mechanical gestures, lifting his feet high in grotesque exaggeration. Many SS followed the group in and were playing along with the joke like country children behind a gypsy with a bear.

The three condemned men, pale as though dead already, naked from the waist up, sunk their chins to their chests. Their suffering had left deep furrows across their features, accentuated by their three-week beards. All the taunts and mockery organized to undermine the solemnity of the execution, the frivolous cabaret music, the coloured paper, only intensified its atrocity. These German common criminals about to be hanged took on the character of martyrs in the eyes of the multitude. The crowd clenched their fists and the evening air thickened.

The wagon finally came to a halt just below the scaffold and the three prisoners got down from it. The grotesque music stopped. The silence was absolute. The ropes swung almost imperceptibly. Hans Gupper had a rasping voice, more fitting for a Prussian than a Viennese:

—The area authority —he said— is not going to tolerate any more attempts to escape, and the fate reserved for these three who are going to be hung in front of you is the same fate that awaits anybody, regardless of his nationality, who makes a similar attempt. Do not hope for success: all possible measures have been taken, and death will be the inevitable outcome for those who want to test their luck against impossible odds.

Hans Gupper went on with his discourse, pleased by his own oratory. Now he was talking about discipline and about the strong measures he was going to take to ensure it:

—And do not think for a moment that your chances might improve in the event of our troops meeting with defeat, in itself inconceivable. Not even in such a case, altogether impossible, would you escape the punishment that your hostility to the German Reich merits. You should pray to God for our country's continued march to its victorious destiny.

The eloquence of the speech was meant to give a pagan flavour to the macabre performance. The victims were to be offered to the god of war to win favour for the troops of the chosen ones, and the attendants—that is to say, the future victims whenever this god required yet more sacrifices in exchange for his help—were to witness the immolation in hollow silence.

One after the other, the condemned men took their place once more on the trestle of "the twenty-five." The courageous intention to not let their pain show through, common to all three, came undone as the number of lashes increased. The requirement to keep count, out loud, for each of the twenty-five strokes seemed to make their sufferings worse. Even the strongest cried out when, after a dozen lashes, he felt the whip begin to tear his flesh.

The second part of the show was about to start. These same condemned had to position a sort of metal stepladder, topped with a little platform that dropped automatically, below one of the nooses. The first to die climbed the steps. The second accompanied him, obliged to adjust the noose around his companion's neck. Then, as he was coming down, he placed his foot on the trap spring. Its metallic click could be heard in the silence and then the creak of the scaffold. The body jerked and swung as if the rope had become elastic. After a few seconds it swung like the pendulum of a clock running down. The third adjusted the rope for the second, and King Kong did the same for the third.

The procession of the prisoners in front of the three hanged men constituted the final act of the performance. They had to march in Indian file, looking directly at the bodies. An SS, whip in hand, made sure this was carried out, and if somebody lowered his gaze instead of looking up, he was made to go back to the end of the line. From this contemplation of the foaming mouths, the greenish pallor of the naked skin, the swinging feet, the camp command hoped to instill a perfect discipline.

Once the lines had broken off, each to its own block, that day's bread was eaten in the same silence that had dominated the whole evening. Night descended over scaffold and camp alike.

> —They were Germans, they were criminals —said somebody near Emili's bed—, but after all, men, prisoners like the rest of us. If the SS enjoyed themselves, who can be sure that the comedy won't be restaged with others who aren't escapees, nor Germans, nor criminals?

Emili first met Rubio one Sunday when the camp's privileged prisoners had been mobilized to construct a sports ground for the SS. While loading wagons at the same excavation site, they had begun talking just to keep boredom at bay, but the conversation soon turned to a subject that preoccupied them both. The German successes in Russian territory had them feeling pessimistic.

> —I've been thinking we should be doing something to improve the situation for the prisoners.

> —It's no easy task —said Rubio—. I've tried myself, but without much luck.

The draughtsman didn't want to let on that he knew as much already.

—I've been talking it over with some friends of mine. Why don't we all get together one day soon?

Rubio agreed, and they settled on the following Sunday to meet.

The look of the camp on holidays, especially if it was sunny, was altogether different than on workdays. The streets were crowded, there were soccer games going on in the roll call square, barbershops were set up at the doors of the blocks. After spending some time in the camp and becoming acclimatized to it by virtue of the constant deprivation and mental fatigue, that place of torture and death became, in the prisoners' eyes, more like a village, like a distorted reflection of the external world. A monstrous village, certainly, a parody of a village, but still, it had the essential characteristics. All the usual ambitions that propel the life of a community were to be found there, in caricature. The currency was bread and cigarettes; the need to "get along" or for "promotion" was satisfied by any of the jobs in the storage rooms, in the laundry, or with "the potatoes"; ostentation, by wearing a cap with a visor, or pants fitted by a tailor; vanity, by winning the adulation of a few starving men; sensuality, by lying in the sun slathered with some kind of Vaseline; women … With imagination and by erasing certain memories, the prisoners created a substitute existence where all their passions had a place. It was a world with clearly differentiated social classes, even more unjust than those of the outside world because they were not determined by behaviour, or personal merit, or intelligence, or industriousness, or daring, but by luck, favouritism and, very often, by certain unmentionable inclinations. This basic injustice was not coincidental, but part of the penitentiary system. If any one of them were somehow able to save his body, he would still leave the camp deformed in spirit. The Germans had planned well.

That Sunday, Rubio, Francesc, and Emili met. Sitting together on Emili's bed, they tried to reconcile their differing points of view. Emili thought it was a mistake to speak about political factions; Rubio, as a good communist, brought grist to his own mill, proposing that they take advantage of the organizational structure created by the Party as the nucleus for their new enterprise; Francesc, in spite of the lack of enthusiasm he'd found among the syndicalists,[32] was opposed to Rubio's formula "because he didn't want to be anybody's puppet." He proposed the formation of a coordinating committee. Rubio agreed to this in principle, although it would need the approval of his friends. Emili accepted it as the lesser of two evils.

They were talking about the objectives of the proposed work when August came in:

—Conspiring? —he said mockingly.

He wanted to conceal his surprise. Used to being the centre of everything, he took it as a kind of treachery whenever he was left out.

—You've come at just the right time —said Emili—. I guess you know Rubio.
—Yes, we know each other —said the barber.

Rubio was remembering the interpreter's anticommunist activities in the International Brigades.

—We've reached some points of agreement —the draughtsman explained.
—I can well imagine —interrupted August—. A complete waste of time; I'm the one with news.

August needed to be flattered, to be listened to. His megalomania sometimes reached levels of real virtuosity. He would just as soon boast about his supposedly aristocratic bloodlines and his private fortune as pass himself off as a dangerous revolutionary. For him, it was all the same to say he was a dancer, a poet, or a playwright. One day he would claim to have been a medical student, and a week later it would turn out that he was an engineer or the director of the family factory. And when he wanted to really shock his audience, he'd confirm that he had taken a half sister, on his father's side, as his lover.

—Anything that doesn't come from the top is useless to us. Hans Gupper knows he can count on the Spaniards. That's the important thing.
—And the news? —asked Emili, whose curiosity was piqued.
—I was just talking to Hans Gupper, not five minutes ago, and he agreed with me.

All this coyness was driving Emili crazy.

—Come on! Stop beating around the bush!

Now sure of the effect he was having, August began to explain:

—I'm leaving with a group of fifty Spaniards to construct a satellite camp. I'm going along as interpreter and as *Lagerälteste*. It's just going to be for Spaniards, and it's possible that later on as many as five hundred or a thousand will follow.

He set out his program: he would create a camp, a model of good administration, peaceful coexistence, and humanitarianism. He would gain the trust of the SS and demonstrate with actual results that a well-treated prisoner was more productive than one who was not. He concluded:

—Some hundreds of Spaniards will be saved. I'm going to bring them back to the world.
—The bloodbath in Russia! —Rubio exclaimed, triumphant—. The Germans are starting to feel it. The manpower is for war materials.

Francesc spoke to the interpreter:

—Very good. You'll save five hundred Spaniards or even a thousand, but this isn't your whole plan. Those left behind will be dying little by little.

August smiled enigmatically:

—Others will get out, in *Kommandos*, Hans Gupper has told me so.
—You're coordinating them as well?
—You'll see; the question is how to handle it.

A great cheer rose from the square. The Spaniards were playing the Austrian team that afternoon. The four friends walked out of the Block. They left behind a couple of Germans playing chess, a Pole studying German, and three or four Spaniards having a bite to eat. Francesc, who lived in a barracks of pariahs, thought about the differing treatment of the different groups of prisoners. Popeye forbade the prisoners from entering his Block on Sundays until it was time to sleep, so they had to stay outside all evening. Meanwhile, their German administrators enjoyed their "social life," received their "little friends," drank black market schnapps or eau de cologne mixed with sugar, and cooked stews on the stove made from the products of their own little dealings. Their charges dragged their feet along the irregular stones of the pavement, sat themselves down in a corner here or there, collected cigarette butts, or went to the square, not to watch the game but to see if they could find a friend or an acquaintance who would give them a crust of bread, leftovers from the soup, or a cigarette butt. On Sunday afternoons, the social differences became most marked. When Francesc stepped out into the street with his three friends, he thought to himself that Sunday was the saddest day of the week.

—I'll be sorry not to be able to help you out —said August with a touch of irony.

He was convinced of the impact his experiment would have. His dream was about to be realized. "Is it coincidence" —he thought— "or is it that a man of character need only wish for something to happen for it to come true?" Only the limitations of the undertaking clouded his satisfaction a little. At the main camp, the experiment would have had a lot more scope. "It will be small, yes," —he consoled himself— "but it will be a unique initiative: to convert a Nazi concentration camp into a place where life is possible."

—When do you leave?
—Tomorrow afternoon, most likely. Depending on what the railway says.

August said goodbye to them in order to go and speak with King Kong.

—Very smart and very energetic —acknowledged Rubio— and I'll be glad for his success. If he manages to save five hundred men, I'll be ready to forget a lot of stories from other times.

Francesc smiled: "He sure doesn't know my story …," he thought.

At the square the match was still going on, the spectators had kept up their enthusiasm, and the hungry were still hanging around, waiting for the show to end. Their keepers, those with a crust of bread or a dish of soup hidden in their cupboards, retained the right to celebrate the weekly holiday with all the tranquility that a satisfied belly brings.

In the Alpine zone, cloudy days always feel like winter, even in mid-August. A summer storm, so fleeting in our country, goes on for four or five days in the Alps, and the cold really makes itself felt.

Under such conditions, working outside was a terrible torture for the prisoners. It often meant putting up with the rain for eleven hours straight, feeling it first on the shoulders, then as it soaked through the shirt to the skin, finally reaching into one's very bones. The *kapos*, provided with raincoats, made sure that no one huddled under shelter. If someone was caught without having prior permission from his *kapo*, after the obligatory beating he'd be sent to the disciplinary company in the quarry, where only the strongest could endure the work.

It hadn't rained that morning, but the storm the previous night had left a trace of damp and chill that the north wind turned merciless. Hands were soon numb, noses streamed, and ears ached as they always did on the cold days.

Francesc had a good spot in the tool shed. Emili had plied the *kapo* with gifts to get this small privilege for his friend, and the results were these: a roof, a little stove, the job of keeping a few tools in order, and, most importantly, making lunch for his superior. As was his nature, Francesc couldn't stop thinking about his companions outside in the weather locked to their shovels, picks, jackhammers, wagons, pitchforks, and mauls, or carrying the stones, slick with mud, from one place to another. It was sure to rain again before nightfall, and he was going to be upset if somebody came up and put their hand on his shoulder and said:

—What's it like being so well connected!

He took a bucket and headed out to the water pump. He had to go down a hill, across the track at the bottom, skirt around the workshop barracks, and, after crossing a little bridge over a creek, he would come to the main road to the quarry. On the other side, under the vertical cut of an abandoned seam, was the well.

The wind funnelled through this artificial valley that had been carved out by centuries of labour. Francesc didn't find the chill damp air at all unpleasant, in fact it was oddly stimulating. He took full advantage of those gusts that spoke of far-off places and welcomed them with his face uplifted, his eyes and mouth closed, and breathing in deeply through his nose; the scent of elsewhere was the scent of freedom. Through the rents in his clothes, the cold pricked his skin into a healthy sensuality. Vigour, repressed for so long, overflowed from every pore, but Francesc wasn't tormented by it. He didn't need a substitute for life, an artificial world, a parody of normalcy, as did so many others in the camp. His fortitude was enough in itself, and Francesc looked on the present and the future in the same way as he waited for the gusts of wind. He knew how to contain his energies within an absolute, aseptic morality, with the certainty that one day he would be able to draw on them all at once. Francesc was living pure, for revenge.

The bucket filled, he lingered a while longer in the play of the wind. It pained him to have to go back to the cramped, dark shed, and retracing his steps, he couldn't help a sad smile thinking about his companions who envied his good fortune.

At the road, which bordered a stream, his way was blocked by a group of Jews carrying stones to the camp. Francesc put his bucket down and waited for them to file past. But the SS in charge of the *Kommando* didn't seem to be in much of a hurry. One of those unfortunates, exhausted, a living corpse, couldn't keep up with the pace of his companions, and this seemed to be a source of some amusement to the guard. With his face and his clothes mired in blood and mud, the Jew couldn't keep himself upright. He was weaving from one side of the road to the other like a drunk, tripping over his own feet and falling down time and again, as if, in an effort to escape, he wanted to sink into the earth. The SS goaded him with the hobnails in his boots and with a pick handle he had with him.

Francesc couldn't resist the strange fascination of the blood and the torture. His eyes fixed, his muscles tense, his jaw clenched, the spectacle seemed to draw him in with a hypnotic attraction.

The *kapo* of the group had ordered a halt, and the SS, in a paroxysm of excitement, was pressing the heel of his boot into the bloody mud-streaked face of his victim, who, lying defenceless on the road, gave a low, inarticulate moan of agony.

By the time Francesc realized the temerity of his being rooted there, it was already too late.

—*Espanyòler!* —yelled the SS, signalling with his index finger for him to come closer. —Come here. Come.

To resist was useless:

—Come here, I said —the German repeated with a menacing shout.

Francesc went towards him. He did not understand the German words, but their meaning was clear.

—I don't understand —he said as a last resort.

Without lifting his heel from the Jew's face, but instead pressing down with his full weight every time the victim shifted or groaned, the SS repeated his order along with gestures that were perfectly clear. There was no way out; and because the recourse of pretending to be an idiot repulsed him, Francesc faced up to it:

—I can't do it —he said in Catalan—. I can't do it!

There was nothing tentative in his tone. Once the initial perplexity had passed, and he realized that his orders were being insolently disobeyed, the SS started yelling and gesticulating like a madman. The Jew, nearly dead, had ceased to be interesting; now the boldness of this Spaniard who had come on the scene was much more titillating. He clasped his hands behind his back and puffed out his chest as his kind always did when they got worked up; he repeated his orders, stressing the syllables behind clenched teeth. His eyes, fixed on Francesc's eyes, shone.

Francesc stood rooted to the spot and mute. Even though he felt as though he'd been dropped off a cliff, that serenity that had always been his at times of great crisis did not leave him. The decision was made and, no matter the cost, he would not go back on it now.

—If you don't throw him in the water, it'll be you instead, you understand?

Some other SS had gathered and also several *kapos*. The role of the extortionist took on major importance in front of so many spectators. Francesc didn't even blink at the first slap. The SS saw the prestige of his irresistible strength shaken. Some of those present started to snigger. The second blow was made with his fist, and seeing that his victim felt it, it was as though a punching machine had suddenly been set in motion. Francesc covered himself with his arms, and even if the blows were not that heavy, he realized the beating was going to be serious unless he found a way to satisfy the guard's boxing vanity without taking any major damage. The strategy of simulating a fall sometimes worked, but he was afraid the SS would use the pick handle to make him get up. In the end he made a decision: keeping his arms up, he tumbled out of reach and got his back to the creek. The soldier, tired of hitting him for nothing, was relieved by his victim's retreat. He stopped the beating all at once. From

K.L. REICH

above the huddled body of the prisoner poised just on the crest of the embankment, he had seen the turbid waters of the creek. He leaned backwards and raised his foot. Francesc felt a brutal blow on his left side and saw the earth sliding away from under his feet as though someone had pulled a rug out from under him. The mud of the bank gave way to his scrabbling fingers, and the water, yielding and freezing cold, embraced him. Scrambling to his feet among the slick stones at the bottom, Francesc looked up from where he'd fallen. Above him, the SS was laughing like an idiot.

Francesc didn't return to the little tool shed. A *kapo* took him to the disciplinary company and processed the "recommendation" made by the SS. It had been a long day. The gentle breeze of the morning had turned to a harsh wind in the afternoon, and even though he never stopped working with the maul through the whole day, the soaking defeated him. When he finally got to the camp, he couldn't stop the compulsive trembling that ran through his body and made his teeth chatter. Emili brought him dry clothes, rubbed him with oil, and made him drink hot "coffee" and take an aspirin. Nothing worked. Under the blankets, Francesc noticed that a burning sensation was growing in his cheeks and temples and that strange visions were blurring his thoughts.

—For sure I'm up over thirty-nine —he said.

The need for sleep closed his eyes. To sleep for hours, days, years. As if dreams could assuage the measureless hatred that, for the whole day, had smouldered within him.

CHAPTER X

In Block 13 they were getting a change of underwear, and Vicent was one of many, stark naked, dirty underwear in hand, waiting in line for a clean pair. This operation usually lasted two or three hours; one more torment to add to all the others endured during the course of a week.

—Have you noticed, València? —said the prisoner next in line behind him— Your feet are swollen.
—I know. For the last few days the sun has been getting to them and the swelling won't go down.
—What are you talking about ... sun? That's water, not sun.
—It's like the rain. The sun makes the rain. Without sun it would never rain.

His neighbour didn't know how to respond, but he took València's explanation as ignorant fantasy and started to laugh. Vicent shrugged his shoulders. What was the point of explaining? He knew well enough what was happening. He'd observed that it was on sunny days his ankles swelled up. The sun penetrated his parched skin and, like honed chisels, drove into his joints. On rainy days, by contrast, he had less trouble getting up from the stones where he sat during lunch hour, walked more easily, and slept more peacefully.

València looked at the line of men in front of him. He had no particular reason to be anxious: most of them were just like him or even worse off. Their skin was wizened where normally it would be fleshy, the buttocks disappearing to leave just a dark stain of wrinkled skin with a small diaphragm, even darker, at its centre.

"We're growing tails, like monkeys," he thought when he realized he could see a clear outline of the coccyx on each of his companions. However, this thought didn't make him laugh as it might have in the past. He was in a rush to get his clean undershirt and pants in order to go back and lie down on his half of the straw mattress. And the distribution was taking a long time between the incessant bickering and the generous beatings.

When his turn came at last, València tucked the two clean undergarments under his arm without even looking at them and ran laboriously back to the dormitory. His skeletal body was bent forward like a broken cane. His head, wobbling massively at the top of his skinny neck, seemed to drag his whole body along behind it. He sat down on the flattened sacks of straw and soon had his legs threaded into the underwear. He watched his feet pop out at the bottoms, and it seemed that the swelling was worse. The skin, smooth and taut from the pressure of the fluid inside, held the imprint of his fingers for several seconds, like a bas-relief. València sat in rapt contemplation of this interesting phenomenon for some time. He didn't know whether the swelling caused the fatigue, or if it was the other way around; he only knew that the water started filling up the feet, then moved up the legs to the knees, and that from there it jumped to the bags under the eyes and often flooded the whole head. Many of his companions had gone into the infirmary when they reached this state, never to return. València shook his head in silence; he rubbed his ankles with both hands and exclaimed in a low whisper:

—I'm lost, I'm lost. One foot in the crematorium.

He lay down and covered himself with the blanket. It was better in this position; it lessened the fatigue. Other prisoners were coming and going with their changes of clothes. The neighbour with whom he shared the mattress hadn't yet arrived. València closed his eyes, but sleep didn't seem inclined to make an appearance. He didn't feel tired, but there was something else keeping him awake: the rumbling of his empty stomach, complaining as always. He swallowed saliva and, desperate, pulled the blanket up over his head. When he squeezed his eyes shut against the dust, it seemed to him that life itself was flowing out of him. Just for a moment. When he thrust his head back out, he could have sworn he saw Eugènia, Perico, Vicentet … It had been a long time since he'd thought about his wife and sons. And now, all of a sudden, she made her appearance, with her white apron, a corner folded, her taut arms, the sleeves of her blouse rolled up, laughing with her strong, white teeth; the oldest boy was teasing the dog while the little one hid behind his mother's skirts. Without having finished constructing the hallucination, Vicent was struck with an indefinable presentiment. Did they know something of his swollen feet, his hunger, his fatigue, of the crematorium that, sooner or later, would welcome him?

He fixed his eyes on the light and on the men coming and going with their changes of clothes. The sacks of poor straw were terribly uncomfortable with all their lumps and hollows. He turned on his right side and with the effort his fatigue became still more acute and painful.

—I can't go on —he grumbled—. I can't go on! It's too much …

València sunk his head into the pile of clothes that served as his pillow, and, like an olfactory hallucination, he could perceive the exact smell of bread, exactly the smell of the soft brown bread they'd been given that day at supper time and that he'd gulped down all at once. But no, it wasn't an illusion! The smell, very real and very close, was coming from between the folds of the clothes that his neighbour, still absent, had left at the head of the bed. Without thinking about what he was doing, he slid his hand under the blanket. And yes, the bread was there, with its scent, its texture, its rough crust, its moist interior.

"It would be robbing a fellow prisoner," he thought. Not like before; that bread of Popeye's was everyone's bread, and so a little bit his own. "A crime," as August had said long ago. No, no! The bread … he wasn't stealing it! He was just touching it, just caressing the crisp rough crust and thinking of how soft and moist and scented it was inside. His stomach made its presence known through the flood of saliva that he was having trouble swallowing down. Nothing existed now except the bread; neither memories, nor fatigue, nor the owner of the rags that concealed it, and who would return at any moment. In possession of that secret, he had available to him all the voluptuousness of its perfume and of its touch. That was enough. Nobody was aware of the ecstasy that separated him from the world around him.

Someone approached and threw a clean change of clothes on the mattress. Vicent felt the displaced air brush his cheek. He realized at the same moment that he had the piece of bread clasped tightly in his arms. With his eyes open and inexpressive, his body immobile, he said nothing, thought nothing. The smell of that soft bread overwhelmed the smell of the blanket and reached his nose with an insistent exclusivity. He didn't understand what the newcomer was saying to him, nor notice that he was searching through his clothes, the blankets, the mattress. València squeezed the bread even more covetously and felt the crust give way ever so slightly.

—Have you seen my bread? I know I left it here.

Vicent was looking at him blankly and didn't answer.

—Have you seen my bread, yes or no? Answer me!
—Bread? What bread? —muttered València, diving under the blanket.

Surprised, the other didn't know what to make of this reaction. Only when he saw València moving underneath the blanket were his suspicions confirmed. He tore the cover off. Wide-eyed, with his mouth crammed full, his hands tearing at the bread in a frenzy, Vicent didn't even notice.

—My bread! He's stolen my bread!

He was trying to wrestle away the remaining crumbs of his ration. Valencia fought back desperately.

—Thief! My bread! Thief!

At the alarm, the other prisoners got up from their mattresses and settled in to watch a bit of raw theatre that promised to be entertaining. Popeye appeared on the scene and quickly figured out what had happened. Vicent's mouth was still full, and a scattering of crumbs across the tangled blankets accused him. He had the courage to admit his guilt. But the new Block interpreter, a German who spoke an affected Castilian, was more interested in showing his own zeal in front of Popeye than in translating València's apologies.

—August! —Vicent moaned, forgetting that his countryman was no longer in the camp—. Get August!

Excited by the interpreter's yelling, Popeye started to shout as well. Vicent, standing at attention as though before a tribunal, didn't understand anything they were saying, nor was he even listening to them. The situation was so grave, and so clear his awareness of the gravity of his crime, that nothing that transpired could be of the least importance to him. The metallic crash over his left ear didn't surprise him. Popeye's hand was heavy. Just at the moment when he touched the mattress with his back, he felt his head strike the wooden divider. He answered the kicks with moans, but Popeye was unreachable. He grabbed him by the collar of his shirt and, after dragging him across the patchwork of straw mattresses and through the dining room, dropped him like a sack of potatoes on the cement floor of the washroom. The other Germans of the Block had already prepared their instruments of torture.

—Strip —ordered Popeye.

Vicent didn't understand the order. Trapped between the row of sinks and the wall, he flattened his body as if he could perhaps seep out through the wall itself, his eyes fixed on the gloating faces of his torturers.

—Strip! What are you, an idiot?

One of the tormentors made it clear with a brutish gesture. València took off his shirt and then his underwear, and his body was revealed in all its extreme thinness.

—In the shower —they shouted, pushing him.

The litter used to carry the bread—a box made of slats, and big enough to contain the hunkered body of a man—was upended with the victim caged inside. Turned on at full pressure, the water lashed through the slats, and it was bars of ice that scourged the victim's back. The Germans filled buckets at the taps and threw their contents through the openings on the sides. The water was painful and penetrating, but Vicent could not tell if it was cold or hot. Only that he was drowning just as if he was sinking down into it, dense, heavy, crushing, the same sense of asphyxiation—he remembered it very clearly now—that day long ago when he was still a child and had almost drowned in the marshes near his village.

When he opened his mouth to suck in the air he hungered for, a long moan escaped him and changed, without any break, into a sustained and high-pitched scream that for a moment drowned out the roar of the water and the laughter of his torturers. Then he regained his breath, and he felt an irrepressible trembling come into him. His body flailed inside the box which, light as it was, was easily shifted out of the vertical stream of the shower. His howls followed one on the other, each time more terrible. Popeye's assistants were trying to hold the litter in place with sticks, and the broken ends pushed through the slats and pierced his skin already numbed by the cold. It was a strange cold, a cold that seemed to come out of his own body, a cold that weakened his voice until it was a child's whimper. The litter was getting big for the shrunken body imprisoned within it. Between the slats one could see only a brown formless mass shaken from time to time with the first of its death throes.

València was not at all afraid of that death that already embraced him and gradually tightened around him. Its hold was gentle, almost a caress; all traces of violence had vanished, and it seemed as if all the pain accumulated beforehand now dilated and evaporated out through the pores of his skin. It was a pain full of piety that poured out of him, along with time and life. He lost his grip on everything, and the vertiginous images that ran through his mind all shared the same sweetness:

—Eugènia … —he murmured under the noise of the rushing water.

When Popeye ordered the water turned off and two of the torturers removed the litter, the body rolled softly to the right. It was still breathing, but the crying had been staunched altogether. There on the soaked floor, in silence, in darkness, the body slowly uncurled and began to take on the rigidity of a corpse.

Eleven hours in that corner of the warehouse was a long time. The air clouded with dust and heavy with the smell of unwashed clothes, and his table littered with obscene drawings, Emili came to envy his comrades working outside. To give it up would be idiotic, but sometimes he thought he would have to. Even drawing, his lifelong passion, had now become a kind of torture.

That afternoon he had a book open on top of the pornographic drawing he'd half finished; but when Werner snuck up on him, he wasn't reading. His gaze had, for some time, been lost on the grass of the lawns, or maybe on the grey-green walls of the barracks across from his window.

—Lost in thought?

Emili turned and smiled. Werner was a good companion, a good man. His efforts to "de-Germanize" himself vindicated the draughtsman's resentment of all things German.

—Did you hear? Someone stole my suitcase of books …
—Does this mean that somebody here knows how to read?
—Yet another prank from those idiots!

The other Germans in the *Kommando* hated Werner because of his superior attitude, because of his sharp tongue. That he had collected a suitcase full of books, while they were taking the murdered Jews' best clothes, seemed a ridiculous intellectual affectation.

—I'll help you find it.

Werner talked about the value the suitcase had for him, recalled titles and authors, and finished by saying that the books were still very much his own, if only because he carried them within.

—You're looking downhearted —he said all of a sudden—. Is there something bothering you?
—It's not me. It's Francesc. You know he's got pneumonia?

The German made a toothless grimace.

—Has he been seen by a doctor who can be trusted?
—A compatriot. He thinks that he'll make it; I don't.
—But you are not a doctor.

The draughtsman told him some details of his friend's adventure; the other listened in silence.

—What upsets me the most is the stupidity of the whole thing. If he'd been crushed by a rock, or got typhoid …
—We're living in a place where murder is a patriotic duty.
—I just feel disgusted, profoundly and completely disgusted.
—We've got to hold on.
—But I can't take any more of it —Emili burst out—. No more, you understand? Made to sit here painting these obscenities, and to look on passively as those around me die without recourse.

He grabbed the half-finished illustration and tore it in half in a rage.

—It makes me ashamed of myself. Why am I such a coward? Why can't I tell this officer to go draw his own pornography?
—And what would be gained by that?

—No, Werner. The truth is I'd be fine with it.

—Stop now. No more nonsense. Don't you remember the plans you had only a few days ago, to organize I don't know what?

—We won't accomplish anything! Francesc alone could have done more than all of us together.

—What you can do, a little or a lot, is more important than your scruples. When your friend gets better, he is going to laugh at your scruples.

—People are apathetic and selfish. No one thinks it's worth the effort to try.

—The external conditions might change.

—Before that happens most of us here will already be dead.

Werner admitted that a change of fortune on the front lines was not much more than a hopeful fantasy. At best, the USSR would withstand the blow, but it would be a long time before the Allies had the right conditions to start a counteroffensive. The war might go on for years; the prisoners could only hold out for a matter of weeks, if that. The German wanted him to take courage:

> —I don't think you are justified in your pessimism —he said slowly, his eyes shining—. But if the majority of your countrymen die, it shouldn't be because you sat back with your arms crossed. As many as possible must be saved, and the only way that will happen is if everyone tries to be among the ones that survive. Selfishness is the law of the camp, the poison of our existence here, and, at the same time, the only antidote. We have to survive in order to claim justice one day.

Emili heard an echo of his friend Francesc in the German's words; he too had spoken like this! To claim justice one day!

Werner added, his words rich with emotion:

> —I am German and all of this affects me even more directly than it does you. Look …

He tore open his shirt and revealed a lump the size of a fist just beneath his ribs.

> —During the last war —he said—, when I was seventeen, a piece of shrapnel almost killed me. It left me this souvenir. When I came to this camp, when they were beating me up, I protested, telling them I was a

wounded veteran. That made them laugh, and they left me half dead. I also want to be there when justice is done! Not only because I have suffered, but also because I am ashamed. When I am depressed I think about justice. You think about it too. I believe that is good advice.

In the left wing of Block 1, right next to the administration offices, there was a so-called school for masons that, in spite of its many years in existence, had yet to claim a single alumnus. One fine day a bricklayers' *Kommando* arrived with a great hustle and bustle. They tore out the partitions, took up planking, and stockpiled cement, bricks, and sand. The cause of all this activity was more than mysterious. Some were convinced they were building an extension to the infirmary, others thought some isolation cells for new arrivals, and still others thought, because of how it was situated, that it was probably going to be a special guardpost for handling any prisoner uprisings. A German prisoner who had good relations with the SS came up with this sensational explanation:

—It's going to be a whorehouse!

Nobody believed him.

—Why not an opera house?

The joke spread quickly; everybody knew it and everybody kept asking to have it repeated just for the pleasure of listening to something so funny. Little by little, however, they noted details in the construction that made it seem more and more likely. One morning ten sinks and ten bidets were carried in, and since no one supposed that the SS were in need of such equipment, there was little doubt left as to the truth of the story.

This innovation didn't hold much interest for the hungry. New pots for the kitchen would have been another thing altogether! But for the privileged, the news held real significance. It was met with both enthusiasm and censure, with calculations as to the degree of virility that could be expected under a regimen like that in the camp, with responses of all kinds, and finally one imbecile who concluded that "the Germans were humanizing the penitentiary system."

That evening, flashes of lightning lit up the bed where Emili was trying to stifle his bad mood. The rain was drumming against the tarpaper of the roof a few inches over his head, and its murmur mixed in with the conversation on the other side of the row of cupboards. They were talking about the inauguration of the brothel the previous evening. Ernest was talking. He had not gone, personally, because the Spaniards were prohibited, but the *kapo* of the "potatoes," his friend, had been among the first, and had told him all about it, in full detail.

According to Ernest, the *kapo* had shaved, bathed, put on cologne, and dressed in clean clothes just before the appointed time, and when the call resounded through the camp, "Those who have asked for relations, form up!" he presented himself at the door of the special barracks decked out like a student going to meet his fiancée. There he joined about forty other prisoners, almost all of them German, waiting their turn in an orderly queue.

Ernest explained how every client had been given a piece of paper "personal and non-transferable" signed by the SS in charge and clearly marked with a number between one and ten. Just like a raffle. Like every other living being in Germany, animals included (poultry wore them tied to their legs), each of the ten women of the house had been granted the Nazi privilege of having their very own number. In this case, each woman's number was the same as the number of her "workroom." Contrary to convention in this sort of transaction, clients were not allowed to choose; the SS in charge distributed the numbers arbitrarily, only being careful to share the work out equally among the women. Four men per day for each of them and fifteen minutes for each man. An hour of "work" each day, two German marks in pay, and an absolute guarantee against the passions of love. To ask for "relations," it should be said in passing, one had to sign for fifty pfennigs on a current account at the canteen. The canteen was selling love for fifty cents a go, and for the ones with no money ...

Before entering the rooms that fortune granted them, the clients had to pass through a waiting room, done up somewhat coquettishly, where an orderly from the infirmary checked their health; since the space was limited, those who could not fit in had to wait on the street. When winter arrived, the system was not going to be much of an aphrodisiac.

—What's your number?
—Seven.
—The young Gipsy. Too fleshy for my taste. You'll tell me how it goes.
—And you?
—Two, the blond Pole. She's pretty and she seems nice. I've seen her through the window.
—Good, good! Wishful thinking makes miracles happen.

At the end of a corridor a door opened and a client, just served, came out. On the left side there was the row of numbered rooms. A matron called out the available number:

—Seven… I said seven!

The first in line with a seven on his ticket went to the door of the same number. The first thing he'd notice would be the peephole that allowed everything going on in the room to be watched from outside in the corridor. Very encouraging!

—Be warned —the woman would announce at the outset—.
Fantasies are prohibited; they're paid for in the disciplinary company.

If after so many tests the imagination still had the strength to create a propitious environment, not so easy to do, all would evaporate suddenly enough with the knock on the door and the implacable words:

—Fifteen minutes: Time up!

Even worse were the times when an ever-vigilant SS would dash into the room, pad and pencil in hand, and demand with puritanical indignation:

—Give me your number, you pig. Tomorrow you'll be carrying stones at the quarry.

Ernest explained all these details to the accompanying laughter of his listeners. The air had grown heavy, as if the thunderstorm outside had imposed a morbid tone on the men's false gaiety. Emili, in his bed, fed up with their stupid jokes, had been trying to fall asleep, but their ruckus was winning out against his fatigue.

—It's strange that the *kapo* of "the potatoes" decided to pay a visit to the women —one of them said—. I didn't think he was that way inclined.
—Ernest can clear this up for us.

They all laughed. The boy tried to defend himself, but the laughter and joking of the others made it impossible for him to get a word in edgewise.

—And you, Ernest, will you go when they give the rest of us permission?
—Get lost!
—Don't go, my good man, don't go!

There was such an uproar that the *Blockälteste* had to call for silence. They calmed down then. To a question about the girls' origins, somebody explained that they were prisoners from a female concentration camp who had been organized into a work *Kommando*.

—It seems they've been promised their freedom after six months' work.
—Freedom! After six months, they'll be told that after six more months they can come back and talk about it.
—They are volunteers. It's their choice.
—Volunteers? It's easy to find volunteers in a camp like that, even to sign on with the devil. Judge them? No, nor would I judge the boys here that, in order to eat …

Someone interrupted loudly. A voice that hadn't yet been heard:

—The Germans have brought them in to clean up the homosexuality. In some ways they're very revolutionary, these Germans. A move like this wouldn't be possible anywhere else in the world, I mean in capitalist countries … Religious prejudices …

Emili couldn't take any more. He propped himself up and, leaning over the lockers that separated him from the gathering, he snapped:

—You want to stop this nonsense? You're like pigs in shit. Of all the shame we've had to endure, this is the worst, the most humiliating. And now it seems the Germans are revolutionaries! After they've killed thousands of good men, now you find it excellent that they degrade those who are left. Leave this sort of talk to the German thugs themselves and shut your mouths for once.

Emili vanished from his little balcony and stretched back out on his bed. The group was momentarily surprised, but their conversation soon started up again, though now with voices lowered. Emili, meanwhile, felt a little ridiculous for the utter futility of his gesture.

CHAPTER XI

When Emili walked into the infirmary that evening, he wondered why he felt so awkward and restrained at his sick friend's bedside. It was obvious that the nature of their friendship had changed, with Francesc so much weakened in body and in spirit. Emili had always depended on his friend's personal strength, and he found it strange now that he was the one who needed to be strong. Because of this reversal of roles, he felt as if he was on uncertain ground; it was hard to find things to talk about, and the pretense of being reassuring didn't come naturally to him.

That evening he'd come with a prepared topic of conversation, and the prospect of an easy and agreeable talk had had him hurrying to the infirmary; but the airless room oppressed him with the same unease it had on other days. Some of the sick, wearing only their shirts, dragged their skeletal bodies, their corpse-grey skin, through the Block's dining room. Their bald heads, out of all proportion to their bodies, made him think of the crude drawings of children. The stench of festering wounds and disinfectants came in waves from the dormitory. The German prisoners who held the nursing posts were shoving the patients out of the dining room and back to their beds.

The Spanish doctor came up to him and shook his hand. He was young, he seemed knowledgeable, and he was known to make every effort to alleviate the suffering of the sick. Emili was grateful to him for all the attention he'd given to Francesc.

—How's the patient doing?
—The same, with a slight fever. He's not eating.

And in response to Emili's silence, he added:

—It doesn't look good. Pneumonia has a bad outcome here.
—You mean that ...

The doctor hesitated a moment before answering.

Emili interrogated him with his eyes. He grasped defensively at the lapels of the white coat, perhaps to deflect the blow that was about to fall. The sentence had been written; was it necessary for the doctor to pronounce it?

—The left lung —said the doctor; a serious lesion.

The draughtsman needed to find somebody to blame, someone on whom to vent his useless rage:

—You told me it was nothing. You've known all along …
—You think it would have helped to tell you? I'm saying it today because the diagnosis is now official. I mean —and he stressed the words— that the danger is now much greater. Do you understand?
—Can it be avoided?
—In the long run, nothing can be done. You know that. I'll try to postpone the end as long as possible. —And after a moment, he added—, Do you want to see him?

Emili shook his head. He turned back towards the door in a daze. Something inside him was tightening his throat, and his legs had gone weak beneath him.

—I'll do what I can —the doctor repeated.

—You'll find this letter interesting.
—Who's it from? —asked Emili.
—From a friend of mine who left with August.

The draughtsman took the letter that Rubio held out to him and began reading it:

After so many months in the *Casa Gran*[33] (this is what we call your camp here), to get into a camp like this one feels a little like the first step toward freedom. The camp dominated the landscape; here it is the other way around. We are closer to the Alps, and the mountains are steeper and not only enclose the river that runs beneath our plateau, but also ourselves, who are here to build a dam. These are barriers too, but more tolerable than yours. Not the grey of quarry stone, but autumn's faded greens. The camp is small, the barbed wire is not electrified, and in total there are probably less than two hundred men here. Our mission is to do the preparations for the work to come. When the construction starts in earnest, there will be a demand for workers, and I think this will be a relatively secure refuge for Spaniards. Apart from the two Germans in the kitchen, all of us speak the same language. And we get along fine.

We have all understood, instinctively, the need to obey, to work, and to lead a life to the liking of those that keep us here, and so far I don't think August has had many problems. Now is the moment for him to assert his authority and shift the old routine set up by those *kapo* blockheads. If he manages to, it seems to me that everything is going to run as smooth as silk. August counts me among his deputies—who knows why—and I've been made *Blockälteste*, though everybody here with a rank still works the same as the rest. The food is not as bad as in your camp, and it's shared out with strict equality. If there are leftovers, they are set aside for the skinniest ones. The basic services are also handled with rigorous fairness, everyone taking their turn except the sick and those with a fixed role, who are exempt. Trade between prisoners is forbidden, and the barbers, tailors, shoemakers, etc., offer their services free of any exchange of cigarettes or food.[34] There is a real camaraderie, and no talk of politics, which prevents divisiveness; the austerity of our life here and the continuous work at one thing or another makes rest a necessity, and so people don't want to waste their time in stupid talk. All of us understand that an experiment has been set in motion in our camp that might save the lives of many men. August says that the Germans will have to be convinced by results. So used to violence, they don't understand that with humane treatment they can draw on a greater measure of our strength. It is to fight against this incomprehension that August feels it is necessary to organize disciplinary actions in the middle of the square. He yells a lot, gesticulates even more, divvies out some blows and, for no reason at all, makes you stand facing the barbed wire for a couple of hours. If he did not do that, likely the SS would think his authority too weak, and it's certain that the German prisoner who'd replace him would not be play-acting. Everybody understands and accepts these performances with a sense of humour. Even I, who in so many ways disagree with him, cannot but …

—What follows isn't of general interest —said Rubio.

Emili gave the letter back to him and asked, smiling:

—He's a good friend of yours, who wrote this?
—Yes. Why?
—He's not going to go very far, your friend. Prosecutors can't be sentimental.

—What do you mean?

—No matter. He's very honest, your friend, too honest.

And not wanting to give more of an explanation, he added quickly:

—It seems that August has made more progress than the rest of us. This all shows he knew what he was doing …

—It's a good experiment, but still very modest. From this to being able to control the whole Spanish contingent …

—It's a first step.

—Don't be too sure; the Germans won't give him enough slack. Do you know Metzinger?

—Yes, he often comes into the warehouse, looking for favours, of course.

—He's declared war on me. We won't be able to get anywhere until he's brought down.

—And who's going to do that?

—In the camp things sometimes just happen —said Rubio with a sly smile—. I also have my plans.

The letter of reply concluded thus:

If your next communiqué has the same tone as the one just received, so that to show even a little of it to our enemies would be enough to convince them of the angelic naïveté that, judging by your words, motivates us, consider your services no longer necessary.

He thought the words too harsh. He tore up the page and started writing:

I hope your next letter will be more satisfactory, since the one I am answering serves only to show our opponents that we too know how to value the good things of others. Sincerely … Burn these papers once you have read them.

Rubio got up from his bed and slipped the papers into his pocket. "Having to take such risks to write stuff like this!" he thought. He smiled fleetingly and left to take a stroll, but when he was out on the street he remembered that he still hadn't finished the work he'd had in mind for that afternoon. There remained one very burdensome task to be done. Depending on how things went, a meeting with Ernest could be difficult, perhaps even violent. The boy was getting too cocky, and the amorality of the camp had found in his general lack of scruples a good medium for cultivation.

Rubio had to admit that he'd made a strategic mistake with Ernest. His was a common case: unmanly, no capacity to endure privation, and the necessary measure of shamelessness. With all this and an evident capacity for learning the language, everything had been easy. A few smiles for Germans with privileges and, the first repugnance overcome, he didn't have to wait long for the prize. "I didn't pay enough attention," he thought; and he set himself to refining the details of his efforts to recuperate his protégé—a comrade all but lost.

When he came to the threshold of the kitchen, he stopped for a moment to watch a group of prisoners at work, selected from the youngest in the *Kommando* according to Ernest's particular tastes. Right now they were at the huge sinks washing out the thermoses from the midday meal. The barber was irritated by his first impression. There was too much chatter going on for his taste. He told one of them he wanted to see the Spanish interpreter. He waited some time. Finally Ernest came up from the basement, and Rubio had to repress a grimace of disgust.

> —My apologies for not receiving you in my office —Ernest said with exaggerated emphasis, and extended his hand—, but I only have a few minutes. The *kapo* is waiting for me to make a report. —And, fickle, he added—. For him, the Spanish names might just as well be Japanese.
> —My congratulations on having an office and Spanish names to report —said Rubio with a hint of irony—. I won't keep you but a minute.

And Rubio started his assault with the obligatory "I hope you weren't upset the other day …" He then launched into a paean on friendship in the most generous terms, and finished by asking help for an old comrade who had arrived two days before and was very sick.

> —Hold on, hold on! —protested Ernest—. For you guys, everything seems easy. It's not enough just to want things done, you know. I've got a lot of commitments. I don't know how I'm going to manage everything as it is. And now you want me to take on something more? I can't do it, believe me, it's impossible.

But he wasn't putting up much of a fight, and Rubio felt that he'd struck on the right moment to put the question. He had to insist, to convince him.

—It's a matter of effort —he said—. The case is worth it—a party militant from the old days, the good days. I've known him for years. Your brother knew him too …
—I'd do it —conceded Ernest—, but I'm doing so many favours I'm going to be called on it, and then everything will be over. No, it can't be done.
—We know you are doing great work —Rubio assured him with his charming smile—. The whole camp is talking about you, and I've even heard rumours … I don't know if they're true or not, but …
—Rumours? Again these stories?
—No, no. A very favourable rumour.

And leaning in close to his ear, Rubio added:

—They say that you will soon be in charge of a *Kommando* "like August's." You'd know if it was true or not.

The interpreter felt light-headed, and his legs faltered.

—I don't know anything about it —he confessed quietly— and I wouldn't want it … too much responsibility.

Rubio now renewed his attack:

—We need men like you. Friendship apart, I think you'd be an excellent choice.

The barber was really enjoying himself now. Notwithstanding the results he might achieve by it, he felt that his little lie was really pushing the limit. "Poor Ernest," he thought.

—Or perhaps I'd be the first to know —said Rubio, with an air of complicity. You know I'm very well connected, and with Gupper too, who holds me in his confidence … This without even considering the fact that *we* have certain resources which, sometimes, … well, you see what I mean.

The youths washing the thermoses were making more of a ruckus than ever. The bitter smell of fermented potatoes wafted up from the basement. The cooks with their white aprons came and went, finishing up their work. Rubio let his words fall carefully:

—I'll send you the comrade I've mentioned. To the Block, right? His name is Fuentes.

And he quickly took his leave before Ernest could come up with any new objections:

—I've taken enough of your time. Don't forget what we've talked about. I'll see you again soon.

Ernest had one more thing to say:

—It's just that I've got things running really smoothly here ...

Rubio was already at the door and limited himself to a smile. Human vanity is a first-class political weapon, he thought, and all in all, his afternoon had been very well spent.

Hans Gupper came to the evening roll call, and before they broke ranks, he asked that all the prisoners who knew Russian present themselves. From among the Germans and Poles who stepped forward, only the ones with a real gallows look were chosen. A second call was made for guards to run the disciplinary company, and the same selection criterion was applied. With those chosen off to one side, all the prisoners waited for the arrival of an SS loaded up with a jumble of mismatched clothing. One of the selected villains was stripped down in no time and dressed in the clothing the SS had brought in. He put on a navy blue jacket and a pair of red pants, adorned with fancy stitching and yellow laces, and was crowned with a white enamelled helmet from the Great War, topped with a Bismarckian spike. And last of all, he took up a cavalry sabre of impressive dimensions. The SS started to laugh out loud. Perhaps it needed a few finishing touches, the right shoes, a belt, a little tailoring here and there, but one could solve these things in time. Hans Gupper was very proud of his knowledge in sartorial matters. Was it possible to find a more appropriate uniform for the Internal Police? These clothes had come from the Royal Yugoslav Army, and certainly the Russians about to arrive, and for whom these police were destined, were going to marvel at having such flashy security.[35]

True, the camp was not for prisoners of war but for political prisoners, and under international law ... But where there's a will there's a way. To section off a row of barracks with barbed wire and post a sign on the front of one of them, "Work Camp for Prisoners of War," that would be enough to keep everything within the strictest regulations. Hans Gupper was a resourceful man.

The following morning was very windy. In the early hours preparations were under way for the largest reception in the camp's history: the arrival of two thousand Russian men. They were not expected until ten in the morning, but long before that, the most extraordinary measures had been taken: the reinforcement of the external guard, a prohibition on setting foot in the roll call square, the mobilization of all *Blockälteste* ... Two thousand Russians or two thousand wild animals.

Only a few minutes past the appointed hour, they could be seen from the camp gates, a dark, reddish stain snaking its way up the road. A little while later the lead guard made its entrance, armed with machine guns and grenades. Then the "hussars of the special police" made their operatic appearance and began the task of getting the column of prisoners in line. These "monsters" passed slowly through the Chinese gate; none of them weighed more than fifty kilos. Gaunt, dirty, half naked, mostly barefoot, they shook like leaves each time a gust of wind found its way between the barracks. The SS laughed with satisfaction, with glee, at the catastrophe before them.

—This is an army? —exclaimed Hans Gupper with sarcasm—. No wonder we're advancing so quickly!

It was the first time he'd seen Russians.

In spite of their being almost naked already, the operation of gathering up their clothes was drawn out long enough for some of those unfortunates to collapse from the cold. They undressed in groups, leaving everything in a big heap, and then went down into the boiling shower, from which, still wet and naked, they were turned back out onto the street and driven along it to the barracks of the special camp. And naked they would remain for three or four days, waiting to get back the clothes they had come with—now all jumbled up, obviously—cleaned and disinfected. They were prisoners of war and so could not wear the striped uniform. A matter of international law ... Four days naked, formed up in ranks on the street most of the time! Many of them never got dressed again.

The villainous internal police took the occasion to show off their uniforms as well as their ferocity. The anachronistic sabre was replaced by a length of rubber hose filled with sand: a symbol. In that hole of five barracks, hunger, cold, terror, and death reigned all through the winter.

The arrival of the Russians opened the gates for countless other deportees from eastern and southeastern Europe: more Russians, groups of Yugoslavs, Czechs, and Jews from all over. Because of his position, Emili had to be present through the interminable rounds of these receptions. Above all, he'd never be able to forget the arrival of the first Czechs.[36]

It was an evening in autumn, still and sweet for those who lived outside the barbed wire, when that group of one hundred condemned came in, among them some twenty Jews. The little square where the exchange of clothes took place was in a corner of the wall that enclosed the interior precinct, very near the Chinese door. There were floodlights at intervals along the wall, throwing their light on the polished pavement below and giving the scene a hallucinatory air. Above their heads the infinite dome of the night descended, while beneath their feet the ground shone. The characters in this scene, some in stripes, others in grey-green, and the newcomers, in muted tones, were moving here and there with no apparent purpose, strangely illumined as though on a stage; their voices seemed afraid of silence and at the same time afraid of echoes. The Czechs were lined up and ready to file past the tables where they would leave all their belongings and be registered. The Jews came behind.

—Strip! —ordered the officer.

And to make them hurry, he came up to the line and started punching them and kicking them.

Hans Gupper arrived followed by his staff. His entourage were highly animated, their faces flushed and their steps uncertain after a dinner celebrating some German victory. Being drunk made the SS even more dangerous. Werner had once said that to facilitate the Third Reich's search for recruits, the SS had learned how to transform wine into blood and blood into wine.

First on the camp authorities' order of business were the Jews. The procedure for these capricious interrogations, always an excuse to mete out blows, this time took on the proportions of an orgy in the after dinner haze.

Hans Gupper approached the table where the first man in line, naked and with chattering teeth, was answering questions:

—And you are?

—Czech, sir.

—Say *Obersturmführer*, do you hear? Are you a Jew?

—No, sir.

—Didn't you understand me, pig?

—Yes, *Obersturmführer*.

—Why have you been arrested?

—I don't know, *Obersturmführer*.

—You don't know, idiot? I'll jog your memory.

The Czech was thrown flat against the wall with a punch directly on the chin. He got up, stunned, his eyes wide with fear. He kept rubbing the painful spot with the back of his hand.

—Communist! —the Commandant was shouting at him—. A communist dog is what you are! Who shoots our soldiers in the back! A communist murderer, saboteur!

He threw himself on the prisoner; he lashed out blindly, falling down drunk as he was and in a paroxysm of fury. The Czech protected himself as best he could, all the while denying that he was a communist. At the sight of the blood gushing from the poor man's nose and mouth, Hans Gupper's anger only increased. Then he tripped and fell forward, all of his weight crashing down on his victim's naked body.

—Communist shit! —he shouted, struggling to his feet. Believe me, I'll teach you what it means to be a Bolshevik! Stand up, do you hear me?

And with that, he sank his hobnailed boots into the man's ribs.

—Bring me a whip —he ordered.

The other SS followed their superior officer's example, each with his chosen victim. Howls of pain, shouts and insults, the crack of blows, all resonated between the walls. The raw light of the floodlights struck into relief a monstrous deformation of bodies and objects. Overcome by the horror, Emili watched the phenomenon as if in a dream. The light reflected from the ground cast their shadows up against the great vault of the night.

When one of his acolytes gave the whip to Hans Gupper, the Czech had backed himself into a corner and curled into a ball, sobbing.

Amidst the chaos, naked bodies, already dead or in agony, were tangled up with piles of clothing and torn-open suitcases. Pools of coagulated blood stained the pavement. In their drunkenness, the SS finished with one victim only to begin on another, and would certainly have exterminated the whole hundred new arrivals if Hans Gupper, himself tired out, hadn't ordered a stop. His only instructions were to intern this group of Czechs, and he didn't want to draw a reprimand from his superiors. The change of clothes recommenced. But the SS found it difficult to abandon the game altogether. They placed themselves in two lines between the tables and the stairs leading to the shower, each of them with a whip in hand, and they obliged the novices to pass between them. The game consisted of aiming their whips at the eyes and the genitals of those who passed through. When the wretches arrived at the top of the stairs, an SS was there to send them tumbling down to the floor below with a shove from his boot. Other SS waited for them in the shower room with a hose of boiling water running at full pressure. A number of those who had survived the orgy outside would die here, burst apart when they were forced to open their mouths ...

At dawn, when he finally got into bed, Emili couldn't sleep. A world of spectres shifted behind his closed eyes through a silence even more shrill than the howls of terror a little while before. The movements of those mouths, those eyes, legs, and arms, now that he could hear only the calm breathing of his sleeping comrades, took on a fascination as disturbing as it was absurd; the gestures without the words made the atrocity still more incomprehensible and rendered his silent rage ridiculous. Everyone around him was sleeping; he felt like he was alone in carrying the weight of it all. Only he smelled the acrid stench of those viscous pools; only he could attach to each gesture of the sacrificed its corresponding scream. Having gathered in all the visual and aural impressions like a recording machine, his brain struggled in vain to set them in order. He'd had the most shameful revelation of his life: he'd felt the jolt of hot blood, like a lightening bolt; the ecstasy of human brutality, quick to mount when the spirit is left to sink into the mire ... He wouldn't sleep! He couldn't let go of the clotted ties that bound him to those images of naked, warm, and bloodied bodies. He too was a part of the wreckage. He didn't feel guilty for any of it, but he felt ashamed.

That night, and the nights to follow, all would be uncertain, presided over by that same madness, until the blood that stained his striped uniform had dried, dried completely. Only then would he think about the hour for justice.

The "lice inspection" consisted of a painstaking search for parasites of all kinds in the seams of underwear and clothing and through the hairy regions of the body. Twice a week, the *Blockälteste* would place a stool at the entrance to the dormitory and oblige his charges to stand naked on it, shirt and underwear in hand. While an assistant searched through the clothes, the German, in person, would scrutinize with particular attention the most hidden zones, a powerful light in one hand and a spatula in the other. At the discovery of a little creature or a clutch of eggs, the prisoner would be put through a general shaving, shower, and rubdown with disinfectant, and receive a clean uniform. The following day, the *Blockälteste* would report the results of the inspection to the secretariat.

With the windows of the dining room shut, the air grew thick with the odour of naked bodies. Exempt from the inspection thanks to his post in the clothing warehouse, Emili had been observing the scene from his bed. The performance made him remember something Werner had said about the imbalance that results from valuing one of the two basic human characteristics, body and spirit, over the other.

—We Germans —his *Kommando* companion had said—, create an ideal out of this imbalance. We make nature, the body, health, physical strength the highest aims of human perfection, and obviously, like all materialists, we oversimplify things. It hasn't occurred to us that the world, and especially for us Germans, is headed for a new Middle Ages, but with its values reversed. Today, the spirit is a nuisance and we concede to the body the same exclusive and pernicious cult with which the medievals embraced the soul. We talk about race, practise euthanasia, play at mind-numbing sports, introduce corporal punishment as a form of social control, we despise the elderly, we put the barracks before the family. That's to say, in the name of the collective, we crush the individual, and ultimately it seems that nudism is going be the great scientific discovery of the age. Idiotic, the whole business! Adam and Eve discovered long ago that going naked was complete nonsense.

The scenes played out in the "lice inspection" were the best illustration of these words. At that very moment, a young man was standing on the stool and his nudity was being thoroughly examined. The *Blockälteste* touched the hot bulb of his lamp to the most sensitive spot on a man's body.

—You're very fat —he told him, suggestively—. You must "requisition" a lot.

With his free hand, the *Blockälteste* prodded the man's chest and flanks, to the insinuating laughter of the Germans present. "Not long before he gets some propositions," Emili said to himself, with a grimace of disgust.

The cult of the body and of physical strength led exactly to this. From the anti-Christian boarding school to a pagan youth camp, from there straight into a military barracks, and later on, off to war: thus was the life of the average German youth laid out. Always among men alone, taught that women were just machines to make children for the Fatherland, believing that nudity and sports were not only a path, but also an aim, that the strongest was the best and that physical beauty was the highest ideal. A perfect climate for every kind of aberration! Sensitivity, modesty, pity, were negative qualities that had to be banished from a strong people.

For the masters of the camp, though, nudism was something more than just a vehicle for the immoral behaviour intended to destroy the individual. While he lay there observing the embarrassment his companions suffered under the inspection of their keepers, Emili thought how disarmed a person is when forced to offer up his naked body to the curiosity of his masters (even more so when this curiosity is perverse). The myth of our first parents was repeated. A naked man is humiliated, brought low, and surrenders to the mercy of those who can give him back his clothes. In a group of naked men, when one is not brought up in the cult of the body, misery and shame achieve a balance that is the beginning and end of the collapse of all principles. Lucid thought, self-respect, defiance, everything that distinguishes men from beasts becomes impossible; and if any of these were to show themselves, they would be quashed instantly by the sense of ridiculousness that is borne of nudity.

The air was so dense that it was starting to get hot. Emili continued observing the scene from his vantage point. In general, when people climbed up on the stool their faces were inexpressive, and they stepped down quickly once the inspection was done. Some, though, took on a submissive and servile attitude, smiling if the German said something to them, even though there was no cause for smiling, and exaggerating the fact of their offering themselves up. More disciplined than their elders, the young men largely rebuffed the Germans' jokes, but even among them there were many who went along with it in the hope of finding a solution to their personal difficulties. To be "protected," to be one of the *javas*, as they were called in the Spaniard's camp slang, meant not going hungry, finding good contacts, getting good clothes. It was often the first step up towards the ranks of the "privileged."

The draughtsman thought that evil was making inroads, that the "Ernests" were increasing in number at an alarming rate. All of those who died without surrendering their principles could not conceal, with their sacrifice, the repugnant faces of the debased. And Emili wondered, despairingly, how the relentless incursion of the *spirit of the camp* could be halted, how the collective will might be raised against it, how the pervasive apathy might be overcome.

He got out of bed and went out to the street, hoping that the cold might be more agreeable than the suffocating dining room. In fact, the contrast gave him the sensation that something had been erased from his thoughts, leaving a comfortable vacuum. The breath coming from his mouth was at first visible, then slowly diffused. Emili looked up at the sky; it was as if the lights of the camp sullied the ceiling of clouds. A man, obviously cold, with his hands in his pockets and his head pulled down between his shoulders, came out behind him.

—Snow tonight —he said—. If we wake up to a white morning tomorrow, it's going to be a long winter.

Emili answered with a groan. He felt irritated, not by the spectacle of a moment ago, but by his own stupidity in wanting to redeem others. He sensed his motives had no real human warmth, that they were, above all, the product of a sense of duty. Why not take refuge in his inner world and try to find the stability there that the exterior world denied him? This uneasiness had been lingering for too long, a disgust for his fellow man, a longing for nullity, for oblivion. Rubio worked for partisan ends, likewise the syndicalists. But not Emili. To fulfill one's duty! Ridiculous. No, he was no apostle. "I am as weak as the others," —he thought— "my egotism is a kind of impotence, just the same as the servility of the cowards and the perversions of the weak." Egotism was another of the weapons that drew its power from the *spirit of the camp*.

That same morning, just a couple of hours earlier, a young Spaniard had left the camp, repatriated as a minor. He was the only one among all the thousands to have such luck. In spite of the oath that the boy had had to swear in front of the SS, he'd taken Matilde's address with him, and he'd promised to go to see her. Emili knew that the boy would hold true to his promise no matter what the risk. And were there not many men here capable of making such a gesture? Most of all those men he found so repugnant, wouldn't they do the same thing if the opportunity presented itself? Can one judge a man for clinging desperately to life? The logic of it made him go back to where he'd started: one had to understand, to be compassionate, and to help. It was all the same in the end if it was out of a sense of duty or out of honest caring: it simply had to be done. To fight, no matter how, to sacrifice everything not to be drawn in by the *spirit of the camp*. To do otherwise was to collaborate with Nazism.

Only the really desperate cases were admitted to the *Isolierung*, a tiny room designated for quarantining infectious cases. The room was crowded with bunk beds, badly ventilated, and abandoned by the doctors and orderlies. One might say there was only one way out of it: to the crematorium. If his frequent hemorrhaging, his high fever, his extreme weakness were not enough to make his fate clear to Francesc, admittance into this room told him that his sentence was final and without appeal.

Emili had sought desperately to find someone of influence who could stop the transfer out of the general ward of the infirmary. But all his efforts had been in vain; it was the personal directive of the SS doctor. The interest shown by the draughtsman served only to win Francesc the gentler treatment generally reserved for those who had prominent friends in the camp. In spite of the regulations, Francesc continued to be provided with food and injections; the draughtsman bought these with the clothes, money, or tobacco that he took from the storeroom.

> —Don't waste your time bringing me these things —Francesc would tell him— you know that I can't eat them. They'd be of more use to someone else.

A depressing serenity, Francesc's. He had courage without making a fuss, a quiet struggle against the destruction of the spirit; facing death, he held on to his capacity to reason. In front his condemned friend, Emili felt inferior, hollow, he felt worthless.

> —In a way, death is a compensation —Francesc said one day—.
> When they kill us, they show that we were right: they justify our long years of fighting.
> —Don't talk like that. It's not as bad as you think. You're going to be all right.
> —There's no point in making grand statements. I'm not going to. But secretly, I hope one day you'll feel proud to have been my friend. You'll remember me and say, "He was a dignified man who didn't give in."
> —Shush —said Emili.

Once in the *Isolierung*, Francesc got worse very quickly. The fetid odour of the sick, the accumulated filth, the bad air, the cadaverousness of his bedmates, the lamentations of the dying, their death rattles, the scene each morning when they took out those who hadn't made it through the night, all of it together was too much for his weakened spirit. Despite his self-discipline, he was sometimes overcome by a profound sadness; the constant company of death was burdensome and exhausting. If he'd accepted death as a friend, its actual presence was exasperating. In that room, Death could take no other form than death-made-manifest, not that death which he had come to love when, its hideousness concealed, it signified the peace he'd so long desired.

During those interminable days, Francesc thought back over his own life, and despite the conviction that he had always acted according to the imperatives of his conscience, he discovered a terrible emptiness. He had the first notion of it the day he realized, to his surprise, how important Emili's visits had become for him. Always a solitary person, he'd never known any real affection. No doubt out of a human instinct to find it, he'd taken up the set of beliefs that, besides monopolizing his youth, now demanded the little he had left. A beloved who had asked much and who gave back only a sterile sensation of "duty done." Until now, in the *Isolierung*, he had not been aware of the real value of a friendship like Emili's. He had ignored what is best in life; and, too late to turn back the pages, he clung desperately to his friend's visits whenever Emili could flout the severe infirmary rules. And it was then that the draughtsman's presence would become, for him, the only real, tangible compensation for his sacrifice. Although his voice had weakened so much, and his words came only with difficulty and in short gasps, his mouth always open because of his asthma, it was on these occasions that he was compensated for the silence of all his days of solitude.

—Don't speak; it tires you out —Emili told him.

More than anything, it was the wracking fits of coughing that often interrupted their conversation, which made the draughtsman wonder whether it did his friend any good to let him talk. Francesc's euphoria was transitory, and the depression that followed was deeper every time, but Emili had come to believe that the happiness found in their exchanges was more important than any pointless conservation of energy.

—It's been hard enough for them ... to catch me ... Now I'm finished, completely finished ... The only thing that bothers me is being burned

... If I could keep my body whole, I'd reappear ... once in a while ... to annoy them ... to demand justice ...

Emili forbade him to talk nonsense.

—It's not nonsense ... not at all ... More than one of them will be pleased ... down there, in the village ... Believe me ... I regret having to give them this satisfaction!
—The doctor says you'll get better ...
—The doctor doesn't know anything.

And after a pause, his gaze fixed on the slats of the upper berth, he said in an even fainter voice:

—Remember ... remember all of this ... when the war is over. Remember me! It's so sad to leave no memory, no trace ...

Emili squeezed his hand in answer. The stench of the sick was suffocating him. Beyond Francesc's bed another patient was speaking Polish to a visitor. On the top berth someone was weeping. Emili decided to leave; he wasn't sure he could keep hold of himself.

—I shouldn't tire you —he told Francesc to explain his sudden departure—. The doctor says I should let you be. Rest now.

One day, as he headed over to speak to the Spanish doctor after one of these visits, the draughtsman didn't make it as far as the consultation room at the other end of the Block.

—Leave right now —an orderly said to him—. The SS doctor is coming, and if he sees you here ... Go on, go. Hurry!

Emili obeyed. The torpor that always came over him in the quarantine room clung to him despite the gusts of cold air that funnelled between the rows of barracks. A heaviness weighed on his chest. He sensed that something bad was about to happen, that the situation couldn't go on much longer as it was. The hour of reckoning was coming. Would it be tomorrow, in a week, a month? What difference did it make! He had no doubts about the real meaning of his presentiment; but it was impossible for him to imagine Francesc dead. Without him, the continuation of life in the camp, the defeat of the Germans, and even the end of the war itself all became incomprehensible. All in a flash, the draughtsman saw that Francesc's resignation before fate was nothing other than the certainty of survival at a higher level, perhaps in another world, where that marvellous strength would find a better place in which to apply itself. If this were so, physical death was a sublimation of life, a desirable consecration. Emili had unconsciously begun to understand many things.

If, better informed of the infirmary's routine, Emili had known that the SS doctor only came in on those afternoons when he needed to make a selection of registration cards; if he had known that the cards selected would be marked with a bold X in red ink; if he had known, finally, that the total number of sick men at that moment surpassed the quantity officially allowed ...

Tomorrow the sun would not come out. The dawn mists would gradually lift, but a dense and threatening cloud cover would persist the whole morning. Possibly, later on, that fine dry snow would fall, brought on by a sudden drop in temperature.

Francesc had slept well until woken by a sensation of cold. His feet felt as though they were frozen, and his whole body was trembling. In the hope of warming himself up, he covered his head with the blanket, but he couldn't stay like this for long; he had to come up for air. Strange, but it was not the same kind of cold as usual. The trembling had something to do with his nerves, and his palms were clammy. He tried to go back to sleep. Useless. That stench! That insistent underlying stench that seemed to be part of the cold itself. It must be coming from one of the neighbouring bunks. And how it stank! No, no, he was exaggerating ...

He covered his head again, trying to escape that stink of decomposing corpses. But he could smell it all the same, even more strongly. The whole room must be impregnated with it. He stuck his head back out of the blanket and had a quick look at the beds on either side of him. The bits of straw, the thin sackcloth covered in terrible stains, the dusty, sweat-stained blankets ... everything around him was tied to a long story of cruelty and sadness. How many of his captive comrades had lain here before him and his neighbours? Without companionship, without tenderness! Only loathing and fear. Francesc understood: it was the smell of death that seeped nauseatingly from the beds all around him, from his own bed, from his own body. "Hallucinations, decay," —he thought—, "fevered imaginings." He resolved to resist, but it came to him that this wasn't just one more test of his courage in the face of death. The atmosphere was charged with something indefinable. The room, usually abandoned by the infirmary workers, was crowded that morning. Not only were they taking away those who had died in the night, but the nursing *kapo* was coming and going with a list in his hands.

Francesc had been too long in the infirmary to be able to share their feigned indifference to the situation. "No one visits the dying," he thought. As for the transfer, yes, that was a certainty. He didn't know anything about the cards with their red X's, but he was sure he wouldn't escape this selection. Strangely enough, all of his anxiety evaporated. He had to wrestle with himself to face the fact that this might be his last morning. He had imagined it a thousand different ways, but he had never thought it would come with the sense of inner peace he felt in those moments. Perhaps a few hours from now he would lie stacked and naked at the crematorium depot, one cadaver among hundreds, but even so, he wasn't afraid. His heart was beating evenly, and however much he tried, he couldn't sense the proximity of any abyss. On the contrary, he saw before him a gentle slope without end, where all his senses ceased their torments. The suffering, the injustices, the thanklessness, erasure, hatred, murder, and the always painful self-discipline ... everything faded away to be replaced by a rare sweetness. The taste of nothingness? He'd shaken off that feeling of regret that sometimes took hold of him for not having put a quick end to his misfortunes by standing up to the SS with a defiant gesture. A new light shone on all things, and revenge, as a passion, now seemed just an overwhelming and exhausting tension. He felt far above all of it now! The certainty that this sacrifice was, in truth, a way to affirm the very reason and essence of his being allowed him to accept death as a necessary end. Without it, his years of fighting would have no meaning. Why wish for anything more if infinite peace was within his reach? "Not nothingness, but infinite peace ..."

—*Qu'est-ce qu'il y a?* —asked his neighbour in the next bed, alarmed by a movement that he'd made.

He was seventeen, a Dutch Jew sick with typhus.

—*Il y a que nous avons eu le gros lot, voilà!* —answered Francesc, enigmatically.
—*Je ne comprends pas ce que tu veux dire.*
—*Ce soir ... j'aurai le temps de t'expliquer ça ... Maintenant j'ai sommeil.*[37]

The nursing *kapo* came in along with two of his subordinates and headed directly to the Pole's bed.

—You're due for a check-up —he said to him—. These two will help you walk. You're number 27-65, yes?

He made a mark on the list. The two orderlies lifted the sick man by crossing their arms to make a sort of chair for him. The unfortunate burst out in a piercing scream. His eyes popping from their sockets, with a voice that didn't seem his own, he yelled:

—You're taking me to slaughter … No! I don't want to die!

This was the signal that unleashed the maelstrom. Some started crying with great, wracking sobs, others screamed that they were well and healthy, that it was murder. Some spat out curses and insults, others prayed aloud or spoke the names of their loved ones, invoking them one by one. They spoke as many different languages as there were patients in the room. Francesc covered his head with his hands against the desperation that assailed him from all sides. Shutting his eyes, he tried to close down all of his senses; he didn't want to see death manifested in any other way than that which he'd already accepted, and which had seemed benign, almost desirable.

When the Pole had gone, there was an oppressive silence, as if they were waiting for a miracle. All that could be heard were some muffled sobs that seemed to mark out the passage of time. No miracle came: after a few minutes, the *kapo* came back with the list in his hand.

The Dutch Jew was the third. Francesc took his hand:

Rappelle-toi … ce soir … j'ai à te parler … Courage, mon cher! —he told him with a weak smile—. *Nous causerons longuement ce soir.*[38]

The boy was brave. He hadn't opened his mouth since their short conversation a little while before, and now he looked at Francesc with a serious expression, but still without a word.

A great number of the beds were empty by the time the *kapo* came in and called Francesc. Francesc took his blanket off. He wanted to get out of bed without any help and to present himself at the "liquidation room" on his own two feet. But he couldn't do it. Steadied by two orderlies, he took a long look around the room. "This is the last time I will see these beds, imagine, this ceiling, this door, this corridor." Very little remained to him.

The room he entered was big, like one of the Block dining rooms. Seated behind a table, the SS doctor was looking through some papers. In the middle of the room, under a broad lampshade, an operating table, articulated and covered with a burgundy oilcloth, and beside it, a little glass table on wheels that was crowded with bottles and some nickel-plated tools. An orderly Francesc recognized was wearing a blue smock. Other doctors—prisoners—some of whom he knew, were standing around the big table. Francesc found himself lying there, naked. He had the feeling that time was running on ahead of him and that the movements of those around him were brusque and mechanical. The shade, with the concave mirror inside it, seemed to physically gather in his attention. He felt cold, and he noticed that he was covered in goose bumps. What did it all mean? He had to wrestle with himself to focus his mind and remember that he was going to die. A few minutes, perhaps seconds ... "I'm an idiot"—he thought—"I'm dreaming. There are no doctors, no tables, there's no lampshade, no self, even." The only real thing was the concave gaze that was absorbing him, and annihilating him, that erased from his mind all trace of time and the dimensions of space. Death was a mirror! Cold, shiny, virtual, an illusory image, the inverted reflection of an absurd world, of men working with jerky movements around a table where another man was lying down. Francesc thought that that fleeting moment, insubstantial, unreal, was the one moment that weighed most heavily on a whole life. He found that the past had taken on something of the grotesque. The struggle over so many years only to avoid that moment, to delay it, seemed out of all proportion, and in the end ridiculous. Fear. Of what? Of this light that was blinding him with the flash of revelation? The deforming mirror was Death, and he held it in his gaze, fascinated by its magic, the serenity it imposed. He could touch it just by reaching out his hand ...

He must have been lying there for some time, because when he rubbed his thigh he noticed it was icy. Getting cold! It didn't matter. The words came out of his mouth without difficulty, without his even intending to say them:

—Come on, what are you waiting for?

He hadn't seen that the Spanish doctor was talking in a low voice with the officer. He didn't realize that his friend was trying to save him right up until the SS approached the operating table. A hermetic face appeared before him. Francesc noticed that the doctor had had a very good shave and that he had a strong smell of wartime cold cream. The doctor gave him a quick look and went back to his papers. Francesc didn't notice the doctor's signal to the orderly wearing the blue gown. He did hear, a few seconds later, the clink of the instruments against the glass top of the little table. Without turning his head he could see clearly that the orderly had a huge syringe in his fingers, a syringe armed with a very long needle.

—Are you going to hurt me? —he asked with pretended interest. In fact, he couldn't have cared less.

The orderly was German and didn't understand him, but the Spanish doctor answered:

—With this treatment you're going to get better. Don't be afraid.
—I know —Francesc said, smiling—. How long before it takes effect?
—Not long —said the doctor in a sombre tone.

And he placed his hand on his arm.

The lampshade's attraction became irresistible. Somebody was raising the table slowly up towards the concave mirror, and the mirror no longer reflected light, but instead the inverted images of all the men and everything around him. Francesc felt pierced to the heart. The weapon was cold and expanded infinitely within his chest. A vivid pain, but not unbearable. Everything was disappearing little by little and only the mirror held on to the vague shadows of an almost maternal night. A great clamour inside his head was deafening him, a noise that turned into a long shrill whistle, sharp and piercing. Meanwhile, the table never stopped rising, slowly …

—I'm not going to have enough gasoline —said the blue-gowned orderly.
—Decrease the dosage —replied the SS doctor—. With less they die just the same.
—It lasts longer and they suffer more.
—It doesn't matter. Decrease the dosage.

CHAPTER XII

Vain and not the sharpest knife in the drawer, Max thought that Jenny, one of the prostitutes in the camp brothel, was in love with his great thick head. In exchange for this love, he brought her stockings and dresses from the Jews, from the Jews who, while the camp slept, were murdered in the basement of the crematorium in unimaginable orgies of blood.

When Hans Gupper interrogated Jenny and wanted to know who had given her the gold watch they'd found under her mattress, the girl clenched her teeth and cursed "that jealous Hilda." It must have been her who told! Jenny confessed without much asking:

—Max gave it to me.
—Max?
—Who works in the *Effecktenkammer.*

Hans Gupper smiled. He'd wanted to do a search of the civilian clothing warehouse for some time now. A propitious opportunity: the officer in charge was on a fifteen-day leave. There'd be no conflicts of authority.

With an assistant at his side, he swept into the barracks where they'd set up the clothing depot. He asked for this "Max" and ordered him to produce all the keys for the drawers and files. Once he'd pulled the documents that looked interesting to him, he took them back to his office.

For the warehouse personnel, Hans Gupper's unexpected visit was like the storm's first bolt of lightning. Panic stations: compromising labels were torn from the sacks the workers had set aside for themselves, inventory lists were burned in the stove, cupboards were emptied. In half an hour they did more work than they'd done in the two months previous. Probably Emili wouldn't even have noticed what was going on, tucked away in his corner, had Werner not hurried over to warn him.

—The hour has come. We have not a moment to lose. Hurry!

Emili asked what was happening.

—Be sure to not leave a trace; burn everything!

—I'm only surprised they've taken so long to find out —said the draughtsman.

With the hundreds of condemned who came through every day inexorably converted to smoke and ashes, civilian clothing, money, and jewels formed the basis of a highly productive trade for everyone involved in it. The time had come for an exemplary lesson. The warehouse workers had just drawn the winning ticket in a dire lottery.

Max, the right-hand man of the officer in charge, handled vast quantities of cash and valuables. Given the morality of the place, it would have been idiotic not to profit from the situation. Everybody accepted it as the most natural thing in the world. What was unpardonable was that he'd risked everything for a whore! Hans Gupper was explaining this to him with the blunt end of a stick. Max, a coward, confessed to everything that his torturers asked him, and then some.

It had been more than three hours that Emili, in canvas shoes and a sweater like his co-workers, had been standing at attention in the roll call square just in front of the offices. They'd been placed at a distance from one another to keep them from talking. A cold breeze carried smoke from the crematorium, with its stench of burned wool, all through the camp.

As they were to find out later, Max had incriminated Werner as the main accessory to the abuses committed by the officer, since he was the one who did the accounts. Werner was the first to be called in to make his statement. The tortures lasted a good hour. He was a man of almost fifty, a wounded veteran, and with his poor health he wasn't going to survive the standard beating. When, at last, he came stumbling out of the office, his clothes torn and covered with blood, Emili's heart tightened. It was truly admirable the way his companion managed to hold his head high.

One by one, they went through the trial of the "twenty-five," and all came back so broken that the draughtsman despaired of his earlier hopes of escaping the torture. When, last of all, he was called in by an SS, he promised himself to say nothing, even if it meant suicide. Not so much from a wish to protect the others as out of a desire to demonstrate to himself that he was capable of withstanding this test.

Inside the office it looked like the aftermath of an earthquake. Upended furniture, papers scattered everywhere, abandoned clothing, bloodstains. Hans Gupper was sitting on a corner of a table, shirt unbuttoned, his hair in front of his face, a whip in his hand, and with his feet swinging back and forth. The same face that Emili had seen on the night of the Czechs. The draughtsman came to attention with a loud slap of his heals.

—Espanyòler? —asked the German, after studying him for a long time.

—Jawohl —answered Emili.

—You don't know anything, obviously. None of you ever know anything —and in the same breath, he yelled— Out!

All the accused Germans were transferred to the *Arrest* that same night. Emili, on the other hand, moved freely through the camp until the afternoon of the next day. An orderly came for him after lunch and handed him over to the guard on duty. A little while later, an SS took him to the same place the others had been held since the early hours of the morning.

The *Arrest* and the crematorium were part of the same building, the only one in the camp built of brick and mortar. The incinerators were on the first floor, while the *Arrest* occupied the floor above, divided into two wings with a special guard between. Each wing had a wide corridor, clean, bright, and airy, with a row of individual cells on each side.

Emili was taken to a cell already occupied by a German he didn't know. When he got used to the darkness, he noticed the "pink triangle" on his shirt: a homosexual.

—I'm Heinrich. You're Spanish, yes?

He spoke very good French. "Suspicious" —the draughtsman was thinking— "A classic setup." Emili listened skeptically to the explanations the man gave. In charge of a tool shed in the quarry, he had been incarcerated now for eight days because of an underground traffic with civilians. Emili outlined his own case as well, but just the bare bones.

The cell was eight square metres, and its furnishings consisted of a wooden bench for sleeping (stood on end against the wall during the day), a radiator that was turned off, and a bucket to relieve oneself.

—It is forbidden to sit on the floor, to pace, to smoke, to talk, or to sing —announced the homosexual with a wry smile—. You have to stay right here at the end, exactly underneath the open window, and you can't lean on the wall. Delightful! If you don't obey, the guard will see through the peephole in the door and ... you'll find out. There aren't any blankets to sleep under, but don't let the cold worry you because the heater comes on at night. Your belt has been taken away, hasn't it? And your sweater, evidently. To eat, a daily piece of bread, and a quarter litre of murky water. Twice a week they give us a litre of hot soup. You'll see what it is to be hungry and not able to say a word about it.

—You're never let out?

—Only early in the morning, to go to the latrines to empty the bucket and wash it. We all go out together and we are like a troupe of ballerinas moving along to the music of the whistle. The steps are learned through beatings. It's really fun!

Emili didn't understand why he'd been sent to the *Arrest* after a twenty-four-hour delay. Had they found out that he was drawing pornography? Was he going to be interrogated, tortured? After he'd thought he'd been spared … All in all, he was in a terrible position: his ignorance of the situation, the drawings, and, to top it all off, the picturesque companion with whom he'd just been billeted. "He doesn't look the part," he thought. And up to now he hadn't asked any dangerous questions.

—Last night they "suicided" one of your companions.

—Was his name Werner?

—I don't know what his name was. The guard told me he was the oldest.

—He was a good friend. The only one of the lot who was really honest.

The homosexual shrugged his shoulders.

—It's those the SS are most interested in silencing forever. The honest ones are a nuisance.

—I'm sure he didn't talk.

—Sooner or later, even the bravest talk. Their methods are infallible. And to make sure of it, they thought best to hang him from the radiator valve.

Emili looked with horror at the cell wall: the valve for the radiator was only one metre off the floor.

—It's not possible —he cried—, a man's body …

—For the SS, everything is possible. The more complicated things are the happier they are.

The pain that Emili felt was visceral, and he covered his face with his hands.

—Why such cruelty?

—*Je regrette.*

The "pink triangle" could not have expected the death of a fellow prisoner to mean so much in a camp where hundreds died every day.

—*Je regrette* —he repeated—. You were good friends?

The draughtsman uncovered his face, looked directly at his interlocutor and clenched his fists:

—I am crying from rage, do you understand?

It was at one of the meetings of the camp's miniature Communist International that Rubio met Frantisek, a Czech medical student who worked in the infirmary. That he belonged to the same Party and knew Castilian became the basis for a long relationship.

One of the Czech's duties was the periodic disinfection of the crematorium.

—Have you never been there? —he asked the barber one day.
—No.

One morning Rubio slipped out of the barber shop on the pretense of going to the infirmary to have a boil lanced. Some minutes later, lugging a big bottle of disinfectant, he and the Czech made their way along a half-underground corridor towards the building's metal staircase.

—A house of many secrets.

The corpses came in through a door on the other side of the building. They were brought in naked, a tin tag with the prisoner's number tied around the neck, and while waiting their turn in the incinerator, were stacked in a large refrigeration room. The oven was not all that big and could hardly burn a hundred bodies in twenty-four hours, a number often surpassed by the mortality rate of the camp, so it was not unusual for some corpses to stay in the cooler for weeks on end.

It was more repugnance than pity that Rubio felt before this macabre spectacle. Frantisek was spraying the two neatly stacked pyramids of corpses with his fumigator. In one pile, heads were visible; in the other, feet. The weak light that came through the ground-level window seemed to augment the volume of the two mountains. The stench of death mixed with the sharpness of the disinfectant. "Fallen soldiers of the revolution," thought Rubio; but he knew at the same time that to say so meant nothing. Is it only suffering that counts? There was enough of that accumulated in those skeletal bodies, purple from bruises and lesions! The sum of all their pain surpassed his too disciplined imagination: "A new order will make these monstrosities impossible." Needless to say, to establish such a "new order" would necessitate ... one more time, but the last time ... an extermination of the exterminators! And justice would reign ever more in the world!

—Not so cheerful, is it? —said the German doing the "honours"— Come with me. If you like, I can show you our operating room.

The oven was in the middle of the room, big piles of coal on each side. Just beneath the round iron door where the corpses were introduced was the firebox. The iridescent flames of the coal showed their tongues to the dead and the living together.

—You won't get cold in here —commented Rubio, to see if the sound of his own voice might calm him down.
—In winter this is the best *Kommando*.
—You can keep it.
—Look at this —invited the German, pointing to a peephole in the round door.

Inside the cylinder, Rubio saw a pile of incandescent matter in which he could vaguely make out the shapes of several tibias. He stepped back, overcome with the feeling that his curiosity had violated something sacred. He'd always thought that cremation was a progressive, hygienic, and pragmatic procedure. Now though, seeing it up close, he expressed his doubts to Frantisek. Who replied:

—In ancient civilizations, cremation was a ceremony carried out with grandeur. Here they burn the dead to erase any trace of their murder.

Rubio noticed a table in the far corner of the room.

—The "operations" are done there —the German explained, trying to make a joke of it.

The barber gave a quick look: there was a pile of bloody limbs from a quartered cadaver.

—We have to take them apart like that before they go into the
oven —the worker explained calmly—. The bodies won't fit in whole.

On another table there was a row of tin cans that looked like food
tins. Rubio remembered someone spreading the rumour that the Germans
canned human meat.

—They're for the ashes. The remains from each firing—six bodies in
each—are put into six of these tins. Each of them is labelled with the
name and number of one of those cremated. The families have the
right to claim them ...
—But this is a fraud: the ashes are all mixed up ...
—Obviously, but it's of no importance when no one knows.

The Czech had finished his job, and when the German invited him to
go down to the cellar, he said:

—It's not worth the trouble. It's more like a druggist's storeroom than a
real columbarium. It's of no interest to you, not even to philosophize ...

When he got out on the street, Rubio walked for a little while in
silence.

—The Inquisition had nothing on this —Frantisek began—. Lambs
compared to the Germans.
—I don't understand why they have to hide their crimes so carefully.
Sooner or later everything will come to light: they'd be better off
justifying what they're doing as a political necessity. The Nazis would
approve completely. But doing it this way, it will be an embarrassment
for them ...
—If all this is discovered one day, Nazism will already be dead and
consequences will be of no importance.

Rubio was silent for a moment, thinking:

—A very unpleasant job —he said.
—The position has many benefits.
—What do you mean?
—That fellow you just met chopping up human flesh belongs to one
of the most lucrative networks in the camp. I told you there were
secrets. You don't know about the gold market?

—Teeth? I thought it was completely controlled. The SS in the infirmary and in the crematorium are personally responsible, right?
—It's a question of profit.

They had arrived at the entrance to the infirmary. Rubio wanted to know more.

—Drop off the tools and come back out. We'll go to my Block and talk more freely.

A little later, sitting in the middle of the barracks' empty dining room, Frantisek explained how it all worked. According to him, the *Blockälteste* would begin by determining which of their men had gold teeth. With a lot of tact, and always keeping in mind whom it was they were dealing with, they'd do their best to hasten the decline and death of their chosen victims. Once in the infirmary, a sick man with gold teeth wouldn't last long, and needless to say, impunity was absolute. The gold was pulled out at the crematorium.

—The SS at the crematorium is in charge of redistributing it. He gets the best portion, obviously.
—And Hans Gupper? As suspicious as he is …
—There's gold for everybody.
—And you, how do you know all this?

Frantisek smiled, with an air of self-importance:

—The walls of the barracks are very thin, especially when people are careless and drunk on ether.
—Have you reported it?
—Yes. We have to talk about it at our next meeting.

Rubio wanted more details.

—The "brains" of the organization is a guy with a unique position in the camp that allows him to create the best conditions for business. It's he who puts the victims in the most dangerous *Kommandos*, who organizes the "workplace accidents," who writes out the death certificates quickly and quietly, who links everything together and has tabs on everything when the alarm has to be sounded.

—Carry on —cried Rubio happily—, I can just imagine who that might be. Metzinger, right?

—It can't be denied that he'd be the best director one could find.

Rubio told him it was Metzinger who had accused Emili of being an accomplice in the warehouse affair. From his position as interior camp secretary, Metzinger was using his influence with Hans Gupper to discredit Spaniards and stop them from moving up into better positions. Great or small, Emili's contributions to fostering solidarity among the Spaniards didn't suit Metzinger, who, in denouncing him as a thief, was hoping to stop him.

—I was afraid —said Rubio— that this particular character would be too honest or too cautious to take part in networks like this. Now I can relax: sooner or later he'll be caught.

As he took his leave of the Czech, the barber was already lost in thought as to how, one day, such a thing might be brought about.

Next to the quarry wagon and with a shovel in his hands, Emili thought over the ten days he'd spent at the *Arrest*. It was like a hypnotic world of shadows that now, out in the open air, he found difficult to believe had been real. Nevertheless, it was a world very much alive in his memory: the sound of the prison guard's boots going up and down the corridor still rang in his ears. Emili was looking down at the stony ground before him. The effort it took to shovel was hard on him. "I ate too much at lunch," he said to himself. He'd been through ten days of hunger. His companions in the *Kommando* would have to go through forty. And after that, a year—a full year!—in the disciplinary company. The officer too ... In such cases, a council of honour. Other SS, thieves themselves, but not having been caught, would judge him and send him to a concentration camp wearing the green triangle of a "common criminal." Emili imagined him laughing like a schoolboy at the pornography he'd drawn for him. He was the same man he once saw tearing off the nose of a Polish priest with a pair of tongs. A prick like all the rest, but ... And Werner dead. First, Francesc; now, Werner ...

He stopped shovelling. The others were giving him sour looks because he was working too fast.

Ten days of standing under the window. The nights were a relief, despite the cries of all the Werners who died hanging from radiator valves, despite the thud of boots going up and down the hallway. Ten days! Seven in complete solitude. "Heinrich was good company," he said to himself. At first, he didn't trust him. The cigarette a guard had given them—they'd smoked it in turns, making sure the smoke clung to the lime of the white-washed wall. And his suspicions had evaporated. Emili had made himself dizzy. "Never again will I smoke with such pleasure." In the cell there was a little sign on the doorframe, right next to the bucket. "The only word that I read for ten days, and I read it hundreds, thousands of times. Where does it come from, this need to read? The addiction to letters." Heinrich had warned him of the danger: "If you look at it too much, you'll be tempted to ring the bell." Call: call for what? The fascination with the little sign grew stronger and stronger. Push the button and the steps of the guard would approach, the bolt on the door would clatter open to reveal a man, a man with a voice, with eyes and hands … "Even if you are dying, do not ring the bell. They'll finish you off."

Emili was shovelling fast. His hands were starting to blister and his back was sore. "I won't be drawing anymore after this, not with these hands," he thought. The wagon had to be filled to the top. Like he'd filled his bowl at lunch. "People congratulated me as though I'd broken a track record." A hero. He knew that with enough days filling the wagons, he'd soon weaken. He noticed the *kapo* watching him. "If I told him that I need my hands to draw, he'd think I was crazy." *Kapos*, in fact, were just people without much in the way of brains. "If they were intelligent, they would understand, and understanding, they would have compassion."

On the ninth day he had almost rung the damned bell. The dark brown letters against a café au lait background: *Rufen*. He'd lain down to try to sleep; "the temptation was getting hold of me." If someone had caught him lying down, things would have got worse. "Why didn't they interrogate me?" Rubio's version was that Metzinger had wanted to break him down. Nobody had said a word to him for ten days. "Now I'd like a cigarette." At the warehouse he'd smoked whenever he wanted. "When I finish the tobacco I'll quit for good." He smiled. The wagon was full. The others had less in them and they'd passed muster. Emili realized that his companions were giving him evil looks. "I'll have to get used to collective work, so they don't think I'm a scab."

The *kapo* gave the order to link the wagons, and while waiting for the "diesel," the engine that would haul them away, he had to move on to another spot and begin again. The new site was not so calm. Emili found himself in the middle of a terrorized crowd. Reminiscing wasn't possible anymore, nor even thinking. The *kapos* were giving out blows left and right.

—You get calluses on the eyes —one of his companions said to him.— It's the eyes that do the real work.

A Pole of about fifty was being made to dig out a stretch of frozen earth which in the event of a collapse would bury him completely. Farther along, a soldier was pushing a Jew out against the barbed wire where a sentry would shoot him for "attempted escape." A Yugoslav had been buried alive under a big pile of snow, and from time to time, his head was being uncovered to check if he was dead.

When the draughtsman returned to the barracks after the evening roll call, he could barely move from exhaustion. The secretary of the barracks informed him that he was being transferred. He would have to go back to Popeye's dominion, leaving behind the individual beds to return to the dusty, sweat-stained, straw palettes. Once again the great heap of hungry, exhausted, and desperate men. Once again, Popeye's humiliations. Emili gathered together the books he had kept safely tucked in the straw of his cot, the little piece of soap, a spoon, and a card given to him by the secretary stating his credentials. Popeye's welcome was friendly. "Punished for theft —the monster must have been telling himself—. One of my own."

Sometime later, Popeye called Emili in.

—If you want to draw for me, you'll have everything you need. You'll be spared many days of work.

So Popeye knew what Emili had thought to be a "secret." He replied evasively. He had decided: he wasn't going to draw any more pornography.

And then came the procession of friends. Offers, promises, fine words. All in all, more exhausting than the afternoon's work. He knew the procedure well: the generosity of the first days would gradually cool, and when your uniform was once again a dirty rag and your skin rough and dark, these *lifelong friends* would avoid you as if you were a mangy dog.

Rubio came by later on. Emili didn't like his protective tone: there seemed to be a hidden agenda in the warm words. But the news about Metzinger was interesting:

—There's not one Spaniard in the new *Effektenkammer Kommando*. Metzinger has got away with it.

Later, Rubio invited him to come to supper the next day. It would be Christmas Eve.

—Some fried potatoes, what do you think?

On his way out, the barber bumped into Popeye.

—He's my friend; see that you treat him well?
—I am always a good comrade —Popeye replied, with a stupid laugh.

Emili was to sleep on one of the mattresses in the dining room. That was a privilege. He had been feeling for some days like a puppet swinging in the wind. Not now. He had to begin the test all over again, and for that he would need all his moral strength. He preferred a little solitude to those old friendships that would evaporate soon enough. He would have time to think, and that in itself was good fortune. He wouldn't go along to Rubio's supper. Christmas, some fried potatoes and Rubio's friends. His black mood made Emili smile: "Look how historical materialism comes to an end." He rolled over on his mattress and closed his eyes.

CHAPTER XIII

And time passed. Winter, spring, summer, fall, winter … many lives cut short all the while to a clockwork rhythm both indifferent and unstoppable, every death a milestone left behind by time on the long road. Every day the calendar seemed to have more pages. Each page was a man who had given up the fight and slipped away to find shelter in the all-consuming darkness. The ranks, decimated by the weather, were repopulated and grew ever larger with the new contingents that came into the camp day after day. And each day was as the day before: the same gestures, the same words, the same suffering, the same horror. And none of the days to follow brought with it any real change. And if there was change, it was so slow, so imperceptible, that eyes habituated to a constant round of petty incidents and to profound and immediate suffering could not see it. The law of the camp imposed on each individual a necessary disregard for his fellows. Selfishness was the only effective weapon against the actions of time; the selfish alone retained the right to hold the pages of the calendar in their own hands. The selfish, and also those whom luck decided to clothe in its armour. These watched the dry or the soft snow come down, they warded off the cold, they bore up under the heavy burdens of fatigue and hunger, they escaped the onslaught of abuse, and, in short, they lived. The hammer beat of time wore out their neighbours, but these, whose destiny it was, were not touched by it. But why them, exactly? They weren't necessarily the best, they weren't necessarily the strongest. Who had given them this gift of one day bearing witness to the deaths of all the others? Why did they survive the winter to be dazzled by spring and warmed by summer, and, with the arrival of fall, to fear again the return of winter, which would, again, not bring them any harm? No one could know. The universe is held together by caprice, its secret law.

It seemed slow, the lethal march of time, but looking back one could see its withering passage measured out in the terrible mounting piles of corpses. These were numbers that no one would ever call, names that no one remembered, smoke swept up by the broom of the wind, ashes joined in a chorus of silences on basement shelves. All those firings of the crematorium had dried up the air and more so the hearts of those still alive. But this counted for little if the days passed, if the snow melted from the most shaded corners, if spring brought forth its greenery onto the earth, if, in coming back to life, nature itself proclaimed that hope for a better future was not in vain. The sun triumphed as it did every year, and those men who could still look at its luminous smile felt the echo within them of its eternal message of hope.

Emili went through the cold and the heat; the hard labour mangled his hands, and, always, starvation made its honed claws felt. As the months passed, he left a good portion of his own flesh at the quarry. But he always ignored the voice of animal realism, proper to an instinct for self-preservation, that urged him to get back to drawing pornography.

He couldn't do it anymore. He was keeping alive the memories of Francesc and Werner. He could withstand the hardest of trials if it revealed, sooner or later, the mystery of his own destiny.

Only Rubio kept Emili in mind, and this only when his more pressing commitments allowed him to do so. But his attentions came at a price. The barber was a master of insinuation, and with every piece of bread Emili got from him, Rubio's proselytizing was so clear that any consolation he might have taken in being cared for quickly evaporated.

The months were passing by faster than the days, and perhaps from this paradoxical inversion of time's value was born the terrible indifference Emili found himself sinking into without analyzing either its causes or its effects. In the middle of so much madness, what better position to take than to sink into madness oneself? Emili's madness was the search for spiritual peace, even at the cost of his body withering away under the scourge of privation.

Nothing interested him apart from that peace. True, the brutishness of the inmates around him was only increasing. It was depressing to see them formed up in the roll call square to witness the execution of forty Yugoslav Resistance fighters, among them five women, and lamenting only that the slowness of the operation delayed their supper. It was depressing to see some of them spending their rest period at the Block windows watching the collective tortures inflicted on the Czechs and Jews in the open square, or tracking the murderous line of SS as they filed into the crematorium armed with axes for the liquidation of "special transports." It was depressing to see the indifference with which they greeted the daily spectacle of carts laden with the bodies of Russians who had collapsed at their work. It was depressing to see the senseless flare-ups between fellow prisoners. It was depressing to see the rapid spread of vice, like oil on water, among the young … Emili was fully aware of all of this, and he lamented that the camp was more and more a jungle, but he held before him Destiny's blunt reminder that it was not up to him to prevent it. He also stayed on the margins of the war talk. The Germans were in the Caucasus and in Egyptian territory, and supposing everything went well, it would still be two or three years before an Allied victory. Just as he didn't ask himself if the thousands of Spaniards who were still alive could hope to survive so long, neither was he preoccupied with the question in regard to himself. War and all its consequences were a chrysalis from which to emerge, in the event that emerging from it was his fate, in a form dictated "by the superior forces of History." Courage meant facing up to raw reality; as of that moment, he believed he had it. He wanted to make it through to the end.

One day, Emili saw himself naked. Like many others before him, he'd made the discovery of his own terrible thinness. His buttocks had vanished completely, and his feet were starting to swell.

—Listen, Emili —Rubio said to him some days later—. Come by my Block every evening and I will keep a bowl of soup for you from lunch.

The draughtsman understood the significance of the offer. "He can see Death is keeping me close company," Emili thought. He started going the very next day. When working in the warehouse, he had considered speeding the end with a proud gesture. Nothing more stupid than the idea of committing suicide, whether through action or omission! To force time's hand? No: he had to hold steady to his course. Only then would he know what was waiting for him: the Light or the Darkness. Time wasn't the enemy.

A selection of Spaniards was made for an external *Kommando*, and Emili was one of the chosen. Once he was dressed in new clothes and formed up with some fifty companions ready to head to the train station in the town, Rubio came up to him to say goodbye:

—Congratulations —he said.— You're going to August's *Kommando*.
—You're sure? That's what the rumours say, but I don't buy it.
—It's certain, and believe me, I'm happy for you. You'll see, at August's side you'll cheer up a bit. —And after a short pause, he added— We have a good friend there. His name is Castro, and you can trust him with anything. You can send me your news through him. I'd like that.

Even though Rubio's help in the past had been important enough for Emili to feel obligated towards him, their friendship had always been a little strained. The draughtsman regretted the coolness of that farewell:

—Thank you for everything. Some day we'll meet again and maybe then we won't be poor prisoners anymore. Once free, our conversation will be richer.

The retinue left the camp. It had been almost two years since the draughtsman had entered by that same door, and not until now had he passed through it again. Marching down the hill from the camp, uncertain of this new enterprise, he was thinking that if somebody had cared to ask him, he would have preferred not to leave this place he knew, not because he was really used to it, but for more personal reasons. Now, a vague feeling of protest welled up in him. If this transfer meant a new test, if his new *Kommando* was one of those destined for a precipitous end, a quick and certain death, why was he denied the right to choose his own scaffold? Why should his can of ashes be denied the company of the ashes of his dear friends?

In contrast to his thoughts, his companions were making a huge uproar. The women and children were, above all, the objects of their noisy commentary.

—Shut up! —one of the guards ordered— you're just like Jews.

The men obeyed, and there was only the rhythmic tramping of their wooden shoes against the cobblestones. The townspeople came to their windows, looked out, and without revealing any kind of feeling, would turn away and disappear. The children tagged along behind the retinue and looked up at the soldiers with respect and envy. At the train station, two railcars were waiting for them, *8 chevaux—40 hommes*, along with Hans Gupper himself. Once they'd boarded the train, they were granted permission to keep the doors open. Gupper went along with them, and throughout the journey, showed himself to be most friendly. He told them straight away that they were being sent to August's *Kommando*.

—And to think that I put so much into not being transferred! —exclaimed a transportee sitting next to Emili.

Not knowing if the comment was addressed to him, he answered back with a smile just in case. One had to show satisfaction like the rest of them. One had to chat, to laugh, to sing … He didn't answer when his neighbour asked him:

—Aren't you glad?

Emili felt out of place. He remembered Francesc's lively spontaneity in such situations. "If Francesc were here, he'd take me to task," he thought. But wasn't the death of his dear friend the very reason for his feeling so low? The loss of Francesc had meant the collapse of any possibility for optimism. In times when the individual meant nothing amidst the great turmoil that stirred the world, optimism inevitably gave way to disappointment and bitterness. To live was to shut up, to suffer, and, ultimately, to die. Right then, Emili came to understand that this change of place required something of him, that he would have to bring himself around. The commuted sentence that the transfer represented for him and for the others had a price that he would have to accept. He decided to start work on it immediately, and confessed that yes, indeed, he was happy.

The train soon left the Danube plain and climbed south through a valley no wider than one of its tributaries. Small industrial towns showed off their massive factories from which emerged every kind of armament. In the stations, the platforms were crammed with tanks, artillery, trucks, and airplane engines. The pale blue of the sky was smeared with smoke from the innumerable chimneys.

—The next station —announced Hans Gupper.

And not much later, the vaguely Byzantine top of the bell tower appeared, and around it, the dihedral peaks of roofs, some with red tiles, some with slate. A spread-out little village tucked into the valley where it narrowed and steepened. The river coursed between the station and the village. The air was so clean that the snow on the surrounding peaks seemed more than white. A great peace reigned there: there was no weapons factory to be seen.

—We're not going to get bombed here —someone observed.
—Who knows? Maybe they've got factories underground.

After walking half an hour, the group reached a small plateau where there were four weathered barracks and one other, more presentable, that, judging from the chimneys, must have been the kitchen. The open space had been put to good use by planting vegetables. Barbed wire, but not electric, created a labyrinth of divisions everywhere.

August was waiting for them at the entrance with two SS officers. He looked different, Emili thought. And then he realized it was because of his hair, which was long, but with a part three centimetres wide shaved from the forehead to the back of the neck. This was a new fashion for the camps implemented from Berlin, with a view to using human hair to make felt. Instead of being shaved, the prisoners were obliged to let their hair grow long. August's, thick and black and straight, with that wide part down the middle, gave him a vague resemblance to certain insects with divided heads.

After the necessary formalities, it was time to embrace. August took the draughtsman by the arm:

—I'm very glad you've come. This is a paradise. Compared to what you've left, I mean! You look a bit worn out, but you'll recover, rest assured.

August had started talking non-stop. Regarding things at the *Casa Gran*, he just wanted confirmation; describing this project of his own, he spoke passionately and included every possible detail.

—The summer was bad. There was only enough food to aggravate their hunger. The men were dropping from exhaustion. They were eating field greens raw. That the pace of production had to be maintained was the only argument I had in my favour. For a moment, I thought I'd failed, but my records and the control I have over the work done was enough for me to show that our productivity is higher than the prisoners of war and even higher than the civilian workers. One day I put on a real show. I ordered all my men to strip in the middle of the roll call square and asked the Commandant to inspect them. They were skeletons. I asked him: "Are you interested in our productivity? Well, you can see that if these men don't get more food, they will soon disappear altogether." For a month now, they've been stuffed with cauliflower and potatoes.

They had supper together. Emili did honour to the miraculous cauli-flower. August's vanity offended his own finer sensibility, but it was obvious that the calm, the order, and the conviviality that reigned in the camp were more important than its organizer's lack of modesty.

—Here we are all equal —August was explaining—, but I'm the referee. Understanding or severe, depending on the situation. And always well informed. I know what everyone does, what everyone says, what everyone thinks. There are some who think I'm the incarnation of the devil himself. Mine is a patriarchal system …

The draughtsman remembered the letter that Rubio had let him read and smiled to himself. August's greatest quality was, without doubt, the mesmerizing effect he could have on those around him, and Castro, Rubio's agent, was one of its victims. Emili looked carefully at that face: it was not the wide part in his hair that had changed his look, but a swagger, a certain satisfied self-assurance that, although he wasn't sure if it pleased him or not, explained many things.

Later on, when Emili went to bed, the rest of his barracks mates had been sleeping for some time. The silence there was calm and settled, without the weight of the silences in the *Casa Gran*. He lit a cigarette; here he didn't have to fear punishment for taking a small liberty like this. On the table in the middle of the room there were a few books and a chess-board. Was it really possible that this camp was a branch of the other? It seemed that something had shifted inside him. The Emili smoking on his bed could not recognize the Emili who, just a few hours ago, had left the main camp with a feeling of abandonment and renunciation.

—I am counting on your help —August had said to him just now.

The work of defending the men against the *spirit of the camp,* for-gotten for many months, had come up again. This time he had been given a subaltern role, as if the *superior powers* wanted to put him to another test.

—*Sursum corda*[39] —he said to himself, content.

CHAPTER XIV

While the Allies regained the upper hand on the Volga and in North Africa, the nations of Western Europe began to turn against their German occupiers. The arrival of Belgian and French Resistance fighters in the main camp was a barometer for the growing efforts against Nazi oppression in these two countries.

Pierre, a metalworker from a town in northern France, had been accused of sabotage and detained by the Gestapo. Having passed through many prisons along the way, he arrived in the camp physically destroyed; the first day he was overcome by sunstroke, common among those who had gone for months without ever seeing the light of day. This crisis opened the door to others; after just a few weeks he was in the grip of starvation edema. In such cases, the usual prescription was to spend a few days in the infirmary until the swelling had gone down enough to get back to work ... a third round was most often the last.

German science had come up with potent solutions to the problem of euthanasia. The benzine injection, the cold shower, and beatings were all very slow; it was more efficient to pass the sick along to the "sanatorium" camp at Dachau, for instance, where they served as guinea pigs in chemical and bacteriological labs or in institutes of vivisection.

The "ghost truck" also gave good and efficient results. It was a bus with seats for twenty passengers, its windows replaced by steel plates. From time to time, it would come into the camp to pick up the sick. While under way, the driver would release a lethal gas from his place in his own sealed compartment. At first the bodies were delivered to the huge crematoria at Steyr, but later on, when the shortage of primary resources was getting critical, the bodies were rendered into grease for making soap.[40]

Nothing was as expeditious, however, as the gas chamber that had recently been installed in the basement of the camp's crematorium. To all appearances it was just an ordinary shower room: a mosaic floor, walls with a frieze of glazed tiles, and some very bright light bulbs hanging from the ceiling. Shower heads were spaced evenly along a grid of pipes. The door was heavy and closed tight against a rubber pressure seal. Through an observation port of thick glass, one could watch from outside what transpired within.

If the condemned were new arrivals and unaware of the mysteries of the camp, they were told to undress in a waiting area lined with clothes hooks. When they were ushered into the chamber itself, they were even given pieces of soap and towels. These shipments didn't fall under the jurisdiction of the camp command, but were subject directly to the Gestapo. They consisted of whole families, men, women, and children, and came from a wide variety of nationalities. Once the door had been locked down, these unfortunates, naked and completely exposed, waited in vain for the water to be turned on. Instead, it was gas that poured out of the shower heads, and soon the air was saturated by it. Their agony was horrifying: maddened by desperation, many would smash their heads against the walls; others would throw themselves on their own companions and, with teeth and nails, take an absurd revenge; some would shove their fingers right down their throats as if trying to get a gulp of air that didn't exist ... Gradually, they would start to drop, one on top of the other, until they became nothing more than a pile of greenish corpses.

Meanwhile, their eyes shining and their muscles tense, the gas specialists, SS officers, and Gestapo agents watched the spectacle from the other side through the glass of the little observation port.

When it was a question of exterminating the sick from within the camp, the refinement of soap and towels was unnecessary. The chosen exited the infirmary completely naked and were sent to their ordeal like sheep to slaughter, by force of blows.

Pierre, the Frenchman, was condemned to the gas during his third stay at the infirmary. The terror with which these selections were greeted by the sick gave a jolt to his system, revitalizing him from a state of almost total exhaustion. Naked and lined up with the rest of the condemned, he suddenly grasped the monstrosity of his fate. The resignation of days past, when he had thought coolly about the inevitable end of his suffering, now vanished before a flood of desperate rebellion. He had no right to let himself be killed like a rabbit! He was young, there wasn't anything wrong with him but hunger, and he had a wife and two sons waiting for him at home. It was his duty to live, to save himself no matter how.

The group started the trek through the roughly cobbled streets of the camp. Pierre noticed that, unlike most of the others, who leaned on one another for support, he was steady on his feet and walking on his own. Why did he have to die? What was the point of it?

—Hey, you! —a Spaniard walking beside him shouted to someone he knew who'd stopped to watch the procession—. You're seeing it now! If you get out alive, tell them when you get home.

When they entered through the side door of the crematorium, Pierre managed to fall a bit behind. Where was he going? He didn't know. He didn't need to know. The first thing was to escape, to run, to get away from this flock of sheep. When he crossed the threshold … he tried to jump back out, but a German pushed him roughly into line. The swirl of men drew him in and made any effort to free himself useless. Shouts, moans, curses uttered in every language filled the thick-walled basement with terror. There was no escaping it. But just at the door of the gas chamber, as though propelled by a spring, Pierre regained his strength. He gave a shove to the German who had been behind him all the way in. Surprised, the German staggered just long enough for the Frenchman to make his escape by the outside door.

People had not yet returned from work, and the Blocks at this hour were mostly empty. Pierre crossed the square in a breath and lost no time disappearing among the barracks. He snaked himself in through the first window he found open.

Once the alarm was given, all the administrative personnel of the camp were mobilized to search for the fugitive. All the Blocks and interior annexes were combed from top to bottom, but without finding a trace, and when the prisoners came back into the camp, the roll call lasted a good hour. Only after having searched a particular Block for the fourth or fifth time did one of the Germans hear the dull thud of a body falling from a height. He soon discovered the corpse of a naked man on a top bunk. He was curled up, knees touching chin, eyes popping out of their sockets, the hands taut; death had taken him in the middle of a supreme effort. The German couldn't understand how the body had ended up there until he remembered that it was the sound of something falling that had caught his attention. He looked up at the ceiling of the barracks. There, directly above the corpse, was the box-like opening of a ventilator with louvred sides. One might be able to hold on there, with fingers and toes hooked into the slats of the louvres and the back, arms, and legs pressed outwards with superhuman tension, for a bare half hour. The Frenchman had been there for three long hours!

He had died from cold and exhaustion, possibly some time before, but not even in death had he willingly surrendered his body to his executioners. With his muscles rigid, his body folded into the narrow shape of the box, he had fallen like ripe fruit from a tree.

In the crematorium, he was reunited with his companions.

In August's *Kommando*, each day was exactly the same as the others. The measured repetition of their tasks and their meticulous schedule allowed the men to preserve their strength and stay healthy. A simple question of addition and subtraction. The food ration was so closely measured that the secret of physical self-preservation was based on a disciplined conservation of energy. Why bend over to pick up a shovel if stepping on its blade would bring its shaft up to hand automatically? Why make one trip to the urinals and then another to the sinks to wash up, if one could go by both places in one trip? And if one took along a dirty plate in one hand and muddy clogs in the other, two more trips could be saved. The monotony of their existence was enervating: get up half an hour before dawn, go out to urinate and wash; then get dressed, make the bed carefully, get the soup, drink it, go out into the street while the Block is swept by those on cleaning duty, smoke half a cigarette when one has it, forget the accumulated fatigue of the days before, and wait for the nightmare of the eleven hours of work about to begin. Then, forming up, roll call, and setting off in work groups.

Emili got used to it. He discovered in this daily routine a positive manifestation of that same spiritual calm he had conjured in the last days at the *Casa Gran* out of renunciation and fatalistic passivity. The difference, though, was critical. Gradual physical and moral annihilation had given way to a reinvigoration of his capacity to reason. The work was hard, the weather bad, the company dull, the food boiled, but a humane atmosphere reigned overall. There was pity and help for the weak, and death was fought from all sides. The SS only intervened in the camp through August, so their actions lost their initial venom. The usual concentration camp regimen was so attenuated by the time it got to August's *Kommando* that it was barely recognizable. Emili bore up under it with the patience of a convalescent trying to readapt to a long-forgotten state of normal health. Without having noticed it, he had been freed from that state of contempt for others that was the instrument the Nazis deployed for the moral extermination of their captives. In August's camp, he was not just a number, but also a man.

—For now, you're going to have to go out to work. Nobody's allowed to stay in the camp unless assigned work here. In the evening, after supper, come to the office and give me a hand.

The office was a bluff designed to impress the Germans, who were, here, more attentive to appearances than to reality. Mounds of papers, registers, records of meetings between *kapos* and *Blockälteste*, bound reports on personnel, file cards everywhere, percentages of productivity, statistics, graphs ... for August, all of these were weapons that, in addition to creating an impression, ensured he always had a ready argument to hand. In another department were prisoners who did skilled labour: making furniture, trinkets, rings, and medals, repairing clocks and watches, everything designed to tempt those with whom August had to maintain good relations: engineers at the works, officials, higher-ups in the Party, ordinary guards and foremen. Emili, as a draughtsman, went into this special section.

—My hands won't answer me; I can't draw anymore.
—It doesn't matter —argued August—. None of these idiots are going to notice.

Once his ability was recognized, Emili was spared many days of cold and damp outside. The Commandant, for instance, commissioned him to do drawings from photographs of his wife and seven children, with permission granted to stay behind in the camp until they were done.

So time went by without any emotional upheavals, without leaving any trace. They spent the days waiting for the night to come, and with it, sleep; and they waited for the night to bring them dreams by which to escape the sad reality of day. The tedious succession of the hours would have become unbearable for Emili had he not taken refuge, once more, in that interior world that, little by little, he was now rebuilding.

One evening, when entering the camp at the end of the day's work, Emili saw that everyone was unusually excited.

—We've got letters! —somebody announced as they broke ranks.

Emili ran to the office.
—You have a letter from your wife —August told him.

It was only a month before that each Spaniard had been authorized to write a postcard, the same dictated message for everybody, and now the first replies had begun to arrive. The address of the camp had been cleverly altered to give the impression that they were prisoners of war rather than political prisoners. The fact of their illegal detention remained; nobody beyond the border could know the truth about the arbitrary and inhumane treatment of those men who could not be accused of any anti-German activity.

Emili held the letter in his hands, unable to bring himself to open it. The weight of those two years, counted out day by day, hour by hour, minute by minute, overwhelmed him now as if he had suddenly found himself buried under the great mountain they made.

That letter that he had not dared to hope for suddenly made real the distance in time and space between him and the world outside. And naturally, that world continued to turn as always: out there, a woman was waiting for him. Keeping him from ripping the envelope open was an unspoken fear of finding himself a stranger in a world so far away. The few lines of a letter, could they fill the vacuum of those two lost years?

—What are you doing, standing there like an idiot? —August laughed.

Emili tore open the envelope. The words were very few, in fact, and Emili read them three times before he could take his eyes off them: "With your postcard in my hands, I have run like a fool through the apartment, to the neighbours, into the street ... I have shown it to everyone, to everyone I've been saying how happy I am ..." Needing to be alone, he went to his room and took refuge in his bed. The image of Matilde took on an uncanny clarity in his memory. The future was inside him.

The next day he didn't go out to work. He was drawing in the office when August came in on his way back from the Commandant's office.

—I've just been listening to the radio —he said, rubbing his hands together.
—And? —asked Emili, without looking up.
—It's fantastic! The Germans have lost the Sixth Army in Stalingrad. They're going to declare a state of national mourning through all of Germany!

Emili jumped to his feet. His stool fell over with a clatter.

—Thank God! —he cried. The Sixth and the Seventh, they'll all fall in a row. It's going to go fast now. The war will be over soon.

August looked at him, surprised by such enthusiasm in someone usually so subdued. Emili was, himself, a bit embarrassed by his spontaneous outburst. "It's the letter" —he thought, while August explained the distant battle—. "The letter has got me all worked up!"

—Come into the office, will you? —August asked, looking serious.

The draughtsman entered, and once the door was closed he sat on the stool offered him.

—What I have to say is confidential —August began—. If it interests you, take it on, if not, I ask you not to make any use of it.

Emili nodded.

—You know that I have a network of informants here. Well, I've been able to confirm something I've long suspected. I'm not the type to be taken by surprise by this kind of thing. When others are just finding out, I already know all about it.

Emili watched the shadow that August's head cast against the back wall. The lamp on the table had no shade.

—From the *Kommando's* very beginnings —August said—, the communists have been receiving directives from the *Casa Gran* ...

The draughtsman remembered Castro's letter that Rubio had once read to him.

—I didn't worry too much about it, since Castro, their agent, was personally attached to me, a puppet in my hands.

Emili made an involuntary nod of his head.

—These current orders aren't like those in the beginning. As expected, they're not wasting time.

Somebody knocked and opened the door.

—Don't bother me now —yelled August—. Shut the door!

He got up to lock it. While walking across the room, he added:

—There are some who have broken our tacit agreement not to be political. I won't tolerate it, you know? It won't be the first time I've confronted them. If they want a fight, they'll get one.

Emili's calm voice was in contrast to August's agitation:

—And what does "being political" mean for you?

August looked at him, surprised.

—What do you think? It means undoing before my very eyes everything that I've struggled to get done. It means meeting behind my back and turning the men against me, it means creating cells, troikas, and all kinds of other idiocies, proselytizing and putting everybody else at risk. Is that enough?
—Apprentice conspirators.
—They buy people. They buy them with food that belongs to everybody.

And without letting the draughtsman get a word in, he went on to explain:

—The chief problem in this camp is that I don't have control of the kitchen. The German *kapo* answers directly to that imbecile of a Commandant, and they take advantage of that.
—It's all communists in the kitchen?
—One is enough.
—Have you tried anything?
—I've talked to the *kapo*. He told me I'm hallucinating. I've also talked about it to the Commandant and made it clear that if I don't get control of the kitchen we'll soon have conflicts. He told me that he's there to solve them. A very German approach! Bunch of idiots …

He raised his voice again and started pacing back and forth in the little office.

—But they shouldn't expect an easy time of it! I've still got a few cards up my sleeve, and I'll defend this peace I've made, with my teeth if I have to. I don't want the unscrupulous few destroying things for everyone else. My regime means equality for everybody before the law. And the law is me—me who eats the same as the rest. Do you think, for the sake of politics, I'll put up with some of them eating more?

—How do you think it can be prevented?

—With whatever it takes! For now, what I need is information, a lot of information. This is why I've called you in. I need your help. The men I've got working on it are useless.

—I don't know anything about these things. It's not a job I'd like.

—You have to stand up for harmony within the camp. You, more than anyone, have reason to appreciate that.

—Emili, annoyed, understood the allusion: "This is the bill I have to pay," he thought.

—It will be a defensive campaign —August continued—. It's fair enough for me to defend myself, for me to defend the men I'm committed to saving. I need to know what this bunch of troublemakers are up to.

—And why not talk it over with Castro and make him see that ...

—Don't be so naive! They tell you one thing and then carry on just as they want to. They follow orders from people who have no idea what we're trying to do here.

—I can tell you, they have.

—They play at their politics and could care less if people die. I could tell you thousands of cases.

And while August began his account, Emili was thinking that the position he'd been offered might give him a chance to soften the blows and forestall a pointless battle between one side and the other.

—I accept —he decided—. Now help me get a better sense of my mission.

And that same evening, not long after his interview, he wrote a letter to Rubio by which he hoped to make him see the dangers that would follow from any hostility shown toward August's work.

Some three weeks later, Castro came up to Emili and, with an air of great secrecy, gave him a letter. It was the barber's reply:

The difficulties in maintaining any sort of correspondence will have to justify my long silence, and I hope that the length of the letter I send you now will be some compensation.

Things have changed a lot since you left. In these ten months, we have gone through a good deal and, after encountering every headache imaginable along the way, we can't complain about our luck. As you might guess, the source of our troubles was Metzinger. I myself, who had been working to undermine him, have to admit that if things are running a little smoother now, it's more due to his own mistakes than to the efficacy of our opposition. I thought I saw an opening after a disagreement he had with a man named Otto, the assistant secretary of the camp. Remember him? He was telling everyone that Metzinger was up to no good and that he had enough stories about him to send him to the gallows. I offered my help in exchange for his. Nothing came of it because Otto got nervous of the German faction that Metzinger controlled. There was always the last resort of going directly to Hans Gupper, but it would have been a very dangerous move. If Hans Gupper didn't help us decisively enough, we'd find ourselves caught up in a war between Germans and Spaniards that we'd be bound to lose. Even though Metzinger set about us with increasing fury, nobody could do anything but wait it out.

One day in the quarry, a Czech took the rag he was using as a handkerchief out of his pocket and a gold dental bridge fell from it onto the ground. The *kapo* saw it and tried to lay hold of it for himself. The poor Czech started to yell and an SS who was hovering nearby came over to intervene. I should say in passing, the SS here have mostly been replaced. Now we have guards from the Balkans, more or less of German ancestry, and they are very different from the pure Hitlerians we had before and who have now been sent on up to the front. These ones are, generally speaking, politically indifferent, and they're not especially happy with the "forced volunteerism" to which they've been committed. The guard that intervened was a good type. He ordered the Czech to open his mouth and verified that he was in the right. He asked him, in all good faith, why he hadn't gone to the camp dentist to have it fixed, and in response to the Czech's evasive answers he pressed with still more questions. Finally the Czech confessed that he hadn't gone to the dentist because he didn't want to be murdered. When they got back to the camp, the SS reported the case to his superiors. An inquest was begun, but before Metzinger was implicated, the Czech was killed by a *Blockälteste* for "having stolen some bread." The Germans know how to organize themselves. As might be expected, nothing more happened.

Metzinger carried on calmly as before.

Some weeks later it was my turn to intervene with Metzinger. A Spaniard had been selected to work in the camp shoemaking shop, but Metzinger made a deal with the secretary of the Block where the fellow lived, and arranged it so he didn't know when to present himself at his new post. They sent a note to say the man was sick, and a German that was next in line for the position got it instead. I objected to Metzinger, but I didn't get anything out of the interview except a faceful of slaps.

Things reached a peak when Hans Gupper left the camp for an indefinite period of time. He'd been put in charge of organizing a big external *Kommando* of some twenty thousand men, and the impression was that he wouldn't be coming back. Metzinger took the opportunity to get Hans Gupper's substitute to let him remove a lot of Spaniards from their positions. I was among them. And I'm proud to say that it was due to me that Metzinger finally fell. When Hans Gupper returned to the camp, he missed "his barber." He went to the secretary in a fury. Metzinger's explanations did nothing to appease his rage, and a new secretary was appointed immediately. Otto took his revenge by explaining to him many of his predecessor's irregularities, though the matter of the gold teeth was kept secret because of the many complications, and in high places, that it carried with it. Metzinger spent a number of days in the disciplinary company, until his own old associates decided to eliminate him. I had occasion to witness how they forced him, with blows from their sticks, up against the electric fence.

After that everything turned around. The Spaniards regained their lost ground and went on to gain more. Metzinger was replaced by a Czech, a very good type. And an old companion of poor Francesc, Manuel, works in the administration. There are Spaniards in all the good *Kommandos*, and even Ernest has moved up, now that he's been made *kapo* of the "potatoes." With so many among the privileged we are on the verge of reaching our initial goal, that no Spaniard go hungry. Now we're moving to establish links with the exterior *Kommandos* in order to be prepared for any eventuality. Tell August that we need everybody working together for what comes next, and that he needs to stop seeing ghosts everywhere. What you've told me is absurd. Castro is just a good friend of mine, nothing more."

Emili read the postscript:

Having just reread my letter, I think I may have gotten a little carried away and given you the wrong impression of our situation. For the

Spaniards, the situation is good; for the rest the camp it's as it was, or even worse. There are the quarantine camps full of people and they die at a rate of hundreds each day. The gas chamber works non-stop, and the "ghost truck" is always coming and going...

The letter was interesting, but Emili had the feeling that Rubio was avoiding the issue. The call to reason that the draughtsman had sent him was being answered with vague generalizations. As for the important questions, he was trying to set him at ease while saying as little as possible.

He woke from his midday nap earlier than usual. The heat from outside, once it got down into the basement, was suffocatingly humid. His shirt soaked with sweat, he left the office and took a turn around the outbuildings.

Ernest had been in paradise since he'd been made *kapo* of "the potatoes," and at this high point in his Germanization, the boy abided strictly by the rules of deportment that seemed to come with his position, and did so with the added zeal of the parvenu. It was no surprise that the basement of the kitchen had become a den of corruption and abuses of authority under his reign. Discipline was rigid for the older men; the young ones, as long as they knew how to smile and be compliant, did what they wanted. Ernest chose among them for his favourites of the moment without even bothering to disguise his turpitude.

The Spaniards in the camp, who had become more and more interested in moral reform so as to make a good impression as a collective, openly repudiated Ernest's conduct. Many, when they saw him, more or less turned their backs. The newly minted *kapo* could have cared less. Modelling himself on the German common criminals, old prison rats that they were, he had built a world apart, with its own particular social and moral code, and he learned to do without the others.

He strolled lazily between the lines of the potato peelers. Some were selecting cauliflowers and turnips, others carefully preparing the potatoes destined for the troops, still others were going through mounds of spinach, and, in a corner, a few others were quartering the unpeeled potatoes that the prisoners would eat the next day. The work was showing the effects of the oppressive heat, and a drowsy silence hung in the air of the vast room. Ernest was entering an adjacent storeroom when, just as he crossed the threshold, he saw someone slip out through a door that led to the section ranged with sinks. He chased after the fugitive and caught him easily. He was a Spaniard, about fifty years old, who had been allowed to stay in the Potato *Kommando* thanks to having a son whom Ernest considered a friend working in one of the warehouses. The man was carrying a bucket with a few kilos of potatoes in it.

—Where are you going with that?
—I was taking them to the Block.
—Don't tell me they're for you.
—No ... well, that's to say ...

The *kapo* took him by the collar of his jacket and shook him.

—Tell me who they're for, you hear? Who told you to steal them?

Ernest, his vanity wounded, forgot all about his friendship with the son and wanted to see the interrogation through to the end.

—It's my boy who ...
—Liar! Your son doesn't need them. You're stealing for someone else. And you are going to tell me who! Don't think you're going to get away with making a fool of me on account of your age, old man.

He grabbed the bucket and threw it in a corner.

—Come with me. You'll explain in front of the officer.
—Please, don't. Beat me, if you wish, but don't tell the officer. I can't tell you who they're for, do you understand? I just can't, please don't force me.
—Fine.

He had taken the man by the arm and was trying to drag him to the stairs. The prisoner was desperately pleading with him, as a fellow Spaniard.

—Please, don't —he begged—. Let me go and I will explain everything. They're for a friend, you understand? He's sick. I'm helping him
...
—Tell me his name. I want to know if you're telling the truth.
—I'll tell you in private.

They crossed the room of the potato peelers, all now alert with expectation. Everyone knew what it meant to be old and have dared to steal potatoes. Only the young were allowed to steal, those who could count on

Ernest's protection, those who stole for profit. Stealing to help a sick man was costly. According to the code that Ernest had adopted, the young had the right to protection, the little friends of little friends, links in the chain of corruption that was, with the connivance of the SS, spreading through the whole camp. The young men who could do the work had to be kept alive, and at the same time they had to be corrupted: if they were freed one day, it would no longer be as men.

The old man didn't come out of Ernest's office for a long time. He passed among his curious companions in silence and sat down at his work station.

—Were you beaten? —his neighbour asked.
—Yes —the old man replied, clenching his teeth.

One could hear the peelers scraping over the skin of the potatoes and the occasional "plop" of a peeled potato dropping into the tub of water.

—Did you tell him the truth? —asked a companion.
—I was afraid. He wanted to send me to the officer. I didn't want to make things more complicated ...
—And him?
—He said he thought we were a bunch of idiots to take part in it. I tried to make him see that it was part of my duty as a communist, and he started to laugh and push me around. "Idiots" —he said—. "This is what he gets you to believe. Can't you see that he wins points at your expense?" He's a nasty piece of work.
—And where did you leave things?
—He said tomorrow I'll be sent to the disciplinary company.
—He wouldn't dare.
—I think he's up to it.
—Presumptuous idiot! One day someone's going to break his nose and then he'll cry like the little girl he is.

When Rubio got back to the camp that afternoon, he hurried right over to the kitchen.

—Have you completely lost your mind? —he asked Ernest—. Do you have any idea what you're doing?
—I do indeed. It's the rest of you who don't get it.

With his eyes fixed on the desk, the barber took a deep breath and said very slowly:

—What you've done today feels like a personal affront to me. The man told you clearly that it was I who had asked for the potatoes. Not only did you stand in his way, but on top of that you've threatened him. Explain this to me, will you?

—Why didn't you ask me for them directly?

—It's been a long time since I've asked you for anything, Ernest. Do you know why? Because the last time I asked you for protection for a comrade, he lasted just three days.

—Those were different circumstances.

—There's also the fact that you're doing whatever you please here. Look, Ernest, as for the personal affront, I can set it aside, but for your own good, I'm asking you not to report this afternoon's case. He is an old man and the disciplinary company will be the death of him. A German *kapo* would do it, I know, but you are different. You're not a common criminal …

When Rubio learned the next morning that the threat had been carried out and that the old man was carrying stones with the disciplinary company, he could only shake his head in commiseration.

—Senseless! —was all he said.

Ernest was physically stronger than the old man's son and easily fended him off when the youth went at him with his fists. The bystanders separated them and so prevented the incident from having any further consequences.

—One day I'll get you —cursed the aggressor, trying to free himself—. Coward! Pussy!

Sitting under the window, Emili mends his only pair of socks. They have patches of every possible colour, but they'll serve for a good while yet; they have to last until the end of the war. At the table nearby, two companions play chess, and a third, with a book open in front of him, is being distracted from his reading by the game. Emili can't stop turning things over in his mind: the Normandy offensive is drawing on too long, he thinks. The final battle, it seems clear, but … it's been a month now since it got under way. In the camp, after a full year of political infighting, they're having a stretch of peace. August has let himself get carried away with the Allied assault in Europe. All of us united, as a military force, he says, could be the axis of armed revolt against the Germans in retreat. "National Union Government," "Army," "General Staff." All of it just as ridiculous as the political struggles of a month ago. August wants a new slant: every day new preoccupations. At the moment, preparing for armed conflict is all the rage. For as long as it lasts. Maybe he'll be done with it this very day. There's a meeting at six o'clock. Emili has time to mend his socks. To weave a net of threads is a delicate operation. He thinks he might make a good doctor. August was briefly obsessed with becoming a surgeon; luckily for the sick, it only lasted for a few days. He was friends with the camp doctor at the time. The political mania lasted a year. Once life in the camp was up and running, idleness opened the door to temptation. Throughout history, conspiracies have been cooked up in backrooms; August was finding them cooked up in kitchens. Leader of the State! Saviour of the masses! Emili realizes now that it was a bad idea to take on the role of organizing August's secret police. Every day he's asked for evidence of a new conspiracy.

The chess players have ended their game and are now arguing about it. It's hot. Things are quiet. Here's one, crossing the courtyard, who needs to urinate. At home it's not like this. Just a few steps across the hall, that's it. And at home you don't have to mend socks either! What does August want? He'll talk and the rest will nod their heads. The communists will say that his representation of things is self-serving, that this fantasy about their organizing is just looking for trouble where there is none. Castro is weak; he's not going to move up. Dirty politics, direct from the communists at the *Casa Gran*. With all their political agitation to win acolytes, they're helping August in his game. The doctor wasn't any sharper than Castro. When August publicly appointed him as the head of the communist group, he was completely satisfied. Vanity. The urge to fight just for the sake of fighting itself. The real enemies, the Nazis, are unassailable. Have to settle for the *ersatz* … Now, government, army, and General Staff … Now, at least, the enemy is the real one. That's a step in the right direction. What does August want? To make things even more complicated?

The chess players are talking about "France." A real man! The son of Spanish parents, born in France, officer in the International Brigades. From time to time he gets packages from home. The Spaniards aren't allowed to get packages and their envy is palpable. August can't bear him. A rivalry that began with the Spanish Civil War. The day "France" offered August something from his first parcel from home, August told him that the sick in the infirmary were in greater need than he was. A fine answer certainly; but when August confiscated one of the parcels later on, that was a mistake. The communists made their "France" a *martyr to tyranny*. The political struggle was getting poisonous, and aggression towards the doctor was one of the consequences. Had others not prevented it, that hothead Camps would have had him skewered. And August was happy, that afternoon. The manipulator of the masses would say that political struggle invigorates the individual consciousness, that he did not want to lead ewes into freedom, but men. "The monotony is crushing them. What's needed is a distraction from their personal worries." "So that they go at each other with knives?" Enough of politics! Now, "Head of Intelligence for the General Staff." A much flashier title. The farce gets more entertaining all the time.

Now the chess players are talking about the "Turk," who was "France's" servant for a while, then his right-hand man, and who, now that there are no more parcels coming in, has returned to searching through the garbage for cabbage stems. Emili considers how difficult it is to keep people like the "Turk" in line. And there are so many of them! August wants to make them into men by giving them a political struggle! What a joke! And when his authority starts to slip through his fingers and he sees that it's his own game that's pulling him down, he steps back. After political infighting, a national union government. Today's meeting is going to start late. What's he want now? Probably he's tired of governments and armies and wants a fresh approach. If the war doesn't end ... This Normandy operation is taking too long.

Emili folds the socks, puts away the needle and thread. The patch is perfect. He promises himself never to tell his wife. The chess players have started a new game. The people in the room are starting to rouse themselves, and while some make a bite to eat, others go out to wash their faces. A group sequestered in the corner, and taking all the necessary precautions, reads a Pétainist newspaper that's been smuggled in.[41] Outside, the sun has lost its strength and people start to move about. In a little bit, the soccer game will start. The draughtsman goes out and heads over to August's office. Some of his companions with positions in the "General Staff" are waiting for the Chief of Staff to let them in. Ten minutes, and August lets them enter.

—Operations in the north of France are lasting longer than expected. The Germans are resisting and I don't think they'll be defeated as long as ...

Emili wonders how he's going to bear up under the flood of clichés. A preamble that's going to go on for some time. "I don't think he's called us in to tell us what we already know."

—The "National Union Government" has mistaken its mandate. I needed a government that would give us the moral strength essential for armed conflict. But instead, it seems to be wholly preoccupied with scrutinizing my administrative decisions. You understand that I can't switch tactics. The SS must not suspect anything. If they learn that we've created a "National Union Government" and that we're preparing for the hour of their defeat, they'll finish us off first. The "Government's" mandate isn't divvying up the work group assignments, or distributing the midday soup. Until the right moment comes, its role has to be purely symbolic. I've tried to explain this, but it seems nobody has understood. The thing that concerns me most right now is the organization of a camp militia. Since it's clear that political interference from government representatives is going make this difficult, from now on all government functions will be assumed by the General Staff. To unify the command even more ...

—And the 'Government'? What are we going to do with it? —asks the Head of Operations.

—Dissolve it.

—This is a coup d'état!

The "new slant," Emili thinks. "A *pronunciamiento* was the only thing missing!"[42]

The communists protest. August says that unless the "Government" is constituted in the way he suggests, he'll dissolve everything, Government, Army, General Staff, all at one go!

—We should never have started it!

—I'm fed up with this farce!

The Head of Services gets up and leaves the room. The meeting is over. The protests drown out the scraping of the chairs and everybody, except Emili, leaves the field open before the new dictator.

—It had to be done —August says later, when he's alone with the draughtsman—. The camp is asleep and we need to whip it back onto its feet.

—After this the only thing left is to proclaim you Emperor.

August bursts into laughter.

—I think you're going too far —adds the draughtsman—. It would be better to leave things as they are. For my part, when the time comes to act, I'll do what I think best. I'll do what I want!

August goes on for quite a while, explaining his own position. Emili hardly listens. He's in a hurry to get back to the relative calm of his Block. He finally manages to escape. "There's nothing for it" —he thinks on his way out the door—. "August: the name of an Emperor and a clown. August, your very name is against you!"

The picture of the main camp that Rubio sketched in his letter to Emili was excessively optimistic. It was the letter of a communist to the uninitiated, and naturally, the content related to reality only in those aspects that interested him politically. Above all, it was inaccurate in everything to do with relations between the two large Spanish groups. Even though a state of relative well-being had been achieved for all of them, now they fought between themselves more than ever. Emili sometimes thought that when equality for all mankind was finally realized and the quality of life had reached its pinnacle, the fighting would still not cease and people would argue and plot against one another in just as Byzantine a manner as ever. The human instinct for quarrelling is only set aside at certain moments, when consciousness of a common interest miraculously emerges.

In the *Casa Gran,* just such a moment came. With the relative abundance being shared among the Spaniards, political infighting between communists and anti-communists reached an unprecedented intensity. So many years of confinement and isolation distorted reality like a bent mirror. They had discovered that generosity towards the weak could be turned, with time, to political advantage. And so it ceased to be generosity. The cook who could give out food, or the warehouse worker who had clothes to give away, imagined himself as having ministerial responsibilities. And since the parties and the organizations functioned only insofar as they could win converts, that cook and that warehouse worker automatically became leaders even if they were completely unschooled. Leaders and followers alike were passionate in their search for converts, as if the future of their homeland and of the whole world depended on the hegemony of the Spaniards in the camp. The undecided, the neutral, and the self-serving took advantage of this rivalry and could sell themselves to one side or another just as they liked.

The communists started this strategy for winning support in accordance with their principle that adherence was what counted most and that conviction would follow. The syndicalists, afraid of letting opportunities slip away, took the same route. The competition to get into positions of economic power was fierce and pitiless. The currency for buying acolytes, influence, or even SS guards, was all generated from theft. Everybody stole, and they stole everywhere. To make things vanish was a civic duty, and the people who stole the most were celebrated as heroes when they were caught. Everyone in the administration knew what was happening, but measures to control it were rendered useless by indecision. The relaxing of discipline born out of this general degradation was put to use by the Nazis with an eye to posthumous revenge. The poison spread without limits. The wretched and the privileged, the hungry and the satisfied, the selfish and the generous, they all became victims, each of their own circumstances. The spirit of the camp kept a man broken and oppressed and, short of some miracle, there was little chance of redress.

Among the Spaniards, who were generally more long-suffering and more austere than other collectives, the "evil of the camp" took the form of petty politics. A well-known Mediterranean disease! The intrigues, the disputes, the loathing sometimes led to irreparable damage. Rubio and Manuel, in charge of their respective sectors, were likewise dragged into the torrent despite their efforts to keep the peace. The reason for the clash had been insignificant: a supposed lack of diligence on Manuel's part in his duties as secretary and as the person responsible for the Spanish mail. Rubio thought his little oversight had been calculated. They'd argued and left things unresolved. Even though they both realized almost immediately that it had all been a misunderstanding, any possibility for reconciliation evaporated in the climate of discord that reigned in the camp.

The main thing, the common interest that brought a truce after so many months of ridiculous, pointless fighting, was the arrival of some dozens of Spaniards who had been detained in France because of their work in the Resistance. They brought the fresh air of the Maquis encampments with them.[43] Shaped by the self-sacrifice and heroism of the underground resistance, they were the heralds of a wave of liberation that was starting to break through the Atlantic wall. The creed they brought with them was the union of all against the common enemy. The camp opened its arms. The newcomers' deeds were on everyone's lips, told and retold, discussed and envied. Everybody felt ashamed of their past bickering when the newcomers talked about machine guns, "plastique" on bridge footings, and spectacular attacks carried out on German officials or collaborationists,[44] about detentions and tortures in Gestapo prison cells, about the sacrifices of those who refused to talk … They were a gust of fresh air, the heroic life, active engagement!

Little by little past disputes were forgotten, and the day came when it seemed impossible that they'd ever existed. The words "fraternal concord" were taken up with the same passion as previously had been the provocations to civil strife. The miracle had come, and the Spaniards had won a clear victory over the "evil of the camp." They were saved, and they would become the very model of brotherhood, of altruism, and of decency. A new kind of vanity had come into fashion: the puritanical.

The Spanish doctor in the infirmary, who had stayed on the margins during their ridiculous fight, wanted to patch together a reconciliation between Rubio and Manuel. He invited them to supper, and when Rubio arrived at the infirmary, Manuel stood up and went over to embrace his ex-enemy.

—Don't you think maybe we've been a couple of idiots?
—I've being wanting to ask you the same thing?
—A Vergara embrace! —added the doctor, laughing.[45]
—But I'm not the Carlist —protested Manuel.

There were out-and-out fights to get into the "Russian Girls *Kommando*."[46] August had to set up a strict rotating schedule to keep everyone satisfied. Emili's turn came around one day, and he could attest that the bizarre scene was worth the visit.

By then, the Americans' airbases had moved much closer, and the massive incursions from Italian territory were affecting all of the manufacturing centres along the Danube. Among many other weapons factories, a particularly important one that produced ball bearings had been destroyed in a nearby town. The machinery left undamaged had been moved to an estate five kilometres from August's camp. To build the workshops to house it, they brought in prisoners of war, civilian deportees, and Spanish prisoners. The work had been completed in great haste, and soon everything was ready to go. Having got the machines in place, the Spaniards stayed on a bit longer to construct connecting roads and to build extensions as they became necessary.

It was all women working at the machines: German women who had been mobilized, French "volunteers," but above all, Ukrainian girls, young single women who had been torn from their own country and forced into a shameful slavery. These girls, usually very young, had but a few rags to conceal the shapeliness proper to their race. Thrown together as they were with odds and ends of clothing, patches of every colour, shod with wooden-soled clogs like the prisoners, filthy and smelling like sheep, all the misery of which they had been the victims shone through. Unable to speak German, they would spend the entire day being yelled at and shoved around by their section foremen. Confronted with this repugnant spectacle, the Spaniards soon forgot their own difficulties in a flood of compassion for the girls, and when any of the girls came out of the workshops and passed by where they were working, they were inevitably the objects of sympathetic looks, kind words and gestures. The Spanish *kapos*, employed as interpreters rather than as real *kapos* and freer to move around than their subordinates, visited the workshops under any pretext whatsoever. The Russians soon responded to these demonstrations of sympathy, fixing themselves up as much as possible under the circumstances. The eternal feminine triumphed yet again.

Days when the guards seemed in a generous mood were put to use overcoming any initial shyness. Little notes started to circulate discreetly, and either openly or in secret, every Spaniard had chosen his own Natasha. Very few, on either side, were without a sentimental attachment. The letters were written in the delightful German of their respective interpreters and in the inflammatory terms appropriate to the situation. Likely unintelligible to a native German speaker, they were clear and eloquent to those strangers from opposite ends of Europe. On holiday Sundays—that is, every fifteen days—the girls would gather at the perimeter of the Spanish camp dressed up as best they could, and through the barbed wire, under the sleepy eye of the sentries, carry on conversations based on the four German words they knew and a torrent of signs and gestures. The Spaniards, leaning out the windows of their barracks, jostled for position to exchange a word or a smile with their visitors. And when the girls left again on the last train, the Spaniards didn't have any time to get depressed: it was then that heated discussions about the qualities of their respective "girlfriends" began amidst the jokes of the unattached, the sermons of those who still had some sense, and the boasts of the Don Juans.

Such a strange story out of a German concentration camp can only be explained by the special indulgence granted the Spaniards by the SS. The Spaniards didn't try to escape, they had the special consideration of Hans Gupper himself, and, during that time of defeat, the Nazis' zeal had cooled enough not to take such things so seriously. Their remonstrances were limited to semi-official recommendations of common sense, just enough so that the guards themselves would not be compromised.

On the train that took the prisoners out to the *Kommando* of the Russian girls each morning, Emili observed the full extent of the erotic epidemic. The men had been transformed from the months previous; they joked like schoolboys headed off on an excursion to the countryside. Young and old alike shaved twice a week, washed their clothes regularly, and never went out without having first polished their clogs with lard. Lost in thought, the draughtsman gazed out the window at the landscape rolling by. He was trying to come to grips with that strange reversion to the frivolities of youth. The men of August's *Kommando* had overcome a period of physical and moral decline; their lives were now stabilized at a minimal level that would probably see them through to the end of the war. An impatience to return to normal life presided over that final period of waiting. In the meantime, they sought substitutes for the joys, the desires, the worries, the dreams common to that normal life, by creating a sort of parody of their old patterns of behaviour, as if all the years of privation had been only some sort of painful vacation. They played at politics, for example, just as they had while sitting at the café in their home village before the Civil War; they organized "governments" and "armies" without giving a thought to the absurdity of doing so. They were passionate about almost everything, and they constructed and deconstructed and reconstructed their plans just for the sake of escaping the presence of the barbed wire and the feeling of being caged and powerless. A child's game played by grown men!

Once they'd arrived at the works, the *kapo* said to him:

—Stand here and you'll have a good view.

The spectacle was worth seeing. For the men, nothing was more important than the relative proximity of the Russian girls. Their posture, conversation, even the work itself, depended on what the girls were doing just a little way off, at work inside the barracks. Some would get dreamy-eyed when they realized they had been seen by "her"; others would quickly wash the mud from their clogs when "she" was about to pass by; the most daring would sling a tool across their shoulders and head off towards the forge on the pretext of having it sharpened, in order to manage a secret rendezvous, exchanging a few furtive kisses and ardent words with the beloved.

—Come on, boys; let's see you work just a little —the *kapo* begged from time to time—. You've been standing around now for more than an hour.

The men would briefly pick up the pace until their chief preoccupation found occasion to reassert itself.

—Yours is coming now —one would warn another—. You see her? She's not wearing her kerchief today. What chubby cheeks she has!

The interested party would feel his heart lift but would pretend indifference. The girl would pass by and, if convenient, would let a little piece of wrinkled paper slip from her hand, her eyes announcing its presence. The paper would lie there amid the clods of earth untouched for a little while and be collected later, when there was no risk of being caught.

—She's too Rubenesque for me —said someone down in the ditch—. In a few years she'll be a sack of potatoes.
—Just right —said another—. So there's something to get hold of ...
—Now work a little —pleaded the *kapo*—. You're going to start attracting attention, and then ...

The air raid siren started up. Everybody had to head over to a little forested hill about five hundred metres from the work camp. The guard that day was a good one; none of its SS had a reputation for being strict or ill-tempered. The Russians had found a spot close to where the Spaniards were sitting surrounded by their sentries. In the beginning, while the planes were still far off and they could see the artificial fog rising up and starting to conceal the town nearby, the conversations between lovers took place across the cordon of the guards, who remained indifferent, perhaps even pleased by this show of trust. However, when the first swarm of planes appeared in the sky and, following the river, flew directly over those hidden beneath the trees, some resolved to take advantage of the soldiers' distraction and cross over the line to sit openly next to their loved ones. Since the guards pretended ignorance, more worried by the enemy air force than by youthful ardor, others soon followed the example of the most brazen. Under the trees and amidst the menacing drone of the planes, some couples were kissing just as though they had emerged from an idyllic postcard; others exchanged photographs and addresses; still others stared closely at each other, searching out the gestures that would make up for their deficiencies in language. The men, clean and shaven; the women, carefully coiffed (only a few still wore the classic shawl on their heads) and dressed with the best rags they'd been able to gather together. Some of the women were trying to get their men to accept half the frugal breakfast they'd been given, and even though more than one would have eaten with pleasure, all felt like gentlemen and refused with ostentatious displays of good manners.

With the all-clear, everyone returned to their work, and none found the hours of toil interminable, nor felt the heat of the day, nor found the task too heavy. All of them lived in hope that the guard would be as easy-going the next day and that the Anglo-American planes with their pay-loads of bombs would not forsake them.

The love virus is highly contagious for anyone immersed in its atmosphere. Even the German girls from the Hitler Youth, who had at first been contemptuous of the Spaniards as an "inferior race," ended up in jealous competition with the Ukrainians, although they kept themselves for the tidier *kapos* with their peaked caps. August himself was captivated by one of them, a Bavarian, and with the excuse of inspecting the works, would often head over to the "Love Kommando" to take her poems and little gifts made by the workers in the special section. This love affair had repercussions in the camp, for the more he fell in love, the more eccentric was his behaviour, not only in inconsequential things like the way he dressed, but also in his implementation of internal policies. The men, a little cynically and always maliciously, started calling his Bavarian "the Pompadour." The bizarreness of the situation only increased. The impassioned prisoners alternated the ecstasies of love with waves of pure hatred for August, Castro, or the doctor, depending on their politics, and would condemn them as the lowest of criminals who must be liquidated as soon as liberation came:[47] "The bastard, I'll finish him off." Or they would talk about the Ukraine as a paradise where they would go to live with "her" once the war was over; or they would assure one another that they would carry their Natashas off to Cordova or the Lavapiés quarter of Madrid. Some Andalusians who would have had trouble making themselves under-stood even in Castillian were making desperate efforts to learn Russian. The most romantic ones were already imagining the military preparations of the "National Union Government" and of the "General Staff" as a fan-tastic epic in which they themselves would play the most heroic roles, committing deeds that would liberate all the oppressed and that would culminate, as in the cinema, with their reunion with the loved one and the endless kiss of happiness that comes before the words "The End."

Their foolishness was understandable enough. The long internment, the end so near at hand, the mirage of the liberation just at the point of becoming a reality. There was a frenzy of feelings, of changes, and worries. What seemed brand new one day was old news the next, and the day after it was thrilling once again. The air was electric, and the threatening storm could as easily end in a little thunder and lightning, or in a genuine cataclysm.

It all blew up one day in September, in a crisis that was christened the "*pronunciamiento* of the cabbages."

That afternoon a truckload of tender cabbages had arrived at the camp. Although hunger was not as rampant as it had been, there were always a few who gathered when the trucks were being unloaded in order to steal a head or two of cabbage, either to eat the whitest of the leaves raw or to cook them on Sunday with a few stolen potatoes, or simply for the practice, so as not to lose their touch. That evening the Commandant inspected the camp outbuildings and found the toilets blocked with cabbage leaves. August—under pressure from the Commandant—asked the men formed up for roll call who was responsible. Nobody answered.

> —Formation won't be broken until the perpetrator, or perpetrators, come forward.

The more serious the situation became, the more reluctant were the guilty to confess. August had a flash of self-love as he never had before. Among other repressive measures he broke up the lines and started arbitrarily lashing people across the buttocks. In addition, the internal police were sent to the trestle of "the twenty-five" for not having been more vigilant; and he probably would have gone through the whole camp if, in the face of so many speeches, threats, and punishments, and, above all, the coming nightfall, the Commandant hadn't decided to intervene in person. To August's laments about the men's lack of discipline, the Commandant replied with an order to break ranks and leave the show for another day. He was in the habit of leaving for the *Gasthof* every evening at this time to meet with friends.

When Emili came into the office to finish up a job, he heard August raging:

> —This has to come to an end —he yelled in a fury—. I will take back up the sword. Is that what you want? With these people it's impossible to achieve anything worthwhile. Who do you think I am? I'm August, and before the Russians get here, I still have time to show you how far I can go. Today I really hit someone for the first time in my life, but I assure you, it's not going to be the last time. To begin with, to hell with governments and armies! Here, I'm in charge, whatever the communists do or say.

Emili smiled to himself. His prophecy of some weeks before was coming true: August was about to proclaim himself Emperor.

Superficially, life continued as before; however, everyone also showed careful good judgment. That day, August lost the little disinterested support he still had. The communists hated him so much that even in establishing more or less cordial relations with the anarcho-syndicalists they decided to leave him out of it. Military developments were coming fast: the Anglo-Americans had reached the Rhine and the Russians were poised to take Warsaw and Budapest. The wave of good sense also did much to quench the bonfires of love, and aside from some four or five eternal sentimentalists, the lovers soon forgot all about the Russian girls. August continued, now and then, to receive the "Pompadour," an exceptional privilege accorded him by the Commandant, and he would pass by, always alone and pensive in his black and white pyjamas, no doubt philosophizing about the complex problems caused by love and power.

One day in October the order came to suspend all work unless it was war related. The dam being considered unnecessary, August's whole *Kommando* had to return to the *Casa Gran*.

This long parenthesis in time, which for many had made up the greater part of their captivity, had come to an end. They had left the main camp at a time when three out of four Spaniards were dying. They had ended up in a corner of the world where, with a few exceptions, everybody had been able to survive. After this good fortune, the prospect of going back to where they had started was not much to anyone's liking. Everyone knew that the end of a war in a small camp, without electric barbed wire and with little in the way of surveillance, would be less bloody than at the *Casa Gran* with its stone walls and large garrison. Someone suggested joining the Maquis and waiting for the imminent arrival of the liberating forces before rising up in rebellion; but good sense had struck its roots deep enough among them that such a half-baked idea wasn't taken up.

The day they took the train, the sun shone sweetly. The four hundred prisoners walked through the village on the road to the station with the feeling that they were losing a little piece of paradise. Was that the last stage?[48]

Emili too, although he knew that life for the Spaniards in the main camp was better than it had been, shared these feelings. The village houses, the river, the station, they all had a certain something of the familiar. They had not been happy years, but in their course he had regained his hope for freedom. He had arrived destroyed in body and spirit and was leaving with his taste for life restored. The countryside was beautiful, and he had to admit that it would have been nice to have known that quiet, tidy little village in other circumstances. Destiny didn't want it thus, so he was being carried off to who knew what new trials. True, an end in the *Casa Gran* had its own attractions, and the draughtsman remembered that during the bitter hours he had wanted to be there when justice was done. The ashes of his friends were there on a shelf in the basement of the crematorium— scrupulously classified and ordered in their respective tins among thousands of others—and they were expecting him to bear witness for them. The routine and relatively tranquil life in August's *Kommando* had held back all the massed hatred. Thousands, dozens of thousands of murdered men were claiming vengeance; but ...

The people of the village came out to watch them. They were silent, but one could read the sympathy on their faces. They had been watching them march back and forth to work for so long now! It was only natural that Emili, wrapped in that caring silence, could not call up any imperative for justice. How was it possible to think of revenge, of blood flowing yet again, of revolution, of upheaval, if the sun that afternoon was so sweet and all the people came out to wish them farewell?

CHAPTER XV

The train arrived at the same station where, four years before, Emili and the rest of prisoners in the expedition had been greeted with kicks and blows from rifle butts. The sky, now criss-crossed in every direction by searchlights, took on a metallic sheen. An entirely useless precaution, since the enemy planes preferred the light of day for their incursions ... The only effect was to darken the night still further on the ground. The four hundred Spaniards made their way uphill, stumbling over stones, treading on the heels of those in front of them, and often enough finding themselves in an intimate embrace with one of the trees that lined the road. The sentries who kept them in line were having an even harder go of it; from time to time one heard the clatter of rifles and cartridge belts along with curses from those who had tripped and fallen into the ditch.

—A good moment to escape —somebody said—. We'd have their throats slit before they could say "ouch."
—Escape where? —Emili commented.

Apart from the Danube, which shimmered in the darkness like satin, no other point of reference could be made out. When they had first climbed that path, everything had been white with snow; now, in contrast, all was blackness. All the same, their feelings were not in keeping with the colour scheme. The old fear of the unknown was gone now, and once they had taken in that they were indeed going back to the main camp, the idea of it even seemed attractive: to end the war where great danger would give rise to great emotions. It wasn't a thirst for blood or cataclysm, but the need to re-enter normal life through a burst of emotion that would make the moment of change palpable and clear. A rebirth without pain wouldn't seem like a rebirth at all.

All of a sudden the camp appeared in front of them like a castle in a stage set. Their eyes had become accustomed to the darkness, and the spectacle was blinding and magical. The high, tiered walls were lit up by floodlights just like the monuments on special holidays at home. Below the road on the left, like a row of sleeping beasts, the barracks of the "Russian camp" were ringed by the glint of barbed wire. That "supplementary" camp, finished just a few months before and in principle destined to house the "innumerable Russian prisoners who had built it," was now an enormous camp hospital. Thousands and thousands of sick men without any medical treatment, without food, lying four to a bed only seventy centimetres across, waited there patiently for the hour of death. No one had time to finish them off. The sentries, like mobile punctuation marks outside the barbed wire, kept vigil over the silence of the condemned.

Above, the exterior precinct with its annexes echoed with the unreal sound of the four hundred men marching in. A strange effect for both ear and eye, as if at that hour of the night the camp was not itself, but an elaborate model constructed of papier mâché. The foreground was illuminated by the street lights, while the background disappeared into the darkness as if of no interest.

The gate with its oriental silhouette swung open once more. The whole prospect of the roll call square, under the harsh glare of the floodlights, seemed welcoming to those returning. Such images were evoked by that desolate solitude, that harsh light!

The SS on duty and some prisoners came out to meet the procession. Emili searched for friends among them. He couldn't tell if it was because their faces were all unfamiliar, or if their civilian clothes had made them unrecognizable, but he found no one he knew. One of them spoke to him:

—Maybe you don't remember me; Rubio will have mentioned me. I'm Manuel.
—Yes, I remember you —Emili replied vaguely.
—I had a servant's position in Popeye's barracks. Francesc was a good friend of mine.
—So long ago ...
—Rubio waited up for you for a good while, but he wasn't feeling well and he's gone to bed. He'll see you tomorrow.

The draughtsmen asked him how things were going.

—Spirits are high. The war is almost over and here things have changed a lot. Spaniards are well treated now.
—And the rest?
—For the rest it's worse than ever ...

August, meanwhile, was walking up and down like a general preparing his forces for battle.

—People are sleeping —came a loud voice—. Try to keep quiet crossing the camp.

—And August, how's he doing? —asked Manuel—. I want to hear it from someone impartial. Here he's the subject of much debate.

The group started to march to the barracks assigned them. The chimney of a new electric crematorium showed its tongue of flame, and the black smoke, reeking of burnt wool, drifted down around them and brought that burning in the throat that Emili had nearly forgotten.

It was a bad night. In a space meant for a hundred men, four hundred were jammed together. Some went on complaining the whole night through, and when the reveille sounded, Emili had only just managed to fall asleep. Waking, he remembered that other first waking, four years before. The same pain in his bones, the same sticky sweat; only now the *Blockälteste* let them get dressed calmly and was both considerate and friendly towards the newcomers. That difference was fundamental, and Emili thought about its price: five thousand of his fellows had paid for it with their lives.

The first visitors arrived while they were having their prison "coffee." It was then Emili learned that they were living in Camp Number 2 and that the walls surrounding their enclosure signified a quarantine. The visitors were dressed in civilian clothes with a wide red stripe down the middle of the back and around the cuffs of the pants. The clothing was of good quality and even fit properly. Once the uniform striped pyjamas had run out, they'd been replaced with civilian clothing from dead prisoners. The long hair, parted with a shaved band three centimetres wide from the forehead to the nape of the neck, still made Emili think of the divided heads of some insects. They also wore civilian shoes, generally well polished. The visitors came with loaves of bread under their arms or with packets of margarine or sugar; the procession lasted that whole day and didn't let up on the days following. The Spanish group had mobilized all its resources to put on a good welcome for the "outsiders."

Emili received visitors as well, and gifts, but not always with the same high spirits as the others. For all he recognized that his companions from the old camp (now Camp Number 1) were doing well for themselves to make up for the hard years, it seemed monstrous, this law that said so many had to die so that just a few could survive. Those living skeletons from other nationalities, shabby in their filthy rags, barefoot, coatless, their heads covered with the most bizarre caps, hunched against the cold despite the mild weather, those unfortunates who had come in from the evacuated camps of Lublin and Auschwitz and now swelled the quarantine camp and hovered with hungry eyes around the circles of Spaniards, they carried with them all the horror of the last hours in which nothing that was human counted. Above all, it was the young Jews who obsessed Emili: only twelve or fourteen years old and with their own monstrous experiences of human cruelty.

He was feeling overwhelmed with revulsion when Rubio came in.

—I can't understand your indifference to all this. —He spat out as soon as he saw him—. Have you all really sunk so low?
—You're shocked, eh? You and the others, maybe you're just back from Paradise!
—Your wealth, it's a provocation.
—No Spaniard has dinner twice. We're keeping ourselves alive, that's all. What we steal from the warehouse doesn't affect the camp ration. If we didn't steal it, nobody would benefit from it; the kitchen would cook up the same soup as they do now. The problem is the flood of new arrivals, which never stops. People with nothing, corpses barely able to drag themselves around. What do you want us to do?

The draughtsman realized that his scruples were out of place and let it drop.

—These ones staring at us as though we're responsible for their hunger —Rubio continued— have just arrived in the camp and don't know a thing about how we manage here. I can assure you that in the camp down below, nobody has anything to say against the Spaniards. It's cost us to get to this point, believe me, but …

And then Rubio talked about the good cooperation among the Spaniards.

—That doesn't mean a thing —Emili countered, still upset—. With a full belly everything looks rosy …
—To our credit, we've overcome the prison environment. We've spent four years among criminals, in a climate of limitless self-interest, under constant threat of death, and we have managed to hold on to our principles.
—Maybe so —admitted the draughtsman—. I know I've forgotten a lot.

—And August? —the barber cut in, before their conversation got too heavy—. I'm anxious to talk to him.

—You're going to have a fight.

—It doesn't matter. I have to see him and tell him what I think. He's gone too far. That is —he added— if what's said about him is true … I trust you'll set me straight on that.

Emili laid out his point of view: without defending August's often arbitrary decisions, he underlined all the good that he'd done.

—I don't understand why, at the last minute …

—Neither do I. I've been wracking my brains for an answer to that. He's like a circus performer drunk on applause who keeps adding more and more complications to his balancing act until everything comes tumbling down around him. He began with some useful innovations and he's ended up with absurdities …

—I'm anxious to talk to him, to make him understand …

—There's no point. You'll be wasting your time; I know him well.

When Rubio left, Emili took a turn around the barracks. They were talking about August in many of the groups of Spaniards, and he could see that those who had been most servile to him before now spoke most harshly. He went back to his Block, disgusted. At the door, the *Blockälteste* was pounding away furiously at a Russian, accused, according to the others, of stealing bread from a Spaniard.

It had been only a few hours since Emili had entered the camp with the intention of waiting out the war there, if it was possible, but now he had an overwhelming desire to turn and go. In August's *Kommando* he had neither civilian clothes, nor much bread, nor margarine, but he lived quietly. It was true that the main camp had improved a lot for the Spaniards, but Death was reaping a more abundant harvest than ever among those who, although not Spanish, had not stopped being men. The war might last for months yet; would he be able to shut his eyes, hunch his shoulders, and wait?

The Spaniards had been at Camp 2 for over two weeks, and still nothing had been settled about their final destination. There was nothing for them to do. With the onset of the spring rains, the camp was an impassable sea of mud, and they stayed crammed inside their barracks, so cramped for four hundred men that most of the time one couldn't even find a place to sit down on the floor. The close quarters, the inactivity, and, above all, the exhausting spectacle of surrounding misery soon had a demoralizing effect on the men, used, as they were, to regular work in the open air. Tedium led to moodiness, irritability, to scheming and misunderstanding, to curses and arguments. The atmosphere became suffocating.

At the beginning, as a temporary solution, the Germans had divvied up small groups of Spaniards among the other barracks of the quarantine enclosure. However, the huge influx of various nationalities from concentration camps being evacuated before the Russian advance had necessitated packing the four hundred Spaniards into a barracks meant for one hundred. Sleep was an illusion. The men had to be positioned one by one, standing up and in rows. At a given signal, each pair of lines lay down together, alternating head to toe and all of them lying on the same side. The bodies fit together like a jigsaw puzzle, and it looked as though you could walk straight across this living carpet without any fear of slipping through. Getting up to go out to urinate risked losing one's place. This system was relatively convenient in the neighbouring barracks, where the *Blockälteste* always carried a whip and could squeeze the men together with a swift kick to the kidneys. But the Spaniards had to be handled with special care, by order of Hans Gupper. The nights were a prolonged torture.

One morning after "coffee," Emili stepped out of the barracks. The fog was icy, but he needed the fresh air. The population of the neighbouring Blocks, turned out onto the street at the sounding of morning reveille and not let back in until evening recall, fought against the cold. It seemed impossible that living bodies still pulsed beneath those scarecrow clothes. They searched in vain for shelter from the bitter wind; hunched, their hands thrust deep in their pockets, they stamped their feet and shivered uncontrollably. Some of them, like bees in a swarm, pressed in against one another to stay warm. When it was large enough, the mass of their bodies started to sway slowly this way and that, like a mound of gelatine, in hopes that the friction of rubbing against one another would add to the heat. The Slavs, above all, took up this strategy, clustering together like grapes swaying on the vine. And soon they would be carried off by the natural melancholy of their race and, keeping time with the motion, would sing their songs of infinite sadness. Patriotic songs, religious songs, folk songs caught between the walls and barbed wire, a sad and tender longing. From the morning when Emili first witnessed this way of enduring the hours of cold outside, he felt an even greater repugnance for his idle companions with their excess vitality. He could not fathom, for instance, the barbarity of those who, just for their own amusement, would launch themselves against those tight clusters of Slavs with an idiotic whoop, and break them apart.

Emili felt ashamed of the instinctive scorn that many of the Spaniards now showed towards those who were helpless and destitute. It seemed normal enough that the Germans in charge of the Blocks, criminals from the margins of society to begin with, and who on top of that had been poisoned by the racist theories of the *Herrenvolk*, it seemed normal enough that they would allow themselves to get carried away by bigotry; but for the Spaniards, it was a completely different case. Not because they were Spaniards, but because they were "men of ideas." They had fought in a civil war and were now enduring captivity for a cause. Certainly none of those behaving so badly would have owned up to their unconscious contempt for the people around them: they would all be offended to be placed on the same moral level as the German scum who ruled over them. But the facts don't lie. Misery is always repulsive; to be clear-sighted about it takes an integrity of character that is difficult to maintain in such circumstances.

The same collective exultation brought to the defence of a French boy being pursued by a *Blockälteste* with dubious intentions confirmed it. This sentimental, quixotic impulse, pointless from the outset, came more than anything out of a desire for some form of redress. It is a phenomenon to be found in many Spanish collectives, which often get more caught up in a petty incident close to home than in some real catastrophe that happens at a distance. Things unfolded like this:

The German *Blockälteste* would choose the youngest of their subjects to make up the cleaning crews for the barracks. This was a kind of protection, since the boys selected got a double ration of food, but it was very often an ignominious arrangement. The *Blockälteste* would choose a favourite from the harem, and any resistance was useless.

Among the boys serving in the Spaniards' barracks there was a French sixteen-year-old who had been arrested as a *maquisard*. He was delicate in his manners, rather sad and shy and with a nearly canine subservience that verged on annoying. The boy limited himself to performing his prescribed duties and timidly evaded his protector's advances. One evening, the man made him sit down at his table and gave him a good meal. When the German told him what he wanted, the boy ran from the table and, trembling and sobbing, sought refuge among the Spaniards, asking them for help.

The next afternoon, when the *Blockälteste* made a show of asking who had cleaned the windows, which he knew perfectly well, and the French boy had to present himself, everybody had a pretty good idea what was going to happen next. Right on cue, the German started screaming like a madman that the windows were filthy and he didn't want useless people in his service, that it was necessary to work in order to eat ... From words he progressed to blows, and the boy came out of it with his face bruised and swollen. He spent half the afternoon huddled in a corner until the *Blockälteste* invited him for an afternoon snack, because he was "sure that from now on he would be more reasonable." The boy burst into tears and the Spaniards were furious. The *Blockälteste*, insulted and threatened, objected to this interference in his affairs, went into a paroxysm of rage, and finished by saying that from that moment on he would not give any deference to the Spaniards and would treat them just the same as everybody else. The boy's protectors found the incident stimulating, and the scandal took on unexpected proportions. August decided to intervene, but, perhaps to counteract the campaign against him, he complicated the situation by openly taking the side of his companions.

With nightfall, when it was time to get them into their places, the German arrived to carry out his threat, whip in hand. He did not have time to raise it because a single blow to his chin laid him out flat on the floor. A very serious breech of discipline. The German went to King Kong with his resignation. King Kong did not accept it, afraid that Hans Gupper, already well disposed to the Spaniards, would use the occasion to remove the German common criminals from their positions of authority. Instead, first thing in the morning, King Kong went directly to the quarantine camp, met with the Spaniards, and tried a little diplomacy:

> —The camp is as it is —he said, among other things—. Your wish to reform it is noble, but useless. Your companions in camp 1, who have been living there for years, know it well enough and don't waste their time on what can't do any good and, frankly, causes a lot headaches for everyone. Forget the incident; let the *Blockälteste* organize things his way and let each individual solve his own problems. We all want to go home where life is not cruel as it is here, but we have to be patient until then. And not complicate life unnecessarily in these last hours.

The Spaniards realized that turning a blind eye as King Kong proposed, even if it resolved nothing, was the best way to deal with the mess. After all, the camp was full of similar stories ... and worse. If they wanted to be saviours, they'd be at it for years … August asked that the boy be transferred to Camp 1 in order to avoid reprisals. King Kong agreed to this, and the case was considered closed.

Emili thought that despite appearances, the *spirit of the camp* was still carrying out its destructive work. The bestiality of the German penitentiary system had brought them to the point of finding "reasonable arguments" to justify selfishness and indifference in the face of evil. The brutalization was cunning and implacable.

The next day everybody had forgotten the French boy. They had found another subject of conversation: cannibalism. A Slav, at the ultimate extreme of hunger, slipped into the washrooms where the dead were left at night until they could be taken to the crematorium in the morning. With a knife improvised from a piece of a saw, he opened the stomach of one of the bodies. It was not the first such case, nor would it be the last. The anthropophagus was caught because, the next morning, the corners of his mouth were still caked with dried blood. Some hours later, half dead from the beating he was given, he was hanged from one of the barracks' beams.

Even rigorous security couldn't keep people from hearing the gruesome details of what was going on in Block 20, a small enclosure completely surrounded by high stone walls. It was said that the internees of that barracks were subject directly to the Gestapo and that the camp administration had no say over them. Even so, it was the SS who watched from atop the armed towers that rose at the corners of the wall.

Block 20 was reserved for those condemned to death, charged with high treason, guilty of major attacks on the Nazi regime. They were brought in at night dressed only in the summer uniform, without underclothes or shoes, and while the normal capacity of a double-winged barracks was two hundred people, here the same space was being used to contain upwards of fifteen hundred. Without heat, or blankets, or bunks, or mattresses, without any furniture whatsoever, and with only a single meal of watery soup each day at noon, the population turned over continuously as the prisoners dragged their way through a slow agony of starvation, cold, sickness, and terror. Often there was a need to "make room," and then they would be culled into large groups and taken to the gas chamber, or they would be shot or hacked to death with axes by the Gestapo or by SS looking for a little excitement. The prisoners were so densely packed together that they could neither stretch out nor even sit down. The indifferent silence of that human mass, reduced to the most extreme level of deprivation, was sometimes broken by shrieks when one of them slipped into madness and lashed out at a neighbour until one or the other of them lay strangled.

The two SS who mounted the guard inside the Block could only impose their authority with pistols in hand. These would have been of little use, obviously, except for the complete physical annihilation of the prisoners. Nonetheless, one of the SS shifts was going to pay very dearly for its faith in such an insignificant weapon.

It was snowing heavily on that Sunday morning in the middle of December when twenty Austrians were brought into the "barracks of Death." Among them was a man of about forty, tall, distinguished, who seemed to have a certain ascendancy over his comrades. It was said that he was an officer of the old Austrian Imperial Army, now Germany's, accused of high treason. When the twenty Austrians were shoved into the barracks amidst a hail of blows, nobody was sleeping. A few SS had just left. They had been trying out some newly issued submachine guns on the defenceless multitude. At that moment, under order of the two SS guards, the corpses were being dragged outside, leaving trails of blood across the floorboards. Some of the wounded were hiding in the traumatized crowd so as not to be dragged out along with the corpses, and they hid their cries of pain amidst the shouts of hate and terror. The newcomers could hardly make sense of their situation, overwhelmed as they were. They were just trying to stay together, and they huddled in a corner. Meanwhile the SS were imposing silence with their whips. In the dark, the cluster of bodies seethed like a pile of worms struggling for some impossible relief. Muffled complaints, prayers from believers, curses from others, sighs, laments, the rhythmic breathing of someone who, despite everything, had managed to fall sleep, all seemed to speak, in their monstrous harmony, with one single voice of desperation. From time to time, the screams of someone who had lost his mind tore through the silence.

The Austrian officer didn't sleep at all that night. The following morning, he proposed to his comrades a plan he had devised. Their various roles were assigned, and more accomplices were sought among the rest. Then they waited for their opportunity.

Everyone had just finished drinking down the watery midday soup when the conspirators started making a huge ruckus. The immediate appearance of one of the SS was their opening. The guard opened the door with a kick of his boot and stood on the threshold with his whip in one hand and his pistol in the other. His shout for "Silence!" had no effect. He raised his whip and, full of rage, struck out against the mass. It was then, with the agility of a tiger, that one of the conspirators got him by the neck, while another struck the hand that held the pistol with a piece of wood torn from the wall. As if by magic, suddenly everything was silent as the grave. One could clearly make out the row going on in the other wing of the Block, where the second SS was falling victim to the same trap. The Austrian officer took the gun, another comrade took the whip, and after telling everybody to stay calm, they ran over to the other side. The revolt here had not gone so well. The SS was standing at the door of the dormitory and was threatening to shoot if they didn't shut up. However, when the dining room door opened behind him and he turned to see armed prisoners running at him, his momentary confusion gave those to whom he had now turned his back an opening. He found himself suddenly disarmed. They fired one shot from his own pistol; the bullet went right through his body and lodged in the wall. He had not even had time to die before one of the prisoners was putting on his uniform. The Austrian stuffed his pistol into the waist of his trousers. One of his lieutenants did the same with the other weapon, while the multitude took their vengeance on the guards' corpses.

The officer gave his instructions in German, a Russian translated them, and, with the spontaneous discipline that is only possible in moments of tremendous gravity, everybody obeyed in complete silence. Those who still had the strength to go through with the sensational adventure got ready to act at the agreed signal. The sick and exhausted tried to get up and follow their comrades, but many had to give up.

Once half a dozen men had been chosen from among the strongest, the officer handed out shovels from the barracks' small storeroom and went out into the street with them, while the false SS remained at the door. The sentry in the tower could only see the uniform he wore. The officer was giving out orders like a *kapo*, yelling himself hoarse and from time to time meting out discipline with the whip. Everything looked so normal that the sentry suspected nothing.

—Faster, faster! —yelled the Austrian—. In ten minutes everything has to be absolutely cleared. Completely, you understand? All the snow into the corner. The corner, I said! Don't you listen? Get at it now. Faster!

The shovels worked frantically. The snow on the road, deep from the last storm, went from shovel to shovel and was heaped up in the corner of the wall next to one of the armed towers. The pile rose bit by bit. One of the men packed it down with the flat of his shovel. The fake *kapo* yelled non-stop, and the fake SS stood at the entrance of the Block shouting and brandishing his whip. The men, meanwhile, were waiting in the dining room and the dormitories with their hands on the latches of the doors and windows, ready for the signal.

The officer came into the Block when the task was almost done, when the snow formed a ramp that ran right up to the top of the wall.

—Do you know how to work the extinguisher? —he asked his companion with the gun.

He could see that he hadn't understood and insisted, impatiently:

—Yes, you. The fire extinguisher, the Minimax.
—Yes, of course —replied the other—. Why?
—To charge the sentries. Don't you see? We're not going to use our fingernails!
—And the pistols? They'd be a surer bet.
—I don't think so.
—But …
—You grab one extinguisher and I'll take the other. Your target is the guard over the ramp. Go out the back window, the one closest to the wall. At the same time, *you* —he pointed to the fake SS— will give the signal for the attack. We have to act swiftly and decisively. No hesitation! Aim the jet at their eyes.

One of the two Minimaxes was taken down and hefted by the man put in charge of it.

—Your mission is to take out the machine gun in the tower —said the officer while grabbing the other extinguisher—. Don't give him time to fire the machine gun. I'll do the same with the other sentry.

After shaking hands, they parted and headed to the windows nearest their respective targets. The multitude watched the operation with both curiosity and emotion. The silence in the room was so complete that one might have said that all those hundreds of men held their breath as one.

194   K.L. REICH

With the precision of movement only possible at moments of life or death, the two leaders opened the windows almost at the same time and jumped outside. Before the sentries realized what was happening, the caustic jet of the extinguishers had already reached their eyes. The fake SS gave a sharp whistle and the men poured out of the doors and windows. The officer threw away his Minimax and ran to the corner across from the wall, up the ramp of snow. He saw that his comrade was coming down the stairs from the tower with the machine gun slung around his neck. The sentry was nowhere to be seen; he'd probably been thrown from the top. The two friends were reunited on top of the cornice. The lieutenant took aim at the sentry in the opposite tower.

    —Let's see if I can calm you down, you idiot.
    —Don't shoot —said the officer—. Save the bullets.

The men rushed up the ramp of packed snow, too soft to support the weight of so many. They were tripping over each other in the rush to jump first, and the ones who had made their way over didn't spare a thought for those coming behind and pleading for a hand up. The two leaders stationed themselves astride the wall and, for a while, did nothing but hoist men and then more men, up and over. All were escaping from one certain death to another almost as certain, but at least they would die on the snow, under the open sky, among the trees, where they could run, where they could show that they were not resigned like sheep to the enormity of their slaughter.

The sentry kept shouting. He could not shoot because he had lost his machine gun down the tower when the spray of the extinguisher burnt his eyes, but he did, all the same, manage to alert the camp with his cries. The siren started to sound and the first of the SS started running to the end of the wall from which the men were escaping in a steady stream. Bursts of machine gun fire started up from all the other towers; the officer and his companion could hear the bullets whistling over their heads. The ramp had become impassable, churned by so many feet; the men now had to be pulled all the way over.

    —Let's go —said the officer—. There's nothing more to be done here.

Hundred of arms reached up for help, cries, weeping, and curses all mixed together in a dull roar of lamentation. Those left behind at the base of the wall fought furiously among themselves.

The officer turned his head. Because of the slope of the hill, enamelled with snow, the moving black dots of the fugitives could easily be made out, a scattered multitude, specks that at last blended in with the black smudge of the pinewoods on the opposite hillside. To wait any longer would mean losing everything. The two men jumped from the wall with their weapons in their hands, ready to shoot. Now the SS were running down the hill, and machine gun fire crackled from the various emplacements. Some of those black specks became suddenly still on the white blanket; others slid eagerly towards the protection of the woods. The officer and his companion also ran for the trees while the soldiers' gunfire intensified from all sides. One of the two men fell; from the camp it was impossible to see which it was, but when they saw that the man left standing turned back for a moment, grabbed something, and then continued on his way, they decided it must be the officer, who had not wanted to abandon the machine gun that his fallen companion had been carrying.

Some seven hundred men had escaped. The hunt lasted two or three days. Some died of cold and exhaustion, others were cut down by SS guns. The neighbouring woods were sown with corpses; but despite the mobilization of the whole countryside, once the threshing was done, two hundred men were still missing, and they were never found, neither dead nor alive.

It was later learned that five or six of those brave men, Soviet soldiers trained to wage guerrilla warfare in the rearguard of the enemy, had managed to reach the advancing lines of the Red Army and survived. Today they are heroes of the Soviet Union. As for the rest, there is no trace. The civilian population, probably out of fear, did not help them. In some cases, quite the contrary. For instance, there's a story that one of the men knocked at the door of an isolated farmhouse. It was night. The farmer seemed to take pity on him and invited him to sit at his table. While the fugitive, shivering from the cold and sick with hunger, was gulping the soup that had been offered to him, the farmer smashed his head in with a shovel.

At the camp, special security measures were implemented. The prisoners were confined to their Blocks for a week, and the SS patrolled the camp non-stop with the order to shoot anybody who was outside his barracks or who even stuck his head out a window. The cooks and the food carriers were the only ones who continued to work, and they were constantly escorted by guards with machine guns. Obviously, nobody made a move. Those already condemned to death could take such risks; not the others.

The prisoners of Block 20 who didn't manage to escape, or who had been too weak to attempt it, were shot that same night, with no exceptions.

A week later, the camp returned to its regular rhythm. People went out to work, lived their miserable lives, and died their usual slow deaths. And Barracks 20 filled, emptied, and filled again without cease. All of the fire extinguishers were gathered up and locked away. Somebody joked that, as a result of this surprise, the Germans had discovered a new secret weapon.

CHAPTER XVI

The end of the war was expected by the following spring but might come anytime. So those last months, those last weeks, perhaps last days, went by unbearably slowly. The question was always and obsessively the same: What would the SS do when they found themselves beyond hope? Would they avenge their losses on the thousands of unarmed prisoners? There was talk of a camp in Poland where the Germans, in retreat, had poisoned the food; when the Russians arrived, they found only a sea of corpses. In another camp, it was said, all of the prisoners had been gassed during the final days of German control. True or false, this kind of news ran all through the camp, and the fear it created spread like a fog.

An underground "International Committee for Protection and Offensive Operations" was constituted. Rubio and Manuel stood as the Spanish representatives. Their meetings were held out in the open, in plain view, as though nothing more than a group out for an innocent stroll; or, when circumstances dictated, they would meet in the basement of the disinfection unit. All eventualities were taken into account, and every plan of action was reviewed down to the smallest details. They secured liaisons with the external *Kommandos*, honed their information about the situation at the front and rearguard, and even counted on the help of some sympathetic SS who monitored the attitude of the camp authorities. Everything had been anticipated, although not the day of the final collapse itself nor what would actually result from all of the complex machinery that had been put in place.

Hundreds of times a day, thousands upon thousands of men asked themselves the same questions: How? When? A penal population of forty thousand souls (one of many in Nazi Germany) caught in the ebb and flow of hope and despair: the sick in the "Russian camp," who ate nothing but potato peelings and spent all day, every day, out on the frozen snow; the men in the quarantine camp, at the last degree of physiological deprivation; those in Camp 1, who didn't know if their tolerable situation would last long enough. Would the body hold up? Would it be put to further tests? Would the Nazis' monstrous ingenuity not discover, at the last minute, a technique for universal and rapid extermination?

In the end, Emili was to remain behind in the camp while his old comrades in August's *Kommando* were sent out to do war work. Rubio and Manuel had insisted that he stay. Everything had been put in place to transfer him to the SS photo laboratory, where, he was told, he would be given a very delicate mission.

—I don't see what good I can do there —the draughtsman had protested.

Some days later, Emili was transferred to the lab as a photo refinisher. As soon as it was clear that the transfer had gone through, Rubio put him in charge of securing a set of proofs of any interesting photographs in the lab's archive before the SS had it destroyed. The task was certainly dangerous; the slightest slip could mean death. But if he could manage it without being discovered, the result would be an extraordinary graphic condemnation of the Nazi regime.

Emili found negatives of all the violent deaths that had occurred in the camp. All were presented as suicides or accidents; the camp authorities thought they would be able to *justify* themselves with the photographs! Perhaps while the Reich endured, when some parent or friend of a victim with enough influence, and as an isolated case, asked for information; but before the whole archive, before the thousands of identical suicides, the lie would soon be uncovered.

The archive, like all things German, was admirably organized and systematized. There were thousands of negatives in the file marked "Suicides against the wire"; thousands more under "Suicides by various means," and still more thousands under "Deaths while attempting escape." Everything carefully numbered. Not much perspicacity was needed to guess the significance of those rows of emaciated men lined up along the base of the electric fence; or the terrible desperation that might lead a man to hang himself from a radiator valve or from a washroom faucet; or the cynicism that would credit an attempted escape to a skeleton that could not possibly walk more than ten steps in a row.

Emili, by now accustomed to the caprices of his fate, decided to embrace his new role; he understood that his field of combat was going to be determined for him by others, by those predestined, it seemed, to play the major parts. He was to stay behind in the main camp, the point of departure and arrival, the circle that closed around his own adventure. He did not know exactly why, but this seemed to him like a good sign. And it was a good mission: a collection of graphic evidence would be of greater value in the final accounting against Nazism than all the chatter of the camp conspirators.

Big, soft snowflakes were coming down, like feathers from a torn pillow. Emili, sitting at his worktable by the window, was keeping himself busy retouching the photograph of an SS officer in a Napoleonic pose. The presence of the *Kommandoführer* made it impossible for him to do any work on the collection with which he'd been entrusted. It was unusual for him to still be there so late. Abandoning himself to the sweet sensation of not being rushed, able to let the time slip by secure in the knowledge that the future could only bring change for the better, Emili thought back to that corner of the clothing warehouse where he'd once worked on pornographic drawings for the SS head of the *Kommando*. At that time his view had consisted of the green lawn and the wall of the opposite barracks; now it was of an open horizon beyond the tiers of forest-clad ranges. He had a strong sensation of déjà vu, of things coming around again within him or all around him. Perhaps this too was a kind of pornography: retouching a photograph of an SS officer striking an arrogant pose.

The *Kommandoführer* was speaking. Emili could only understand some of the words, but enough to make sense of what he was saying.

> —Yes, the work is coming to an end for us —the man said—. We've been ordered to destroy the archive. Tell this to no one. Do you understand? To destroy the archive!

Emili feigned indifference. The SS's insistence that he understand this secret directive wasn't normal.

> —I'm in no rush —said the SS—. The slowness with which I intend to proceed will not, I think, be such a bad thing for you. Since it is you yourself who will carry out the destruction, I suggest that you begin thinking about how you will approach it.

The draughtsman looked at him in astonishment.

> —I'm going to tell you the truth. I'm in the SS in just the same way that I might have been in the Infantry or the Paratroopers. Don't believe for a moment that everyone who wears an SS uniform is a Nazi!

His story was long and a little difficult to believe. According to its chief protagonist, he himself had been able to do more harm to Hitler's regime than all the allies together. Emili was hardly listening. Logically, this complicity of the SS, so feared up to now, should have made him happy: he would be able to finish his work more easily and safely. Nor was it so strange that the man sought some form of extenuating circumstances that would, at the last moment, make a place for him on the side of the victors. The thing that deflated Emili was the sudden diminishment of his role: he felt ridiculous. Destiny's cruel joke had brought him face to face with his own sad mediocrity: his mission was entirely free of danger!

The draughtsman watched, mesmerized, the softly falling snow, and he started to feel that it wasn't actually falling, but swirling randomly up and down. He was just one snowflake more, at the mercy of the wind, insignificant, melting away, lost among thousands and thousands of others. He thought about the years of civil war when ordinary political rivals became mortal enemies, when he, a pacifist by nature, also took up arms to add to the carnage, although without much enthusiasm. And afterwards in France, where the hunger and the lice in the refugee camp had propelled him into the "Work Company" only to be captured by the Germans a few months later with the collapse of the French army. Still later, in the prisoner-of-war camp, he hadn't had the courage to escape like some of his companions had done.[49] And now, finally, in this Nazi concentration camp, where thousands of unfortunates, as removed as he was from the course of events, were dying in the most horrifying ways. He couldn't come up with any justification for his life. Why? "Who am I?" he asked himself. "Why am I alive?" Once free, he would find himself in the same world from which the civil war had torn him nine years before, and he would be just as vulnerable and naked. All the horrors he had witnessed, the suffering that had toughened his skin and aged his spirit, were they all for nothing? Was it all meaningless?

The *Kommandoführer* got up and got ready to leave:

—If you have to put something together, you can do it in front of me. Don't waste time. There's no need to fear me. I'm on your side.

When Emili left his work later on he came upon three men lined up facing the wall just inside the entrance of the camp, their heads uncovered in the still falling snow. Manuel, whom he met by chance crossing the roll call square, started to give him the latest news picked up on the foreign radio stations. Emili interrupted him to ask about the three men being punished.

—Two of them stole some dog food —the clerk replied—. The other one, I'm not sure. It seems he's a Polish priest who said mass in secret with some of his compatriots. Complete nonsense.

Thinking about it later on, Emili came to realize that there were two worlds there, intermingled, but without contact. For the two starving men who had broken into the dog food, freedom had a concrete meaning: to satisfy hunger. The priest, on the contrary, had found his freedom in the restoration of his right to celebrate a mass. A material world and a spiritual world. Emili hadn't wanted to belong to either. He had pretended to find his balance in a kind of resilience that was far beyond him. "Snowflakes don't pretend anything," he thought; and he agonized over having walked such a long and painful road only to find himself a failure.

August had left for a new *Kommando* with three hundred fifty men. It was a camp that had been set up a couple of years earlier on the Linz–Salzburg railway line. Just then it consisted of some five hundred prisoners of various nationalities, and was run by German common criminals and organized along the same lines as the *Casa Gran.* It was said that the camp population had turned over completely five or six times. Despite their being a group apart, totally autonomous, the Spaniards had not been unaffected by the move. Their bodies, up till then relatively well preserved, had quickly become emaciated as hunger returned to wreak its havoc. Veterans as they were, though, they were not going to resign themselves to death from hunger in these last days of the adventure. Soon an action was started against the supply depots, and it was skill as a thief that determined the division of classes: on one hand, those who stole and were provided with everything; on the other, those who were nervous or careful and had nothing. After the living conditions in the *Casa Gran,* the current inequality created envy, resentment, disputes, out-and-out hatred, all channelled soon enough into political confrontations, which is where differences among Spaniards generally surface. Each group tried to gain control, blaming the others for their privations. For some, the fault lay with the communists, who placed proselytizing above the interests of the people in general; for others, August was the only one responsible, because of his tendentiousness and favouritism.

To counteract the campaign that had been launched against him in the *Casa Gran,* and suffocated by the climate of conciliation that reigned in the new *Kommando,* August had had to accept that Castro and the doctor, leaders of the rival group, would be joining him in a "triumvirate" in charge of the Spanish group. In reality, he was planning to get rid of them as soon as circumstances allowed, that is to say, once the strong opposition he intended to bring to bear against the German prisoners running the *Kommando* won back the goodwill of his men as well as that of the SS Command. But times were different now and so were the men. When August made his move, he found no supporters, only hostility and indifference. So he too lost interest in things, or at least pretended to, thinking that a little more time and the pervasive discontent would make the "strong hand" he'd imposed before, with so much success, once again desirable.

The other two "triumvirs," seeing him lose heart, wanted to finish him off. Since it was only a few days until Christmas, they hit on the idea of organizing a celebratory meal that would bring all the Spaniards together at the same table. "To anticipate victory and to forget our differences," was to be the order of the day. They asked for August's authorization and collaboration; however, seeing the trap, he replied:

—Go ahead and organize it if you like; I won't stand in your way.

The situation was awkward. If he attended, he would be ridiculed for seconding the initiative of his communist rivals, he who had never marched to the beat of anyone else's drum; if he did not, it would be seen as a rejection of "harmony and brotherhood among compatriots."

When the day of the celebration arrived, the communists performed the miracle of converting the barracks' wide passageway into a dining hall for four hundred men. They worked hard, begged more; the organization had been perfect. They managed to get hold of some cigarettes and underwear to raffle, they improvised an "orchestra" with a couple of guitars, an accordion, and a clarinet, and they even managed to have a few "guests of honour" in the persons of some of the camp's higher-ups: some SS and German criminals.

Just as things were about to begin, the communists went to August and invited him to preside over the head table. He offered this diplomatic excuse: "I'm not feeling well." The dinner went ahead all the same. They served up baked potatoes with a quarter litre of thick gruel each; for dessert, they had an apple and a biscuit. While some were finding that, on thinking about it, they'd finished up hungrier than on other days, the head table was delivering a flood of inflammatory speeches in support of a union among Spaniards. The Germans clapped enthusiastically without knowing why. The musicians played a "pasodoble," those who knew how to sing tried to prove it, and by the end everyone felt that the festivities had been first-rate. The organizers, above all, were delighted: August's absence had been an unforgivable rebuke to those in attendance, and whatever prestige he'd had left was gone.

The real flourish came the next day during roll call when August, in front of the entire camp in formation, tendered his resignation as Spanish leader.

—Have you lost your mind? —the officer asked him, stunned.
—The Spaniards are not satisfied with me and they won't obey me. Just to get them formed up this afternoon took me half an hour of hard labour and yelling. I don't have the means to impose my authority.

To the astonished objections of the SS, August added, as though measuring his words:

—There is somebody who can do the job better than I can.

And so Castro found himself leader of the Spaniards. He didn't know German and didn't have any sense of how to deal with the SS. As a good soldier, he obeyed orders and he gave them. However, the flexibility and the charisma that had been key to August's success were qualities that Castro lacked. With the men undisciplined, and hungry, and cocky under Hans Gupper's protection, on the one hand, and excited by the proximity of the Russian army, on the other, the new leader's every effort to re-establish a brotherhood of Spaniards ended in failure. The raids on the potato stores became scandalous, and the SS had to intervene and impose heavy sanctions.

August came out of it very well. From his new position as secretary to the Commandant—a more important post than his last—he could do and undo things as he pleased, and he couldn't stop laughing at the disasters brought on by his successor's attempts at management. The communists accused him of interfering secretly with Castro's authority, but August only laughed some more.

Meanwhile, with the completion of the urgent work that had brought the Spaniards there in the first place, the order came for a reduction in personnel; a hundred men were to be pulled out of the *Kommando* and transferred elsewhere. August's great moment had arrived: after a few days, the hundred most prominent communists in the camp were put on trucks.

—You'll pay for this! —Castro threatened from the back of one of them.

August smiled and shrugged his shoulders.

—Maybe they thought I was kidding —he said afterwards, walking with a few friends—. For three years they've made my life unbearable. Enough is enough! If I'm to be murdered in the end, I want at least to spend these last days with a bit of quiet. You'll see how all the conflicts will evaporate from now on.

And external events helped prove him right. The Russians reached Vienna, the Anglo-Americans pushed into German territory. These military blows had repercussions in the up until then undisturbed region where the *Kommando* was located. Rail lines and roads were clogged with the tragedy of civilian evacuation. Allied aircraft bombed the transportation and communication hubs relentlessly. Lines of trucks, wagons, bicycles, carts of all kinds—even baby carriages—loaded with furniture, boxes, and bundles, dragged by women, old people, children, the sick and war wounded, spent day on day going just a few kilometres. The more clearly marked these "Aryans" were with signs of hunger, fatigue, and terror, the more the spectacle lifted the prisoners' hearts. Their captivity was coming to an end; liberation would follow close on the heels of the evacuees!

There were also material advantages. All the military provisions threatened by the Soviet advance were being gathered in the zone crossed by the Linz–Salzburg railway: warehouses, stables, all available empty spaces were suddenly filled to bursting with articles of the highest quality. The prisoners had been put to work maintaining these improvised warehouses, and as one can imagine, they were stealing everything they could lay their hands on. Other prisoners were being sent out to rebuild the bombed-out stations, where provision trains packed with food and ripped open by bombs offered up their entrails to their greedy hunger.

Sacks full of provisions were coming into the camp; a horn of plenty poured forth in front of men who had not filled their bellies once in five years. A general obsession with hoarding reserves against possible privations to come found fertile ground in the Divine beneficence of those storerooms stuffed with food and clothing. Jars of *pâté de foie*, pillowcases filled with sugar, slabs of bacon, and paper sacks of soy spilled from straw mattresses everywhere. Everybody had socks, leather snowboots, and woollen undershirts. Some kept heavy military greatcoats against the day they might have to break through the barbed wire. They weren't thinking about politics now; they were most interested in getting a turn in the kitchen and laying hold of the few pots and pans available in the camp. It was only in the post-prandial hours that anyone talked about the progress of the Allied armies, and then it was with the same amiable contentment that might have been the case in any of their café gatherings at home in Barcelona.

The end came. One morning Hitler was presumed dead, and by the middle of the afternoon all work had been suspended because the Americans were only thirty kilometres from the camp. As a security measure, the Commandant arranged a general transfer to a *Kommando* farther behind the lines, and because of the lack of transport they would have to get there on foot.

They were called to form up. Everyone carried whatever he could. Some had mattresses stuffed with food. The general intention was to escape at the first opportunity. The Commandant gave a speech, which August translated:

> —The war might be finished, but you cannot be left here on your own. I have orders to deliver you to a safe location under the protection of the International Red Cross. Here the war may put your lives at risk. I give you my word of honour —and here the men started to grin— that you will not be harmed. Obey orders and do not try to escape. It would be a pity if, in these final hours, the guards had to take harsh measures against you. I don't want you to take a bad impression away with you of the time you've spent in this camp. I believe I've dealt fairly with you and I have appreciated your value as workers. If anyone feels dissatisfied, please speak openly now, as to a comrade. I will try to explain why I've not always been able to act according to my wishes ...

There were bursts of laughter.

August added on his own account that he would be staying behind "because his work was not yet done."

> —What you want is to evaporate, you bastard —said a voice in the crowd.

Night fell on the long column of prisoners withdrawing on foot from a liberation that lay less than thirty kilometres away. August did not stay in the camp. He left just after his comrades, without a trace. His enemies would not have the pleasure of bringing him to account.

It was a shame nobody noticed that spring's awakening. An April in which no one thinks about the magic of the world coming alive once more is an April wasted, in fact, a wasted year. For those in the main camp, consumed by anxiety and by hope, another April meant little. Their spring was of a different order altogether.

One evening after supper, under a clear sky tinged with dusk, Emili and Manuel were strolling through the roll call square. The tension of these final hours showed in their gestures and their voices.

—It's time for the final round up —said Manuel—. Nazism may be defeated, but it won't give in; it will die killing. You know how I sometimes talk with the prisoners arriving from the East; well, I've seen a lot but the things they say still make me tremble. They don't come by train anymore. They come on foot, and they're rare, the ones that can take it. All of them have the shock of what they've seen etched in their faces.[50]

—I don't know which is worse —said Emili—. Have you heard about the "death trains"? A Frenchman told me about them, and while he was talking he had a nervous attack. Out of a hundred fifty men crowded into a railcar made for forty, only twenty survived. All the rest suffocated. The poor wreck spent the last twenty-four hours of the journey unconscious, squeezed in among the corpses.

After a moment, Emili added:

The Germans can't even claim the excuse of eleventh-hour desperation; they've been doing the same thing all along.

Manuel nodded as though he'd reached some final understanding:

—There's not much difference between dying from suffocation in a railcar and dying from exhaustion during a forced march by road. But dying during these final days is maybe even stupider. So many have been evacuated with liberation just four steps away, the roar of the Soviet artillery in their ears ...

—Do you think we'll be evacuated too?

—No. If it's the Americans that make the advance, the Germans won't have us marching out just to meet up with the Soviets, and if the Soviets get here first, I don't think there will be any rearguard left. To be equidistant from both fronts is great luck for us.

—Nothing new, today?

—For us —Manuel replied— there's only one piece of news that's important; we'll know all about it without anybody having to tell us.

—They say Munich might have fallen.

—It doesn't matter! If it hasn't fallen yet, it will soon enough.

In general, all conversations were reduced to questions that had no answers and replies that answered no questions. Memories of better times, anecdotes from the day at hand, plans for the future, the usual topics of conversation between prisoners, were all set aside as colourless and dull. They sought out war news the way addicts seek the drug that will tranquilize them, and they felt unsatisfied if the dose was insufficient. Once heard, the news was already "old news" and immediately lost any value in the rush to know the latest.

There were some exceptions: those who were in the last stages of organic decay. They thought only of the present moment, a present without any news at all and that adhered only to the materiality of their suffering. The war, which was the beginning and the end of that suffering, was something remote for them, of no interest. Theirs was an indifference both pathetic and majestic, as though they shared among them an esoteric secret of far greater importance than war and peace.

Emili spoke of the contrast between this indifference found in the most unfortunate and the agitation of the rest:

—It's as if the proximity of death inoculates them with a sort of elevated disregard.

—It's their only defence —said Manuel.

Emili thought for a moment:

—I feel absent too, sometimes. I don't know if it's the same for you, but I often have the sensation that nothing we hear about the war is true. It's difficult to explain. There's something in me that doesn't let me see beyond a bizarre administrative continuation of the camp, as if the only thing that could possibly interest me is the idea of the camp functioning normally, that all the forms and papers be dealt with and filed, that the supply of provisions, good or bad, not fail, that the work carry on, that the SS continue their abuses and murders as if nothing has happened.

—Sheaves of compromising documents are being destroyed every day —said Manuel, who hadn't been following Emili's line of thinking—. There's also the worry about the SS when they're overwhelmed …

—What is about to happen is of such magnitude that we're only going to be able to grasp it with real effort. What I mean is that those who can't make the mental effort are going to be dragged along like clouds on a windy day, taking on the shapes the wind chooses …

—The routine has tainted you —said Manuel, who definitely hadn't been following him—. That day will call for fighting and … that's it.

After a pause he added:

—I haven't told you about the talk I had the other day with Hans Gupper, have I? He came into the office and spent about an hour shuffling papers. When he got tired of that, he sat down across from me at my work table. He lit a cigarette and then offered me one. I was pretending to work. "Yes" —he said—. "It's obviously hard for you to hide your satisfaction. You know there is no point to this work. You keep at it just to avoid looking at me." I wanted to protest. Hans Gupper is an executioner like the rest of them, maybe the worst, but I felt like I should try to draw him out. Completely idiotic! But he didn't give me a chance; he did it all by himself: "No, Spaniard, no" —he carried on, little by little—. "There's no need now to hide your feelings. I know that all of these years in the camp haven't changed you and that you are just as you were before, only tougher." He'd talked to me lots of times about things related to work, always in his dry, cutting tone of voice. That day, if he hadn't recounted all these details from his family life that made him seem more human, I'd have thought that the defeat had completely unhinged him. He sat in silence for a moment; then he crushed his cigarette in the ashtray and got up wearily. "You're right to be happy" —he said in a dark voice—. "For you, life is about to begin." And from the way he looked at me, I understood what he was leaving out …

—It's a bit grotesque —said the draughtsman—. The Jews he slaughtered with an axe didn't particularly move him …

—You're right, but Hans Gupper is important as a type. Monsters make up part of humanity too, and …

—I see I'm not the only one who's been tainted by the routine.

Any insignificant incident, a phrase spoken or an attitude struck by an SS, a word misunderstood, any little thing was capable of arousing veritable waves of panic in this time of high anxiety. Equilibrium hung by a thread, and the sounding of an alarm, well founded or not, could plunge the camp into a catastrophic situation, into a suicidal revolt, for instance.

A few words uttered by Hans Gupper that morning, when they spread through the camp, were just such a jolt to the system.

Passing through the roll call square, Hans Gupper had apparently asked a Spaniard:

—Are you a communist?
—No, sir.

And the officer had smiled, mockingly.

—If you are not a communist, then it only follows that you would want to fight them, yes?

The Spaniard pretended not to understand.

—If you're ready to wear the German uniform, tomorrow you are a free man.

The alarm provoked by these words grew even greater an hour later when the proposal became public. There were three nationalities that merited the trust of the SS: German, Polish, and Spanish. The volunteers were to present themselves that evening at the door to the office.

Many took the invitation as a joke, while others were offended by it; however, the leaders of the Spanish political groups, in seeing that a general abstention was not as guaranteed as it needed to be, decided to act jointly and called for a meeting of representatives in the dining room of Block 13, right after lunch.

Taking all due precautions, a dozen men gathered to make "important decisions." Emili had been invited as an "independent." He didn't want to miss a show that was bound to be highly entertaining.

No one but those convened stayed in the dining room. The draughtsman smiled to look at them, all of them just the same. Sunshine poured in through the windows. It all passed for nothing more than an after-lunch chat.

Manuel had said: "Even if the meeting gets us nowhere, it's always worthwhile having an exchange of opinions." "Worthwhile" doubtless meant having the opportunity to make speeches. Manuel, as chair, set out the reason for the gathering:

—There is a risk that some Spaniards will volunteer. We cannot come to the aid of our enemies, even if it means getting free of the camp. We are pariahs, we have nothing, but we will hold on to the one thing that nobody can take from us: our dignity!

"Lawyer's rhetoric," Emili thought, amused.

—Let's imagine for a moment what would happen if Hans Gupper, confronted by our total abstention, asked us one by one.

"By tomorrow everybody would be in the SS," the draughtsman laughed to himself.

—What would we say then? How would we answer? We know that the question has been posed to two of the external *Kommandos*. Would it be unusual for the Germans to turn to coercion? You'll tell me that their proposal is absurd, that we will never fight for those who have murdered thousands of our friends …

"This is complicated" —thought Emili—. "Now is when they remember that the SS are still in charge. Nothing's going to get done!"

—To say that we're not communists would be to say that we're ready to wear the German uniform. To say that we *are* exposes us to immediate reprisals …

When Manuel had finished spouting, Rubio got up. He was a terrible orator: an oily voice, no sense of structure or form, a household manner. He maintained that, in the case of individual coercion, it would be necessary to accept the SS proposal.

—If they give us weapons —the barber said icily—, we can always use them against the SS.

The declaration was greeted with an explosion of protests.

—Never! —yelled a syndicalist—. I'm not going to sully myself with the green of our executioners!
—When the Russians take us prisoner —said another—, you're going to explain to them why we're all dressed up as Germans?

None but Spaniards could make so much noise among so few. Manuel couldn't impose order. Rubio, always so cool and measured, was making himself hoarse in his own defence. His voice was getting strident.

—You syndicalists, who love direct action so much, are you afraid of being left on your own? Maybe you need assistants to shoot your weapons for you?

—Let's not start bickering like fishwives —shouted Manuel, finally managing to make himself heard—. Rubio's solution is as worthy of consideration as any other. Myself, I don't agree with it. Even if it's for tactical reasons ...

—We have to be realistic —interrupted the barber.

—We have to be worthy —corrected Manuel—. To set out the alternative, I, who am not a communist, propose that all of us, absolutely all of us, answer that yes, we are communists, that we be ready to set aside our differences for what's essential.

—That's stupid. Suicide.

—It's just what the SS want —added Rubio, for his part—. It does their work for them.

—Over my dead body will I put on a German uniform —protested an anarchist—, but I'm not going to say that I am a communist either. I'd die of shame!

The bickering began all over again. It was like a burlesque: syndicalists ready to die rather than say they were communists, communists pretending to be enemies of communism ...

—Between dying in the gas chamber like a coward and dying with a weapon in my hands, I've made my choice —said the barber—. I don't want to surrender so easily.

—Quiet, quiet! —pleaded Manuel.

—When are you going to have the courage to say what you are? —asked a Syndicalist.

—And why are all of you pretending to be what you're not? —Rubio answered back.

Emili stood up to speak. The disputants looked at him with hostility. What could this one want, who belonged to neither side? The draughtsman took advantage of the momentary attention that he'd been ceded:

—I only wanted to ask those in the know, if, given a desperate situation, a revolt in our own defence might succeed. I don't want to wear an SS uniform, but I don't think dying like rabbits is the only alternative. I understand that the "International Committee" has foreseen many eventualities, and I ask if it has also foreseen this one. If this is the case, we don't need to be fighting among ourselves.

—This is precisely what I wanted to clarify —said Manuel—, but nobody's let me.

—Our problem now doesn't affect the other nationalities —interrupted Rubio—. The Russians, the Czechs, the French, nothing has been said to them. We can't drag the whole camp into an act of desperation. The moment for revolt is not yet upon us. The fronts are still too far away and the sacrifice would be pointless.

—I will never say I'm a communist —yelled the anarchist, not backing down.

Manuel wanted them to see that all this was unimportant, that communists and anarchists, according to the Nazis, were all the same.

—For five years now your file has said *Rote Spanier*.

The meeting continued more calmly than it had begun. The possibilities for carrying out a violent action were carefully reviewed, and all agreed that nobody would respond to the call from the camp authority. A plan of attack on the armoury was discussed down to the smallest details, and in the end they decided, pending the results of their non-compliance with the call-up, that they'd put the whole matter before the International Committee.

—Hans Gupper's coming! —one of the men posted at the door called out.

The meeting dissolved quickly, and in an instant, the dining room took on its habitual aspect. The brooms, retrieved from their nook, obediently swept the floorboards, the dusters caressed the tables and the cupboards.

When the hour came for volunteers to present themselves, only a few of the German common criminals showed up, in a bid to avoid probable retaliation within the camp, and some Poles as well, in a sudden fit of Russophobia. As for Spaniards, none.

Hans Gupper understood that times had changed and that, in these final hours, it was probably better not to rely too much on volunteers obtained by force. And nothing else happened.

CHAPTER XVII

For the first time in the life of the camp, the bell failed to sound its reveille. The men were roused from sleep only by the increasing din made by those already awake around them. Nobody mentioned going to work; nobody had a thought for the black concoction usually served for breakfast. Everything they said was sensational! Everything had been transfigured by this change that, no matter how long anticipated, still felt like winning the lottery. The colours of things, the morning light, the faces of friends and of enemies, everything was new. And like a piece of ice next to a bonfire, discipline melted away. They came and went as they pleased, those who had tobacco smoked in bed or right under the nose of the *Blockälteste*, the *kapos* tried to suck up to the very people they would have been beating to a pulp just twenty-four hours earlier, and the SS had become invisible. The only thing left of the women in the brothel was a trace of their perfume and of last-minute confusion: they'd escaped.

The German and Polish anti-communist "volunteers," equipped as *Volksturm* (people's militia) and armed like real soldiers, had left before dawn. King Kong was one of the eleventh-hour volunteers, although it was hard to believe that he'd get very far with his enormous belly.

With the changing of the guard, regular soldiers from the auxiliary service had been substituted for the SS. From their turrets and towers, these new sentries—mostly not so young—chatted away with the prisoners snooping around the barbed wire.

—The Americans will be here soon —they said, trying to be friendly—. It's only a question of hours now. You can rest easy with us. When they get here we'll put down our arms and … head for home! Like you.

For any one of those guards, a prisoner's friendship was worth as much as a government minister's might normally be.[51]

The International Committee had been meeting all night; Emili had had to stay up as well since he'd been put in charge of night-time security for his Block. He hadn't slept more than half an hour when one of Rubio's friends unceremoniously shook him awake:

—Get up! —he told him— and get over to Block 3. You'll find Rubio in the washroom;[52] he wants to see you right now.

The washroom of Block 3 was, at that moment, the Spanish headquarters. The draughtsman wasn't allowed in until he was announced by a lookout at the door. The barber and Manuel were surrounded by some fifteen Spaniards.

—We are almost certain —said Rubio— that today is our last day of captivity. Early this morning, German radio gave the official announcement of Hitler's death. The hour has come, then, to brace ourselves for whatever happens next.

All in attendance, stirred by the news, nodded their heads in agreement.

—The International Committee is entrusting you with a mission more dangerous than any thus far. Manuel, who has obtained the instructions, will set out your duties for you. Those of you who consider yourselves my friends, I beg you not to shirk your responsibilities now.

He went on to explain that Hans Gupper had ordered that the entire camp form up at ten o'clock, in less than an hour's time.

—We don't know what his intentions are —he added—, but don't count too much on the regular army soldiers having replaced the SS: they are still under Gupper's orders and they'll do what he tells them to. And there are still many SS in the exterior annexes. There's no risk of an evacuation. The Americans are closer than the Russians and it's absurd to think we could be evacuated to the East. Why gather everyone together, then? It's not the time for a roll call. No matter what, we've got to be alert: these people, they could get carried away with some sort of last desperate act. We need to anticipate them. Here are the instructions: each nationality is to mount a separate shock troop with a designated mission. Our troop will be made up of us here, and our objective is to attack the main entrance to the camp. Each of you is to choose two men in whom you have complete confidence and go to Block 2, which is closest to the main gate. We have two pistols. If we have to shoot them, it will be at Hans Gupper, and the moment you hear the first shot, get to the gate as quickly as possible, open it any way you can, and head directly over to the armoury. I'll go with you with my gun. It's not much, I know, but a pistol is still better than fingernails …

An hour later when the bell rang for forming up in the roll call square, the atmosphere in the camp was electric. The committee's agitation and the preparations for the mutiny had infected the whole camp with that fever that precedes moments of great heroism. Everybody knew that with any German move to exterminate the prisoners wholesale, the call for an all-out revolt would be given. There was talk of the machine guns at the tops of the sentry towers, of an SS company formed up and awaiting orders, of the gas chamber prepared some days before, of the committee's cache of hand grenades …

The prisoners formed up as usual. Each Block had its *Blockälteste;* those who had been incorporated to the *Volksturm* had been replaced by substitutes, all of them German common criminals who had had a sudden change of heart and become the most zealous collaborators with the committee. The shock troops in place and ready to carry out their orders, discipline was at that moment a most valuable weapon that had slipped from the hands of the SS into those of the prisoners. To all appearances, nothing was going on.

Hans Gupper made his entrance followed by four sergeants of the *Kommandantur*. King Kong's replacement asked him if it was necessary to take roll call. He replied with a gesture, no, and immediately, in a flat, controlled voice and with a visible effort to contain himself, began to speak to the crowd about the camp's delicate situation in relation to the fronts and the possibility of making it a centre of resistance against the enemy advance.

—It is my duty to look out for your safety —he added—, and it is to spare you the risks posed by bombing that I propose that you let us direct you, in an orderly manner, into the underground factories of the quarry.

The president of the International Committee, the infirmary orderly Frantisek, stood in the front row of Block 2. He stepped forward and asked permission to speak on behalf of the prisoners. Hans Gupper stared at him fixedly for a moment before granting him permission. One could see from his expression, and from the way he gestured with his hands, the disgust he felt for this improvised democracy the prisoners evidently felt was their right.

—Speak —he said dryly.

—What you have just told us, is it an order or a suggestion? —the Czech asked evenly, but firmly.

—It is a suggestion, and I make it in your own best interests. You are free to decide and I have no intention of forcing you. If you are not all in agreement, I will direct that those wishing to be transferred to the underground shelter will be, regardless of those who prefer to stay. Talk to your comrades and let them decide.

The Czech turned to face the impatient multitude. He explained Hans Gupper's proposal and judged it an unnecessary precaution.

—Close at hand as the American troops are —he added—, we don't believe they are going to meet the kind of resistance that the *Obersturmführer* is suggesting. It's been three days now since we've seen an American plane. The International Committee (here Hans Gupper looked at him with curiosity) is here to ensure the safety of the internees and advises against leaving the camp when there is no need to do so.

—The shelter is mined —someone yelled.

—It's a trap —someone else asserted.

—We're not moving!

—The Americans are our friends! They're not going to bomb us!

The shouting was getting out of hand, and Hans Gupper smiled disdainfully, obviously nervous. The Czech finally managed to impose silence.

—Say whether you want to go to the shelter or not.

The square resounded with a unanimous "No!"

—Anyone who wants to go, raise your hand.

He repeated the question in Russian and in French. No hands went up. Hans Gupper shrugged his shoulders and, without relinquishing his contemptuous smile, said that in the event that something unpleasant happened as a consequence of military action, he would not be held responsible. He added that he was asking for calm, and he gave his assurances that for his part, no repressive measures would be taken as long as order was maintained.

The Czech replied that an organization already existed that was responsible for order and discipline, and that it could guarantee calm within the camp as long as no actions were taken that compromised the prisoners' personal safety. He asked that the food ration be increased, especially in the quarantine camps, where the situation was desperate.

The German affirmed that these orders had already been given, and recommended prudence in regard to the administration of the food since the warehouses were not all that full and the American troops might take longer than expected.

That afternoon, Emili didn't eat a thing. It was the second day that he'd forsaken his lunch and subsisted on just the morsel of black bread that was distributed at night. The black market had suffered in the face of a decisive outcome, and anyone who had anything at all was holding on to it against tougher times. Emili didn't have access to anything other than the inedible daily ration of soup. But he wasn't hungry anyway. External events, the great hopes of those moments, were far more important than the gnawing in his stomach.

When, after collecting his soup, Emili went to the door of the Block intending to give it to anybody who wanted it, he found a desperate crowd fighting savagely for that charity. He emptied his portion into the first receptacle held out to him, and, on returning to the barracks, wondered about the point at which hunger becomes all-consuming. It was a soup of rotten potatoes, peel and all, boiled with nettles that had been picked near the camp. That they would fight so fiercely for just one more serving and could not wait those few days, maybe just those few hours needed to win their freedom, could only be explained by the damage done to their ability to reason. Those few hours, the last, seemed harder to endure than all the years before. There was a heightening of the senses and the emotions; hunger became bulimia, fear of not making it to the Final Hour became outright panic. It was the last push of the runner a few metres from the finish, the final wager that makes up for all the rest. The instinct for self-preservation was out of control now and their behaviour was human only in what humans share with beasts.

Emili took a turn through the camp. At the doors of all the Blocks, and even inside some of them, crowded throngs as never seen before. With the opening of the quarantine camps, the multitudes who had been locked inside were taking their first steps towards freedom. They were free, at least, to walk around with an aluminium bowl in their hands, knees shaking, eyes popping out of their sockets from hunger and covetousness;

they were free to cluster around the entrances of the Camp 1 barracks where they might manage to get the dregs of some putrid soup, leftovers that nobody else wanted.

Emili arrived at the roll call square. He was looking for some space and fresh air. He sat down on the stoop of the warehouse next to the kitchen. He wanted solitude; he felt tired and disinterested in everything going on around him. Others were running here and there searching for food or, without moving from the fug of the barracks, discussed the themes proper to those hours. Nobody else was sitting on the stone steps. Only him. He was trying to make himself understand. None of the things that were stirring his companions, politics or the thirst for revenge, signified real freedom. From the solitude of his little lookout, he had a presentiment of the change that one day, who knows, might reveal the fullness of understanding he needed now: to understand! But, to understand what?

He was getting cold and stood up. He took a deep breath. The crisp, clear air made the chimneys of the crematorium stand out more sharply. The stink of burnt wool was gone. That was the truest sign of freedom.

Emili crossed the square slowly; he stopped in front of the office where the committee had kept its headquarters since coming out of hiding. Many people were coming and going. The draughtsman wondered what they were doing now that the safety of the camp seemed beyond doubt. A window opened and he heard Manuel's voice:

—Why don't you come inside?
—You're very busy. I don't want to get in the way.
—No, no. We've got a job for you.

Coming up with an excuse had been too complicated, and so for some time now he had been busy painting an inscription in English on a white sheet: "Welcome to our Liberators!"[53] He was surrounded by curious onlookers, and they were distracting him with their chatter. In the small room next door, the committee was holding a non-stop meeting.

Emili smiled to think that they could go on and on for so many hours in a row. They prattled away, first one camp leader and then another, and had spent the whole night at the table; the lack of sleep had made them feel worthy of the moment. Some were hanging around, just out of curiosity, others were hoping for "missions" that would bring them prestige. Nor was there any shortage of opportunists, or of the fatuous, or of those who needed to be pardoned for one thing or another. Had some real danger arisen at that moment, most of them would have disappeared as if by magic. Emili knew them well: those who gave their canteen tokens to the *kapos* in order to avoid work; others who condoned, with an abject smile, the cruelties the Germans visited on the Jews or the Russians; the informers; the ones who traded with the food of others; those who had sold a brother for a plate of turnips. Now they were tripping over themselves to be useful, to make themselves visible, pretending to be self-sacrificing, now, when it cost them nothing. Ernest was there too, in one of those groups.

Now Frantisek came in. He was in a rush, pushing his way through the crowd. His closed expression made it clear that he had important news. Silence fell a few minutes later when another member of the committee came out and stated loudly in German:

—The only enemy we had to fear can no longer do us any harm. Hans Gupper, along with his wife and sons, committed suicide about an hour ago.

The murmuring silenced him for a moment, and then he continued:

—All the SS staff have fled the camp and given over command to an army sergeant. Spread the news and advise everyone to stay calm. Our safety is now almost assured. All that's left is to wait for the American forces. Long live liberty!

They garlanded the camp's pagoda gates with fir boughs and the flags of all the Allies, presided over by the Stars and Stripes of the United States. They draped welcome banners all around the roll call square to greet the victorious armies. Emili and everyone else who knew how to handle a paintbrush had spent the whole night painting banners, banners, and then more banners.

From first thing in the morning, the square was full of people awaiting the arrival of the motorized units of the vanguard. Rumour had it that the liberators were not meeting any resistance at all and that they might well reach the camp by mid-morning. The cooks too had worked valiantly through the night, so the breakfast soup was plentiful and thick and the prisoners grew noisy with excitement. The group from the quarantine camp, their stomachs full for the first time in a long time, began to take an interest in the unique spectacle being played out around them. The appearance of the camp was sufficiently unusual that the certainty that change was coming made itself felt even in those most numbed by physiological misery.

But the hours of that clear morning in May were passing by and no one had yet come. The beneficial effects of the thick morning soup faded and, little by little, lunch, which also promised to be extraordinary, began to gain more importance than the arrival of the Americans. The crowd gradually dissolved, each person setting off for his respective Block to watch out for the soup pots, and it is possible that some even started to think they had been duped by the story of the liberation. Very few were still left at the pagoda gates when the kitchen thermoses came out at noon.

Emili ate with appetite, but he hadn't yet finished his bowl of gruel when he heard people shouting and saw them running towards the camp entrance. He rushed out. The multitude poured from every corner of the camp, all following the same route. All the languages seemed to have been fused into a single and universal one, such was the ease with which everyone understood:

—They're here! The Americans! They're coming in! We're free! The tanks!

Those who were not strong enough to walk dragged themselves along. Running, many lost their wooden clogs. Others were throwing their striped caps into the air or ripping the numbers from the fronts of their jackets.

When the draughtsman got near the gate it was impossible to turn back. Caught in the crowd that was thrown against it, shaken by this human avalanche, he felt himself dragged along as though by a torrent. He couldn't see anything; neither could the others, and they stood on their toes and scrambled up onto the shoulders of their neighbours. The outcry was deafening.

—Please … —he protested to somebody who was using him as an anchor.

Since he could see only the backs of heads in front of him, he turned to look behind. The spectacle was worth it. Crowds of prisoners were tumbling down the gentle slope from the square. Some who couldn't move quickly enough were being pushed aside by the others, and if they fell, they got right back up without seeming to have noticed. Nothing was more important than those gates, now open and never to be closed again. And the roaring tanks that laboured up the hill. And the marvellous upwelling of thousands and thousands of the condemned, who pressed forward to witness the entrance of the first tank, to receive this final reprieve. Some volunteers linked arms, trying desperately to contain the cresting human wave and preserve a path, however narrow, through which the victorious tanks could pass. The noise of the engines grew more distinct, and Emili, peering between the heads of the men in front of him, saw the members of the committee climb on top of the first tank and fly flags from the barrel of the cannon, like a steel finger pointing to the sky. They hugged the soldiers, whose khaki uniforms and oversized helmets were covered with dust, and they opened their mouths wide with shouts and cheers that nobody could hear.

The clamour of the crowd grew louder still when the tank passed through the pagoda gate:

—Hurrah, hurrah! —cried out some voices, hoarse and weak, near Emili.

The cry spread like the first word of a new language, of the universal language that would be needed in a world of peace:

—Hurrah, hurrah!

It was the cry of those reborn.

The tank advanced with some difficulty through a crowd that seemed to open before it like living flesh under the blade of a scalpel. Its white, five-pointed star stood out against the khaki green. Only the metallic shriek of the tank tracks could be heard through the uproar. There was joy beyond hysteria.

Behind the first tank came another, and then two more. After these, a jeep with officers. All had passed through the gate that for five years had admitted only the condemned and their executioners. The draughtsman managed to reach the sidewalk, where the going was easier. The spectacle was delirious. The Slavs were kissing one another over and over again, the Latins were yelling, jumping up and down, and raising their arms. Some Yugoslavs had unfurled their flag and climbed on top of a tank, where one of them was improvising a speech, making his powerful voice heard; everyone applauded whether they understood him or not. The American soldiers smiled constantly, just like in the ads, and looked with astonishment at the scene before them.

—They're cold, these Americans —Emili said to an acquaintance.

—What do you want them to do, dance?

—Hurrah, hurrah! —yelled thousands of hoarse voices.

The Yugoslavs had finished with their oratory and now were singing hymns in chorus. Some of the curious examined the tanks and equipment. The sober dress of the Americans, somewhat casual, pistols strapped on cowboy-style, helmets tipped back, all of this made an extraordinary impression on eyes so used to the rigidity of the German uniform. The jeep attracted a good deal of attention with its cobbled-together look, the antenna dangling like a fishing rod, and the headphones the drivers wore.

—It looks like a Ford from a slapstick movie.

A thirteen-year-old prisoner was being introduced to the soldiers. They kissed him and gave him chocolate while the people shouted themselves hoarse with more hurrahs. Another prisoner had the idea of getting an autograph from one of the soldiers. The example was taken up, and soon everybody was searching for bits of paper to be signed. For a long half hour, the Americans did nothing but sign little pieces of paper, and they were starting to look like they'd had enough when a bloody incident gave them an excuse to be done with it.

Emili was having a look at those war machines as well, and the soldiers who ran them, when he heard screams of rage behind him. An arm shot past his ear, and when he turned to look he saw the hand of that arm grasping the throat of a man who was waiting his turn for an autograph. He just had time to see the green triangle stitched to the man's chest before he had to step back because of the tumult around him. The German had lost his cap to the first punch, and now the blows rained down on his face. An American got down from the tank and tried to intervene. The aggressors yelled their explanations in Russian, without for a moment letting up on the beating. The soldier asked for an interpreter. Somebody who could string together a few words of English managed to explain that they were dealing here with the very worst kind and that he deserved everything he got. The American opted to get back in his tank and let it go. One of the prisoners went to get a huge rock, and between all of them they crushed the man's skull and killed him.

Emili asked one of the Russians who the lynched man was.

—Assistant to the quarry *kapo* —he replied in German—. A murderer. Many Russians and many Jews. We do not forget.

The officer in charge of the American patrol came back from a brief tour of the camp accompanied by some members of the International Committee. He'd had a look at the "Russian camp," the infirmary, and the crematorium. A bit pale, he climbed back into the jeep while the tanks started up their engines. They turned around to go. Then a German soldier, about fifty years old, protected by a group of prisoners, came up to surrender his rifle to the victorious forces. That must have been the only such case, as all the camp sentries had slipped away when the tanks came in. The committee interpreter confirmed that the man was just a hapless recruit. The American officer, smiling, extended his hand and the men around them started clapping. The German, confused and emotional, started hugging all the prisoners within reach.

The Yugoslavs never tired of singing their revolutionary hymns; the Poles sang religious ones; the Spaniards pretended that nothing could phase them and that this wasn't anything compared to their Civil War; the French got emotional and made speeches; the Italians were exclaiming "*Porca miseria!*"; and the Russians hunted down their assassins of the day before. The few Jews lucky enough to have made it through to the end, hunched over and dragging their feet, rubbed their hands together and took everything in, sharp-eyed, saying not a word.[54]

The tanks with their white stars abandoned the camp, and the great doors stayed open. Many ex-prisoners followed them along the road and the square began to empty; and, just as when the water of a stream diminishes and the riverbed is revealed, so appeared five horribly mutilated corpses, each in its respective pool of blood. Nobody looked at them.

Just to rest a little. Somebody has taken the blankets from his bed, so Emili lies on top of the sack of straw. When the fatigue is so extreme, he needs silence more than ever to sleep. His companions in the barracks are singing, yelling, bickering, and breaking up the cupboards to feed the stove. The chaos is universal. When the sentries abandoned their watchtowers with the arrival of the tanks, a mob of prisoners cut the barbed wire and raided the warehouses in the exterior precinct. While the others were yelling their "hurrahs," the looters were providing themselves with food, clothing, and weapons. A drunken Russian has started shooting salvos from a rifle, and the loud reports have awakened in the mob an explosive sense of their new freedom. His example has found imitators, and even the swift intervention of the committee hasn't been able to prevent disaster. Blood has been spilled. There is shooting everywhere: from those who find the noise entertaining, from those busy exterminating imaginary enemies in a haze of alcohol, and from those actually giving themselves over to the pleasures of revenge. The population is out of control. Many have abandoned the camp and, loaded up with bread, a blanket slung across their shoulders, are setting out across country in search of adventure, perhaps to hunt down the SS hiding nearby, perhaps to raid farmhouses.

It's useless trying to sleep without a blanket to block the light. With all this ruckus ... Emili gets up. He goes out to the street. A contact from the committee stops him and tells him he has to get to the office. What do they want now? The two men walk down the street. Turning a corner, they almost trip over a corpse. Its skull is crushed; a scribbled note identifies it: "Popeye, no more spinach for you." Emili stops to look at him: this shapeless mound of flesh and bloody clothing is the man who first laid a hand on him, the first to make him feel the reality of the camp. An important person in his life! The hatred he once felt now seems pointless. He tries to evoke the memory of that beating, but the images that surface don't answer to present circumstances.

—As it should be —the contact says—. He was a prick.
—I don't remember him very well —Emili answers quietly.

Perhaps he should say he thinks it's a good thing too, like everybody else; to put himself in line with the rest. During all these years he's wanted this moment to come, and now he doesn't know what to do. He changes the subject and says he can't remember. Does he pity Popeye? He just feels nauseous, and when they start to walk again, he realizes that he's hurrying.

A little farther along is a group gathered around another lynching. The draughtsman moves along still faster until he reaches the office. A group of men go in ahead of him, loaded up with rifles and machine guns.

—This is all we could find in the armoury —says the leader—. The looters have taken everything.

Emili starts in with Rubio, a strange violence in his voice:

—Why have the Americans gone? We'll see who's going to contain the crowds now!

He himself is surprised by his tone. His hands are shaking.

—Don't worry —replies Rubio, smiling—. The bulk of the troops won't be long coming. We've phoned the village requesting guards, but they can't send them. They say that it's up to us; that's why I've called you.

—Me?

—It won't get any worse —Rubio continues, as if he's not heard him—. There's nothing more exhausting than acting like an idiot. With these few weapons we'll have enough. Each national group will contribute some men. For our part, the Spaniards, we're in charge of the nine to twelve shift. The kitchen warehouse is the only one still intact; if it gets attacked, nobody's going to eat tomorrow. Make sure it doesn't happen. At twelve, the French will come relieve you.

—You realize I haven't slept for two days now?

—I suppose not; for me it's been longer than that.

—You mean I have to accept?

—Tomorrow you can sleep for a whole year if you want to.

A little later, Emili goes in and out of the Blocks looking for "his" men. He doesn't find any, anywhere. Only after running all over the place does he stumble onto two of them by chance. If he lets himself go now, he'll fall asleep. He keeps his eyes open. But all the images that come through have the vagueness of dreams. A chaotic nightmare! Everywhere the same gutted sacks of straw, the same furniture smashed to pieces, the same scattered blankets and abandoned clothing. Huge bonfires are burning in the square and in the streets between the barracks. The tables in the Blocks are being used to knead flour and make rudimentary cakes. People everywhere are boiling cauldrons of gruel or preparing dried vegetables or macaroni. A man with barely enough strength to stand carries a huge sack of flour on his back that threatens to squash him completely. Two others are being carried out of a barracks, killed when a hand grenade that one of them was fooling around with exploded. A lunatic amuses himself throwing rocks through the windows of the *Arrest*.

—Now the Nazis will stay nice and cool when they get locked up —he shouts.

And everywhere the music of gunfire. Emili realizes that the groups walking around in only their shirts and underwear are the sick from the "Russian camp." A starving man, holding himself up against a wall, eats raw flour in handfuls.

—Do you know if Enric is inside?

—Enric? I think he's gone to the village.

—Why's he gone there?

Some peal potatoes and fry them on the stove they've brought out onto the street. At the door of the Block, two skeletal men are wrestling furiously over a loaf of bread. Another has tucked himself into a corner to suffer through a most difficult digestion.

Emili drags himself through the camp not knowing what he's looking for. His thinking is muddled, and he's trying to grasp the meaning of this nightmare. The words *reaction, compensation, resurrection* dance around in his head among others, but they don't make anything clearer. In the mix there are always the absolute extremes: good and bad, hunger and abundance, life and death. What has triumphed might just as well be the other side of the same coin of what has been defeated. People can only see change if they see the blood of one paid for by the blood of another, if what was once prohibited is now permitted, and vice versa. More than anything, the draughtsman feels repugnance and fatigue. He's angry without knowing towards what or towards whom. Certainly none of this is new to him: the ignorant have weapons? They're not going to miss out on a chance to shoot them! To understand … understand what? The rationalizations seem clumsy: "Spring floods tear asunder, but bear fruit in the end." Just pedantic phrases that fix nothing. Tomorrow the occupying troops will arrive, order will be restored: that's all that counts! To judge? His only duty now is to be useful. Emili shuffles from Block to Block, searching for two more men.

Rubio makes him sit down. A radio is giving the latest news in French. German cities destroyed, astronomical numbers of prisoners, generals and Nazi leaders surrendering. He listens to the announcer's voice and finds its timbre pleasing. No one has to hide to listen to the radio anymore! He's a free man. He smiles and continues to drink in the rich voice that never stops speaking. The voice of a man from outside who wants to welcome him as one of his own, as one of the victorious. Victorious? He wants to laugh.

"General Bradley's troops have discovered another charnel house on the banks of the Danube near Linz, where thousands of political deportees of all nationalities have been held under unimaginable conditions; the crematoria contained hundreds of corpses in an advanced state of decay due to the insufficient capacity of the furnaces."

The committee discusses how to find replacements for the cooks who have resigned; they fall silent from time to time to listen to the news. This report that refers to their own camp is particularly well received:

—It's the same as they had on the Italian broadcast —one of them comments.

Everyone knows they've heard it before, but it's pleasing to the ear, listening to it again. To imagine freedom, not as it is, amid chaos, crime, and blood, but as it's evoked in the entrancing voice of the announcer thousands of kilometres away.

The dial of the radio suddenly goes dark, and the spell is broken.

Somebody tries the light switch.

—The power's out.

An expert in electrical matters, who has been charged with the repair, comes back after a bit to say that he's not going to be able to locate the problem before dark.

—It might be something outside the camp —he supposes.

—No lights! —exclaims Frantisek—. That's all we need!

—Nor water —adds Rubio.

—There's nothing I can do —says the electrician.

While Manuel is enumerating the dire consequences of a lack of lighting on a night such as they have before them, a Spaniard rushes in and addresses Rubio's group. He's so out of breath, he can hardly speak:

—What's happened? —asks the barber two or three times.

—Ernest ... they've got him ... right in front of me ... I saw it just as I see you now ...

—Who? —asks Manuel, while Rubio gives no sign of even having heard.

—The son of that old man, the one who died in the punishment detail. The one who stole potatoes from the kitchen.

—Yes, we know who that is —Rubio cuts in quietly.

—Ernest was walking alone past Block 6. The boy came up to him and said: "You don't remember my father, eh?" And then he shot him in the stomach with a pistol.

—Is he dead?
—I don't know. They've taken him to the infirmary.

Rubio gets up and goes out. The day is darkening and the fading light coming in through the window etches Manuel's face in shadow as he starts to speak:

—Rubio is going to take this hard. They'd reconciled, you know? Ernest had been behaving himself lately. The death of the old man made an impression on him …

Emili lets him talk. Fatigue has tied him to the chair, and everything spinning around him seems unreal. Ernest has been attacked. He remembers him, always well dressed and with his peaked cap, the striped suit tailored and his shoes well polished. Dead like Popeye, like so many others. Blood and mud. He feels no pity, just repugnance and fatigue.

The ex-barber of the SS soon comes back.

—Alive?
—No —Rubio answers without emotion.

He pretends to search for some papers on the table. After a while, he looks at the clock and clears his throat.

—A quarter to nine, Emili —he says softly—. Go and get your men. Let me know when you're ready.

Then he lifts his eyes to look at Manuel:

—Don't forget about the cooks.

The draughtsman leaves the room. Outside, people are coming and going through the darkness, the bonfires send up their columns of smoke, and one can hear the rhythmic, tireless gunfire of someone far off. "Blood and mud" —he thinks—. "Raw, stinking death." The radio has confirmed that he is now a free man.

—SS patrols are attacking the camp —or so ran the rumour.

And in the dark, the panic has started a shootout; two men have been wounded.

Apart from this stupid alarm, the watch has been quiet. Now, Emili leaves the office with the prospect of catching a few hours sleep. The night is darker than ever. One can see the glowing points of the fires dying down in the streets, still watched over by men wrapped in blankets. Many are still moving around the camp. They come and go through the main gate, perhaps because they can't yet get used to the idea that nobody controls it. At the bottom of the slope that serves as the foundation for Block 6, a man writhes in pain and moans. He begs for water. Emili goes over to him and when he goes to help him up, he's almost weightless. A sticky foam drools from his mouth. He has eaten too much and now he is dying. Everything is dark in the infirmary where the draughtsman takes him; they're all asleep, and however much he searches and calls out, he finds no one who can help the dying man. Water! Impossible to find. That evening many parched with thirst had abandoned the camp in search of it. Emili goes back to the office to see if there is anything left of the "coffee" he had been drinking. A candle casts a flickering, rosy light about the room. Manuel tells him that the "coffee" is gone but that they are waiting for a tank of water that's being sent up from the village by the Americans. He promises he will sort out what to do for the sick, of whom there are many.

—Go to sleep, go on —he tells him—. You can hardly stand up. Drink a little of this; it'll do you good.

The alcohol is very strong and he almost chokes.

—Look —cries Manuel all of a sudden, pointing at the window.

They go out on the street. The word "Fire!" is being shouted in many languages. The smoke settles over the camp and makes for a different kind of burning in the throat than that other smoke, the smoke from the crematorium that everyone is used to. The few men available are mobilized to keep the fire from spreading. A warehouse for furniture and clothing in the exterior precinct has gone up in flames. The barracks' dry wood burns like kindling. An improvised fire brigade provided with picks and shovels and some extinguishers fights desperately to get all the combustible material they can out of reach of the flames.

Emili makes a superhuman effort to keep up with the rhythm of his comrades, who, in a human chain, are clearing out the sections of the barracks the flames have not yet reached. Parcels of clothing, sheets, towels, shirts and underwear, lengths of wood, cupboards, tables, beds, all these pass incessantly through his hands. By the light of the fire, his eyes carry an image to his brain again and again—repeating like hammer beats to the rhythm of the human chain—the stamp borne by every object in a German concentration camp:

$$\boxed{\text{K.L. REICH}}$$

Printed in ink on all the clothing, burned into the wood, Emili has had it constantly before his eyes for four and a half years, and he knows it is the stigma with which they wanted to mark him too, the only epitaph his dead comrades have been given. But now that he is wrapped in the torpor of fatigue, his senses dulled by the automatic movement of his muscles, he forgets the significance of the words *Konzentrations Lager Reich* and is left only with an obsession over the lettering itself and the border that encloses it. The mark passes in front of his eyes over and over, and when a package comes through backwards, or a length of wood upside down, he sets them straight so that the rhythm of the images is not broken. All of a sudden he realizes what he's doing and he's frightened by the symbolic truth that might be buried within his obsession. Is he marked? Is he really just the detritus of a concentration camp? A revolt against what is being asked of him wells up within him: "Why save this stuff?" Let the camp burn, and with it all the barracks, all the furniture, all the clothing marked with this stamp! Who is to say that freedom isn't the fire itself? A great and invisible weight bears down on his arms, and the chain is broken. He doesn't bend to pick up the parcel he's dropped on the ground; on the contrary, he turns and goes.

—Hey, what are you doing? —they ask him.
—To hell with it! —he shouts as his only reply.

He enters the camp. The roofs of the barracks are illuminated by the wavering glimmer of the fire. The wall that separates the two precincts casts the sidewalk along the square into shadow, and for a moment Emili has the feeling that he is walking into a vacuum. The embers of all the little bonfires glow phosphorescent like cat's eyes. Smoke hangs in the air, immobile, like a red fog, a smoke that, however acrid, smells good for not coming from the crematorium …

Where now? He doesn't know! The darkened barracks get confused in a labyrinth of shadows, and he can't remember which one is his. People are still coming and going on the streets, indifferent, in a sort of somnambu-lism that makes them absent and unreal. Drawn in by a strange attraction, the draughtsman stops in front of one small brazier. A man wrapped in a blanket wakes up and instinctively puts his hand over the can where he's keeping the remnants of the gruel he's not been able to finish. Emili sits cross-legged on the ground, still warm from the fire.

—Want a smoke? —he asks, offering one of the cigarettes that
Manuel gave him.

The man doesn't understand German but puts out his hand. He lets out a huge belch and grins because he realizes that his "treasure" is not at risk. They light their cigarettes from an ember. Emili feels as if the warmth from the brazier is moving down into his belly, carried by the smoke from the tobacco. And surprisingly, under the influence of the surrounding nightmare, his need for sleep has evaporated; the fatigue is now just a faint tickling sensation, ineffable and sweet, and the silence between him and his companion fills him with a serenity that nothing can disturb. He watches the man as he smokes, he watches him for a long time, until the sweet sensation makes him drunk like strong wine. Then he sees it clearly: he has found peace, and it is personified in this man. The Man! The Man who is above everything accidental, beyond race, nationality, political party, beyond the nucleus of friends or individuality. The average Man, one of the multitudes walking the streets and pathways of the world without knowing where they lead; who has been through hunger and thirst, who has known fear for years, and today burps, full and brazen in the impunity of a night of interregnum; who is propelled by unchanging primal instincts the moment any external act tears away his cloak of civilization.

He contemplates how his companion, with a pinch of his fingers, extinguishes the butt of his cigarette and stashes it behind his ear, and how he looks greedily at the can of soup, and how he finally succumbs to the temptation, not without the courteous gesture of offering it first to his friend. The man gulps voraciously at the thick, still warm gruel. He wants to feel even fuller!

This stranger, whose features he can't even make out, with his gluttony and his hunched shoulders, has more symbolic weight than all the important personages the radio talks about non-stop these days. Millions of men like this one have won the war with their suffering and humility, and above all, with their indestructible instinct for self-preservation. It is not states that determine the winners, it is not a certain politics, nor an economy, nor a leadership, nor a revolutionary working class, nor political parties; it is a mass of millions and millions of men made up of farmers, workers, bourgeoisie, priests, aristocrats—a mass of men and women from all races, all religions, and all ideologies, a mass that has given everything of themselves without complaint, a mass ignorant of the value of their own sacrifice, a sacrifice that is the deepest heartbeat of the world.

And the Man grows huge in Emili's mind as if he was creating him out of his own breath, and he sees him framed within the era in which he has happened to live. It is this man who now fills himself up on gruel with a fatalistic courage, without fantasies about happiness or absolutes. It is He who, a puppet in the great convulsions of the world, determines the final balance of the scales with the weight of the sacrifice imposed upon him. Being flesh and blood, the Man knows that to live is to suffer.

Emili takes a final drag on his cigarette and throws it on the fire. He feels good here in the company of this silent man he has found and with whom he feels a growing kinship; and the repugnance he felt for the throng just a few hours before has turned to tenderness and to love for humankind. In his need to commune with what is permanent, he finds that everything else is beside the point.

The man has come to the end of his gruel and scrapes the bottom of the can with his spoon. The draughtsman feels a shiver run up his spine, not knowing if it is from the metallic scraping or from this tenderness that invades him. He thinks now of Werner's silence when they tortured him, and of Francesc's serenity on his deathbed. Both often talked to him of their faith in justice, but clearly their courage before death wasn't born from this faith but from an internal peace they had managed to find, the same peace that Emili is finding now. A peace that is not passive, that is not founded on resignation, but is instead an active moral condition, like a state of grace. With this conquest he has made, the four and half years in the camp might not be pointless, just as the war itself has not been pointless if, scattered around the world, there are other men who have also won this peace within. The great peace of the world will only be born on the day that every man feels within him this little peace within his own soul. And this is not beside the point. That there will be more conflicts among men, that other wars will follow, is more than certain. But with each new test, each more horrifying than the one before, the greater anguish among men will scatter more widely the seeds of serenity. The length of the road should not make us despair. When each of us has triumphed, so will humanity as a whole. All that is needed is that we feel, deeply and humbly, an integral part of this humankind worthy of pity, as Emili feels now. All of the other satisfactions that life has to offer follow on this.

Emili gets up; the fire is going out and the night is cold. The fire at the barracks has also died down, and the camp is submerged once more in darkness. Behind is a past of horrors; in front opens a future full of hope. The smoke still clings to the earth as if to affirm its triumph over that other smoke from the crematorium. Dawn must be very near; Emili is impatient for it to come. He needs to know for certain that this night's victory has not been a dream but the real triumph of the Man over the *spirit of the camp*, over the *spirit of a national-socialist camp*—the enemy that lies dead, but still warm.

NOTES

Notes to A Note on the Translation

1 Amat-Piniella, "La novela popular," *Tele-Expres* (26 de maig de 1966); our translation.
2 http://www.memoria.cat/amat/content/lopini%C3%B3-damat-piniella-sobre -la-seva-novel%C2%B7la-klreich; our translation.

Notes to Introduction

1 The history of the French camps is complex; at some point they also served to concentrate the Jewish population prior to deportation. For a detailed account on the evolution of French camps, see Daniel Peschanski, *La France des camps. L'internement 1938–1946* (Paris: Gallimard, 2002).
2 Although the prisoner-of-war camps set up by the Nazis are generally referred to as *Stalags,* a distinction has to be made. While *Stalags* were intended for soldiers, officers were held in *Oflags. Furthermore, Frontstalags,* internment camps established on French soil under German occupation, contained French colonial troops. The first scene of *K.L. Reich* describes the "motley uniforms" of the Spaniards when entering the Nazi camp, and mentions "Senegalese caps," implicitly acknowledging the presence of French colonial units. For a general account of the literature produced in *Stalags* and other prisoner-of-war camps, see "Écrivains au Stalag," ed. Elio Vittorini and Pierre Michon, special issue of *Europe. Révue littéraire mensuelle*, no. 948 (April 2008), Paris.
3 We are using round figures here. For detailed information, see Benito Bermejo and Sandra Checa, *Libro Memorial. Españoles deportados a los campos nazis (1940–1945)* (Madrid: Ministerio de Cultura de España, 2006).
4 This information has been taken from the transcription of Montserrat Roig's interview with Joaquim Amat-Piniella (24 July 1973), published http://www .memoria.cat/amat/, and from David Serrano, *L'hora blanca. L 'Holocaust i Joaquim Amat-Piniella* (Sabadell: Fundació Ars, 2004), 26ff.
5 After the liberation, Josep Carbrero Arnal stayed in Paris and began working for the French Communist newspaper, *L'Humanité*. He created the comic strip *Pif le chien*, which became very popular in France. "Pif" exposed the hunger and the housing crisis that many were suffering at that time.
6 For a detailed account of the castle of Hartheim and the mobile gas chamber trucks, see David W. Pike, *Spaniards in the Holocaust: Mauthausen, Horror on the Danube* (London and New York: Routledge), 103ff.

7   The fact that Mauthausen was classified under Category III has led to the belief that the camp should be considered an "extermination camp." See, for instance, the account of survivor and writer Paul Tillard, *Mauthausen* (Paris: Éditions Sociales, 1945). This confusion is present in the majority of accounts, and to our understanding it has become an important key in the construction of the Spanish imaginary around Mauthausen, for it has enabled a parallel to be drawn between the history of the Spaniards in Mauthausen and the Jewish genocide.

8   Spaniards were already considered "undesirable foreigners" on French soil, right after they crossed the border in February 1939, based on the implementation of Édouard Daladier's regulation issued on 12 November 1938, which ordered the administrative internment of foreigners. See Geneviève Dreyfus-Armand, "Among the 'Indésirables': Catalans in French Internment Camps, 1939," in *Catalan Culture and the French Camps, 1939: Literary and Visual Representations,* ed. Marta Marín-Dòmine, *Catalan Review* 25, North American Catalan Society, 2012, 19–29. It may well be that this designation has gone on to influence the imaginary reconstruction of Spaniards in Mauthausen.

9   Pike, *Spaniards in the Holocaust,* 10.

10 Information on the colour classification of concentration camp badges is available through the various official websites that provide information on the Nazi camps, such as the United States Holocaust Memorial Museum, www.ushmm.org. Among the testimonials and accounts we have found some instances in which the classification of Spanish Republicans is mentioned. See Tillard, *Mauthausen,* 29, where the author states that the blue triangle was given to "Spanish political refugees"; and François Wetterwald, *Les morts inutiles,* ed. and prefaced by Thierry Feral (Paris: L'Harmattan, 2009), a reissue of the 1945 edition, in which note 161 on page 97 reads: "*La désignation officielle de cette catégorie [blue triangle] était 'émigrant' (emigrant)*" (the official designation of this category [blue triangle] was "emigrant").

11 It must be noted, however, that Spaniards were not the only ones to organize themselves. Some international resistance committees were organized in the main camp and in some of its satellites. Among the first testimonial accounts written in French about such clandestine organizations were a fictionalized narration by Pierre Daix, *La dernière forteresse* (Paris: Les Éditeurs Français Réunis, 1950) and that of Paul Tillard, *Mauthausen.*

12 Francesc Boix and Antonio García were key in this operation, as were a group of young boys who formed part of the *Poschacher Kommando.* Much controversy has arisen due to the fact that Boix has become well know for this actions, while García has remained in the shadows. Boix gave his testimony at the Nuremberg trials in 1946. For more information, see Benito Bermejo, *Francisco Boix: El Fotografo De Mauthausen* (Barcelona: RBA, 2002).

13 The Valencian Casimir Climent and the Catalan Josep Bailina were key figures in this initiative, having been transferred to the *Politische Abteilung,* the camp office that kept the prisoners' records. For more detailed information, see Pike, *Mauthausen;* and Pierre Daix, *Bréviaire pour Mauthausen* (Paris: Gallimard, 2005).

14 For footage related to the liberation of Mauthausen, see United States Holocaust Memorial Museum, http://www.ushmm.org/wlc/search/index.php?langcode=en& group=&query=mauthausen&Submit=Search. For a full representation of photographs taken in Mauthausen, see the catalogue edited by the Amicale de Mauthausen, *La part visible des camps. Les photographies du camp de concentration de Mauthausen* (Paris: Tiresias Michel Reynaud, 2005), issued on the occasion of the inauguration of the international exhibit devoted to Mauthausen that opened at the National Archives of Paris in 2005. Previous to this exhibit another had been organized in Barcelona based on the photographic material given by the Amical de Mauthausen to the Museu d'Història de Catalunya in Barcelona. From this exhibit a catalogue was also issued: Rosa Toran and Margarida Sala, *Mauthausen: Crònica gràfica d'un camp de concentració* (Barcelona: Viena, 2002).

15 There are, however, the four photographs taken by the *Sonderkommando* in Auschwitz in August 1944. See Georges Didi-Huberman, *Images in Spite of All* (Chicago: University of Chicago Press, 2012).

16 The most recent Spanish edition was published by El Aleph, Barcelona, in 2009, translated by Antonio Padilla and with a prologue by David Serrano.

17 In Jorge Semprún, *L'Écriture ou la vie* (Paris: Gallimard, 1996) pp. 350–51.

18 Letter written on 2 February 1948, Arxiu Històric Comarcal de Terrassa, Catalonia, Spain.

19 Letter written on 5 June 1953, Arxiu Històric Comarcal de Terrassa.

20 Letter written on 14 July 1953, Arxiu Històric Comarcal de Terrassa.

21 Letter written on 13 May 1958, Arxiu Històric Comarcal de Terrassa.

22 Well known is the poor reception the European Communist parties gave their survivor comrades following Stalin's dictum that a traitor could be found behind every communist survivor. For a very general discussion of this matter, see Daix, *Bréviaire pour Mauthausen*, 58–59; Rosa Toran, prologue Joan B. Culla, *Joan de Diego. Tercer Secretari a Mauthausen* (Barcelona: Eds 62, 2007), 204ff.

23 Régine Waintrater, *Sortir du genocide. Témoigner pour réapprendre à vivre* (Paris: Payot, 2003), 42.

24 We had the privilege of briefly consulting the Archives of the *Amical* of Mauthausen in Barcelona, where we found a number of letters written by ex-deportees asking Joan Pagés, the President of the *Amical* at that time, to send copies of *K.L. Reich* to different places in Spain and France.

25 Especially controversial might have been the image given of César Orquín, easily recognizable in the character August. As noted by David Pike, after the Liberation, Orquín had very poor press among the Communists, "who accused him of having handed the SS, while he was in the Hauptlager, a list of Spanish prisoners who were communists or communist sympathizers." "Thanks to the sinister César," write Razola and Constante, "110 Spaniards were punished and dispatched to Gusen," 96–97. Mention of César Orquín and his bad relations with "republicans" can be found in Etienne and Paul Le Caër, *K.L. Mauthausen. Les cicatrices de la mémoire* (Bayeux: Éditions Heimdal), 90.

26 Our translation.

27 Renaud Dulong, *Le témoin oculaire. Les conditions sociales de l'attestation personnelle* (Paris: Éditions de l'EHESS, 1998).

28 Although this subject has produced a great number of theoretical works, we suggest the reader consult Luba Jurgenson, *L'experiénce concentrationaire est-elle indicible?* (Paris: Éditions du Rocher, 2003); and Alain Parrau, *Écrire les camps* (Paris: Belin, 1995).

29 Jean Cayrol is the author of, among other works, *Lazare parmi nous* (Paris: Éditions du Seuil, 1950), a sort of treatise on the characteristics that literature after the camps ought to take, as well as of the script for the film *Nuit et Brouillard*, directed by Alain Resnais and released in 1955.

30 Cayrol, "Témoignage et littérature," 577.

31 "We had dreamt, in 1943, when we were imprisoned, of describing in fiction what we were enduring, but we quickly understood the ridiculousness of this project. We were not the docile heroes of novels but difficult and disquieting souls" (our translation). Jean Cayrol, "Témoignage et littérature," in *Esprit*, April 1953, 575.

32 Joaquim Amat-Piniella, preface to *K.L. Reich*.

33 Tillard finished writing *Mauthausen* in July 1945.

34 Robert Antelme, *L'Espèce humaine* (Paris: Gallimard, 1978), 9. It is worth mentioning that some of these writings, especially poems and journals, had been begun inside the camps. This was the case for Amat-Piniella, who began writing poems in the camp, which were later collected in a volume titled *Les llunyanies* (Distances), published in Barcelona by Columna in 1999, edited by David Serrano, with a prologue by Jordi Castellanos.

35 Annette Wieviorka, *Déportation et Génocide* (Paris: Plon, 1992), 168.

36 Giuseppe Mayda, *Mauthausen, Storia di un lager* (Bologna: Il Mulino, 2008).

37 "This book is constructed using the technique of the novel, due to a mistrust in words ... However, fiction is not part of this work. The facts, the events, the characters are all true" (our translation). David Rousset, *Les jours de notre mort* (Paris: Hachette, 1993).

38 "Yet another book about the concentration camps! After those by Rousset, Kogon, and so many others, one believed that everything had been said. Even if there is something still to say, we would be happy to have people shut up about it. The War is over. We have the right to savour the peace without its being spoiled" (our translation). In Parrau, *Écrire les camps*, 54.

39 Jean Cayrol, *Lazare parmi nous* (Paris: Éditions du Seuil, 1950), 21.

40 A major debate among historians, negationists, and survivors followed the 1968 publication of historian Olga Wormser-Migot's dissertation in which she stated that there had been no gas chambers in Western camps such as Mauthausen and Ravensbrück. For the truth to finally be established took the work of Pierre-Serge Choumoff, *Les chambers à gaz de Mauthausen (Paris: Amicale des Déportés et Familles de Disparus du Cam*p de Concentration de Mauthausen, 1972).

41 Tillard's early testimonial account *Mauthausen* focuses on this aspect as well.

42 "The gaze of a deportee, you must remember, was that of a man who had seen too much, a gaze that overcomes the obstacles, that sees what blinds it." Our translation.

Notes to *K.L. Reich*

1 Amat-Piniella's first reference to the infamous granite quarry of Mauthausen. (All notes are by the translators.)

2 Workers Companies were equipped with surplus First World War uniforms by the French government. Some Spanish exiles, Amat-Piniella among them, had been enrolled in the *Groupements de Travailleurs Étrangers* (Groups of Foreign Workers), known as *Compagnies de Travailleurs Étrangers* (Companies of Foreign Workers) prior to the Vichy government. Some of the men enrolled in these companies found themselves prisoners of the Germans after the German occupation of France in 1940. They were sent to *Stalags* (prisoner-of-war camps within German territory). Prisoners originating in the French Colonial Forces, and of African origin, were sent not to *Stalags* but to *Frontslags* (prisoner-of-war camps within French-occupied territory) as a way to segregate a potentially "contaminated" inmate population. There is little documentation of the fate of the Spanish prisoners in *Stalags* and *Frontslags;* however, the reference here to the presence of the caps of Senegalese *tiralleurs* suggests a meeting of the two groups, or a transfer at some point between *Frontslags* and *Stalags*.

3 Short for Francesc.

4 In Spanish in the original.

5 It is interesting that Amat-Piniella opts for a domestic word, *menjador,* to refer to the block's eating area. This partitioned section of the block, with its stove and tables, cupboards, and individual beds, was the preserve of a few privileged inmates, largely Germans with administrative positions in the camp structure along with their servants and favourites. The inmates in the general population ate their meagre portions standing up or in their bunks. Using tables or benches, or profiting from the warmth of the stove, was forbidden to them. See David Pike, *Spaniards in the Holocaust: Mauthausen, Horror on the Danube* (London: Routledge, 2000), Chapter 5.

6 Inmates responsible for cleaning the block.

7 Interpreters in Nazi camps had a greater chance of survival than other deportees due to their key role in the camps' functioning; they were also known to ease the lives of their fellow inmates. The disorientation and terror experienced by deportees was heightened by the Babel of languages in which they were immersed. Primo Levi has given a good account of this situation in "Initiation," Chapter 3 of his *Survival in Auschwitz.* For a detailed analysis of the role of interpreters in Nazi camps, see Małgorzata Tryuk, "Interpreting in Nazi

Concentration Camps during World War II," in *Interpreting* 12, no. 2 (2010): 125–45.

8 The International Brigades were comprised of volunteers from many nations who came together to help the Republican cause during the Spanish Civil War. However, their organization came under the wing of foreign Communist Parties. Many non-communist volunteers, such as August, found themselves at odds with their leaders and defected to the Anarchist and Trotskyite militias. The film *Land and Freedom* (1995), by Ken Loach, depicts this conflict.

9 In Spanish in the original. The term refers to the prisoners put in charge of various aspects of the camp's operations. They were known for their brutality. The usual term for them in concentration camp jargon was *kapo*.

10 Graziani was an Italian army officer responsible for a number of African campaigns before and during the Second World War. When Mussolini ordered him to invade Egypt in August 1940, Graziani expressed reservations about the capabilities of the Italian army against the much better equipped British forces.

11 Political deportees used cigarettes as currency, trading them for other goods such as bread. In the literature of camps and incarceration, cigarettes become an iconic element, because they also have a symbolic value as a means to share an intimate moment. See, for instance, the ending of Robert Antelme's *L'espèce humaine* (Paris: Gallimard, 1947), with which *K.L. Reich's* ending has some narrative similarities.

12 The French writer Jean Cayrol, a survivor of Mauthausen-Gusen, describes the dreams one had in a concentration camp as an aspect of the experience too little examined, in *Lazare parmi nous* (Paris: Éditions du Seuil, 1950).

13 Paulino Uzcudun Eizmendi (or Uzkudun) (1899–1985) was a Basque boxer who won many heavyweight titles in Spain and in Europe. The Franco regime used his image for propaganda purposes as an example of the "glory of Spain."

14 The Spanish Legion (*Legión Española*), established in 1920 as a Colonial Army.

15 A very fertile county in the Autonomous Community of Valencia, famous for its rice, oranges, and vegetables. It has become an icon of the meridional zone of Valencia.

16 Poles, with their deep Catholic roots, had tense relations in the camps with the anti-clerical Spaniards.

17 The *Nationalsozialistische Deutsche Arbeiterpartei* (NSDAP): the Nazi Party.

18 The *Anschluss*, or *Anschluß*, refers to the Third Reich's annexation of Austria on 12 March 1938.

19 The Pan-German movement arose in the nineteenth century with the aim of unifying the German-speaking populations of Europe into a single nation-state to be known as *Großdeutschland* (Greater Germany).

20 "These games end up in bed." In Spanish in the original.

21 In Amat-Piniella's 1946 manuscript, this exchange is as follows:

—And why are you here?
—For having fought in the Spanish War.
—I was there too —said the Dutchman, visibly happy to have found a friend—. In the International Brigades

In general, Amat-Piniella's revisions for the 1963 publication of the book downplay any political context for the deportations of the characters.

This change in the text points to an explanation for the internment of the Spaniards that developed after the liberation and that is now part of the collective construction of memory of the Spaniards in Mauthausen. It is said that the Spanish prisoners were not recognized as Spanish citizens in a meeting between Himmler and Spanish Foreign Affairs Minister Ramón Serrano Súñer, although there is no documentation of their exchange. What seems clear, however, is that Franco refused to recognize the Spaniards taken prisoner in Occupied France, and that Stalin did not want to recognize them either, so they were sent to Mauthausen. In Mauthausen, those who had been captured in Occupied France wore the blue triangle designating "emigrant," with an "S" for "*Spanien*" sewn onto it.

22 The quarry at Mauthausen, roughly one kilometre from the camp, was owned by *Deutsche Erd- und Steinwerke* (DEST), at that time under SS control. Its floor was reached by a long and treacherous stone stairway up which the prisoners were made to carry the granite blocks they quarried there. Initially this stairway consisted of 160 uneven stones, some of them 40 centimetres in height. In 1942, the stairway was rebuilt with its infamous 186 steps. Amat-Piniella here modifies the number of steps. Further information can be found in Pike, *Spaniards in the Holocaust*, 89–90.

23 Vegetarianism, along with an inclination to live a healthy life in accord with nature, belongs to a branch of anarchism very popular at that time. Christian Bernadac records a story from Spanish survivor Mariano Constante about the demise of the Spanish anarchist Ramon, nicknamed *El Barbas* (The Bearded). *El Barbas* had sworn not to shave his beard until the day the Republic was again established in Spain. He died of self-starvation in Mauthausen, protesting his right not to be shaved. Constante describes *El Barbas* as an "anarcho-syndicaliste, avec toutes les vertues, les rites, les moeurs que les 'purs' anarchists espagnols possédaient. El Barbas était végétarien. Jamais—avant, pendant et après la guerre d'Espagne—il n'avala un milligramme de viande." See Christian Bernadac, *Deportation 1933/1945* (Paris: France-Empire, 1993), 61. The same story appears in the letters of other Spanish survivors. Archives of the *Federación Española de Deportados e Internados Políticos, Centro Documental de la Memoria Histórica*, Salamanca.

24 Pedro Calderón de la Barca de Henao y Riaño (Madrid 1600–1681) was a Spanish poet and playwright known mainly for his play *La vida es sueño* (*Life Is a Dream*). Codes of honour are key in much of his writing.

25 The Non-Aggression Treaty between Germany and the Soviet Union, often referred to as the Molotov–Ribbentrop Pact, was signed in Moscow 23 August 1939. It pledged neutrality by either party should the other be attacked by a third party, thus securing Germany's eastern border and sealing Poland's fate. Many Communists saw the Pact as an act of Soviet treachery. It remained in effect until Nazi Germany invaded the Soviet Union on 22 June 1941 in Operation Barbarossa. Given this context, Francesc's position, as an anarchist, is understandable.

26　The term "fifth column," coined during the Spanish Civil War, refers to any group that lends its support to an invading force by undermining a regime from within.

27　The question of who was allowed to correspond and when was highly complex; the answer varied depending on the camp, the period, and above all the status of the inmates. Needless to say, Jews were seldom permitted to write letters. For a summarized account, see Jean-Louis Rouhart, "Contribution des lettres illégales à l'histoire des camps de concentration Nazis,"¿Interrogations? 14: *Le suicide* (Juin 2012), http://www.revue-interrogations.org. See also David Serrano i Blanquer. reproduced in *L'Hora Blanca. L'Holocaust i Joaquim Amat-Piniella* (Sabadell: Fundació Ars, 2004), 249–56. See also eight postcards sent by Amat-Piniella from the "Lager Mauthausen (Oberdonau) Deutschland" to his wife Maria Llaverias, living in Barcelona. The postcards were sent between February 1943 and August 1944. We have not been able to access this material.

28　It is thought that the general disinfection at Mauthausen on 21 June 1941, during which all the prisoners were assembled for the whole day in a relatively unsupervised setting, provided the communists with the opportunity to organize the first Spanish Committee of Resistance. Meetings subsequently took place in the latrines of Block 3.

29　Carlos Greykey (José Grey Molay) was born in Barcelona in 1913. His family was from Fernando Po, at that time a Spanish colony. Two pictures of Greykey are held in the archive of the Mauthausen Memorial.

30　Ilse Koch (née Kohler), the "Bitch of Buchenwald," married the Camp Commandant, Karl Koch, in 1936.

31　The scene seems to have been inspired by the execution at Mauthausen of three German inmates in June 1941. Another infamous execution, of which there is a photographic record, was that of Hans Bonarewitz, deported as a German common criminal. Bonarewitz managed to escape from the camp in June 1942, only to be found by local villagers and returned to the camp on 11 July; he was hanged on 29 July. His case was fictionalized by French writer Jean Laffitte, himself a survivor of Mauthausen, in *La Pendaison* (1983).

32　In Spain, Syndicalism was a branch of Anarchism associated mainly with the unions (*sindicats*), in this case the *Confederación Nacional de Trabajadores* (CNT), which played a prominent role in events prior to and during the Spanish Civil War.

33　In various French, Spanish, and Italian testimonial narratives and literary accounts, deportees refer to the main camp at Mauthausen as the "Casa Madre" or "Maison Mère." Catalan speakers likely used "Casa Mare." Here, Amat-Piniella adopts the term "Casa Gran," or "Big House."

34　Amat-Piniella's 1946 manuscript adds here: "in contrast to how it is for you," pointing to the lack of solidarity among inmates in the main camp.

35　The Royal Yugoslav Army surrendered to the Axis countries on 17 April 1941.

36　Resistance was widespread among the Czech population and was generally well organized and effective. This is one reason why Czechs were subjected to especially harsh treatment in the camp. A recent literary account that can be read as an homage to the Czech Resistance is *HHhH* (2009) by Laurent Binet.

37 —What is it? —asked his neighbour in the next bed, alarmed by a movement that he'd made.

He was seventeen, a Dutch Jew sick with typhus.

—We've hit the jackpot! —answered Francesc, enigmatically.

—I don't know what you mean.

—Tonight... I'll have time to explain... Just now I'm going to sleep.

38 Remember now... tonight... I need to talk to you... Courage, dear one —he told him with a weak smile—. We'll have a good talk tonight.

39 *Sursum corda* (Latin for "Lift up your hearts") is uttered by the priest at the beginning of the Catholic mass. In Catalan and in Spanish, the words have evolved into *sursuncorda,* the term for an imaginary person to whom everyone delegates things they don't want to do and at the same time whom nobody obeys.

40 The use of human fat to make soap is one of the *topoi* of narratives of the Nazi concentration camps; however, it has never been proven and is now generally considered a myth. It is interesting that this information is presented as a possibility rather than a fact in one of the first creative documentaries on the Nazi camps, *Nuit et Brouillard* (1956), by Alain Resnais with a script by Jean Cayrol, himself a survivor of Mauthausen. In the film, the voice-over recites: "Avec les corps ... mais on ne peut plus rien dire ... avec les corps, on veut fabriquer du savon. Quant à la peau ..." (With the bodies... but one can say nothing more... with the bodies they want to make soap. As for the skin...). Historians have always found this rumour to be unfounded; however, Raul Hilberg mentions one such attempt to make soap taking place in Danzig. Raul Hilberg, *The Destruction of the European Jews* (Chicago: Quadrangle Books, 1961), 624.

41 Philippe Pétain, the French general who established the Vichy government.

42 The Spanish term "pronunciamiento" was commonly used in Spain around this time in reference to Franco's coup d'état of July 1936 against the democratically elected Second Republic. In Spanish in the original.

43 The *maquis* were guerrilla groups of the French Resistance, based mostly in rural areas. Many Spaniards joined the *maquis* as a logical continuation of their fight against fascism during the Spanish Civil War. Among their number was the renowned Spanish writer and survivor of Buchenwald, Jorge Semprún.

44 Collaborationists included individuals working undercover for the Nazi occupiers. Some of them infiltrated Resistance groups and denounced their members to the Nazis.

45 The "Embrace of Vergara" refers to the treaty that ended the First Carlist War (29 August 1839), signed by Baldomero Espartero (Liberal) and Rafael Maroto (Carlist). Carlists were conservatives, hence the joke of Manuel refusing to take the Carlist part.

46 ... *al Kommando de "les russes."* Amat-Piniella's 1943 manuscript reads: "*Kommando de 'les novias,'*" *novias* meaning "girlfriends."

47 This is a brutal but accurate account. August is based on the historical personage of Cesar Orquín Serra, who escaped from the camp when it was liberated

by the Americans, fearing that some factions of the Spaniards would carry out this threat. He disappeared. From correspondence between members of the *Federación Española de Deportados e Internados Políticos* (FEDIP, Spanish Federation of Deportees and Political Internees), it appears that he went to Argentina with his brother. Nothing more is known of him. Archives of the FEDIP, *Centro Documental de la Memoria Histórica*, Salamanca, Spain.

48 *The Last Stage* (*Ostatni etap*) is also the title of a 1947 Polish film directed by Wanda Jakubowska, a survivor of Auschwitz. The film is one of the earliest cinematic representations of life and death in Nazi camps, and it has served as a reference for many filmmakers since, such as Alain Resnais and Steven Spielberg.

49 Amat-Piniella refers here to a direct personal experience: after he was imprisoned in the *Fronstalag,* his friend Ferran Planes suggested to him that they escape together. Amat-Piniella refused, while Planes managed to escape and thus save himself from being sent to Mauthausen. Ferran Planes wrote an account of his life in the Spanish Civil war and in exile in France in *El Desgavell,* a Catalan novel published in 1969. A long passage in the book is devoted to this event.

50 Towards the end of the war, Britain and the United States approached the concentration camps from the West, while the Soviet Union pressed in from the East. During this period, the Nazis abandoned the camps, retreating into German territory and destroying evidence as they did so. Thousands of prisoners were killed. Those who survived were transferred to the remaining camps, where they endured violence and extremely harsh conditions. This scene refers to one of the so-called death marches, which brought prisoners in from another camp, possibly Auschwitz-Birkenau, to Mauthausen. At this point, women, mainly from Birkenau, entered the camp population.

51 This refers to the guards' well-founded fear of what might transpire with liberation. Americans and Soviets alike were extremely harsh with the camp guards. They also forced the civilian populations of the nearby villages to view the piles of corpses and then to bury them. In some cases, they did nothing to halt the beating and killing of *kapos* by survivors.

52 The Catalan word *lavabo* is used here by Piniella, indicating the washroom with its sinks. Pike and others locate these meetings in the block latrines. Amat-Piniella's account does seem more probable, if privacy is what was sought by the committee in a camp where dysentery was endemic.

53 The actual banner read, in Spanish: "Los españoles antifascistas saludan a las fuerzas libertadoras" (Antifascist Spaniards salute the liberating forces).

54 Although the description in this passage of the reactions of the various ethnic and cultural groups relies on heavily charged stereotypes, it is worth noting the racial stereotyping of the Jewish collective. This description, set off in its own sentence, points to the radical separation, both symbolic and real, between the reality of the Jews and that of the rest of the deportees, and not only within Germany but within Hispanic Peninsular culture with its own history of misunderstandings in relation to Jewish culture. While it is probably true, as some testimonies have stated, that deportees were grouped in accordance with their cultural affinities, the stereotyping in this passage, startling to a

contemporary reader, may also be understood to add a symbolic dimension to the scene that lies very close to the heart of the book as a whole: that "the Man" has survived, beyond all cultural, ethnic, and religious differences. Amat-Piniella would not have been witness to the liberation of the camp at Mauthausen described in these pages. He was at this time being held at Ebensee, a satellite camp liberated the next day, 6 May 1945.